COOL FOR THE SUMMER

A ROSEDALE NOVEL

ELLE WATERS

His Birthday Wish

His Christmas Love Song

His Fake Wedding Date

New Beginnings

Day Dreaming

His Ever After Collection

Rosedale

His Coffee Shop Crush

Rosedale Seasons

Cool for the Summer

Autumn Crush

For Taylor

ONE
DONOVAN

I'VE GOT time to kill. How exactly should I pass the hours until meeting Jack and Pete at their magazine-spread-perfect Cape-style house? I definitely can't show up early. My friends are probably sleeping or fucking, since their wedding party only broke up late last night.

I shudder involuntarily, still processing the fact that Pete's married, like an actual, well-adjusted grown-up. I still think of Pete Blekitny as the fresh-faced, dumb-as-a-brick (in a nice way) kid I met when we both answered the same ad for a roommate in Chelsea nearly a decade ago. Neither of us had gotten the room, but we'd decided to go in on a place together. By pooling our resources and finding a third roommate, we'd been able to afford a shitty walk-up in Chinatown. Pete had been trying to break into the art scene, while I was desperate to put my NYU theater education to work as an actor. Pete had more success as a barista, while I perfected my acting skills waiting tables at an upscale seafood restaurant. It took every ounce of my talent to pretend to be nice to the snobby patrons. At least the tips were good.

But I haven't waited tables in years, and Pete left the city for Rosedale, Connecticut, three years ago now. Rosedale was supposed to be a temporary refuge, a place to lick his wounds from a toxic relationship, but he ended up meeting his creative and life partner, Jack Avery, and stayed put. Together, they write and illustrate a best-selling series of books for middle schoolers. They've done well for themselves. Honestly, the success and domestic bliss couldn't have happened to a couple of nicer guys.

Not that I want what Pete and Jack have. I might be taking care of their house and dog for a couple of months while they're on their boinkfest of a European honeymoon, but their life is definitely not for me. I'm already missing having all of New York outside my front door, not to mention access to the buffet of men that is Manhattan.

The car service that picked me up from my no-frills motel lets me out on Rosedale's main drag. The sleepy small-town vibes of the three-block stretch of two-story brick buildings don't inspire me. Then again, I remind myself the whole point of this house-sitting gig is to get away from the city for a while, and do a favor for an old friend.

I have to take the good with the bad. So there's not going to be a plethora of guys to choose from for the next couple of months—I'll survive. I've been going through an uncharacteristic dry spell, but if I get really horny, I can always fire up one of my dating apps and see what the pickings are like in this corner of Connecticut.

Rolling my suitcase behind me, backpack over my shoulders, I head for the only place in Rosedale I really know, thanks to Pete talking my ear off about it.

Hot Brew is a small but stylish coffee shop smack in the middle of Main Street. The mid-morning sun gleams off the black and white tile interior and the pastry case is filled with tempting golden brown baked goods. My mouth waters at the scent of roasting coffee beans, a hint of spice underneath.

I met Pete's friend Meadow, Hot Brew's manager, at the wedding reception last night, but I don't see the pretty goth behind the counter today. Instead, a diminutive redhead with translucent skin works the register while a hulking bear of a man handles the espresso machine as efficiently as any New York City barista. To my surprise, I may actually get a decent cup of joe in this place.

I set my bags down at an empty two-top in a corner, marking my territory, and get in line behind a woman on a cell phone with a small child at her knee. The kid alternates between coughing and smearing his snotty nose on his mother's jean-clad legs. I take a step back. Kids are also not my thing. Another reason not to envy what Pete and Jack are embarking on. Sure, they have a sweet house, thriving careers, and they *seem* super happy. But wait until they have a rug rat or two—their sex life will disappear, mark my words.

The child peeks around his mother's legs and smiles up at me. I weaken against cute little milk teeth and chubby cheeks and find myself smiling back accidentally.

In self-defense, I pull out my phone to check the weather. Looks like sun for days.

When the kid and his mom have left holding their bag of goodies, it's my turn at the counter. I start with a simple, "Good morning."

The tiny redhead blinks at me. "Good morning?" she responds, making it into a question.

"Can I get a red eye and...something healthy?" I scan the menu on the wall. "How's the veggie breakfast bowl?"

"It's good?"

"Sold."

"Name for the order?"

"Van. And what's your name?" I tap my credit card to pay.

"Ruth."

At least she seems certain of that.

"Thanks a million, Ruth," I say, deepening my smile as I tuck a five into the tip jar.

She blushes crimson and I chuckle to myself as I sit down at the table I'd claimed earlier. I can be charming when I want to be, and there's no reason not to be charming to the woman in charge of my breakfast.

Mindful of the hours I still have to fill, I get my pen and notebook out of my backpack, open to an empty page and lose my smile.

I'm supposed to be writing a play.

It's not going particularly well.

I sigh and close my notebook. Maybe I'll think better after eating.

Ruth brings my coffee. I thank her effusively and it's not entirely a put-on. I worked in food service long enough to know a simple thank you goes a long way. Also, after the watery crap at the motel, I'm grateful for a jolt of caffeine. She blushes again and scurries away. I can't pretend it doesn't do my ego good. I'm enough of a narcissist to appreciate my effect on some people. It comes in handy at auditions, not to mention social situations. I take pride in my pickup game. Lord knows I've had enough practice since—

Nope. Not thinking about that. I take a sip of the red eye, piping hot and pleasantly strong, and let the drink distract me from things that shouldn't still hurt this many years later.

Halfway through my meal, I'm still wondering how I'm going to spend the next few hours until it's safe enough to show up at Pete's house when the chime indicating a new arrival to Hot Brew sounds. I'm surprised to recognize the man who walks through the door. He was at the wedding, but we weren't introduced. I would've remembered.

This guy and Jack have the same thick honey blond hair and fair skin—they've got to be related. But the coffee shop newcomer is slimmer and shorter than Jack. And right now he looks like death warmed over in a preppy pink untucked button-down with the sleeves rolled up over knobby wrists. Ray-Bans cover his eyes. The baseball cap pulled low over his forehead is similar to the one I'm wearing, but this guy's is chalk white, where mine's a simple black.

He doesn't remove the sunglasses as he stumbles to the counter, and I diagnose a world-class hangover. I wince in sympathy as the guy puts a hand over his stomach and whispers his order for black coffee and dry toast.

He pays with his phone and turns around. I realize I'm staring when the guy seems to stop his survey of the room at my table. I drop my head and take a bite of my food. A silly instinct, but somehow I don't want to have been caught looking.

Even though I keep my eyes on my breakfast, I can see him walk in my direction and stop a couple of feet away. Damn my excellent peripheral vision.

"You were at the wedding," the guy says. "Can I sit down?"

I can't think of a reason not to share my table, even though there are a couple of open spots on the other side of the room. I lift my gaze and stare at the opaque lenses of his glasses, then shrug. "Sure."

The man gingerly sits on the wooden cafe chair. "I'm Beck Avery."

Beck. The only other Beck I know is a burly short-haired stagehand who shuns her given name of Rebecca.

"Donovan Eastman," I say, surprising myself by giving my full name. Most of my friends call me Van, even if Donovan's what's in the playbill.

"Pete's actor friend, right?" Beck says. "I'm Jack's cousin."

"You could be brothers."

"You think? Wish we were. Jack's the best." Beck pulls a bottle of ibuprofen out of his pocket and sets it on the table. A thin leather bracelet dangles around his left wrist; it's woven with small beads whose colors make a rainbow. "If I die before the coffee gets here, let Jack know, okay?"

He clearly feels like shit, but I appreciate his self-deprecating sense of humor. "I guess you had fun last night."

"A little too much fun," Beck admits. "Haven't partied that hard since college."

"Must not have been that long ago," I comment. The guy looks young, despite his current ashen pallor.

"A few years," Beck says vaguely. "Anyway, last night was a celebration."

"Weddings are happy occasions, I'm told."

"I'm happy for Jack. Pete's really cool. They're kind of relationship goals, you know?"

I wince. So he's one of those.

Ruth forestalls the mild rant that's on the tip of my tongue by setting Beck's coffee and toast on the table, and I stop her before she can hurry away. "Ruth, honey, can you bring us a big glass of water?" She nods and rushes off.

Beck takes a bite of toast, chews slowly. I feel like I'm getting a sympathetic stomachache watching him force it down.

"Dry toast is a mistake, friend," I say lightly. "You need something greasy."

He groans. "Don't think I can handle it yet."

"Black coffee on an empty stomach won't do you any good, either."

"I have a system," Beck says. "Or at least, I used to. Actually, bacon sounds pretty good."

When Ruth comes back with the water, I ask her for

a bacon-and-egg breakfast sandwich and push the glass across the table. "This is for you."

"Thanks." Beck alternates small sips of water and coffee with bites of toast until the breakfast sandwich arrives. Then he takes the pain meds and devours the sandwich while I finish my veggie bowl. The bacon smells good, and I regret opting for the healthier choice, but I choke it down, anyway.

"Feeling a little more human?" I ask when Beck sits back in his chair and takes off his sunglasses.

"Getting there. Thanks for the assist."

With his glasses off, I can see Beck's eyes are pale blue. A little color has come back to his cheeks, high-lighting strong cheekbones. He's a good-looking man.

"No problem." I turn my charming smile on full force, testing the waters. Gratifyingly, Beck's eyes widen slightly and the color in his cheeks deepens. I'm not exactly trying to pick up Pete's new husband's cousin, but I'm not exactly trying not to. What am I going to do for the next few hours—actually work on my play?

"So, now that you're no longer at death's door, you got plans?"

Beck flicks his eyes to the big wall clock behind the register. "Not for a while. Why?"

"I was going to explore Rosedale a little. Up for a walk?"

Beck puts his hand over his flat stomach. "I think so. Fresh air sounds good."

We clear the dishes to the counter, and I slip Ruth a ten for the breakfast sandwich.

"You don't have to do that," Beck says.

"My treat. Ruth, can I ask a huge favor? I'm a friend of Pete Blekitny. Could I leave my suitcase here for a couple of hours?"

"Sure?" Ruth says. "I'll put it in the back?"

"Thanks, darling." I tuck another five in the tip jar and shoulder my backpack. "You ready?"

Beck slides his Ray-Bans over his nose like he's donning armor. He nods carefully. "Ready."

As we walk outside, Beck laughs lightly. "Does your charm work on everyone? I think that girl was about to offer to have your babies."

"Mostly just on straight women and gay men," I say, affecting false modesty.

"Oh, I hate being a cliché," Beck says with a dramatic sigh.

I'd been pretty sure, but I like getting the confirmation. "Don't worry. My charm is a power I only use for good."

"And for getting hapless men into your bed?" Beck asks wryly.

"That's what I said. I use my power for good. And I'm very good," I say, riding the line between smug and confident.

Beck just laughs again. "Wow. Jack said you were, um, friendly. But do lines like that actually work?"

I stop on the sidewalk outside a thrift store and put a hand on my hip. "Why do I feel like I should be offended?"

"Oh, I'm not judging. But you're an attractive, charming actor. You probably haven't had to work for it in a while."

How did this conversation turn into a critique of my pickup style? But maybe I need it, since it doesn't seem to be working on Beck. Even though he just called me attractive, he seems more amused than interested.

"What about you?" I ask, prickly now. "You never fall for a line?"

"Oh, I have. That's how I know to be wary of them. You want to go in here?" Beck gestures to the open door of the thrift shop, then walks in without waiting for me to respond.

The interior of the shop is much darker than the bright June day outside, and I have to let my eyes adjust for a moment. Beck keeps his glasses on as he starts browsing a table full of kitchen stuff.

"This is nice," he says, lifting up what looks like an ordinary mixing bowl.

"A bowl?"

"It's a great size." Beck turns it over and glances at the price. "A steal." He tucks it under his arm and continues his perusal of the shop, stopping at a rack of used books.

I watch him for a moment, intrigued against my better judgment by this young man with wholesome good looks, a faint Texas accent, preppy clothes, and a predilection for random kitchen tools. "So, you travel far for the wedding?"

"It's complicated," Beck says, taking what looks like an old cookbook from the rack and putting it in the bowl. "I came from Boston, but that's because I've been couch-surfing for a few weeks. Before Boston, I was in Portland. Maine, not Oregon. And before that, Hackensack. I've been putting a lot of miles on my car the last few months."

"I've never met a preppy vagabond before."

Beck laughs again. He seems to do that a lot. He has a nice laugh, not a giggle, but not a belly laugh, either. Somewhere in the middle.

"Preppy vagabond. I like that. No, I'm just" — he pauses as if searching for the right words, fingering the sleeve of a jean jacket with hideous patches sewn all over, then belatedly finishes his sentence — "at loose ends."

That I can identify with. Ever since finishing the run of my last play, I've been at loose ends, too. I'm at a cross-roads, career-wise, and I keep putting off my decision as to which path I should go down.

"Well, you're young," I say, to keep things casual with this near stranger. "You'll figure it out."

"I'm twenty-five." Beck sighs. "Not that young anymore."

I chuckle. "Look, I'm thirty, so don't talk to me about not being young."

"You're only thirty?" Beck says, sounding surprised. Then he must realize how that sounds. "Not that you look—never mind."

"It's okay. I always read older. It's the nose." I resist touching my crooked nose, the feature that pushes my face from handsome to merely interesting.

"I like your nose," Beck says quietly.

"Yeah?" My sixth sense for a possible hookup sharpens. Sure, it's eleven-thirty in the morning, and we've only just met, but those are details. On the other hand, we can't exactly hook up in the alley behind the thrift store. But maybe Beck's staying an extra night in Rosedale and we could get together later. I'm about to ask what his evening plans are when Beck's phone buzzes in his pocket, surprisingly loud in the quiet shop.

"Hold these, will you?" Without waiting for an answer, Beck pushes his finds into my arms and gets out his phone. He glances at the screen, types out a quick message, and flashes me what seems to be a regretful smile. "I gotta get going earlier than I thought."

"Hitting the road?" I shouldn't be disappointed.

"No, but—" The chime of my phone interrupts whatever Beck was going to say. I shift Beck's stuff back to him and get out my own phone to see a text from Pete.

> Hey, can you meet us at the house
> now? If you're not free, 1 still works.

Since my outing with Beck has been cut short anyway, I don't see why not.

I type back a quick reply and order a car from my favorite ride app while I'm at it. Beck chats with the gray-haired lady behind the sales counter as she rings up his purchases. She coos over something he says—clearly Beck has his own skills in the charming straight women department.

The ride app tells me my driver will meet me in front of Hot Brew in six minutes. Outside on the sidewalk, I feel an urge to get Beck's number, which is ridiculous. I'm going to be spending the next two months right here in Rosedale, and who knows where Beck's off to next?

"All set?" I ask when Beck walks out with a brown paper shopping bag with the store's name, Second Time

Around, stamped on the side. The midday sun is brighter than ever, and Beck pulls the bill of his hat down a little farther over his forehead.

"Yeah, that was fun. Sorry I have to run." Beck smiles and again, I want to ask him for...something. I'm not sure quite what I'd ask for, and not knowing throws me off.

Finally, I say, "Keep drinking water."

"I will." Beck doesn't move, but I can't think of anything else to say.

"Well, nice meeting you." I hold out my hand.

"Nice meeting you, Donovan," Beck says, shaking my hand. His skin is warm and dry, and it occurs to me this is the first time we've touched.

Then he lets go, crosses the street, and unlocks a spiffy little black European hatchback parked at the curb.

I turn my back on him reluctantly, but I have to hustle back down the block to meet my ride, a big gray SUV.

I ask the driver to wait while I collect my bag from Ruth, and by the time I'm settled inside the vehicle, Beck's hatchback is gone.

I shake off an unexpected pang of regret. So Beck is cute, and funny, and just a bit mysterious, with all his talk of loose ends and his strange love of mixing bowls. But I'll probably never see him again.

The idea is strangely depressing.

TWO

BECK

I PULL into Jack and Pete's U-shaped driveway and kill the GTI's engine. I pat the bottle of ibuprofen in my pocket to reassure myself it's still there, even though it'll be a few hours before I can take more, and force myself out of the car. The house seems relatively quiet—looking at the charming two-story Cape-style house today, I would never have known a hundred-person wedding reception was held here the night before.

In fact, if my hangover wasn't still making me feel like the sun is actively trying to kill me while I wait for someone to answer the doorbell, I'd have no evidence at all of the big event.

Except for the memory of Donovan Eastman this morning, teasing me over coffee and a greasy breakfast sandwich.

And Jack's platinum wedding ring, which glints offendingly in the sun when he finally opens the door.

"I'm never drinking again," I declare, passing into the cool, blessedly sun-free interior of the house.

Jack chuckles, the jerk. "Feeling it this morning? You were pretty wasted."

I take off my sunglasses and hook them onto the front of my shirt. "Don't laugh. This is your fault. Tell me again why you and Pete had to get married?"

"Because we're madly in love with each other and we want the world to know it," Jack says with a wickedly smug smile. "Come on, there's coffee in the kitchen."

I trail my cousin to the gorgeous space with its clean white counters and handsome dark blue accents and take a seat on one of the blue leather barstools lined up on one side of the big kitchen island. "I already had coffee, but can I get some water?" Donovan's parting words echo in my brain. Sure, the stupid actor hadn't asked for my number, but at least he cared enough to remind me to hydrate.

I swallow a disappointed sigh. It's not like I can get involved with anyone at the moment, anyway. Donovan is probably heading back to the city right now, while I spend the next two months house-sitting while Jack and Pete go on an extended honeymoon. Yesterday, I'd been excited about not having to worry about the future for a little while longer. Today, with my hangover and my strange but intriguing morning with Donovan, I kind of wish I had the freedom to head off to New York if I wanted.

Oh well. That's me in a nutshell. The grass is always greener, and no amount of fence hopping has brought me any closer to knowing what I really want to do with my life.

Jack hands me a tall glass of cold tap water. "There's a ton of leftovers in the fridge."

"Later." I down half the glass gratefully. Donovan was right. The water helps. "So, give me the download. Where is Cleo, anyway?" House-sitting really means dog-sitting for Jack and Pete's cute brown rescue pup.

"Miss Cleo is in the backyard with Pete. They'll be here in a minute. Actually, I need to talk to you about something. There was sort of a mix-up and it turns out Pete and I both accidentally—"

The front bell chimes. Jack shoots me an apologetic glance. "Hang on. It'll be easier to explain to both of you at the same time, anyway."

"Both of us?" But Jack's already gone.

I set my phone down, then lay my head on my arms. The cold surface of the white stone countertop refreshes my skin and eases the pounding in my head. It hadn't been so bad when I was talking and, okay, flirting a little with Donovan. But without the distraction, I'm forcibly reminded how spectacularly I overdid it the night before.

Voices are coming down the hall, but I can't be bothered to lift my bowling-ball-heavy head.

"—he's in the kitchen. Want some coffee?" Jack offers the visitor.

The newcomer says, "Didn't expect to see you so soon." Donovan's voice.

Donovan.

I raise my head too fast and the resulting stab of pain shoots from the base of my skull to my eyebrows. I wince and shut my eyes against a wave of dizziness.

A hand on my elbow steadies me somewhat.

"You okay?" Jack asks. But when I crack open my eyes experimentally, it's Donovan who's six inches away, Donovan's hand on my arm. From this distance, I can clearly see his blue eyes, a darker shade than my own, framed by thick black lashes, and a day's worth of stubble on his cheeks.

"I'm okay," I say after a beat. I shift slightly and Donovan drops his hold. "Sorry. Just got dizzy for a second. What are you doing here?"

Before Donovan can answer, the French doors that lead from the kitchen to the back patio open and a thirty-pound bundle of chocolate brown fur bounds inside, followed by a lanky six-foot-something man with longish brown hair that curls around his ears.

"Van, hey," Pete says, closing the French doors behind him. Cleo sniffs at my knees, then inspects Donovan's sneakers. "And Beck, great. Sorry about the mix-up, but I think this will actually work out well for you two."

"What mix-up?" Donovan asks at the same time I say, "What will work out?"

"I haven't told them yet," Jack says, giving Pete an exasperated smile.

"Told us what?" I'm starting to get a bad feeling about whatever my cousin isn't saying.

"Spit it out," Donovan says gruffly.

"So, we accidentally double-booked the house. Pete asked Van if he could stay here and take care of Cleo, and I asked you, Beck. And since you," he turns to Van, "are such a great friend and you," he points to me, "are such an amazing cousin, you dropped everything to help us out. Which we really appreciate."

Jack doesn't point out that he's doing me a favor by giving me a place to live rent-free for two months, and I don't bring it up.

"So what now?" Donovan asks.

"Well, if one of you wants to be let off the hook, now's your chance to speak up," Pete says.

I'm not about to give up the gig that easily. My fantasies about following Donovan to New York notwithstanding, I don't really like the city. And if Donovan's here, I've lost my incentive to leave. I glance at him, but he keeps his lips pressed together.

"Or you can both stay here," Pete goes on. "Which I think is the ideal solution. That way, if one of you has something come up, there's a backup to take care of Cleo. She'll get twice as much attention, and the house is big enough that the two of you don't even have to see each other much if you don't want to. I know it's a little strange to have an unexpected roommate, but, hey, we've had worse living situations, right, Van?"

Donovan's lips curl. "Don't remind me." He glances my way, seeming to study me. I'm overly aware of my wrinkled shirt, my battered boat shoes. I was in too much pain to be self-conscious this morning, but now it feels as if I'm being inspected and will be found wanting.

It doesn't help that Donovan, even in a casual T-shirt, jeans, and a plain black baseball cap, emanates a sort of rugged magnetic beauty, the kind that makes you want to never stop looking at him and shy away at the same time. I've never seen him act, but I can imagine a camera loving him, an audience hanging on his every word.

Maybe he'll bail and I won't have to figure out how to

live in close quarters with a man I have a hard time simply looking at.

"Well," Donovan catches my gaze for a split second, then turns to Pete and shrugs nonchalantly, "I'm cool with it if Beck is."

I've never regretted my love of tequila more. My brain is too foggy to think this through. I don't want to find somewhere else to live for the summer, but is it such a good idea to share a house with a guy I'm attracted to? On the other hand, outside the thrift shop, I gave Donovan an opening to ask me out—and he hadn't taken it, so that answers that.

Donovan is just a guy. I try to remember the way we bantered in the coffee shop, the thrift store. We'd gotten along, right?

Besides, I really don't have much choice. I have nowhere else to go.

"I'm cool with it." My voice sounds far away to my own ears.

Pete and Jack share a relieved smile and Cleo barks once, as if to signal her approval as well.

I lean down to scratch her behind the ears, and the dizziness comes back with a hefty dose of nausea. I gingerly let myself off the stool. "I'm going to throw up now."

"You don't want to throw up that delicious breakfast, do you?" Donovan asks, sounding amused.

I put a hand on my stomach. "Might not have much of a choice."

"Jack, do you have an ice pack?" Donovan asks quickly.

A moment later, a cold pack is being pressed to the back of my neck, and I'm being led to the living room couch.

"Better?"

I blink up at Donovan, my nausea receding. "Yeah. Thanks."

Donovan winks. "No problem, roomie."

My stomach swoops and it has nothing to do with my hangover. Shit.

"I'll get the info on Cleo and fill you in later. Take it easy."

"Thanks," I say again, and Donovan leaves me to suffer in peace. I'm not at my best right now, but I have to believe that when I get the poison out of my system, I can handle spending two months living with a guy who presses all my buttons. It doesn't have to be weird. I'm a grown up. I can totally handle this.

I close my eyes, move the ice pack from my neck to my forehead, yawn.

I'll handle it just as soon as I wake up from my nap.

THREE
DONOVAN

"AND IF SHE doesn't poop in the morning, she usually gets a little fussy around lunchtime, so really try to get her to go on the morning walk."

I glance at Cleo, curled up and snoozing in her bed in the corner of the kitchen. Seems the dog has a bed in almost every room of the house.

"You guys are going to spoil your kids so bad," I say, instead of making fun of Pete for the overly detailed instructions. He's printed everything out on three single-spaced 8 1/2 by 11 sheets of paper and has been going over it word by word. I'm all for doing a good job, but this seems like overkill.

Pete doesn't rise to my bait. "And the vet's number is here, but there's also an animal urgent care on Route 7 if something happens after hours."

"Pete, I've got this. *We've* got this," I say, remembering I'm not the only one taking care of Cleo, and suddenly grateful for the extra pair of hands to share the load of taking care of Pete's fur-baby.

"Yeah, I know." He smiles self-deprecatingly. "We've just never left her for longer than a weekend before."

"It's going to be fine. Beck and I will take good care of Cleo and the house." There are an additional two pages detailing the security system, the landscaper's schedule, trash collection, the names and numbers of local handymen, and how to turn off the gas and water hookups in the basement.

"Speaking of Beck, are you sure you're okay with this? I've only met him a couple of times, but Jack says he's a great person."

"Oh, yeah, sure." I sound more confident than I feel. Acting skills for the win. When the driver had pulled into the driveway earlier today and I'd seen Beck's car parked there, I suddenly felt like I'd been stabbed with a syringe of adrenaline. Was the universe telling me to take another shot at the cute blond? It hadn't occurred to me that Beck was there not to say goodbye to his cousin before he took off to parts unknown, but to stay for the summer, just like me.

My attraction to Beck seems more like a liability than a perk now. We're going to be living together, and I've never broken my own rule about not shitting where I eat. That means never hooking up with a co-star, at least not while the show's still running, and never *ever* hooking up with a roommate.

Sure, the circumstances are a little different considering we'll have separate rooms in a 2,500 square foot house instead of sharing a bedroom in an 800 square foot New York apartment, but the principle is the same. I've had enough roommates to know it's usually best to keep them at arm's length.

So Beck's cute. Doesn't change the fact I'm here for a specific reason—to write my stupid play. I'll just have to scratch the itch with someone else.

"By the way, is there anywhere to meet guys in this town?"

Pete shakes his head, as if my question disappoints him. My shoulders stiffen. I don't have to explain myself to Pete or anyone else. I'm a thirty-year-old man with a healthy libido and I haven't gotten off with anyone in three whole weeks, which may not sound like a long time, but for me is a new record. It's a legitimate question.

"There's Sparkle, the gay bar in Midville. They have live music sometimes on the weekend. Which reminds me, you can use my car if you want. The keys are in the cupboard. But promise me you won't drink and drive."

"I promise, Dad."

Pete rolls his eyes. "Okay, fine. I get it. Have fun."

He puts his hands up in surrender, but I'm not done being defensive.

"Just because monogamy turns you on, that doesn't mean we've all been brainwashed into thinking we have to be with only one person for the rest of our lives."

Pete frowns. "I'm not saying you have to get married, but when was the last time you stayed with a guy for even a week? You might actually like it if you tried it."

"I've tried it," I say sullenly. Pete's one of the only people who even remembers that far back.

"You mean Aidan? That was eight years ago," Pete says gently.

The gentleness rankles. I'm not a delicate flower. "Yeah, I learned my lesson and I'm perfectly happy; thank you very much."

"I know you got burned. Hell, I was there helping you pick up the pieces," Pete says, still with the soft voice. "But what if I'd let what happened with Kurt stop me from trying? I'd never have found Jack."

"That's completely different." Pete's toxic ex stole from him, gaslit him, and cheated on him, and is now serving time for embezzlement. Aidan hadn't been a literal criminal—he'd just taught me the valuable lesson that the more you love someone, the more they can hurt you.

Pete stares at me, his eyes melting like chocolate coins in the sun.

I sigh. Pete's superpower is he can say whatever he wants and get away with it. He's too good to stay mad at. "You got lucky, okay?" I try on a smile. "I'm fine. You don't have to worry about me."

"Let me just say one more thing and then I promise I will leave you in peace for two whole months," Pete says.

"Except when you're texting me to check on Cleo."

"Which I promise to do no more than once a day. Twice at most," he amends. "Anyway, I just want you to know that I admire your stubborn streak. It's what's gotten you where you are—an honest-to-god working New York actor. You did it. The thing you wanted to be— you made it. And I think that the play you're writing will be amazing. Stubbornness can be a good thing when you aren't giving up on your dreams, but don't let it stop you from going after other things, too."

"Things like long-term relationships?" I ask sharply, stubborn enough to be unwilling to let him get the last word.

"Maybe. Or maybe just more than a one-night stand. It doesn't have to be all or nothing. Keep an open mind. Isn't that what writers should do, anyway?"

I roll my shoulders to relieve them of the anxiety that's locked them up. "Come on, Pete, I'm not really a writer."

"What are you talking about?" He waves his hands and knocks the printed instructions to the floor. As I bend down to pick them up, he keeps talking. "I read the one-act play you won that award for. It was freaking good. Which reminds me—The Rosedale Art Center puts on a Shakespeare comedy every summer. I think they already cast it, but maybe you'd want to ask them if they need any help."

I straighten up and heroically refrain from wincing. Add community theater to the list of things I don't dig. But Pete means well, and he is giving me a place to stay rent free, even if I have to share it with a too-cute, currently hungover, off-limits boy.

"Yeah, maybe," I say noncommittally. "Look, you and your man go have the time of your lives and don't worry about anything—especially me."

"I'm good with that plan," Jack says, coming into the kitchen dragging a giant rolling suitcase.

"I thought you were packing light?" Pete's eyes widen when he takes in the size of his husband's luggage.

"I tried, sweetheart," Jack says plaintively.

"Where are we going to put all the clothes you said you'd buy me?"

"I guess we'll just have to get another suitcase while we're there." Jack sidles up to his husband and gives him a sickeningly besotted grin.

I absolutely do not make a gagging noise. I'm thirty, not thirteen.

"We better get going. You got everything you need?" Jack asks me.

"Pete has thoroughly briefed me. You two crazy kids get out of here. Europe is waiting."

"Thanks for doing this. And thanks for being cool about Beck. He doesn't really have anywhere else to go right now, so I'll feel better knowing he's set for a little while. And between the two of you, I know Cleo will be well taken care of."

"Sure, no problem," I say, wondering again why Beck is so transient. "Now get."

Pete and Jack take turns giving Cleo goodbye kisses, then they each give me a goodbye hug. We all tromp out of the kitchen and down the hall toward the front door.

"You guys leaving?" It's Beck, standing in the doorway to the living room. His pink shirt is as wrinkled as yesterday's newspaper, and he has matching pink sleep lines from the couch pillows etched into the side of his face.

As I hope the nap has done him some good, a wave of fondness hits me low in the chest and throws me off-balance.

"Hey, sleepyhead, just in time to say goodbye," Jack

says, pushing past me to give his cousin a bear hug. "You be good this summer, you hear?"

Beck yawns expansively. "I promise."

Pete takes a turn hugging his cousin-in-law, and then the newlyweds are gone, whisked away by the car service they ordered to take them to the airport.

The house suddenly feels extra quiet. I glance at Beck, who's rubbing his eyes like a little kid. "I bet you could eat a horse."

He groans. "Oh my god, I've never been so hungry in my life."

"Come on, let's see what's in the fridge."

OKAY, so maybe this summer won't be a total shitshow.

After Donovan and I raid the fridge for wedding reception leftovers and serve ourselves a curious, but not unsatisfying, early supper of mini quiches, fruit skewers, and carnitas from last night's taco bar, my headache is almost gone. The liter of water I down helps, too.

We manage to feed Cleo her dinner according to the comically detailed instructions left by Pete. Next up— escorting her on her evening walk.

I don my sunglasses again, but that's because the sun is still high in the sky this close to the solstice, not because I'm going to die if I don't.

Still, I happily let Donovan take charge of Cleo's lead while we walk on the grassy shoulder of Wild Rose Lane. Pete sketched out a couple of his and Jack's favorite walking routes, and I study the directions. "If we turn left up here, there's a long street that ends in a cul-de-sac."

"Left, got it," Donovan says easily. He's been pretty easy since I woke up from my nap. He gave me the short version of Pete's care guide and cleaned up the kitchen after our meal. I'm still getting my bearings, but so far it doesn't seem like this co-house-sitting, co-dog-sitting thing will be a huge problem.

"So, tell me your life story," I say as we veer onto Turner Street.

Donovan stumbles but rights himself before he actually falls. "Excuse me?"

"Your life story," I repeat. "We're going to be living with each other for the next two months. Let's skip to the good stuff."

"I'm pretty boring."

"Well, that's a total lie," I scoff. "You have a super cool job, for one thing. Did you always want to be an actor? Where are you from? Do you have any siblings? What about college?"

He laughs and pauses to let Cleo sniff a mailbox post in front of a colonial-style house. I slow to wait for them.

"You really want to know? Or are you just being polite?"

"'Stop being polite and start getting real,'" I intone.

"You're too young to have watched *The Real World*," he says skeptically.

I grin, pleased he picked up the reference. "I had cool older cousins, remember? I watched a lot of shit I probably shouldn't have." I think about waiting out hot Texas summer days in Jack's parents' basement watching TV and playing video games with Jack and his brother and sister.

"Where were your parents while you were rotting your brain with reality TV?" Donovan asks.

At the mention of my own parents, I suppress a grimace and deploy my well-practiced deflection technique. "Nope. I asked you first. Come on, pony up the deets, Donovan."

Cleo, done with her inspection, ambles on, and we follow obediently.

"Fine. I wanted to be an actor from the first time I saw live theater. I grew up in Upstate New York and—"

"Where upstate?"

"This tiny little town near the Finger Lakes. Beautiful and boring. Kind of like Rosedale, actually. Anyway, in seventh grade my mom took me to see a touring production of *Phantom*. I was hooked. Unfortunately, I can't carry a tune in a tote bag, so I stick to plays."

I eye him and try to picture an adolescent Donovan being captivated by a romantic eighties-era musical. It's hard to think of him as anything but effortlessly charismatic, but it's comforting to imagine he was a theater dork before he was Donovan Eastman, Broadway star.

When I realize I've been looking at his charmingly crooked profile for too long, I rush to fill the silence. "I'm not that into musicals, no offense."

"What? Don't they revoke your gay card for that?" he asks with mock severity.

I smile wryly. "I know, I'm such a disappointment." If only it were that easy.

"Anyway, what were your other questions?"

"Siblings? College? Big break?"

Donovan shakes his head, as if he can't believe he's letting me bully him, but he answers anyway. "One sister, married with kids, is still upstate. I went to NYU, did the theater program, waited tables forever, finally broke out a few years ago with a great part in a hot play that got nominated for a bunch of Tonys. I've been supporting myself as an actor ever since, mostly theater but some commercials and guest spots on TV. I've been lucky, but I also could have quit so many times and I just...didn't."

"That's cool." I admire him for sticking with what is no doubt a demoralizing job with more lows than highs. "You don't seem like a quitter."

"According to Pete, I'm stubborn."

"Huh. Don't like people telling you what to do?"

"Hey, I can take direction. When called for," Donovan says with a sly smile.

I purse my lips. He could be referring to the directors of his plays, but it kind of sounds like he's talking about taking direction in the bedroom. I hastily push the mental images that crop up as far to the back of my brain as I can.

"So, why are you here?"

"Why are any of us here?" Donovan answers facetiously, gesturing grandly to the tree-lined street of large grassy lots and well-kept post-war houses.

I give him my bitchiest glare and Donovan relents, dropping his hands to his sides. "I'm here because Pete asked me to take care of Cleo, and he never asks me for anything."

For the first time, it occurs to me that maybe he and Pete have a romantic history. I swallow. Should I press my luck and ask? It really isn't any of my business, and Donovan and I are getting along so far—I don't want to make the next two months any more awkward than they're already going to be.

Instead, I say, "That was nice of you, to upend your life like that."

He lets out a little huff. "Well, if we're being honest here, I was kind of excited about the chance to get out of the city. I lost my lease about a month ago and I've been imposing on another friend ever since. My last show ended around the same time, and my agent's working on setting me up with something for the fall, but in the meantime, I'm supposed to be writing a play."

"You're a playwright, too?" How many layers does this onion have?

"Not really." Donovan seems uncomfortable at the term. When I lift my eyebrows, he elaborates. "I wrote a little one-act on a whim and, without telling me, my agent entered it into a contest. Somehow it won. Suddenly, I had producers wanting to talk to me. I never thought about writing seriously before, but Joan thinks I'm getting burned out, told me to take a break from the grind of auditions and eight shows a week and stew in my creative juices. Whatever that means."

The irritation in his voice doesn't distract me from the vulnerability on his face. It's strange to see him uncertain about something, since he's projected effortless competence all day. I want to be reassuring, but despite this accelerated get-to-know-you game, I really don't know him well enough to be sure what to say, so I keep it light. "Stewing in creative juices—sounds delicious."

He laughs a little, making the corners of his eyes crease attractively. I deliberately turn my gaze away and land on a house at the very end of the street. It's different from the others we've passed—the front yard is an overgrown tangle of grass and rose bushes, the windows are dark, and there's no car in the gravel driveway. A yellow newspaper sits disintegrating on the front step. The dark blue paint on the charming two-story wood frame house is peeling around the windows and the front door looks like it was once white but is now mottled green with some kind of moss.

"A fairy-tale cottage," I whisper, pushing my sunglasses down my nose so I can see it more clearly.

Donovan squints at the property. "A dump," he says flatly.

"A fixer-upper," I correct him. There's something about the house, clearly unlived-in, that makes me ache a little. Every other house on the street is tidy and neat. Boring. This one has gone to seed but has more character than all the rest. "I wonder if it's on the market."

"You looking to buy?" He makes it sound like a joke.

I open my mouth, then think better of it. People tend to treat me differently after I explain about my family. Instead, I shake my head. "You're right. I shouldn't tempt myself with things I can't have."

Donovan stares at the house for another minute, letting Cleo explore the overgrown flowerbed outside the split-rail fence that separates the front yard from the sidewalk.

"Wonder what the story is," he muses. "Squabbling relatives? Maybe it's haunted."

"Ah, your writer's imagination is showing," I say, delighted.

He shrugs. "More likely the owner got moved to

assisted living and their kids don't know what to do with it."

"Way to take the romance out of it," I say dryly. "Well, anyway, you're right. It would be a lot of work to fix it up."

"You know about that kind of thing?" Donovan asks when we turn back toward home, Cleo leading the way.

"Not really. I once painted my dorm room purple—other than that, I'm not really handy. But I could learn." I picture myself as a house flipper, rewiring and, uh, doing plumbing...things. It doesn't exactly appeal. But I could hire people—that's what Jack and Pete did when they bought their house. They redid the kitchen and bathrooms, added a studio for Pete, and completely overhauled the pool.

I wonder what the kitchen's like in the dark blue house. I might not be handy, but I like to cook, and I love to bake. The kitchen is usually the only place I can fully relax.

"Purple?" Donovan sounds appalled.

"Yeah, it's the color of passion. I thought it would help me get laid." I laugh, remembering the irony of my first college boyfriend being color blind.

"Wouldn't have thought you'd need much help," he says mildly.

I glance at him, surprised. He was definitely flirting with me this morning, but now it's hard to tell if he means anything by that. Our little coffee klatch feels like a million years ago.

"Thanks, but it was harder than you might think. I

went to a small college in a small town. The odds were not in my favor."

"Shoulda gone to college in the city."

"I'm not really a city person. I grew up in one and it didn't exactly work out, either."

"What city was that?" he asks.

"Austin."

"Was growing up gay in Texas the nightmare I'm picturing?"

"It was okay." I'm not lying. It wasn't great, but it could have been much worse. But high school sucks for everyone, and I don't like to live in the past. "I wasn't out, so it was a little lonely."

"Yeah," Donovan says simply, as if he knows what I mean. I can't imagine growing up gay in Upstate New York was much better than my experience. We don't talk for a while and I enjoy the breather. I started the twenty questions routine, but my headache's coming back. I want to go to sleep and wake up feeling like a different person.

Which reminds me—"Hey, where are we going to sleep?" I ask as we near the turn back to Wild Rose Lane.

"Where are we...oh, which rooms?" he asks, his brow clearing as he figures out what I mean.

"Yeah. What did Jack and Pete say?"

"Well, there are three bedrooms upstairs, if you count their room, and the one off the kitchen."

"I'll take that one," I say quickly. "If that's okay with you."

"Sure. I'll take one of the guest rooms. Probably the one in the front."

"Sounds good."

"They said Cleo gets up early to be let out. You want me to do it tomorrow?"

"No, you've already done more than your share. I'll get up with her."

"Okay."

Negotiations concluded, we walk in silence back to the house. Cleo flops on the bed in the kitchen. Donovan disappears upstairs, and I bring my bags out of the car where they've been roasting all day. I set the paper bag with the mixing bowl and eighties-era cookbook I bought that morning on the kitchen island and let my shoulders drop. My lungs expand as I breathe in deep, then let the air out slowly.

This day has not gone at all how I thought it would, but after waking up with the worst hangover of my life, I'm ending it in a pretty good spot. I have a place to live. I have a gorgeous kitchen to bash around in. And I've made a new friend.

Sort of.

FIVE
DONOVAN

I ALWAYS SLEEP BADLY the first night in a strange location. But after a shitty night's sleep at the motel, I sink into the comfortable guest bed at the front of Jack and Pete's house and fall into a rare deep sleep, waking up to birdsong outside my window at the civilized hour of eight o'clock. I'm weirdly rested. I wasn't woken up by emergency sirens or upstairs neighbors or slamming doors.

Huh.

Maybe there's something to small-town life after all.

I take a quick shower before checking the weather on my phone. We're due for another warm, sunny day. Aside from the lightweight suit I wore to the wedding, I packed mostly jeans and T-shirts. I did remember my swim trunks at the last minute, but maybe I should have brought more shorts. I throw on the only pair I have, army green ones that accentuate the olive tones of my skin, and tug a plain dark gray shirt over my head.

I wonder how Beck's doing. I assume he got up with

Cleo because I haven't heard anything to the contrary, but I steel myself to find a hungry dog and a still-hungover man when I get downstairs.

I'm still adjusting to the idea of spending the next two months living with Beck. We've gotten along so far, but then there's the pesky attraction that pops up at seemingly random times. Like last night—we'd gotten through a picnic-style dinner of wedding leftovers. Then while we walked Cleo in this Stepford-perfect neighborhood, Beck stopped to admire the most rundown house on the block and I wanted...well, I'm not sure what, exactly. I'm used to wanting sex—and yesterday morning, that's exactly what I was picturing with the guy.

But twenty-four hours later, Beck isn't just a random guy. He's my roommate. And that means it doesn't matter what I want, even if I could figure it out. Roommates are a hard no. I'm going to keep things purely friendly for the next two months. Easy as pie.

I grab my baseball cap, sunglasses, phone, and wallet, and carry my shoes downstairs, enjoying the novelty of bare feet on the cool hardwood floors. I rarely go barefoot in the city, even in my own apartment.

My plan for the day, such as it is, is to take Pete's car into town for breakfast and a trip to the grocery store. Maybe Beck wants to add a few things to the list, or even come with me.

Provided he's awake and functional.

Picturing Beck rumpled and sleepy, I'm stunned by the sight that meets me in the kitchen when I walk in, Beck at the big six-burner stove with his back to me, working on something emitting an appetizing smell. He's gotten the shorts memo, too, and is wearing dark blue ones that hug his rear and stop just beneath the full globes of his ass, showing off pale, lightly muscled legs that move in time to the strains of classical music coming from the built-in wall speakers. He has on a loose sky-blue tank top that exposes bony shoulders. The back of his neck is bare, and I'm hit with an unexpected desire to run my nose along the shorn hair there, to find out what he smells like and how soft his skin is.

No. Friendly thoughts only.

"What's all this?"

Beck whirls around holding a spatula like a weapon. "Oh, you startled me." He leans over and hits a button on his phone. The music stops.

I can differentiate scents now, something sweet and cinnamon in the pan on the stove and the welcome bitter aroma of coffee coming from a machine on the counter by the window.

"You're cooking?"

"I like to cook," Beck says, smiling. "Didn't I mention that before? And bake. And they might have a Nancy Meyers-esque kitchen, but Jack and Pete barely have the basics, so I'm definitely going to the store today. I started a list if you want to add anything. Oh, and I got the coffee machine figured out. Help yourself. Do you like cinnamon? I wanted to make waffles, but I didn't have the right ingredients, so this is just French toast with my own little twist. It's almost ready. They do have real maple syrup at least, the brutes."

I stare at Beck until I'm sure the flow of words has come to a stop. "So you're feeling better," I say.

Beck laughs. "So much better. The bed down here is amazing. Cleo and I got up around six. I am a new man."

"Six?" I feel vaguely guilty for getting up late, even though eight is barely sleeping in by my usual standards. I glance at Cleo, who's gnawing on some kind of complicated dog toy in her bed. "Thanks."

"No problem. She's an angel. But I think she needs to go out again. Maybe you could take her while I get the food on the table. Scrambled eggs okay?"

I'm still slightly baffled by this new energetically domestic Beck. But I'm not going to turn down a home-cooked breakfast, especially one that smells this good.

"Yeah, okay. Thanks." I slip on my shoes and open the French door that leads from the kitchen to the patio and the fenced-in backyard beyond. Cleo automatically trots to the door at the sound, and the two of us go outside. She jogs around the big lawn—they have two acres, Pete told me once, about an acre for the house, garage, and the yard, a rectangle of lawn abutting the generous stone patio, with the fenced-in pool off to the side. The other acre is deciduous woods that surround the house on three sides, shielding it from the neighbors, at least during the leafy months.

Pete's done well for himself. I'm not exactly jealous. But I am a little surprised at how good it feels to be here, pulling fresh air into my lungs, the only sounds the snuffling of Cleo in the grass as she locates a good spot to do her morning business and the ambient noise of birds and the occasional car passing by on Wild Rose Lane. I have the day ahead of me to do whatever I want, starting with breakfast waiting inside. I shake off the feeling that things are too good to be true.

Cleo squats and I chuckle. That's the reality check I need. It's a beautiful morning, but there's still shit to pick up. I grab the scooper Pete showed me yesterday and take care of the mess.

I throw a tennis ball a couple of times for Cleo, but she seems to lose interest just when I fear I might pass out if I don't get an infusion of calories. She follows me inside without a fuss and I wash my hands at the big white porcelain kitchen sink.

"Perfect timing," Beck says sunnily as he emerges from the walk-in pantry with a glass jar of dark brown liquid. Maple syrup. Probably from some tiny local farm.

There are two places set at the island, complete with two plates filled with fluffy-looking scrambled eggs, golden French toast, and the last of the fruit from the wedding.

"No bacon, but I put it on the list," Beck says. "You do like bacon, don't you?"

"Do I look like someone who doesn't like bacon?"

"I don't know; aren't actors all healthy and stuff?" Beck asks as he takes the right-hand seat.

I have a sip of the coffee Beck already poured for me and take the other tall, dark blue leather barstool. "Excellent coffee."

"It took me a second to figure out the machine, but glad you like it."

"And I do try to keep in shape," I say, picking up my fork. "But bacon is a basic human necessity. Though I usually go for turkey bacon if I have a choice."

"You did order bacon for me yesterday," Beck muses. "You probably wouldn't have done that if you were vegan or something."

"Not vegan. Though I do like vegetables."

"Vegetables I can get behind. You want anything in particular?" Beck nods at the pad of paper on the other side of the island and I drag it toward me while I eat. The French toast is crispy-soft and perfumed with vanilla, I think, while the eggs are light and perfectly salted. I try not to inhale them as I read Beck's list, printed in neat block letters, a far cry from my own hasty scribble.

"Besides the bacon, there's no food on this list."

"What are you talking about?" Beck pours a generous amount of syrup on his French toast.

"Baking powder, lemon extract, ground cloves, almond flour—what's AP flour?"

"All purpose," Beck says. "I take it you aren't a baker. Those are all ingredients."

"Ingredients aren't food," I say, sticking to my guns.

"You mix them together, heat them up, and then you get food," Beck explains, a smile in his voice. "Trust me. What kind of cookies do you like?"

"Cookies?"

"Cookies are my favorite thing to bake."

"Oh. Well." I try to remember the last time I ate a cookie. "I don't know. I guess I don't eat a lot of cookies. Oreos are pretty good."

"Oreos are very good," Beck agrees. "But I can't make an Oreo. Didn't your mom bake?"

"My mom can't boil water," I say, "but I love her, anyway." I'm struck by a sudden memory—opening a box at Christmastime from my Aunt Sharleen. "My aunt used to send us fudge and some kind of spicy cookie at the holidays. Those were pretty good. She died a couple of years ago. I haven't thought about those in a long time."

"Like a gingerbread cookie?" Beck asks, leaning closer, his face lighting up. "Or more of a molasses?"

"What's the difference?"

"Was it cut out in a shape or was it round, like your typical chocolate chip cookie?"

I close my eyes and think back. My parents were always busy with their full-time jobs. Christmas was one of the few times they were off work. The holiday was usually a bit of a rushed affair, but cozy. We'd all sprawl on the living room rug, watching movies as we snacked on those delicious cookies. I open my eyes and Beck's closer than I thought, his clear light blue eyes trained intently on my face. He has a small mole at the edge of one eyebrow that lends him a nice asymmetry. I swallow. "Round. They definitely had cinnamon in them, but other flavors, too. Don't ask me what they were."

"Okay." His gaze seems to drop to my mouth for a split second before he turns his attention back to his plate. "That gives me something to go on." He grabs a pen and adds a few more items to the list.

I lean over to see he added cardamom, nutmeg, allspice. And Oreos.

I ignore the warm feeling flooding my chest and finish my coffee.

"I had planned to go to the store, too," I say. "Why don't we go together?"

"Okay," Beck says. "What else is on the agenda, Mr. Playwright? You going to write today?"

I groan. "And we were getting along so well."

Beck waves a hand. "Forget I asked. None of my business. Just tell me if you want dinner here tonight. I might as well cook for two."

"You sure you don't mind?"

"Nope. Especially not if you take dish duty."

"Seems like a fair enough trade." I think about the rest of the summer stretching ahead. "And what about the morning shift with Cleo? I'm not much of a morning person, but you want me to do tomorrow since you got up with her today?"

"Oh, I don't mind," Beck says, throwing a smile at the pup, who looks up as if she knows we're talking about her. "She's actually pretty easy."

"You're making me feel like a freeloader," I say. "I've got to pull my weight, or Pete will find some way to make me regret it."

"How about I do mornings and you do evenings? And if one of us has something come up, we can trade."

"Deal."

We finish our breakfasts quickly and I clear the dishes into the dishwasher while Beck ducks into his room off the kitchen and emerges a couple of minutes later dressed in a short-sleeved white button-down embroidered with tiny pink flamingos, holding his Ray-Bans. We decide to leave Cleo behind while we go shopping, since Pete said she doesn't like car rides.

I go upstairs to brush my teeth. When I come back down, Beck's arms are full of canvas shopping totes.

"You got the list?" I ask.

"Got it. You want to drive?"

I hesitate. "I can, if you want me to."

Beck looks confused for a moment, then the furrow between his eyebrows disappears. "Oh, you're one of those New Yorkers who doesn't drive."

"I know how to drive," I say, feeling defensive. "I have a valid license and everything. I'm just a little rusty. It kind of stresses me out."

Beck laughs. "No worries. I love driving. I just thought you—" He stops before finishing the sentence and I have no idea what he was going to say. Before I can ask, Beck pushes the load of bags into my arms and snags his keys from the little table by the front door. "You can navigate," Beck says, putting on his sunglasses and activating the alarm system behind us as we leave.

"Nice car," I say once we're on the road and I open my maps app. "Had it long?"

Beck smiles. "You don't know anything about cars, do you?"

"So?"

"This is my baby," Beck says. "Got her as a graduation present."

I whistle. "Nice present." When I graduated from NYU, my parents took me out for a steak dinner and handed me the paperwork for all the student loans I had to start paying back.

I can't figure Beck out. I might not know anything about cars, but I know this isn't a cheap commuter car, not with its sleek dash and powerful engine on display as we race down the back roads heading for the market.

Beck is college-educated, wears decent clothes, owns expensive sunglasses, drives a sweet car. But he doesn't have any discernible job and is a self-proclaimed couch surfer. The dissonance bugs me.

Have we established enough of a rapport that I can ask for more details? It's not as if Beck has been shy about asking me anything that comes into his head. But I'm strangely reluctant to upset our equilibrium.

"Turn up here," I direct, and soon we're pulling into the parking lot of a medium-sized grocery store. Some kind of local chain, I guess. Beck grabs a cart and plops the bags in the front basket.

"Want to split up or stick together?" Beck asks.

I blink. I imagine trying to find some of the things on Beck's list by myself and shake my head. "Let's stick together."

Beck grins and pushes the cart through the automatic doors. "Good choice."

SIX

BECK

GROCERY SHOPPING with Donovan is surprisingly fun. Everything with Donovan is surprisingly fun.

I'm not sure how well I'm managing the little crush I've been developing on my roommate. I'd wanted to do something nice for him, and making breakfast seemed like the obvious choice, but eating elbow to elbow, breathing in his freshly showered scent and trying not to ogle his legs, dark hair covering firm muscles, while bantering over the shopping list, well, it felt intimate. Like boyfriend behavior.

My logical brain knows that whatever intimacy is growing between us is the byproduct of sharing a space and having to get to know each other quickly, not any actual chemistry. But my lizard brain hasn't gotten the memo, because every time Donovan smiles at me, tiny little fireworks go off in my belly, and today I can't blame the hangover.

We might be living together, shopping together, taking care of a dog together. But we aren't boyfriends.

And I need to remember that before I do something to embarrass myself.

I always do this—leap into things, relationships, schools, new towns, thinking this time I've found the perfect fit, the thing that will stick. And then the guy isn't The One, it turns out I don't want to be a teacher/nurse/lawyer, and the seemingly perfect little towns no longer appeal.

Nothing has stuck yet, but that doesn't mean I'm going to stop looking for the right place to put down roots once Jack and Pete come back.

I've got to remember everything about this particular arrangement is temporary. If I keep my head screwed on, then Donovan and I can just have fun, and I won't end up hurt and leaving Rosedale licking my wounds.

But it's hard to stay indifferent when I go a little crazy in the baking aisle and he only lifts one thick black eyebrow and says dryly, "I'm going to have to start working out more, aren't I?"

I sweep a critical eye down Donovan's trim but muscular frame. He looks good. It doesn't help he happens to be just my type. Handsome but flawed, a couple inches taller than my five-eight. All man. I force myself to keep my tone light. "If you want to partake of my baking guilt-free, then you just might. Aren't there a couple of workout machines in the basement? And there's the pool, of course."

I'm fully intending to spend my afternoon poolside. Why the hell shouldn't I? I'm in hyper avoidance mode. Pools were designed for procrastination.

"Right, the pool." He sounds less than enthused.

"You don't like swimming?" I try not to pout—maybe it's better if I don't have to see him half-naked and wet.

"Swimming is okay, but I've been living in Manhattan for twelve years. We do other things for recreation."

"Oh, yeah?" I can imagine. Donovan has the air of a guy who indulges himself—when it comes to men, at least.

As if to prove the point, he says, "I was thinking of going to the gay bar in Midville tonight. Pete said it's a good time."

I tamp down the flare of jealousy. So he wants to go out. He's got every right. I keep my voice neutral when I say, "On a Monday?"

He frowns. "I forgot it was Monday. Well, I'll check their hours later. Do we need pasta?"

Almost an hour later, we get in the checkout line with a cart loaded to the brim.

"We're only staying for two months," Donovan says as he surveys our haul.

"And believe me, we'll be back in a week to restock." I start putting things on the conveyor belt, but he stops me.

"Wait. Should we split it up somehow—or just settle up after?"

"Oh." I hadn't thought about money. It's typically my last concern. "So much of this is stuff I want. I'll take care of it, and you can get the next grocery run."

"Are you sure?" He looks doubtfully at all the food.

"I'm sure. You bag." I shoo him to the end of the conveyor belt.

"New in town?" the woman scanning our purchases asks with a friendly smile. Her name tag reads Annie.

"Yeah. Temporary residents," I say, smiling back.

"Welcome to Rosedale," she says.

Donovan lets out something like a snort as he puts the celery in a canvas bag. I glare at him.

"Thank you, Annie," I say, injecting my voice with all the Texan sweetness I can muster.

She finishes ringing us up, and I tap my credit card. I wait until we've pushed the cart out of earshot to admonish him. "You were kind of rude."

He winces. "Sorry, but I don't buy all this small-town hokeyness. There's something in the water here that makes everyone overly chummy. I'm all for politeness, but I'm not here to be indoctrinated into the cult of Rosedale."

"I think it's nice," I say. "Small towns are charming. Not like cities—all smelly and confusing and dirty."

Donovan smirks. "What about the lack of—uh—options?"

I know what he means. "I don't need a different guy every night," I say shortly. I regret it as soon as I say it. Just because I'm not into casual hookups, it doesn't give me the right to judge.

But he doesn't seem to take it personally. "Different guy? There aren't *any* guys."

"Not true," I say, arguing and not exactly knowing why. "Jack's agent Kingston is gay, and he has a house here."

"He doesn't live here full time," he counters.

"What about Shay?" I open the hatch and we load in the bags.

"Who's Shay?"

"The guy who did the flowers for Jack and Pete's wedding. He just moved here. I didn't meet him, but Jack was going on and on about how great his eye was."

"One gay guy in a town of, what, a couple thousand? Nice odds."

"I'm here. You're here," I say, running out of patience.

"Yeah, but we're not—" Donovan stops, the implication clear. I don't count because he isn't attracted to me. Which is totally fine and not at all demoralizing. I leave him loading the last few bags to drop into the driver's seat and slam the door.

A few beats later, he gets in the car. "Look, as much as I like hooking up, I've never hooked up with a roommate. It's just asking for trouble." His voice is hatefully kind and mortifyingly apologetic. "I've had so many bad roommate experiences, and this one has been really good so far. So can we just—"

"Of course," I say quickly. "That's not what I meant, anyway." I hope the heat in my cheeks doesn't betray me. "I just meant you might be surprised at the options in a town like Rosedale. Not that *we* should—" To avoid having to finish that sentence, I start the car and turn the AC up to full blast. "Anyway, Jack and Pete met here, didn't they?" Why can't I let this go?

"Turn left," he says as we approach an intersection.

"I think I can get back home," I say as I make the turn.

"Anyway, Jack and Pete are not normal," he says flatly. Maybe he can't let it go, either.

"Why exactly aren't they normal?"

"For one thing, they actually seem happy."

My heart twinges at the sour note in his voice. "I think they are happy." I feel defensive on their behalf. "They have the whole package. Great house, great relationship, great career. Isn't that what everyone wants?"

"No." Donovan doesn't elaborate, and I can practically feel the bitterness radiating off him.

"Well, some people do," I say quietly, then switch on the stereo, effectively ending the conversation. The air fills with Top 40 radio and we drive back to the house on Wild Rose Lane without talking. The only good thing to come out of that excruciating exchange was the knowledge that if he doesn't hook up with roommates, he and Pete probably never messed around, which makes me feel irrationally better.

Cleo greets us with a wagging tail, and I let her out into the backyard while Donovan unloads the groceries. By the time we get everything put away, it's lunchtime.

"I think I'll take a sandwich upstairs and try to work," he says, taking the sliced turkey right back out of the fridge again.

"Sure," I say breezily, trying to recapture some of the ease of the morning. "I think I'll eat later. I'm going to try out the pool."

I go into my room and change into my swimsuit, berating myself for harboring the silly idea that the mild interest Donovan had shown in me meant anything. His no roommate policy actually makes a lot of sense. Why would we want to complicate an already unconventional living situation with sex?

I shake off the melancholy that settles over me knowing that's all I'll ever be to Donovan—his roommate. But I take solace in knowing if he's that touchy about it, he's probably had some pretty crappy roommates. Well, challenge accepted.

I'll be the best roommate he ever had.

SEVEN
DONOVAN

I'M BORED.

After retreating from Beck I opened up my laptop with the best of intentions—to look at the scenes I've already worked on—but somehow I spent the last few hours reading random news articles, texting a few friends, and checking my bank balance. I haven't written a word.

Something's off. Maybe it's that if I was in the city, I'd have all manner of distractions to fill my day. I could go meet up with friends for a drink, or catch a movie, or visit a museum, or just walk around the park. I'm not sequestered in this house—it's not a prison—but what is there to do in Rosedale, honestly, besides get coffee at Hot Brew or walk around Main Street? It might be fun to do those things with someone. With Beck, specifically. But I've managed to offend him somehow, and it rankles.

Okay, so that's what's really bothering me. Beck's a nice guy, but he's been throwing up red flags all day. Starting with the cute—and tasty—breakfast for two, and then the cozy little shopping trip. Beck has boyfriend material stamped on his forehead. Even if we weren't sharing the house for the summer, I wouldn't want to hurt the guy by dangling a relationship in front of him that's never going to happen. Beck obviously thinks Jack and Pete's marriage is something to aspire to, and he's clearly unimpressed with my attitude.

Well, that's fine. I don't need Beck to approve of me. I just need to coexist with the guy for...one month, three weeks, and six days.

I push away from the little desk in front of the window that looks over the driveway and the street beyond and collapse on the navy blue quilt covering the guest bed. This isn't going to work. Beck doesn't actually need anybody to help with Cleo—he's obviously capable of doing the job single-handedly. I'm completely superfluous.

Pete might be disappointed, but he'll get over it. Beck will probably be happy to get me out of his hair. Then he can have the whole place to himself. I picture Beck here alone—baking cookies for no one. I sigh.

My phone vibrates on the desk. I consider ignoring it, but it buzzes again and I force myself up. I grab it and take it back to the bed, sliding open my notifications.

PETE

Hey! Sorry for just now checking in.
How's the pup?

I forgot to tell you I got a new pack of
chew toys if you need them. In the
pantry.

I shake my head and type back a reply before he can barrage me with more mother-henning.

> Cleo's happy as a clam. How was the flight?

> Great. We're trying to get on London time. Need anything before I sign off for the night?

> Nope, we're good.

I hit send before I can rethink that wording. It's not as if Beck and I are a unit. We aren't a "we." But maybe Pete will think I mean me and Cleo. Whatever. It doesn't matter.

> Another thing I forgot — even though she doesn't like car rides, she's usually okay if I take her to the loop in the woods by the cemetery in town. It's pretty short, and she loves that walk. Just keep her on the lead.

> And don't give her too many treats before bed.

> And give her lots of kisses for me.

I laugh and type as fast as I can to stem the tide of texts.

> I'm taking good care of her, promise. Hang on.

I jog downstairs to the kitchen but don't see Cleo in her

bed. I panic for a second, until I realize Beck must have taken her outside. I slide into shoes I left by the French doors and head outside across the patio. The afternoon sun is a stark contrast to the air-conditioned house, but the heat feels good on my shoulders as I cross the lawn to the fenced-in pool area, where I hear classic rock coming out of a poolside sound system. The gate's latched, so I let myself in. Cleo is here, as predicted, gnawing on a tennis ball under the shade of a sand-colored canvas patio umbrella. Beck is here, too, lying on his front on a towel draped over a deck chair.

I stare shamelessly for a long minute. Beck is practically naked. The only scrap of fabric covering him are black briefs that barely cover his ass. His exposed skin is shiny, and there's a lot of it. I catch a whiff of sunblock and hope the kid was smart enough to slather himself with it, though his shoulders look a little pink. I swallow heavily, remembering why I came out here.

Walking over to Cleo, I drop into a crouch to rub her head. "Hey girl, your daddy misses you." I thumb open the camera on my phone and take a couple of snaps, then rise to my feet.

"What's up?" Beck asks.

Out of the corner of my eye, I can see him turning from his front to back. I concentrate on sending the photos instead of letting myself look at him from this angle.

"Pete texted me. I thought I'd send him some pics to prove we're not falling down on the job."

"Good idea. I'll send Jack more later." He drapes his sunglasses over his face.

I look up from my phone with careful nonchalance. "Well, I'll let you get back to it."

"The pool's really refreshing if you want to take a dip."

The denial is on the tip of my tongue, but the only reason I'd turn down the chance to go swimming on a beautiful summer afternoon is because I'm feeling contrary. And maybe I don't trust myself around a mostly naked Beck.

"You staying out here for a while?" I ask.

"I've almost had enough sun," Beck says. "But I'll go in for a few more laps before starting dinner."

"Okay."

I read Pete's thank you message for the Cleo pics on the way to my room. I shed my clothes and pull on my swim trunks, which seem old-man fogyish next to Beck's banana hammock. I grab a towel from the stack in the guest bathroom, though there are probably pool towels somewhere. I'll have to investigate. A minute later, I'm back by the pool, dipping my toes in the deep end. Chilly.

"It's heated," Beck says reassuringly.

"It doesn't feel that warm." I try to remember the last time I went swimming. Must have been vacation in Florida, a couple of years ago.

"Do you need me to push you in?" he asks, amused. Sitting up to watch the show, Beck's flat abs form little ridges as he curves his spine forward and puts his arms around his ankles.

"No, thank you." I make my way to the shallow end of the long, narrow pool. I don't have goggles or anything, so laps are out. But I can't back out now. I leave my sunglasses on the edge, leap over the side, and plunge in, the cold water hitting everywhere at once, at first a shock and then a delight. I swim a few feet and come to standing in the middle of the pool, grinning at Beck. "Feels good."

"Told you." He grins back and gets up, changing his sunglasses out for blue-tinted goggles that he produces from somewhere. He goes to the deep end and dives in smoothly, takes a few strokes, and easily comes up next to me.

"Of course you're a good swimmer," I say with affected grumpiness.

"My parents made me do a sport. They were picturing football, but I picked the swim team."

"Ah. That explains what you're wearing."

He laughs and glances down at his crotch. "What—you wouldn't wear one of these?"

"Not in public."

"Well, this is private property," he says. "But I guess some of us are more mature than others." And then he splashes me, hitting me square across the face with a spray of water.

I snort in surprise, wipe my eyes. The little shit. "Very mature."

Beck laughs again and I take the bait—I splash water back in his direction, but he's too fast.

He throws himself backward and starts reverse frog-kicking out of the splash zone. I launch myself forward, and a chase ensues. He's fast, darting like a fish to evade my attempts to get him back, but I have a longer reach, and eventually I succeed in pushing a wave of water into his face, leaving him sputtering and laughing and retaliating with his own wave of water.

I ignore the slight ridiculousness of two grown men having a splash fight in the middle of the afternoon. It's too much fun. Beck finally calls a truce and swims to the side of the pool, where he takes off his goggles. I swim up to him, breathless, my cheeks aching from smiling so hard.

"You look like a raccoon," I say, raising my finger and grazing the delicate skin under his right eye, where the goggles have left a pink imprint. At the contact, I yank my hand back. I hadn't intended to touch him.

"I'm sure I do," Beck agrees. He sighs. "You look like a cologne ad."

"Huh?" I look down at myself, waist deep in water, the hair on my chest matted down, my nipples standing at attention. My skin is naturally tinted olive, though if I spent more time shirtless in the sun I'd brown like a roasted almond. Water drips into my eyes from my hair. I sniff and run my hand through my hair to get it off my forehead. I don't get the compliment, if there was one.

"Never mind," Beck says, hoisting himself out of the water with ease on arms that flex with lean muscle. He walks briskly over to his lounge chair and wraps himself in the large towel. "I'm going to get dinner started. Bring Cleo in with you?"

"Sure."

He collects his things and latches the gate behind him, leaving the music playing. I have the feeling I've done something wrong, but I'm not sure what. I push away from the wall, swim a couple of lazy laps, keeping my head above water. It feels good to move, but it's not as enjoyable out here alone.

I force my thoughts away from how much fun Beck is and think about practical matters. Swimming is good exercise. I should order some swim goggles or find the nearest big box store and buy some. I could get some more shorts, too. Maybe a few board games. Unless Jack and Pete have a collection. Does Beck like games? I happen to know Kingston is a poker player. Maybe we could get a group together this weekend—

With a start, I realize I'm no longer considering bouncing and leaving the house and Cleo to Beck. I made Pete a promise, and I'm going to keep my word. But more than that—I owe it to Beck to hold up my end of the bargain. To be the kind of roommate he deserves, even if it means I'm sometimes bored in this Pleasantville of a town.

My mother used to say boredom is good for you—it forces you to get creative.

Maybe I'll get so bored I'll actually write my play.

AFTER SHOWERING off the pool water and dressing in jeans and a T-shirt, I take myself on a belated tour of the house. I find striped blue pool towels in the upstairs hall closet, and in the TV room there's a cupboard with DVDs ranging from buddy cop action movies to foreign romances. There's also a set of DVDs of the television show that's based on the Super Rupert books Jack writes and Pete illustrates. Am I a bad friend for never making time to watch it? The producers based the art on Pete's style, and Pete was consulted heavily, though he and Jack aren't otherwise involved with the production.

In a wooden chest behind the big sand-colored L-shaped couch where Beck took his nap yesterday, I discover a treasure trove of games, from a battered chess board and Yahtzee to more modern cooperative games. There are playing cards, a cribbage board, and a large quantity of poker chips.

Score.

Beck is in the kitchen, seemingly freshly showered,

dressed in the same shorts from the morning and a clean white T-shirt.

"I'm going to feed Cleo."

"Right on schedule." Beck smiles at me and I concentrate on following Pete's recipe—a combination of two different dog foods, both clearly high-end brands. Cleo comes running at the sound of the canisters of dog food opening, and she waits with barely disguised excitement, watching me with soft brown eyes while I measure out her meal.

"Dinner's almost ready," Beck says, closing the fridge door with his hip. He seems really comfortable in the kitchen, and I vaguely wish I knew how to make more than ramen and cereal. Living in New York, takeout is my friend.

"Smells good. What are we having?"

"Steak salad."

"Perfect." I help myself to one of the few beers in the door of the fridge. Beer didn't make it into our cart earlier, so we're stuck drinking what's on hand. Luckily, Pete and Jack have pretty good taste in alcohol and this brand of pilsner is one of my favorites.

Beck takes two fragrant steaks off the cast iron pan on the stove and cuts them into strips. The salad bowl is already on the island, but I don't see any place settings. "Want me to set the table?"

"Actually, I set us up outside."

"Oh. Good idea." The sky's still light and there's a big outdoor dining table on the patio just outside the kitchen's French doors. "Won't be too buggy?"

"If it is, we can come in," he says. "And I thought I'd take a stab at the molasses cookies after dinner."

"What do you mean?"

"I looked up some recipes online and I'm going to see if I can get close to your aunt's recipe."

I freeze. He wants to replicate my aunt's cookie recipe? Seems like a weird goal, but I don't know how to ask what his motivation is without seeming like a jerk.

He seems to sense my unease because he says quickly, "Cookies are my thing. I've been wanting to find the perfect molasses cookie recipe anyway, so you can be my taste tester. If you want."

"Sounds good," I reply stiffly. It's not like he's asking me for anything. They're just cookies. And the guy's making me dinner. The least I can do is try not to be an asshole.

Beck carries the steak outside and I follow with the salad bowl and my beer.

After my first bite of salad—crisp lettuce mixed with the perfect amount of creamy dressing and livened up with radishes, snap peas, and tomatoes—I moan my approval. "Damn, this is good. I didn't realize how hungry I was."

He looks pleased, but only says, "Swimming works up an appetite."

"I'll say."

We eat for a minute and I can't think of anything to say. I've gotten used to Beck jumping in and kicking off conversation by being nosy, but he's quiet.

I take a sip of beer and cast about for a topic. "So, I

feel like you know everything about me, but I don't even know what you do."

"Do?"

"Like, do you have a job?"

"Oh." He wrinkles his nose. "Not at the moment."

Huh. I think about the thick black credit card Beck used to pay for the groceries this morning. "What did you go to school for?"

He laughs at that. "What haven't I gone to school for?"

"What do you mean?"

"Well, undergrad was a mess. First, I thought I wanted to be a film major, then there was the semester I thought I'd be the next great choreographer and switched to dance. Thank god I sprained my ankle and changed my mind before I got around to telling my parents about that particular flight of fancy. Then I considered pre-med. But my science grades were shit." He shrugs, and I wonder if his casual attitude is a put-on or not. "History was the only area I had enough credits in by the time I had to declare a major or risk not graduating."

"A lot of people don't end up using their degrees," I say, trying to be supportive.

"What did you major in?" he asks.

"Uh. Drama."

He grins. "It's okay. You knew what you wanted to be when you grew up. I still don't."

I'm not sure how to respond to that. Knowing what I wanted to do was never the problem for me—it was breaking in. I feel like I'm starting all over again with playwriting, with no clue what I'm doing. But we're talking about Beck right now. "So what did you do after you graduated?"

"I spent six months at a LGBTQ+ nonprofit. But I wasn't actually that good at it. I'm not a big fan of conflict. Or getting myself to an office on time. I always had law school in my back pocket. Figured I could go and figure out what kind of lawyer I wanted to be later."

"So you're thinking about law school?" I lift my beer, but it's empty.

"Been there, done that," Beck says acerbically. "Washed out after a year and a half. That's the thing I actually thought would stick—but I was wrong. I think I have job ADHD."

I'm beginning to understand what Beck meant by being at loose ends. "Hence the couch surfing—you don't have a home base?"

"Nope," he says, sounding unconcerned, but there's a slight shadow in his eyes. "Law school was in Boston, and I have a lot of friends there, but the winters are rough."

"Why don't you go back to Texas?"

Beck sighs. "Texas is fine—to visit. It's a big state, but it's not big enough to hold both me and my parents."

"You don't get along?" I lucked out with parents who were just as supportive when I came out as when I said I wanted to try acting, but I have plenty of friends who aren't as fortunate.

"My parents are very...traditional. My dad is a strapping six-foot-tall straight man who married his college sweetheart. It never occurred to him that his son wouldn't be just like him."

I grimace. It's a common story, but it still makes me ache a little for Beck.

"Growing up, I was on the scrawny side. My parents always told me I'd have a growth spurt and catch up to Dad. Never happened. They also told me I'd meet a nice girl and get married someday. So that shows you how much vision my folks have. They wanted—they *expected* —a six-foot Texas boy who played football and married a sweet country girl. They got a five-foot-eight gay son who likes to bake and dropped out of law school."

"That's tough." My heart goes out to the kid who's clearly still inside Beck. East Coast college must have been a much-needed escape.

"Thank god for Jack, honestly," Beck says. "Our dads are brothers and they're really close. Jack coming out made it so much easier for me to finally tell my parents. And Jack's parents are super sweet."

"So what's your relationship like now?"

"Well, it's not like we never talk. I'm still my mom's baby. But they've got their life and I've got mine."

I wonder what life Beck has exactly. No job, no ambition, no place to live. Just a car and a temporary place to lay his head for the next two months.

Still, the kid seems happy enough. His life might not fit a traditional pattern, but he certainly has plenty of enthusiasm for the small things.

After dinner, I hold up my end of our bargain and do the dishes, then run Cleo around the backyard until we're both panting and tired. While I've been out with the dog, Beck's filled a kitchen counter with mysterious tiny bottles and bags of flour and at least two kinds of sugar.

I wash my hands while he consults the recipe on his phone for his first attempt at molasses cookies to rival my Aunt Sharleen's.

We move around each other easily, quietly, coexisting in a peaceful way I've never experienced in any of my other co-living situations. To me, a roommate means someone who detracts from my peace, whose very existence causes stress and the unsettled feeling of not being able to relax in my own home.

But living with Beck isn't like that. Not so far, anyway.

I sit at the kitchen island and doomscroll on my phone while he measures good smelling things into the bowl of the mixer he'd triumphantly found in one of the many cupboards and plugged in next to the coffee maker. The beat of some French bistro-esque jazz comes over the speakers and provides an acoustic backdrop that I don't feel the need to break by talking. The kitchen slowly warms as the oven pings, ready to be filled with the first tray of brown mounds of dough.

I look up from my screen when Beck lets out a borderline obscene sound. The blond baker licks something off his thumb and moans again.

I shift in my seat, suddenly uncomfortable at the sight of Beck with his thumb in his mouth, making noises that send the wrong signal to my downstairs brain. I look away from him to the dough-covered mixer paddle and speak up. "Can I try some?"

"I don't know—will it mess with your taste buds? I

want you to give me an honest assessment when they come out of the oven."

"Okay. I can be patient." I casually adjust my shorts underneath the counter and go back to my phone, only half paying attention to the article I'm reading. Beck puts the first batch of cookies in the oven and soon an even stronger scent of mingled spices fills the kitchen.

I pretend to read, but out of the corner of my eye, I'm really watching Beck efficiently clean up. He puts the ingredients back into the pantry, hums a little as he wipes down the counters. He finds a metal rack and sets it up just in time for the first batch of cookies to emerge from the oven.

"They smell amazing," I say, eyeing cookies the size of my palm.

"Give them a minute to cool," he says, sliding another tray into the oven.

"I bet milk would be great with these."

Beck turns toward the fridge, but I stand up. "You don't have to—I can get it myself."

He smiles and waves me away. "You're at my cookie counter. I got it."

I feel a little weird about letting him wait on me, but I sit back down. A minute later, Beck delivers a glass of milk and a cookie on a plain white plate.

"Looks almost too good to eat."

"They look nice," he agrees, taking his phone out to snap a few pictures. "But how do they taste?"

He watches anxiously as I take a bite of the still-warm cookie.

All the flavors hanging in the air combine into a

sharp, sweet taste on my tongue. The cookie is the perfect amount of chewy, and I wordlessly grunt my approval, then wash the bite down with a refreshing sip of milk.

"Good?" Beck asks, sounding unsure.

"Great," I say, taking a second bite. "You're a good baker."

"Thanks, but are they as good as your aunt's?"

I consider the question. It's not exactly easy to compare the deliciousness in my mouth to a childhood Christmas memory. "Yes?"

His mouth flattens. "Be honest."

"Beck, it's been fifteen years. These are amazing molasses cookies."

"Were hers lighter? Darker? Sweeter?" he persists.

"Spicier, actually," I say, finally putting my finger on the difference. "They had a bit of heat. And I think they were darker."

Beck hums and types something on his phone. "Interesting."

"But these are honestly delicious." I munch happily on the rest of the cookie and grab another from the cooling rack.

"I'll just have to try again," he says, sounding unbothered by the prospect. He looks at me and points to my mouth. "You've got a crumb."

I dart my tongue out and fish around for the crumb in question. Beck's gaze seems to follow along. I make contact with the bit of cookie and swallow. "Did I get it?"

"Yeah." Beck's voice is low. There's a long moment where no one says anything. I don't know if it's the sugar or the late hour or the sensual jazz riff coming over the speakers, but I very strongly want to know if Beck tastes as good as his cookies.

The timer beeps shrilly and Beck leaps toward the oven. The moment is over, but I wonder how long it will be before the same urge comes at me again.

Later, I'm drifting off to sleep, the air still tinged with the scent of spices, when I realize I hadn't even thought twice about staying in tonight and not hitting the bar. *The sex drought continues*, I think as I fall asleep with a hint of a smile on my face.

NINE
BECK

FRIDAY IS the first cloudy day since my arrival in Rosedale, so I throw on a thin light blue cardigan over my jeans and dark blue V-neck before grabbing my keys. Cleo's happily snoozing in her bed in the kitchen, and Donovan's probably upstairs. He spends most of his mornings upstairs in his room. Supposedly he's working on his play, but every time I ask him about it he turns grumpy, so I haven't mentioned it for a couple of days.

I can't believe it's already Friday. At this rate, the summer is going to fly by faster than a shooting star. Taking care of Cleo isn't a chore, but feeding her, walking her, and sending lots of pictures to her daddies is more time-consuming than one might think. The rest of the week I've spent poolside, cooking, and trying a different molasses cookie recipe every night. So far I haven't cracked the code of Donovan's aunt's recipe, but it's just a matter of time.

We've eaten dinner together each night this week. It's been nice to cook for more than myself, and Donovan enthusiastically eats everything I put in front of him. Not sure how he maintains that body of his, since the couple of times he's joined me in the pool he floats around lazily more than doing actual laps, but I think he's used the workout machines in the basement once or twice. I'm trying really hard to stay on my best behavior and not follow him around like a puppy—we already have one of those in the house, thank you very much.

We don't spend every minute together, but our shared meals have been a bright spot. Donovan tells me stories about his theater experiences, some of them redacted to protect the identities of his more famous friends, and I've made him laugh with some of my more epic baking and higher education fails.

I think we might be getting to be real friends.

And if I still think Donovan is basically the handsomest man I've ever met, well, I can handle myself.

Between all the dog care and cooking and working on my tan (I know I shouldn't, but a guy can't help it), I haven't made it back to town. I've been wanting to return to the thrift store and explore the bookshop Jack told me about. But the first thing I do after parking my GTI in a shady spot on a side street is make for Hot Brew.

I was too hungover the last time I was here to appreciate the cute black and white tile and the array of baked goods in the pastry case next to the clean white counter. The morning rush is probably over, because there are only a couple of people in line, but almost every table is full of chatting, caffeinated patrons. I take my time perusing the short but appealing food menu and what's on offer in the way of croissants and muffins. I don't see any cookies, which is disappointing until I remember I've got about five dozen leftover molasses cookies at home.

I've earned a stimulant after taking Cleo for an extra-long walk this morning, so when it's my turn I ask the petite redhead behind the counter for a matcha latte. I think I recognize her from my previous visit, but my memory of that morning is mostly the splitting headache and Donovan being way too sweet to someone he just met.

Of course, at the time, he didn't know we'd have to spend the rest of the summer together. It shouldn't sting that he completely stopped flirting after he found out he'd actually be living with me. I guess it's good we're getting along, but it makes me sad that he doesn't seem to believe he can get companionship and sex in the same relationship. I wonder, not for the first time, if he's just one of those guys who's not built to settle down, or if something happened to turn him off to the idea.

"What's an Everything Muffin?" I ask the red-haired employee, hoping it doesn't involve caraway seeds. I'm not a huge fan.

"Right now, it's got blueberries, raspberries, and blackberries, with a hint of lemon," she explains. "We change up the flavor every season."

"Sounds delicious. Who does your baking?"

"Who wants to know?" A woman with ink-black hair, painted on eyebrows, and black lipstick leaves the espresso machine to stand next to the redhead.

I'm taken aback by her question until I notice her grin; I'm pretty sure I've met her somewhere before.

"Beck, right?" she says. "I'm Meadow. We met at your cousin's wedding."

"I remember," I say slowly, the memory filtering through the drunken haze of that night.

"Jack told me you were house-sitting this summer. How's it going rattling around in that big house?"

"Turns out Pete asked his friend Donovan to house-sit, too, so it's not as, uh, rattly."

The redhead lets out a small squeak and her cheeks turn almost as red as her hair.

"You okay, Ruth?" Meadow asks her coworker with a hint of concern.

Now I definitely remember Ruth from the other morning, and the way she seemed to melt every time Donovan threw a smile her way. Since I can relate, I give her a sympathetic look. "Anyway, so far, so good. But I haven't had a chance to explore Rosedale yet. I'm fueling up here first."

"Well, the muffins are terrific, but we don't make them in-house. The croissants and other pastries come from the city—some poor schmo drives them up from a bakery in Manhattan every morning. But the muffins and quick breads come from a local baker, Stacy Robinson. She also makes the bread we use for our sandwiches."

"I can't wait to try everything," I enthuse. "But I have to point out a hole in your menu. No cookies?"

"No, we've never carried cookies. I've mentioned it to the owner a couple of times, but she's pretty happy with our current offerings."

"Good to know. Well, this place is adorable."

"Thanks," Meadow says warmly. "Ruth, you can give him the friends and family discount."

Ruth charges me what seems like a ridiculously low amount and passes me a wax paper bag with the muffin inside.

I thank them both and tuck an extra big tip into the jar next to the computer. I nibble on the muffin until the matcha latte is up a few minutes later. The drink is strong and not too sweet, and I'm instantly addicted.

"See you soon," I call to the women when I leave, getting twin waves in return.

Outside, the sky is still overcast, but it's not cold. Still, I'm glad for the warmth of my drink as I saunter down Main Street. The thrift store is up on the right, and the bookstore is somewhere a bit farther along. I see a cute-looking Italian restaurant not yet open for the day, and a real estate firm with photos of local properties in the window. I stop and browse the listings—a twenty-acre farm, a small ranch-style house, a one-bedroom apartment. I look for the abandoned dark blue house I've seen on my walks with Cleo, but it's not there.

Second Time Around, the thrift store, is cool and dark inside. Before I pounce on the kitchenware, I reintroduce myself to the lady rearranging the window display, who says her name is Beth, and that she owns the place.

After poking around for a while, I decide I absolutely have to have some really cute vintage cocktail glasses I find on an out-of-the-way shelf. Beth rings me up, carefully wrapping each glass in tissue paper.

"Where's your young man today?" she asks.

"Who?" I look around as if I can conjure up a boyfriend by sheer willpower.

"Your friend from the other morning," she says, handing me a paper bag with my purchases.

"Oh, him. He's my...roommate," I say awkwardly.

Beth gives me a knowing smile. "It's all right, dear. Rosedale is a very open-minded place."

I'm about to correct her, but figure there's no point and just smile at the sentiment. I guess it's better she accepts Donovan and I are together than being appalled at the possibility. People do like to make assumptions, but since this one is rather nice, I let it go. "Thanks. I'll be back soon," I promise.

Still shaking my head over that exchange, I head in the direction of the bookstore, but my attention is grabbed by a couple of guys attempting to move a large couch through a small doorway. I step out of their way, surveying the building. They seem to be moving someone out of an upper floor apartment, which is over an empty storefront. I glance through the ground floor window. The inside is dusty, but looks like it used to be a shop at one time, with built-in shelving on the walls and unfinished sections of the floor where it looks like a counter used to be. I step back and survey the building. It's attractive, warm red brick on top, big plate-glass windows at street level. This block seems to be thriving otherwise—I wonder what happened to this store. It seems to be the perfect place for a little boutique or—not a coffee shop, because Hot Brew's got that covered—some kind of eatery.

I can't stop thinking about the empty space as I walk

to the bookshop. Cheerful bells sound as I let myself in, and I allow myself to be distracted by the comforting smell of new books.

"Hi there," a tall woman with short wavy brunette hair greets me. "Oh, I know you. Jack's cousin, right?"

I'm still not used to just how small a town Rosedale is. Everyone seems to know me and I've only been here a week. I smile at her, trying to place her. "Beck Avery," I confirm.

"Melissa Sanchez," she says. "Jack told us you were going to be house-sitting. And I see you were at Hot Brew. Meadow's my girlfriend."

"Oh! Cool." I lift my almost empty takeout cup. "Bookstore and coffee shop? Power couple."

She laughs. "Can I help you find something?"

"Cookbooks?"

"Over here." She shows me the section and leaves me to browse. I find two cookie-centric books that have promising molasses cookie recipes and take them both to the counter. I'm about to pay when I have a thought. "Do you have any books about writing?"

"A few." She takes me to the nonfiction section and I scan the titles. Nothing specific about playwriting. Which is probably for the best. Donovan hasn't exactly invited my input on the subject. And I don't want to make him uncomfortable with an unwelcome present.

"Didn't see what you wanted?" she asks when I return empty-handed.

"It's okay. The cookbooks are perfect." I throw in a couple of cute pencils I spot at the register and then notice a plain black notebook in a rack. "Wait, this too," I say, adding it to my small pile. I've seen Donovan write in a similar book. Maybe he needs another one. And if I chicken out of giving it to him, I can use it myself. I usually take recipe notes on my phone, but I can try something new.

While she scans my items, I ask, "Do you know what's up with that empty storefront down the block?"

Melissa thinks for a moment, then her brow clears. "Oh, that was a sandwich shop, but the owner decided to move to Florida. It's been empty for a couple of years now. I keep hearing rumors of things going in, but nothing so far."

"Hmmm." I wonder what the rent would be on a place like that. Not that I know anything about retail. Or even know what kind of store I'd want to run. But the possibility nags at me, just like the possibility of that cute blue house.

"Are you a baker?" Melissa asks as I pay and add my purchases to the bag from Second Time Around.

The question flummoxes me for a second. "Strictly amateur," I say. "Cookies, mostly."

"Well, if you ever need a taste tester, you know where to find me," Melissa says.

I think about the five dozen cookies at home and grin. "Be careful what you wish for."

TEN
DONOVAN

WHEN I AMBLE DOWNSTAIRS around noon for lunch, Cleo looks up from her bed, but when she sees it's only me, she settles down again. I've begun to suspect that she likes Beck more than me, which, fair. I think I like Beck more than me, too.

He's been a constant presence this week, but not in a bad way. How can I complain about someone who cooks seemingly effortlessly delicious meals and keeps trying to replicate my aunt's cookie recipe for fun?

By the third night and third attempt, I had my fill of molasses cookies for about a year, but I haven't had the heart to tell Beck. Each batch has been good, but either not quite like my aunt's or not up to his standards in some way. So he keeps trying, and I keep feeling that if I never have another molasses cookie again, I'll be good.

I glance in the fridge, checking that the leftover potato salad from last night is still there. I pull it out and grab sandwich fixings, then it occurs to me there's no music coming through the kitchen speakers. I don't hear anything from Beck's room, and if he'd gone out to the pool, he'd probably have taken Cleo with him.

So where is he?

It's not like he has to check in with me. Neither of us have ventured far from the house this week. It's been surprisingly relaxing to stay put, and it occurs to me that I haven't had a real vacation since that jaunt to Florida a couple of years ago.

Still, I've gotten used to Beck being in the background. He plays music wherever he goes, and I like his eclectic taste. I don't know how he got his phone to sync up to the sound system, though it was probably on one of Pete's pages of instructions about the house.

But currently the house is quiet. I make my sandwich, dollop a healthy helping of potato salad onto my plate, and wonder where Beck is for the sixth time.

He's an adult, I remind myself as I settle in the TV room and flip on the TV. I decide to watch some of the Super Rupert series and dig out a DVD. I'm halfway through the first surprisingly entertaining episode when my phone dings and I startle myself with how quickly I pause the show to take a look at my messages.

But the text isn't from Beck.

KINGSTON JAMES

> Van the Man! Jack told me about the dog-sitting double-booking. You and Jack's cousin doing okay? I'm coming to Rosedale for the weekend. Want to get together?

Kingston is more Pete's friend than mine, but we get along well. We even hooked up a few years ago. It was fun, but neither of us was interested in a repeat. I've socialized with him a few times in the last couple of years since Pete moved to Rosedale and my circle of New York friends shrank by one. Kingston works in the city during the week but has his Rosedale house for when he wants to get away, or to lend to hapless friends when they need an escape.

> Anytime. How's your poker game?

I'm a little rusty.

> I bet. I'm willing to be schooled if you're up for it.

Sure. Tonight? I have a friend in town who might be interested.

I agree before I realize maybe I should ask Beck before inviting people over for a poker night. Well, if he has a problem with it, then we'll just sequester ourselves in the den or something. I'm spending way too much time thinking about the kid, anyway.

Food might be an issue, but I'm not going to ask Beck to cook for guests. We can order pizza or something. Alcohol might be more of a problem, since we don't have much on hand.

> Where do you get alcohol around here?

Might as well ask a local.

For a curated selection, Wine and Roses on Cross Street. For the mass stuff, there's a big box place on Route 7. But I can bring my own.

I need to stock up anyway. Thanks for the recs. See you tonight.

Okay, I can do this. I can leave the house by myself. I clean up from lunch, take Cleo out for a little exercise, then get my hat, wallet, and, finally, the keys to Pete's car. I open the side door to the garage. The silver hybrid SUV is parked dead center, the lingering smell of exhaust in the stale garage air.

I take a minute to adjust the seat and the mirrors. The location of the garage door clicker eludes me until I find it in a hidden compartment above the center console. I open the garage door, start the car. It's shockingly quiet. I wipe my palms on my shorts and give myself a pep talk. "You can do this. You're a fine driver. It's like riding a bike."

I laugh at my own weak metaphor and carefully put the vehicle in reverse, backing out of the garage and onto the gravel driveway at a snail's pace. I put the car in park while I tap the clicker to shut the garage door. Okay. So far so good. I pull up directions to Wine and Roses on my phone and see that Cross Street is one of the offshoots from Main, just around the corner from Hot Brew.

I put the car in drive. *Here goes nothing.*

Ten minutes later, I'm pulling into a town parking lot behind Main Street and feeling pretty proud of myself. It helps that Pete's car has great visibility, and the directions were pretty simple. But I definitely have my driving confidence back. Just don't ask me to go above forty miles an hour.

I lock the car and head to the shop, missing the sun. Today's warm but cloudy and I hope the gloom breaks for the weekend.

Wine and Roses is a narrow, cluttered store, and a familiar man is inspecting a wall of red wine. He's wearing a cardigan I've never seen on him before and his short hair's charmingly messy. The boho-meets-preppy look really suits him.

"Beck! Guess what?" I bound up to him, and he turns and gives me a surprised smile.

"What are you doing here?"

"I drove!" I know it's dumb, but I'm exhilarated by my minor accomplishment. "I haven't driven in I don't know how long."

He laughs, and I laugh along with him. "Good for you." He doesn't make fun of me and I appreciate the simple acceptance.

"How did you know where to find me?" he asks, smile broad.

"Oh. I didn't—I mean, I wasn't looking for you," I say haltingly. Why should the admission make me feel guilty? "I thought I'd get some beer and wine for the house. Kingston and maybe a friend of his are going to come over later."

"Oh right," he says, turning back to the shelves of wine.

"Hope that's okay."

"Of course. Jack said Kingston might stop by sometime."

"We're getting together a little poker game. You play?"

"Poker?" Beck seems distracted, running his finger over the label of a bottle of merlot.

"Yeah, poker." I don't know how else to describe it, honestly.

"I know how to play," he says vaguely. "I'm looking for some cooking wines. I don't really drink red."

"I'm more of a beer guy, but I thought I'd get a bunch of stuff." The place is too small for a cart, so I start pulling things at random. A couple of bottles of red, a couple of white. I set them on the counter in the back of the shop and nod to the blonde woman behind the register who's helping another customer. I remember Kingston likes bubbles, so I cross over to the sparkling wine.

"Can you get me some Prosecco?" Beck asks, at my elbow again. He's juggling two bottles of red and a bag from Second Time Around.

I take the bottles from him, add them to my collection, then return to his side.

"What did you get?" I ask, indicating his bag.

"You'll see," he says mysteriously.

"So, Prosecco. This look good?" I pick something mid-range, and then grab a bottle of something French and expensive that Kingston won't turn his nose up at.

"Sure. I'm not really an expert," Beck says as the woman from behind the counter walks over to us.

"Can I help you?"

Beck turns his small-town smile on her. "I think we're okay, thanks."

"Where's your beer selection?" I ask.

"Your first time in the shop?" she asks as she shows us a refrigerated case. "We mostly carry stuff from local breweries."

"Cool, and yeah, first time," I say. "What do you like?" I ask Beck.

"Anything," he says, lifting a careless shoulder. "I'm easy."

I get a variety here, too, accumulating a small mountain of booze on the counter. "Anything else?"

Beck thinks and then snaps his fingers. "I was going to get some vodka so I can make penne alla vodka."

"We only sell wine, beer, and cider," the woman says. "But you can get spirits at the place up Route 7."

Beck pouts for a second.

"I can swing by there on the way home," I say. "I wanted to go to that big box store and get some swim goggles and a few other things."

"Oh, that would be great," he says, face clearing. "Thanks, Donovan."

"Sure."

The woman starts ringing us up, and Beck pulls out his black credit card. I put a hand on his arm. "Let me get this." I'm still a little unclear on Beck's finances, but whatever they are, I need to pull my weight. Beck hesitates but lets me get out my wallet.

"You new to Rosedale?" the blonde asks as she grabs a couple of empty wine boxes to organize our purchases into. "I don't remember seeing you around."

Then she smiles at Beck in such a way that has my eyebrows shooting up my forehead. "I'm Ariana, by the way."

"Like Ariana Grande?" Beck asks.

"Yeah." She brightens even more. "You a fan?"

"I've seen her three times live," Beck says enthusiastically.

"That's awesome," Ariana says, leaning forward a little over the counter. Is it just me, or does she tug her shirt down a little in the process? "I love live music."

"She puts on an amazing show. I'm Beck, and this is Donovan."

"Like Beck, Beck?" Ariana tinkles out a laugh, her gaze glued to Beck's face. "I love his music."

"Me too." Beck smiles and I bristle.

"I have the same name as a famous musician, too," I put in, but neither of them seems to care. Probably neither has heard of the Scottish hippie single-named musician. He was a favorite of my parents.

"Well, Beck, I hope I'll see you again soon." She tosses her hair and gives him a flirtatious smile, completely ignoring me.

"Sure thing, Ariana."

I grab the box of wine and Beck manages the beer and his other bag.

As soon as we're out of the shop and heading toward Pete's car, I hiss at him. "She was totally hitting on you."

"What? No." He shakes his head.

"Seriously. She was into you."

"But I'm so gay," he says, as if it's self-evident.

"Seeing Ariana Grande three times live would have

been the giveaway for me," I say. "But I guess she didn't care."

"Wow. I thought it was weird that she didn't pay you any attention."

My ego thought it was weird, too, but I get it. She's probably around Beck's age, and he's cute and approachable, open and friendly. And as I've established already, there can't be that many people to choose from in this town.

Before I can respond, Beck adds, "I would have thought she'd have assumed we were a couple."

I look back over the interaction and have to agree. Is that bad? Are we acting too couple-y?

We're just roommates, I remind myself. And however it looks to the outside world, that's how it's going to stay.

ELEVEN
BECK

JACK

Made it to Edinburgh. How are you?

BECK

At the moment, I'm running around like the proverbial headless chicken.

That doesn't sound good. Everything okay with Cleo?

She's perfect. Donovan invited people over, so I'm getting the house ready.

Not throwing a rager, are you?

Yeah, the kegs are being delivered any minute.

No, Kingston's coming over for poker night.

Oh, that sounds fun. Watch out. Kingston really knows what he's doing.

What about Donovan?

Let me ask Pete.

He says Donovan's decent but conservative.

Good to know.

Everything going okay with him?

It's fine. We're getting along. But I really have to go now. Have so much fun in Edinburgh!

Thanks, cuz.

BY THE TIME Donovan returns with more beer and vodka from the liquor store and takes his assorted bags from the big box store to his room, I'm freaking out a little. I love entertaining, but it activates my anxiety brain. If we're having people over, I want them to have a good time, which means anticipating their needs. I've chilled the beer and wine from the wine shop, tidied the house, taken Cleo out, and made dessert. What else?

I pounce on Donovan the second he comes downstairs.

"What about food? I have some veggies I can cut up, but that's about it."

"I told you; we'll order pizza. You don't have to cook."

"Is the pizza around here even any good?"

"This close to New York, it's gotta be decent," he reassures me. "What toppings do you like?"

"I need to see a menu. We should wait until the guests arrive. What if one of them is gluten-free or something?"

"Beck. Look at me."

I obey because I want to, not because he used the faux-stern voice he uses on Cleo to get her to settle down before she eats. When Donovan's dark blue gaze is latched onto mine, I find myself distracted by the depths of that blue. I've gotten a little used to his handsomeness over the past few days. I don't find it quite so unsettling. But looking right at those pretty eyes and having them look right back at me—as if they can stare right into me and see all the fantasies I'm actively repressing—I shiver.

"We're not having 'guests,'" he says, actually using air quotes and making me remember why I stopped being quite so in awe of his beauty—turns out talented actor Donovan Eastman is kind of a big dork. "It's just Kingston and maybe a couple of his friends. It's casual. Relaxed. Chill. And other words that mean calm down."

I don't bother correcting Donovan that it doesn't matter if it's a head of state or some old college friends coming over; I always want to make a good impression. Instead, I catalog the mosaic of blues that make up his irises while I have the chance. Then he blinks and turns away and the spell is broken.

"Right. I'm calm. I just want to be a good host."

"We have beer, wine, and my nose tells me you baked something while I was gone, so that's already more impressive than ninety-nine percent of poker nights. Throw in pizza and we're golden."

I allow myself to be persuaded. "Where are we going to play? The round table in the living room works, but it's not too hot if we want to do it outside."

"I think inside. Last night was pretty buggy."

"True. Okay. You want to set up the table and I'll slice up some veggies?"

"Since I know you will whether or not I think you should, sure. Oh, and put on some music, would you?"

"What do you want?"

"Whatever you think. You always pick good stuff," he says before heading to the living room.

I find myself smiling as I scroll through my playlists. Donovan liking my taste in music makes me unreasonably pleased. I choose a feel-good alt-rock mix and sing along while I make neat little carrot sticks and orange bell pepper slices. Hmmm. Too much orange? I'm rummaging in the crisper drawer for something of a different color when the front doorbell chime goes off.

"Can you get that?" I shout.

"Getting it!" Donovan shouts back.

I put my hands on a bag of snap peas and grab the fixings for a quick dip. I hear voices in the hall and my pulse goes up a few notches. Jack's mentioned Kingston, but I've never met the guy, not to mention the mysterious friends he might be bringing. I wipe my hands on a dish cloth and put on a polite smile when Donovan brings the newcomers into the kitchen.

"Do you know Beck?" Donovan asks a man of about his height with ebony skin and shoulder-length locs wearing spiffy linen slacks and a paisley print short-sleeved button-down shirt. The man shakes his head no, so Donovan goes on, "Kingston James, meet Beck Avery."

"Ah yes, Beckett, pleasure to meet you. I must have missed you at the wedding." Kingston sticks out a hand and I shake it firmly.

"Beckett?" Donovan says, a wrinkle between his eyebrows.

"My mom's a big reader," I say to him, then I grin at Kingston. "I've heard a lot about you from Jack."

"Don't believe a word of it, dear," Kingston says loftily.

I laugh. He's a character and I immediately feel comfortable around him.

"And this is my dear friend Sergio," Kingston says, putting his hand on the shoulder of the good-looking man with dark brown skin, short black hair, and dark eyes next to him. "Sergio, this is Jack's cousin Beckett and an old friend of Pete's, Van—well, Donovan Eastman, to be more precise. You might have caught him in *Plum Island* or—what was that other Tony-winner?"

"I'm not much of a theater guy," Sergio says apologetically.

Donovan waves away the sentiment.

"Sergio is doing the unthinkable and putting his house on the market. It's a stunner on Beechwood Lane."

"You're moving away from Rosedale?" I ask, surprised. According to Jack, once people discover the town, they don't tend to leave.

"Unfortunately, yes. I probably should have put the house on the market a while ago, but this one—" Sergio points to Kingston "—told me I should wait in case my new job didn't work out. But I'm actually very happy in Seattle, even if it means goodbye, Rosedale."

Donovan gets Sergio a beer and asks Kingston what he wants.

"I would have brought my own bubbly," Kingston says, "but the afternoon got away from me."

"No problem," Donovan says. "We went to that wine shop you told me about. How's this?" He flourishes the pricey bottle with the pretty label he picked up earlier at Wine and Roses and Kingston raises his eyebrows.

"Oh, you shouldn't have. You'll spoil me. Oh well," he says happily.

"If we're opening that, then we have to use these." I pluck two of my new-old cocktail glasses from where I set them near the window after I washed them. "I got these today from the thrift store on Main Street."

"So that's what was in the bag," Donovan says, as if some big mystery has been cleared up.

"Classy," Kingston remarks. "Fill 'er up, Van."

Donovan pulls out the cork with a satisfying pop and the three of us put my new glasses to the test, while Sergio says he's happy with his beer.

"I think champagne tastes better in these," I say, smacking my lips.

"I think you're right," Donovan says, smiling at me.

It's really bad how warm his approval makes me. I turn away and ask Sergio about his job, which he tells me is some kind of nonprofit financial work, while I make the dip.

"Let's take this to the patio until the bugs realize we're here," I say, and we tromp outside, Cleo trotting between our legs. It never did get sunny today, but it's still warm.

"So, you're Jack's agent—how do you know Donovan?" I ask Kingston once we've made ourselves comfortable at the outdoor dining table.

"I was friends with Pete long before he got the job illustrating the Super Rupert books—before I even started representing Jack. And since Pete and Van lived together, we all knew each other back in the day when we were coming up in the city. I was an assistant agent—you were, what? A bartender?"

"Waiter," Donovan says briefly, pouring himself more of the sparkling wine.

"Oh, yes, now I remember." Kingston's eyes flash. And is it my imagination, or does he glance at Donovan's ass? I wonder what Donovan was like when he was younger, before he broke out as an actor, and I feel a tug of jealousy that Kingston has known Donovan for so much longer than I have.

Kingston twirls the stem of the glass in his hand. "Pete inspires loyalty in his friends."

"That's because he's better than all of us," Donovan says.

"Too true."

"So you guys are all friends from the city. But how did you end up in Rosedale?"

"I take full credit for discovering this gem of a hamlet. The city was wearing on me and I wanted a weekend retreat, so I rented a car and just started driving around, looking for inspiration. I stumbled upon Rosedale one morning and I just knew. I walked into the real estate office on Main Street, asked them to show me whatever was in my price range, and I put in an offer on my house that afternoon."

My nose tingles from Kingston's romantic spontaneity. Or maybe it's the bubbles from the wine. "So why don't you live here full-time?"

"I spend more time here than I used to, but I still have to make an appearance at the office a few days a week." Kingston sniffs. "But I've had an absolutely shit week at work, and I want to blow off some steam. Who wants to play some poker?"

"I'm game, but let's order food first to soak up this alcohol," Donovan suggests. He takes charge of ordering the pizza and we put in an eclectic selection.

"We're lucky Sergio is here this weekend," Kingston says, clapping his friend on the back. "He's a terrible poker player."

"We're not playing for real money, are we?" Sergio asks, alarmed.

"Nah," Kingston says. "We play for bragging rights."

Even better, in my book.

We nibble and chat and drink until the pizza arrives, and we're sick of swatting bugs away. I should have asked Donovan to get some citronella candles while he was out today.

"We better move this party inside. Donovan, you go ahead and take the pizza to the living room and I'll bring plates."

"I'll help you," Kingston says. Sergio excuses himself to use the bathroom, leaving Kingston and I alone as I count out a stack of Jack and Pete's heavy white bistro plates.

"Van treating you all right?" Kingston asks.

I'm surprised at his directness. "He's been great. Why?"

"He can be a prickly one. But you two seem like you're getting along." He waggles his eyebrows suggestively.

I laugh and shake my head. "We're getting to know each other."

Kingston chuckles. "Niiiice," he says, drawing out the vowel sound.

"Not like that." Not that it's any of his business. But I get the feeling that Jack asked him to check up on me—this is probably Kingston's interpretation of the request.

"All right." He puts his hands up in surrender. "Van's a player, always has been since I've known him. Just figured I'd warn you."

It's nothing different from what Donovan himself already told me, but my stomach sinks anyway at hearing someone who knows him better, warning me away, as if my little crush on him is painted on my face.

"Yeah, no worries," I say, trying to turn it into a joke. "We're just housemates. He's not even my—" I was going to say type, but I can't make myself lie.

Kingston rolls his eyes, not buying it for a second. "Yeah, with those thick black eyelashes and that mouth and those shoulders? Van's *everyone's* type."

I sigh. He's not wrong. "Doesn't matter if he's my type as long as I'm not his," I grumble.

"Oh, you think so?" Kingston laughs and looks me up and down blatantly. "If he hasn't made a move on you, that's not the reason why."

"Thank you?" I think there's a compliment in there

somewhere. "We're just housemates. He told me he doesn't hook up with his roommates. And I'm not really a one-night stand guy, anyway." It's true that if Donovan wanted to hook up, I'd be hard-pressed to say no. But it might be less painful to pass up the opportunity than to pretend I wouldn't want more.

"Oh, fair young Beckett. Stick to those principles. I admire a young man who hasn't been ground down to dust by the dating scene. It gives an old man like me hope."

Kingston's what, thirty-five? Sometimes I wish I was older and had things figured out already. Kingston has an amazing career and a home—I wonder what his house is like. I'm so far from any of those things, but if I think about that, I'll start drowning my angst in too much bubbly. "You're not old. Grab those forks, will you?"

"You're sweet," Kingston says, pulling me into a half-hug. "I like you, Beckett."

"You know, he goes by Beck." Donovan leans in the doorway, hand on his hip, looking at where Kingston's arm is wrapped around my shoulder.

"Oh, pardon me." Kingston grins at Donovan and then turns to me and bows exaggeratedly. "Forgive me, young *Beck*." He picks up the pile of silverware and flounces out of the room.

"Nothing to forgive," I say to his back, shoving the napkins at Donovan since he's just standing there staring at me. How long was he listening to us? I pick up the stack of plates. "Let's go eat."

TWELVE
DONOVAN

"THE GAME, in honor of my new friend Beckett—sorry, *Beck*," Kingston says with a nod in my direction, "is Texas Hold 'Em. Ante up." He gets Beck to cut and deals each of us two cards.

I glance at Sergio to my right, who looks a little lost. "Put a chip in the pot. Price of admission to play."

"Right," he says, following my lead and dropping a chip in the center of the table. "I'm not really a poker player."

"We'll talk you through it," Kingston says cheerfully. He's to my left, which means Beck is across the table from me. He takes a brief glance at his cards, but his face doesn't change. Which is weird. I've gotten to know a lot of Beck's expressions over the past week. He doesn't usually hide how he's feeling, but maybe he has something else on his mind.

Kingston lays the first card face up on the table. "Beck bets first."

"Check," Beck says calmly.

"What's that?" Sergio asks.

"We're just getting warmed up, so you can say check," Kingston explains.

"Check," he says obediently.

I look at my cards for the first time. Ace of diamonds and four of clubs, with a king of hearts on the table. "Check."

"And I check," Kingston says. He lays the ten of diamonds next to the king.

We all check again. The third card Kingston lays down is the ace of spades. Now we're talking. I've got a pair of aces, which isn't amazing, but it's better than nothing. Beck drops two chips into the pot.

While Kingston explains to Sergio what his options are, I watch Beck. He's ostensibly paying attention to the action on the table, but again he seems subdued. I wonder if Kingston said something to upset him when they were in the kitchen earlier? I went in search of the plates in time to see Kingston putting his arm around Beck and call him sweet. Was that some kind of pass?

Dinner before the game was friendly enough, with Beck asking Sergio all sorts of questions about the house he's putting up for sale. Beck seemed particularly interested in getting real estate agent recommendations from both Kingston and Sergio. Which seems strange.

"You know what? I fold," Sergio says. I tune back into Beck laughing lightly and realize this is going to be a long game if we have to hold Sergio's hand through every play.

"I'm in," I say, because why not? We're not playing for real money. I'm a decent player, but I know Kingston takes his game pretty seriously. We'll all stay friends if it's just for fun.

"I will stay in as well," Kingston says, matching Beck's bet. We get a four of hearts on the turn. Now I have two pair. Beck studies me for a moment before he starts off with five chips. He could have pocket pairs of something on the table and beat me with three of a kind, but what do I have to lose? I stay in. Kingston looks at his cards and considers for a moment, then folds.

The river card is the two of diamonds, which is no help. Beck stays steady, dropping five chips in the pot. I've gone this far, so I call. "Let's see what you got."

"Oh, just a straight," Beck says modestly, showing me his queen of spades and jack of hearts. Matching up with the ace, king, and ten, he's got my two pair beat handily.

"That's a good hand, right?" Sergio says.

I laugh. "I'll say. Beats me." I reveal my ace and four while Beck rakes in his chips. "Nice job."

He grins. "You, too. Thanks for staying in."

Kingston hoots. "This is going to be a more interesting game than I thought. I should have known you'd be a ringer."

"Lots of hot summer days growing up in Texas—we had to pass the time somehow," Beck says with a shrug.

Damn. He's good at poker, too. Shouldn't be surprising. And shouldn't be so appealing.

But it is.

With Kingston coaching Sergio, his game improves after a couple of hands. I'm feeling like I could use some lessons myself. My chips are dwindling while Beck's clearly leading the pack. Then Kingston takes a big pot and they're about even. Sergio goes all in on a pair of kings and loses to Kingston's full house. He gets up from the table with a rueful smile. "Anyone want anything else to drink?"

I switched to beer after my first glass of champagne. It did taste better in Beck's classy vintage glasses, but I'm more of a beer guy, anyway. "I'll take another beer," I say.

"Oh, what about dessert?" Beck jumps up. "Can we pause for a minute?"

"It's your deal, so you're the boss," Kingston says.

"Need any help?" I ask Beck.

He looks a little surprised at my offer. "Sure."

I stand up, crack my neck after sitting so long, and trail Beck to the kitchen. "What have you got cooked up for us?"

"I made mini chocolate chocolate chip cookies earlier, but I just remembered we have vanilla ice cream, too. Want to get out the bowls?"

He softens the ice cream in the microwave, and I get out bowls and spoons. I steal one of the half-dollar-sized cookies from the rack and bite into it. Rich chocolate chunks are studded throughout the chewy cookie, and I smack my lips. "These are amazing."

"Yeah?" Beck perks up. "I was getting sick of ginger and cinnamon, sorry."

I laugh, glad it's not just me who was ready for a change. "Variety is good. And I love chocolate."

"You can't go wrong with a chocolate chocolate chip cookie. I made them mini so we can eat a bunch and not feel like we're overdoing it."

"Brilliant." I watch as Beck assembles four bowls of ice cream and sticks two cookies artfully in each scoop. "You've got a cookie gift, you know."

"Do I?"

"But you're also a poker shark. Is there anything you aren't good at?"

Beck puts a hand on his chin and pretends to think. "Organic chemistry. Pretending to be nice to people whose politics turn my stomach. The butterfly stroke. But maybe that's it."

"If that's it, then I think you're doing pretty well."

"It doesn't feel like it on some days," he says, losing some of the joy from his face.

I scoot closer. "Are you okay? Are you not having fun tonight—I can send those guys home if you want."

"No, I'm having fun. Beating you at poker is surprisingly satisfying," Beck says, and I believe him. "Maybe I'm just tired. Being on permanent vacation is hard work."

I frown. "Permanent vacation?"

"I'm just kind of sick of not knowing what I'm doing with my life. Everyone else has it figured out, and I'm this cliche of a twentysomething with no direction. And I can't even look for a job right now because I have to be here this summer."

"Do you want to leave?" The idea of Beck going off and leaving me alone in this big house makes my chest ache unexpectedly.

"No, I love it here. But I have to admit that I've been running away from making any decisions about my life, and being here is not helping. Instead, it's making me realize that I want the stability that Pete and Jack have—I want the beautiful house, I want to spend my days doing something I love. Hell, I even want the dog. But as long as I keep pretending I don't know what I want, I can put off the hard work of actually figuring out how to get it."

"Sounds like you're getting tired of pretending."

He stares at me for a second. "Yeah. I guess I am."

"You're wrong about one thing, though. You think everyone else has their lives figured out? Look at me. I don't have a place to live or even my next job lined up. I'm pretending to write a play, so I don't have to admit I'm scared I'm never going to work as an actor again."

"What do you mean? Of course you will."

"Every actor thinks they're never going to work again when they're between jobs. It's part of the existential angst of one's profession being predicated on other people telling you they want you, and most of the time hearing they don't." It took time to grow a thick enough skin to keep going, and now that I've worked steadily for a while, it feels ungrateful to not be sure I even want to keep doing it.

"So you're a mess, too," Beck says. "That actually does make me feel better. Thanks."

Making Beck feel better is infinitely more satisfying than winning a hand of poker against him. "Anytime. We can be messy together."

He turns away abruptly, grabbing two of the dessert bowls. "Come on, they're melting."

I feel like I've said the wrong thing, which is

annoying after feeling like I actually did something good for a second there.

But just when I think I've figured Beck out, there's always more to learn.

THIRTEEN
BECK

KINGSTON AND SERGIO love the cookies. Like, really love them. Their unstinting praise helps me to stop thinking about Donovan and how nice he's being to me, and how he keeps saying things that I want to read in a romantic way, even though I know he doesn't mean them that way.

Does he?

No. He's just a supportive friend. And that tracks—he's known Pete forever. I don't know my cousin's husband all that well, but I know he's a good guy who wouldn't be friends with a dick.

So far, Donovan's biggest character flaw is that he's not ready to settle down. Maybe he won't ever be. And that's his choice. None of my business.

I just wonder if my heart's getting the message because every time he says something sweet or thought-ful, I get confused about why, exactly, we're not taking advantage of our situation and getting off with each other, especially when people like Kingston keep assuming we are.

Oh yeah, because he's a player who doesn't mess around with his roommates, and I haven't exactly been subtle about wanting something long-term. God. How cringe can I be?

Instead of going back to the game, we sit around in sugar comas, talking and drinking.

Sergio is really nice—kind of intimidating, since he's clearly successful at his job—and he's nice to look at. Tight black curls, appealing arms, a great smile. He and Kingston have the air of exes who stayed friends, intimate but somehow careful. I'm familiar.

Kingston is a charmer, but he's definitely giving off paternal vibes toward me. Honestly, it's comforting to know there's someone nearby I can call if I need something.

Of course, if I need something, Donovan is right here. But he didn't choose to live with me—I mean, I suppose in a certain sense he did, but he didn't choose *me*. In my quest to be an exemplary roommate, I'm not going to impose myself on him more than I have to.

This whole summer is an accident and we're making the best of it, but I still feel unsettled. I came here at loose ends and the longer I'm here, the more I want to tie some of those ends up.

Like that empty storefront I passed today. I can't stop thinking about it, about the possibilities. What could Rosedale need in that cute little space? And why do I think I could be the one to provide it? I don't know anything about owning my own business. And starting a store isn't something you can just try on a whim. I can hear my dad's voice now, telling me to pick something and stick with it. He thinks I'm a dabbler, and yeah, I kind of am. But maybe I just haven't found the thing I'm meant to stick with yet.

I tune back into the conversation when Donovan throws his head back and laughs at something Kingston's said. I tamp down a stupid flare of jealousy that someone else is making Donovan laugh and then try to catch up.

"I haven't been there in donkey's years," Kingston says. "But I'm not busy tomorrow. What do you say, Sergio? Wanna hit up Sparkle tomorrow night?"

"I guess I'm in," Sergio says. "I have a meeting with my real estate agent at two, but after that, I'm free."

"Sparkle?" The name is familiar, but I can't immediately place it.

"It's what passes for gay nightlife in these parts," Kingston explains. "Though it sounds like the name of a unicorn from a children's TV show, it's actually a pretty decent place. The drinks are overpriced, but the music is good."

"And the talent?" Donovan asks.

Oh yeah. I forgot he's been stuck at home with me and Cleo all week instead of whatever exciting New York nightlife he usually partakes of. He probably has no shortage of willing partners in the city. I know that's standard for some guys, but I've always been uncomfortable with random hookups. Call me a romantic or a prude, but it's probably just because I'm careful. Does this mean I can count my number of sexual partners on one hand?

Yes. Do I care? Sometimes, if I'm being honest. But I don't think it's a bad thing that I want to have feelings for someone before I have sex with them.

Kingston shrugs. "Depends on the night. But it's usually a fairly big crowd on the weekends."

"Well, I'm willing to give it a shot," Donovan says. "I'm currently in a dry spell and it's not a streak I particularly want to extend."

"I'm a great wingman," Kingston says. "I've got some stuff to do tomorrow, so let's just meet there—say eight?"

"Done." Donovan glances at me. "You in?"

I shake my head. "I don't know. I should stay with Cleo."

"I think she'll be fine for a few hours on her own. She's not a baby," Donovan says, surprisingly persistent.

"You mentioned music. Is there dancing?" I ask Kingston.

"Yeah, there's a dance floor. Sometimes they have live music, but they get good DJs the rest of the time."

Watching Donovan hit on strangers doesn't exactly sound like a good time, but it might be fun to get out of the house, and I do like dancing. "I'll think about it," I say finally, and Donovan seems satisfied with that.

Sergio and Kingston leave pretty soon after. We've graduated from handshakes to hugs, and Kingston compliments my poker game, which makes me feel pretty good.

"Shoulda suspected a Texas boy would know his way around a deck of cards," he says, clapping me on the shoulder.

"I'm always up for a game. We need more players, though."

"True. I'll see what I can do. Now, can I ask a huge favor?"

"What's that?"

"Can I get a doggie bag with some of those outrageous chocolate cookies?"

"Oh!" I run to the kitchen and shove half the batch into a paper bag and run back. "Here you go."

He peeks in the bag, and his brown eyes widen. "This is too many, but I'm not giving them back. Thanks, Beck."

"Thanks for coming over, guys," Donovan says. I wish I could stop noticing how handsome he looks, all rumpled and smiling easy and relaxed after however many beers he drank.

After he closes the front door, I set the alarm. He gives Cleo fresh water and takes her out one last time while I put the empties in the recycle bin and make sure the lid on the cookie jar is sealed tight. We have a routine by now, and we move easily around each other as if we've done this a thousand times before, even though it's only been six.

Finally, I switch off the light in the kitchen and bend over to give Cleo a goodnight kiss on her soft nose.

Donovan's hovering by the kitchen door when I stand back up, half illuminated by the light from the hall.

"Fun party," he says, hands shoved in the pockets of his jeans. "Thanks for baking, and, well, being generally awesome."

"You're welcome," I say, taken aback at the praise. "It was fun to have people over."

"You're good at it," he says. "A good host, I mean."

"Thanks."

We just stand there for a second and I wonder if there's something else he wants.

"I was thinking about what you said before—about not having a direction, about being ready to make a decision."

He was thinking about our conversation in the kitchen? About me? The idea warms my belly.

"And I was remembering when I decided I wanted to be an actor—it didn't just happen overnight. I had to take classes, audition for shows, apply to school. It's tempting to think we can just make snap decisions and change our lives, but I think getting what you really want takes time. I don't know. Maybe that's not what you'd like to hear. But I guess what I'm saying is there are things you can do now—small things, maybe—and in a few months, in a year, five years, you'll be somewhere completely differ- ent. But you'll be building what you really want."

I arch an eyebrow. "So you're saying it's the journey?"

He laughs a little at my sarcasm. "Jerk. But yes. It's the process. It's taking a small step and then taking another small step after that. You don't have to be stuck, not if you have an idea of what you really want. There's got to be some steps you can take right here and now."

I think about that storefront, about the blue house with the peeling paint. I think about Rosedale and my cousin, and I think about how of all the things I want out of life. Kissing the beautiful man who's saying such lovely, encouraging things to me has suddenly risen alarmingly close to the top of the list.

"Thanks, Donovan. That's good advice."

"Okay." He smiles hesitantly at me. "Good night, Beck."

I say goodnight, and he turns to go upstairs. I'm still standing in the kitchen, thinking, when the hallway light goes out a minute later.

FOURTEEN
DONOVAN

I SLEEP IN; the combination of the late hour when Kingston and Sergio left last night and the quantity of beer I drank keeping me in bed until almost eleven.

I feel guilty about letting Beck get up with Cleo this morning. He's definitely what I would call a morning person, but he was up just as late as me last night. I should offer to take care of her tomorrow—even if I'm planning another late night tonight.

I'm looking forward to hitting up Sparkle and seeing if there's anyone remotely interesting in this corner of rural New England. Maybe getting laid will get my mind off Beck, and how every day I spend near him, I find him more attractive, not less. And I found him pretty attractive to begin with.

But even if I like the guy and find his Martha Stewart-meets-Michael Phelps vibe weirdly hot, nothing's changed. We live together, and neither of us wants to mess up the good thing we have going. Hence, finding someone else to work out my physical needs with.

Part of me can't help imagining what it might be like with Beck, though. Would he be shy, the way he unexpectedly is sometimes, or would he be as passionately all-in as he is when he's trying a new recipe or trouncing me in a hand of poker? I've seen him nearly naked in his ridiculously small excuse for a bathing suit a handful of times at the pool, but I don't know how sensitive his tight little nipples are, or how his more-than-adequate package, from the looks of things, would feel in my hand.

And now I'm hard in the shower, washing my hair and thinking about my roommate, of all people. Right, roommate, that's why we're not ending our swimming sessions by making out on the deck chairs, jerking each other off poolside. Pete and Jack would probably appreciate it if they knew we weren't fucking all over their house.

Pete and Jack. Their likely disapproval is another reason to keep my hands to myself, even as right now in the shower I can't keep from stroking my cock, wondering if Beck would be mad if I just bent him over the kitchen counter in the middle of one of his cookie baking marathons.

Before I know it, I'm coming as I imagine it's Beck bringing me off, tasting my come on his fingers and declaring it better than his last batch of batter.

I feel strange after I finish washing and turn off the shower tap. There are so many reasons not to hook up with Beck, but that doesn't seem to matter much to my libido, which doesn't feel sated at all.

There better be some passably hot, willing guys at Sparkle tonight, or I'm going to explode.

When I finally drag myself downstairs, Beck's seated at the island, hunched over his laptop. Cleo trots up to me and sniffs my hand.

"Good morning," Beck calls absently. "I fed her, but she could probably use some exercise."

"I'm on it. Any coffee left?"

"Actually, no. But I made muffins."

I snag one and bite into it, cranberry and lemon bursting tangy sweet on my tongue. "Yum," I say with my mouth full. "What did you do, drink the whole pot?" I ask after I swallow and Beck still hasn't looked up from his screen.

He winces. "Yeah. I've been up for a while. Sorry."

"No worries." I remember what Pete said about taking Cleo on the walk in the woods and figure today's a good day to try it. I can get something at Hot Brew on the way. "Wanna take Cleo for a walk? I thought we could try out the loop in the woods Pete mentioned."

He looks up at that. "No, you go ahead. I have a call with Sergio's real estate agent in a bit. Oh, I was thinking fajitas for dinner."

I finish the muffin in two bites. "Fajitas sound amazing. Why do you have a call with Sergio's real estate agent?"

His sky-blue eyes gleam with excitement. "I'm taking your advice. Taking my first step toward what I want. I'm going to get some information on retail spaces in Rosedale and on that abandoned house on Turner Street."

"Wait—what?" I'm not really following the logic. "This sounds more like a huge leap than a step, Beck."

The excitement in his eyes dims and I immediately curse myself for doing anything to dampen his enthusiasm. Just because the things he's talking about seem wildly unattainable doesn't mean I should throw cold water on him. How many of my friends thought me being an actor was an impossible dream?

"I'm just gathering information," he says with a trace of defensiveness in his voice.

"No—no, that's great," I say, backpedaling awkwardly. "Really. I know you love that house. Might as well see what the deal is, right?" Privately, I can't imagine that even if it was for sale that a guy who isn't employed and basically lives out of his car could buy it, but I don't say anything.

"Why do you want to know about retail spaces?" I ask, grabbing a second muffin. These things are delicious —fluffy and light. I wish I had some coffee to go with them, but I'm too lazy to start the machine.

"Oh. Well. I saw this empty storefront on Main Street yesterday and it just...got me thinking," Beck says. He stands up and away from his computer, runs a hand through his hair, which makes the blond strands stick up like a baby chick's fluffy feathers. He seems so young sometimes, but he's not a kid. I repress the urge to pat down his hair. Touching him seems like a bad idea, given what I've just been fantasizing about in the shower.

"Thinking about what?"

He laughs ruefully. "I'm actually not sure. I've never thought about owning a store, but it seems appealing. Being in the center of town, getting to talk to people, providing something they need. Making people's lives a little better through retail therapy."

"So what, like a boutique or something?"

"Or something." He shrugs and frowns. "It's only a kernel of an idea, so it'll probably peter out, like everything I try."

"Don't say that." I go to finish my second muffin, only to realize it's already all gone. I snap my muffin-sticky fingers as an idea hits me. "What about baking?"

"What about baking?" Beck repeats, confused.

"Rosedale doesn't have a great bakery—you said it yourself. Hot Brew has muffins and stuff, but no cookies, no cakes, no pies. You could open a bakery." I disregard the part of my brain that calls up the statistic that most small businesses fail and focus on how freaking delicious everything Beck makes turns out.

"I don't know," Beck says slowly. "There's this woman, Stacy, who provides the baked goods for Hot Brew. She's got that space covered, I think. She has a booth at the farmer's market that I was going to check out tomorrow."

"I'm pretty sure a town the size of Rosedale could support two people who like to bake delicious treats," I say, determined to be supportive even if I'm not actually sure what I'm saying is true.

"Apparently she's not into cookies," Beck says, tapping the counter nervously. "I could specialize. I do love baking cookies. And they're easier to display and package than cakes or pies."

I remember what Beck said to me the first night he made me a batch of molasses cookies. "It could be called the Cookie Counter! Or Beck's Cookie Counter? I like them both. And you could have high top seating and sell drinks, maybe?" I can't help getting into the concept now.

He laughs, and my chest puffs with pride at having made his frown disappear. "Wow, you're full of ideas."

"It's just that it's so perfect for you. And it would fit in with the other businesses on Main Street." I can picture Beck in a cute apron, greeting the denizens of Rosedale with a smile and hooking them on his amazing creations.

"I guess—I don't know." He bites his lip. "Baking for me has always been something I do to blow off steam or make someone happy. What if I did it as a job and it wasn't fun anymore?"

"Or maybe you'd get to do something you love as your job," I say. "Look, owning your own business isn't easy. There's paperwork and permits and taxes and all that— but it could be really rewarding, too."

"Okay, okay. Yeah. I'll think about it. The space I saw yesterday used to be a deli or something, so maybe it's already set up for food?" He goes to the computer and types for a second. "Another thing to ask the agent."

I wash my hands in the sink and rummage in the cupboard for Cleo's lead. I crouch down and attach it, giving her a thorough head scratch in the process. "So— you like Rosedale enough to settle down here, maybe?"

Beck doesn't answer right away as I grab the keys to Pete's car and pat my pockets for my wallet. Eventually, he says, "I like Rosedale, sure. Settling down hasn't exactly been my strong suit, but I'm getting tired of being on the move. Rosedale seems as good a place as any. Maybe better than most."

"But?" I prompt, hearing his underlying hesitation.

"But I'm scared," he says softly. "Nothing I've ever done has ever really worked out. What if I try this and nothing comes of it? I'll just be back where I started—at loose ends."

"But you have to try," I tell him, certain of that if nothing else. "You can't dog-sit for the rest of your life. You deserve to have your own place, your own career, your own life."

We're both borrowing Jack and Pete's life for a couple of months, but I have a life to go back to in the city, even if it's crappy plays and endless auditions. It doesn't make sense for Beck not to go after what he wants—he's too awesome for that.

And his smile and his quiet "thank you" keep me company for the rest of the day.

FIFTEEN
BECK

IT'S past Cleo's dinnertime when I park the GTI haphazardly in the driveway and rush into the house, my brain filled to the brim with information and ideas. After talking to Noelle, Sergio's real estate agent, on the phone, she immediately persuaded me to look at a few houses and the retail space on Main Street. That took up most of the afternoon, and then when I found out her sister owns a bakery in Brooklyn, I lost track of time picking her brain about that.

I should have been home an hour ago to start dinner and make sure Cleo was okay, and my heart's racing with excitement over all the possibilities I've thought of today and with the fact that my actual job right now is to take care of one very cute dog.

When I skid to a stop in the kitchen like a harried cartoon character, I'm astonished to find it completely empty. No hungry pup. No hungry Donovan, for that matter.

I worry for half a second until I spot them through the French doors. Donovan's throwing the ball for Cleo, his tight black tee showing off his elegantly muscled arms as he arcs the ball across the yard. The sun's starting to go down, bathing the backyard in gold. His profile is perfectly outlined by the flare of the setting sun filtered through the leafy deciduous trees that ring the property, making him look more like a sexy model than usual. My heart, still galloping, doesn't slow down as I watch him play with Cleo, but it feels as if it's being squeezed unpleasantly tight even as it tries to hammer its way out of my chest.

I know it's beyond foolish to let myself feel any sort of way about him, but he's making it really, really difficult not to fall for him. It's not just the way he looks, so objectively beautiful that I'm still not sure how he exists—though the more we get to know each other the less his beauty surprises me and the more his goofy, dorky sides come through and humanize him—it's more the things he says, as if we're actually friends and he really cares about me. I have a lot of friends in a lot of parts of the world, but it feels really good to have a live-in cheerleader who takes me as I am and seems to think I'm pretty awesome.

After twenty-five years of hearing I'm not what my parents hoped for, it's a small miracle to have someone accept me for who I am, and who believes in what I'm capable of.

So yeah, my heart doesn't listen to my head as I stare out the French doors and wish that he wasn't my roommate. I wish he was just… mine.

A moment later, Donovan confiscates the tennis ball and rubs Cleo's neck. When they start for the house, I shake myself and flip on the recessed lights in the kitchen.

"You're back," Donovan says with a wide smile.

"Yeah, sorry I'm late for dinner. I got caught up looking at properties with Noelle," I say, yanking open the refrigerator door to remind myself his smile doesn't mean anything except that he's happy to see me. His roommate/friend.

I startle at a touch on my arm and close the fridge door to reveal Donovan standing close. "Hey, you don't have to feed me every night," he says. "And you don't have to apologize. I had leftover pizza. But you should eat. Who knows if the food at Sparkle is any good?"

I stare at him, confounded by the words coming out of his mouth until I remember. Sparkle. The bar. That's tonight. "Oh, right." I glance at the wall clock. "Aren't you meeting Kingston and Sergio there soon?"

"*We're* meeting them at eight," he says easily.

"Oh *we* are, are we?" I put the emphasis on the 'we' the way he did. As if we're a package deal, even though I know he wants to go to Sparkle to hook up, and I can't imagine he needs me along for the ride.

"Yeah. You have to come. It'll be good for you to get out of the house," he says.

"I was out of the house most of the day," I protest.

"And I want to hear all about it. You can tell me on the way."

"I'm a mess," I say, lifting my shirt away from my chest and wrinkling my nose dramatically.

"So take a shower. Please? I'll have more fun if you're there." He blinks slowly, his thick eyelashes sweeping down to almost touch the tops of his cheeks.

It would take a stronger man than me to deny those eyelashes.

"Fine. Heat me up a piece of pizza, will you?"

"Done."

AN HOUR LATER, I'm driving us toward Midville, the closest small city to Rosedale. It has a movie theater, a bowling alley, and, apparently, a gay bar. I've been telling Donovan about the retail space—how it's already set up to take industrial ovens, and how Noelle's face lit up when I mentioned the cookie shop idea. "Sugar cookies are her favorite, so I'm going to drop some off on Monday. She said the owners would look at a lower offer, so we'll see."

"You're going to put in an offer?" Donovan sounds surprised, but not skeptical.

"I know it's kind of rushed." I bite my lip. I have so much to figure out, but something about this feels right. "I don't want to lose this space—it's perfect."

I'm expecting Donovan to say something like, "When you're ready, the right space will come along," but he just says, "Cool." His phone pings with a notification. He checks it and swears.

"Damn. Kingston and Sergio are bailing." He types a short reply and glances sideways at me. "Looks like it's just you and me tonight."

"Right," I respond tightly. I don't have a good feeling

about this. Donovan's goal is to have sex tonight, and I think it's going to kill me a little to see him be physical with someone else. I don't have any claim to him, but that doesn't mean I want to see him all over some random guy.

"What's wrong?" Donovan, as ever, seems to read my mood.

"I'm just not good at bars," I say, which is partly the truth.

"What do you mean?"

"I never know the etiquette. In college, we just drank in the dorms. And I always feel self-conscious in gay bars and clubs, like everyone has an agenda."

"Well, our only agenda is to have fun," Donovan says. "We'll get something to drink, we'll check the place out, and if it sucks, we'll get out of there. Okay?"

"Sure." I promised myself I'd be the best roommate ever, and that means being a good wingman if it comes to that. Donovan's sweet to reassure me, but I know the score. He's looking for something different tonight— someone different.

As I pull the GTI into the parking lot next to the stand-alone brick building with the neon sign, I wonder if maybe I should take inspiration from him tonight. My last boyfriend and I called it quits months ago, and while I don't really mind not having constant sex, being around Donovan—being able to look but not touch—has had me feeling slightly turned on since we met. I'm not a complete stranger to hookup culture, I just don't usually feel comfortable getting physical with someone I just met.

But if Donovan can do it, maybe I can, too. After all, if I'm going to start putting down roots in Rosedale, getting to know the queer scene is a good idea. Maybe I'll hit it off with a local and start working on the Jack-and-Pete-style happily ever after I want for myself. Who knows, I could meet the love of my life tonight.

I push away the idea that the odds are slim I'll meet anyone as interesting, nice, and hot as Donovan and instead try stay optimistic as we lock the car and walk to the entrance. A beefy, bored-looking guy sitting on a stool glances at us and says, "ID."

I hold up mine and he gives me a nod, then he says, "You too, sir," to Donovan, and I snort.

Donovan glares at me and fishes his wallet out of his back pocket, flipping it open to his license.

"Sir?" I mutter under my breath as we get ushered into the cool, dark interior of Sparkle. Despite the name, the inside is fairly restrained. There's a disco ball over the dance floor on one side of the room, but it's not like it's all glitter and feathers. The heavy wooden bar looks old, and I wonder how long this place has been here. Maybe it used to be something else.

It's also pretty busy. Almost every barstool taken—mostly by men, but there are a few women—and a healthy amount of the low tables on the bar side of the place are filled with patrons. The dance floor is emptier, but it's still early, and there's just generic pop music coming from the speakers. I see a DJ setting up, so I assume there'll be more activity in a little while.

Meanwhile, I endure the social anxiety of not

knowing the best place to claim. Should I go to the bar and squeeze in between the existing patrons, or look for an empty table?

Donovan solves the problem for me by striding confidently up to the bar, immediately catching the eye of one of the two bartenders, an attractive older guy with short silver hair and a black tee with Sparkle emblazoned on the front in metallic blue.

As if communicating by telepathy, the bartender seems to indicate to Donovan that it'll be a minute, so Donovan looks over his shoulder at me. "What do you want? I'll get the first round."

"Uh." What do I want? I should have figured this out earlier. "What are you having?"

Donovan's looking over the draft beer menu. "A pilsner."

"Okay. Me too." I don't love beer, but I can't think of anything else, and the bartender is now looking at Donovan expectantly. He puts in the order and hands over a credit card, and a minute later we're carrying our filled-to-the-brim pint glasses to a table that seems to appear magically under Donovan's gaze.

"Cheers," he says, tapping the rim of his glass against mine.

"Cheers." I take a sip and purse my lips involuntarily. It's kind of sour. Probably better with something greasy, like a burger and fries. My stomach rumbles. A single piece of leftover pizza was not enough for dinner.

"You hate it," Donovan says.

"No—well, it's not my favorite."

"Then why did you order it?" He sounds confused rather than angry.

"Because I'm bad at bars!" I wail.

He cracks a grin, shakes his head. I laugh a little, knowing I'm being dramatic. I push my glass across the table at him. "You can have mine."

"Oh, it won't go to waste," he says, "but let's start over. What sounds good? Do you need a menu?"

"I am kind of hungry. And I don't really feel like drinking. I have to drive later, anyway."

"Okay." Donovan looks around the room, then leans over and asks a guy sitting alone at the table nearest us if we can borrow his menu, which is sitting folded on the table. The guy smiles and nods and looks like he's about to say something, but Donovan's got the menu now and he opens it, no longer paying attention to the other guy.

"They have your standard bar food. Burgers. Pizza."

"No pizza."

"Right, we just had pizza. Sweet potato fries? Meatball sub?"

"Meatball sub?" I take the menu out of his hands and scan it. There it is. Meatball sub. Huh.

"You didn't believe me?" He's smiling again, and it's distracting.

"Meatball sub at a gay bar just seems kind of on the nose," I say with a wave of my hand. "I'll have a burger. And fries. And a root beer."

"We're not at a baseball game," he says mildly.

"I'm hungry. You asked what sounded good, and that sounds good."

"You're the boss," he says, standing up from the table.

"Stay here and try not to have a panic attack. It's just a bar."

On his way to the bar, he drops the menu on the table of the guy he borrowed it from. I don't miss the way the guy's eyes track Donovan. Donovan again somehow smoothly puts in the order with the bartender, and I'm a little annoyed at how together he is. On the other hand, he's getting me food, so how can I complain about that? The bartender hands him a tall glass that presumably holds my root beer and Donovan heads back.

I'm not surprised when the guy from the table next to us gets up to intercept him. He's tall and fit and wearing a slim-cut short-sleeved button-down and cutoff jean shorts. His blond hair hangs around his shoulders, and I wonder if Donovan goes for guys with long hair.

"Hey, haven't seen you in here before," the guy says to Donovan.

"First time," Donovan says briefly, but not rudely. He looks the guy up and down subtly.

"I'm Ken," the guy says.

"Van," Donovan says. I always forget that's the name most people know him by.

"I'd love to buy you a drink, Van," Ken says.

I realize I probably shouldn't be listening, but our table is right there, and it's hard to pretend to be doing something else when they're like three feet away. I happen to meet Donovan's gaze when he looks my way, the hint of a smile on his face. I hold it for a second. Do I want him to let Ken buy him a drink? Not really, but I'd be an asshole for holding him back. The most I can do is shrug, as if I couldn't care either way.

"Thanks, but I already have one. Two, actually. And I have to deliver this," Donovan says, holding up my soda.

Ken looks over his shoulder at me, as if he's just now noticing my existence. "Boyfriend?"

Donovan laughs a little, maybe at the guy's transparency, maybe at the idea of me in a role he's not looking to fill. "Friend."

Friend is accurate, which both fills me with satisfaction and leaves a cold little pit in my stomach. But then he goes on, "Again, thanks for asking."

He comes over to sit down and Ken watches us for a second, then turns away, apparently taking the hint.

"Here you go." Donovan slides the drink my way. "They said the burger would take a few minutes."

"No rush." I take a sip of root beer and the sweet drink immediately washes away the sour taste of beer. Maybe the sour taste of jealousy, too. After all, Donovan's sitting here with me, and he's easily the hottest guy in the place.

While we wait for the burger, Donovan drinks and I tell him about Noelle's sister's Brooklyn bakery. It's way too easy to forget my resolution to keep my eyes open for a guy of my own when Donovan's attention is on me, but it's hard to miss it when a cute chubby guy with round glasses and a nice smile asks me to dance.

I've just finished my meal and I'm feeling a little bad about talking Donovan's ear off, even though he hasn't seemed bored—if anything, he keeps asking questions and giving me good ideas for next steps. But when the guy, who says his name is Casey, comes up just as the DJ's starting a set with a song I love, it's hard to say no.

I glance at Donovan anyway, but he's just got a bland smile on his face. I hesitate—he hadn't bailed on me before with Ken. But then he's looking across the room and I see him making eye contact with a muscular guy in a tank top. I guess the friends-hanging-out portion of the evening is over.

SIXTEEN
DONOVAN

THE BUILT guy I'm talking to is telling me about his weight routine, which I'm honestly interested in since I get bored doing the same routines all the time. But my attention's only partly on him. The rest is on Beck, who's still on the dance floor. The burger he devoured seems to have given him a boost of confidence, because he no longer seems like he's "bad at bars." He's shimmying and shaking to the beat while the guy who got him on the dance floor watches, clapping and hollering appreciatively. Beck's flushed and smiling.

"I'm all in on pea protein right now," the guy—he told me his name, but I forgot it already—says. "I add that shit to everything."

"Hmm." Beck's dance partner seems to be introducing him to another man and they're forming a little group.

"You wanna dance?" the pea-protein enthusiast asks.

"Huh?"

"You seem really interested in what's happening over

there," he says, pointing to the dance floor. "I'm not much of a dancer, but I could give it a shot. Or we could go somewhere else to talk—somewhere quieter. I live a couple miles away."

"Oh." I look at him, giving him my full attention for the first time since we started talking. He's attractive, in a gym-rat way, and he smells good, like clean laundry. I drank my beer and Beck's, too, and I'm working on my third. It would be easy to go home with him and end my dry spell tonight.

But I'd have to leave Beck behind.

"Let's dance," I say, draining most of the rest of my beer before I can overthink my decision.

Pea-protein guy follows me willingly, and we get on the floor just as the beat ramps up. He's not lying—he can't really match the tempo of the music, which makes me wonder how good in bed he could be. I could find out —but as I catch sight of Beck in the modest crowd, his hands on someone new's hips as they move back and forth in sync, I realize I don't want to.

Beck's as good at dancing as he is at everything else. The lights in the ceiling must be on some kind of timer, because they're cycling through all the colors of the rainbow, making the disco ball throw panes of red, orange, yellow, green onto the crowd. I should be getting my hands on Mr. Hard Body, but I can't tear my gaze away from Beck, watching his face flash blue, purple, pink.

He's radiant.

And I want him.

I think the last beer must have gone to my head because dragging Beck home right this minute and taking him to bed seems like the best idea I've had in a long time.

"I think I'm going to head out," my dance partner says, leaning close to be heard over the music. "You want to come with?"

I should say yes. There's a reason I don't hook up with guys like Beck, and it's not just because we're roommates. It's because hooking up with someone who I actually like, actually care about, is too hard. Too painful.

Pete's voice in my head says, "Aidan was eight years ago. Move on already."

Maybe it's pathetic to still mourn a relationship that's been over that long, but it's less that I'm still sad and more that I've become so used to short-term hookups that I don't know how to do anything else anymore.

But it could be different with Beck. Our living situation is over at the end of the summer. Then we'll both walk away—I'll go back to the city, to my career, and Beck will, well, maybe he'll stay here, but he knows that I won't.

Maybe we could have fun together in the meantime.

I clear my throat to turn down the offer, but he's already gone. I feel bad for half a second, but honestly, it's a relief to thread my way through the dancing bodies and find Beck. Now he's dancing with a dark-haired guy with blue eyeshadow and painted-on jeans.

I hover for a second. Maybe this is stupid. Maybe Beck doesn't want me like I want him. Maybe he's too smart to get involved with someone as emotionally unavailable as me.

But when he catches my gaze with his, I push away my nerves. This is just Beck. "Hey."

"Hey," he says back, sounding amused. He doesn't stop dancing with the guy, who pays no attention to me.

"Can we—" I stall out, not sure what I want to ask for. A dance? A ride home? Hand jobs in the bathroom?

He raises his eyebrows, and the disco lights flash again—red, orange, yellow. By the time they get to blue, I blurt it out: "Are you ready to leave?"

He looks surprised. "Already?"

"Who's this?" The guy he's dancing with looks me up and down, his pierced tongue peeking between his lips.

"He's my roommate," Beck says, still sounding amused.

"He's delicious," the guy says, invitation in his eyes.

I watch Beck's face carefully, but he doesn't move to agree or scoff at the guy's description of me. Damn him and his poker face.

"Sorry to interrupt," I say, though I'm not sorry in the least. I tug on Beck's arm and he lets go of pierced-tongue guy.

"What's going on?" Beck says, following me a few feet away, nearly off the edge of the dance floor. "I thought you had big plans for tonight."

The song shifts to something boppier. I run my hand through my hair, frustrated that I messed up a perfectly good night to pull, and messed up Beck's game, too. All because I can't keep my mind off him, even when we spend half our time together as it is.

"I'm an idiot."

He grins. "What does that have to do with anything?"

I jut out my chin. "Thanks a lot."

He laughs. "No, seriously. Is everything okay? Are you feeling okay? What did you drink?"

"I'm fine. We don't have to go if you don't want to. I just—I thought—" What am I doing? He doesn't want me. He wants a real relationship. He wants a forever kind of love. The kind I've been telling myself I don't believe in for the last eight years. The kind I thought I once had for myself.

"What?" he asks, more gently.

"I just want to go home. With you." If I sound tired, it's because suddenly I'm exhausted. I can't believe it, but the truth is I'd rather spend a sexless night hanging with Beck, munching on cookies and watching a movie, Cleo curled up between us on the couch, instead of anonymous sex with a pea-protein-obsessed gym rat.

"Oh." Beck looks a little lost, and I feel like the selfish shit I am.

"But you were having fun. You should dance more. I'll get another drink—"

"No." Beck touches my shoulder and I lean into him involuntarily. "It's okay. Let's go."

I settle the tab and we get back in the car without saying much.

"Sorry. I ruined the night, I guess," I say, feeling uncharacteristically self-pitying.

"My night wasn't ruined," he says, but he still sounds quiet, like I've taken the energy out of him. The last thing I want to do.

"That's a pretty cool place. Sparkle," I say, in a weak attempt at salvaging a conversation.

"Good burgers," he says.

"Good beer."

"Nice people."

"I guess," I say.

"What—not up to your New York standards?" He sounds like he's teasing, but I can hear an undercurrent of insecurity.

"It's not that." I haven't missed New York at all the last couple of days. "I'd just rather be with you." Shit. That's both exactly what I mean and not at all what I meant to say.

Beck flips on his blinker, checks his mirrors, then pulls his car into a turnout on the side of the road.

"What—?"

He throws the emergency brake on and puts the gear shift in neutral. "Donovan, you have to stop staying stuff like that."

I swallow hard. Shit.

"Because if you keep on being so supportive and nice and sweet and acting like my goddamn boyfriend, I'm going to get the idea that you want to actually be my boyfriend. And that's not good for my mental health, okay?"

"I don't want to be your boyfriend," I say quickly. It might make me an asshole, but it's the truth.

"I know." In the dark cabin of the car, his face is faintly illuminated by the dials on the dash. He sounds calm, but he looks...sad. "We're friends. Which is awesome. I'm really enjoying being your friend."

"Me too." That's the truth, too. And while I'm on this

truth-telling kick, I might as well confess something else. "I sort of want to kiss you, though."

I can hear his sharp inhale. "Sort of?" I should know he's not going to make it easy on me.

"I do want to kiss you." I owe him that much.

"Just kiss?" he asks, looking not at me, but at the gear shift. Now I can hear the flirtation in his voice and I let go of the anxious breath I've been holding onto.

"No. I want to get you off." I'm dying to know what he looks like when he's turned-on and coming—is it the same face he makes when he bites into the first still-warm cookie from the oven?

"Anything else?"

"I want you to get me off." Fuck, I need to feel another body next to mine—it doesn't have to be anything fancy. I'd happily rub off on Beck in the back seat. For starters, anyway.

"And just to be clear, you want all of these things, and you don't want to be my boyfriend?"

"Is this a trick question?"

"I'm just wondering what this would be. Friends with benefits? A one-night thing?"

I already know he's not the kind of guy who wants the latter. The former is a cliche. But not inaccurate. "We're roommates with benefits," I offer. "Taking advantage of our mutual attraction for a mutually beneficial arrangement. For the summer."

"Hey, who said anything about mutual attraction?" Beck says, but I know he's just giving me a hard time.

"Whatever, you know you want me," I say. And then

I put my hand on his thigh and squeeze. He shivers. "See?"

He bites his lip. "Just for the summer?"

It must be the law school dropout in him that wants to clarify terms before entering into the contract, such as it is.

"Just for the summer. Is that cool?"

He puts his hand hesitantly on top of mine, meets my gaze with his. "Cool."

SEVENTEEN
BECK

BY UNSPOKEN AGREEMENT, we don't seal our bargain with a kiss. Not yet.

Negotiations for a roommates-with-benefits situation for the duration of the summer complete, I put the car back in gear and finish getting us home in the dark, wary of possible nocturnal animals on the country roads.

When we get back to the house, Donovan stops me on the front step before I can put my key in the lock.

"Wait," he says, and then he's kissing me, soft bristles from his two-day-old beard brushing my chin, softer lips brushing mine. It's an unexpected kiss—both the timing and the location—but not unwanted. Kissing Donovan is actually kind of perfect. He's slightly taller than me, but he picks just the right angle, and his hand snakes around my waist while I grab one of his shoulders with the hand that isn't holding keys. I think he just means to tease me, to get the awkward first kiss out of the way, but then he deepens it, and suddenly I can taste the beer on his tongue and saliva pools in my mouth because I want more. I want to taste all of him.

He steps closer, and that's when I can feel his dick through his jeans, pressing against my hip. Holy shit. This is really happening. We're really kissing and he really wants me.

And I'm really letting him have me, even though this isn't ever going to be all I want it to be.

He couldn't have been clearer about not wanting to be my boyfriend. And that's something I'm apparently willing to accept, if it means I get to make out with him under the milky glow of the front porch light, softly grinding my own swiftly filling cock against him, somewhat unable to believe this is really happening.

He pulls back and I'm struck again by the unreality of it. He's just too pretty, those dark lashes, those cheekbones, the crooked nose so dear to me after only a week. Donovan Eastman is fucking hot, and apparently slender blond bakers turn him on.

"Um," is all I can think to say.

"I forgot how good it feels to kiss," he says, with a touch of gravel in his voice, surprising me for the millionth time that night.

I made him feel good. It's bananas.

I laugh, slightly nervous, afraid to wake up. "Yeah. Well. Kissing me on the front step is a little too close to boyfriend territory for me, so."

His eyes widen, and I laugh again. "Just a joke." I'm going to be terrible at this.

But he seems to relax. "You're right," he says lightly. "My bad. Should we?" He gestures to the door.

I unlock the door and disarm the security system, then lock the door and arm it again. "Are you hungry or—?"

"Horny," he corrects me. "Want to come up to my room?"

My dick pulses at the idea of imminent sex, even if I'm not prepared in any practical way. "Sure. Let me check on Cleo first."

"Good idea." We check on her together—she's snoozing in her bed, raising her head sleepily when we come in, then settling back down again. She should be fine until morning.

"Give me a minute," I say to Donovan, who nods and then goes upstairs.

In my room I have condoms and lube, a few toys, but I don't know if any of that is what Donovan has in mind. Or even if I want to go there. I'm kind of an old-fashioned boy. I like to start slow and work my way up to the main event, which is part of why one-night stands don't really work for me. It sounds like Donovan wants this to be more than a one-night thing, so maybe we can afford to start slow. But if I only have one night with him—what do I want?

The fact that I'm even about to go to his bedroom has me wanting to scream into my pillow like an over-whelmed teenager about to have his first date. It doesn't fucking matter what we do. I trust Donovan to make it good, and I just need to let myself enjoy it.

Just because I'm going to have my heart broken at the end of this doesn't mean I can't savor every second of it before that inevitable conclusion.

In the end, I clean up a little, quickly brush my teeth, and change out of my bar clothes into a pair of loose shorts—sans underwear—and my aqua tank top that makes my eyes look electric blue.

Barefoot, I pad up the stairs. Donovan must have lube and condoms if we need them, and if he doesn't, mine are only a floor away. I hesitate outside the door to his room, which is open a crack, faint light showing through the gap. I've never actually been inside. I've been upstairs, of course, familiarizing myself with the linen closet and retrieving some extra dog toys from the floor of Jack and Pete's room. But Donovan's door has always been closed.

I knock lightly, and he opens up right away. He's barefoot, too, wearing the same jeans from earlier, but he's unbuttoned his shirt and it's hanging open, exposing the ridges of his pecs and abs, the light dusting of hair down the center of his chest. My mouth goes dry.

"Hey."

"Hey."

And then we're kissing again, hot and fierce, like we're both starving for it. He stops after way too short a time, removing his tongue from my mouth. I chase it for a second, but he says, "You brushed your teeth. I should, too."

"Don't worry about it," I say, launching myself at him as though if I don't have more of him right now, I might expire from wanting.

He lets me walk him backward to the bed, which is a king, like mine, but covered in a dark blue comforter where my room is done up in shades of gray. When we reach it, we topple over, and I revel in feeling our chests touch for the first time. Greedy for more, I take half a second to lose my tank top, then push aside his shirt and lick a stripe over each of his flat, dark brown nipples. They fatten up nicely under my tongue. He hisses and puts a hand to the back of my head, pushing me against his chest, so I do it again and again until he's groaning a bit desperately beneath me.

Since I'm so hard I could poke a hole in the mattress, I let up on the nipple play and we crawl farther up the bed together. Donovan stays on his back, though, and I straddle him, glad my shorts are loose, allowing me to easily push the waistband down and pull my erection free.

"Damn, I knew you had something going on," he says, gaze glued to my hand on my dick. I stroke it from root to tip, flicking my thumb over the head, and smile. I'm not hung like a horse or anything, but I'm a little above average, which I'm vain enough to maximize by keeping my pubes shaved close.

"Yeah? What did you think I had going on?"

"Teasing me with that tiny little excuse for a swim-suit," he says. "Can I?"

I let him replace my hand with his, and he jacks me a little, fumbling with his other hand to get his own dick out through his fly. I do my best to help him, and then we're jerking each other off, slowly, not really with an end in mind, just learning the weight and feel of each other. He's not small, either, not as long as me, but a little thicker, with a gorgeous dark bush of curls. I love all the hair—I want to shoot come all over his pubes, see them glossy and sticky with me. It feels good—I almost forgot how good sex is. It's been so long.

"Feels good," Donovan says, echoing my thoughts exactly.

"Yeah." I lift my head and we make eye contact. His blue eyes look almost black in the dim light thrown by the desk lamp on the other side of the room. I get a shock of recognition as we look at each other. We haven't actually known each other very long, but, I don't know, maybe living together, accelerating our friendship from the get-go—I feel like I know him better than most of my best friends.

Being with him like this feels good, yeah. I'm ready to come just from this, rubbing our dicks together without even getting fully naked. But it also feels sort of...natural. Like we're supposed to have been doing this all along. That I can be myself with him, that he doesn't have to pretend with me, either.

I flutter my eyes closed, lean forward and press my mouth to his. It's not a frantic kiss, because if I kiss him hard and fast right now, I'll come. Instead, I keep it soft, tracing his plush, sculpted lips with mine, tattooing my mouth against his in gentle pulses. We work each other slowly. A humid dampness blooms between us, the smell of sex and sweat, and, a second later, the addition of a slightly metallic odor as my hand grows wet and sticky with Donovan's come.

I hadn't realized he was so close—the only warning he gave was a slight stiffening of his torso and a low groan. Fuck. I made Donovan Eastman come. I haven't stopped kissing him, and I milk him for a few more strokes, then put my dirty hand over the one he has on my cock and speed up the rhythm. I'm close, but it's when I breach the seam of his lips with my tongue, and he sucks on the tip—hard—that my orgasm overwhelms me and I add my jizz to the party with a groan of relief.

Slowly, I break the kiss and look down, the sight of our mingled come streaking his pubes and both of our hands, his softening cock lying in the crease of his thigh, an erotic snapshot I'm determined to memorize for posterity.

"Fuck," Donovan says, reaching across the bed to a tissue box on the side table. He grabs a wad, and is about to mop us up, but I stop him with a hand on his wrist.

"Wait. I want to—" I scoot backward and bend over, sticking my face close to his crotch, breathing in the heady, musky scent of him, a scent I already associate with some of the best sex of my life when all we've done is rub each other off.

Carefully, deliberately, I lick the come off his cock, cleaning it as thoroughly as if I was scrubbing the counters after a baking session. I look up at him as I start in on the rest, intent on my task, my cock impatient to respond to how the taste of him—of us—turns me on.

He looks down at me, his dark eyebrows drawn together as if he's puzzled by my actions, his mouth parted on a question.

I pause to check in. "Okay?" Maybe he thinks this is gross—in which case I'll be disappointed, but I'll deal.

He responds by growling, "Fuck yes," and pushing me back down with his hand on the back of my head.

Well, then.

EIGHTEEN
DONOVAN

BECK IS GOING to be the fucking death of me. He's cleaning me as if our come tastes like brownie batter and he's got a terrible sweet tooth. His tongue on my skin feels so amazing I'm trying to get hard again, which is the least my cock can do after its pathetic showing earlier. I went from being lost in the sensation of Beck's competent hands on me, kissing me like that's all we had to do for the rest of our lives, to all of a sudden coming like a green kid in a whiteout of pleasure.

What the fuck was that?

I can't dwell on the weirdness of my unexpected orgasm because the sight of Beck going to town on me, his blond head a contrast to my olive skin and dark blue jeans, is too distracting. I thought he'd probably be responsive and enthusiastic, but I didn't know he'd melt my brains with how hot he looks between my legs.

We've only just started, but I'm fervently glad we have the rest of the summer to play, because I'm nowhere near done with him.

When I'm borderline too sensitive to take any more of Beck's attentions, he raises his head and looks at me, licks his lips, and that's it. I surge up, kiss that dirty mouth, and switch our positions. I have to get out of my stupid jeans, and while I'm taking care of them, he tugs his shorts all the way off, throwing them over the side of the bed.

"Nice tan," I say, tracing the provocative line his Speedo has left behind around his upper thighs and lower belly. The line cuts through his light blond treasure trail.

"Thanks." He grins up at me, and my chest makes a funny little twinge. God. I'm in bed with Beck, and it's just as easy and fun as hanging out with him in the kitchen or by the pool. I ignore the overwhelmed sensation that makes it hard to breathe for a second. This is just sex between friends, between two people who have to share a house for the summer. This is about being conveniently attracted to the nearest available guy, and if that makes me a slut or a bad person, whatever. Beck agreed to this, and he seems just as into the physical stuff as I am. So any inconvenient feelings I might be experiencing are really beside the point.

To prove to myself that this is what it says on the label and nothing more, I take my turn paying attention to Beck's nipples, pink little nubs that I've seen nearly every day at the pool. Now I know what his skin tastes like— sweet and salty—and how he sounds when I scrape my teeth over the tender peaks—breathy little moans that send my blood south.

He swears softly when I switch from his chest to his

throat, licking and sucking my way up the column of his neck. I don't usually spend this much time kissing my sexual partners—but with Beck, I want to try everything at least once. Or twice. Like right now, I want to feel his mouth around me again, since I'm almost all the way hard again.

I put my finger on his lower lip. He chases it with a nip and a kiss. "You wanna suck me off?" I ask.

He glances down. "Already?"

I shrug to downplay my eagerness. "I'll return the favor."

"Well, with that offer...how do you want it?"

I think for a second, then pull my bed pillows together to prop him up in the center of the bed. "Comfy?"

He adjusts the pillow behind his head and gives me a nod. "Comfy."

"Good." I rise up on my knees, bringing my dick conveniently mouth-height. I rest it on his lower lip, the same spot I'd just had my finger on. I glance at him, and he nods slightly, then I feed my cock to him in slow inches, letting him adjust, enjoying the feel of a warm, wet mouth and Beck's pretty lips stretched around me. I keep going, checking in nonverbally with him, until he's taken all of me. God, the picture he makes, eyes big, mouth stretched—my balls pulse and I have to hold back from pulling out and slamming back in like the caveman part of me wants to.

He starts moving first, grabbing my hips and using them as leverage to build up a rhythm of smooth strokes. He's being a perfect vessel to fill up over and over again, and thank god I only came a few minutes ago or this would be finished embarrassingly fast yet again. The pleasure builds until I lose control and hit the back of Beck's throat. He makes a strangled noise that has me thinking bad things, but I have the presence of mind to pull all the way out and check in with him.

"Sorry," I say, but he just opens up right away again and swallows me down. Holy fuck. I don't know if he's trying to make a point or show off or what, but I'm not complaining. This is the best head I've had in a long time. When he moves one hand to my balls and starts rolling them, then pressing unerringly behind them, I twitch, my nerves lighting up with the new sensations.

"So you're good at this, too," I gasp, gaze glued to his pink lips, shiny with spit.

He pulls off for a second. "I'm better than good," he corrects, then sucks on the tip, pulls off again. "And I swallow. So."

I groan as he sucks me in again, and a finger circles my rim. "Of course you fucking swallow." Makes sense, after the show he'd put on of licking me clean earlier. "You seem all sweet, but you're a dirty little fucker, aren't you?"

He hums his assent, wiggles the tip of his finger inside me. Shit. It's tight—I haven't had anything in there in a while. Still, he doesn't overdo it, and the small intrusion just makes everything that much better. I don't last much further after that, hips stuttering as my second orgasm of the night rolls through me, longer and deeper than the first one, which had just sort of happened.

True to his word, Beck swallows everything I give

him, and when I finally pull all the way out, he licks his lips. His jaw must be fucking sore after that performance, but he kisses me anyway on my way down to the bed, my joints currently in a gelatinous state. I flop next to him, stealing one of the pillows. My hand somehow finds his dick, which seems ready for round two.

"I'll get you back in a second," I say, stroking him idly as he turns on his side to face me.

"It's okay. We've got all night." He smiles at me like we're sharing a secret.

I smile back. "And all summer."

Does his smile dim a little? "Right. All summer. So no rush."

"I'm not leaving you hanging," I promise. "So, where'd you learn to give head that amazing?"

"My second boyfriend was really talented in that area. He taught me a lot of tricks."

"Ah. Well, thank him for me."

"What makes you think I'm still in touch with him?"

"You seem like the kind of person who stays friends with their exes," I say.

He makes a face. "I don't know if that's a good thing or a bad thing. But it's true either way."

"It's a good thing. It means you're mature enough to not let relationship status change the fact that you liked that person enough to be with them."

"Or maybe it means we weren't really passionate about each other if we're fine being just friends," he says. "That's definitely how it was with my first boyfriend, Michael."

"College, right?" I try to remember the little Beck's

told me about his dating history. He mentioned having a handful of boyfriends over the years.

"It was one of those 'we're both gay and we want experience so let's be together even though we're not that attracted to each other' things."

"Oh, one of those." I have to admit I've never been in that position, but I get the gist.

"But experimenting with him did give me confidence, so when Aidan came along, I had the balls to ask him out, even though he seemed way out of my league."

At the name Aidan I can't help but freeze up. Obviously, it's not the same Aidan. Different state, different dates. But Beck notices, because of course he does. "What? You okay?"

"Fine. Tell me more about Aidan's great blow jobs," I say, forcing myself to sound normal.

"Well, he was hot, and nice, and we dated for like two years. But when we graduated, he wanted to go to grad school in Europe and I did not, so we broke up. He's still over there. I keep threatening to go visit but I haven't yet."

So definitely not the same Aidan. My Aidan was scared of flying and had never gone anywhere west of Chicago.

Besides, he hasn't been my Aidan in forever.

Maybe Pete's right and I have been letting him stop me for too long.

To keep the conversation going, I ask, "What happened next?"

"What do you mean?"

"After you and Aidan broke up."

"Oh! Well, I moved to Jersey and took that nonprofit job. That's when I discovered that casual flings were not for me. I got hit on so much, and sometimes I was tempted, but whenever I tried it I was too stressed to enjoy myself. I know that sounds totally stupid."

"It's not stupid," I say, even though I've never had any trouble enjoying myself with a stranger. "You know what you aren't into, and that's valid."

"Thanks."

"That also explains why you gave me such a hard time when we first met."

"What do you mean?"

"In the coffee shop, or afterward. I was hitting on you and you wouldn't give me the time of day."

"I knew you were hitting on me." Beck sounds triumphant and I laugh. "I wasn't sure," he admits, sitting up. He's not really hard anymore, but it doesn't matter. I know I can change that when the time is right. "I was so hungover, I thought maybe I imagined it."

"You were pretty hungover," I agree. "Anyway, I'm glad you're making an exception for me."

"Am I?"

"With the casual sex thing," I clarify.

"Oh. Well. I guess there's an exception to every rule," he says.

I like being Beck's exception.

"What about you?" he asks, folding his legs underneath him.

"What about me?"

"I told you my dating history—well, most of it. There was one more guy in law school. Now it's your turn."

"What was the deal with the law school guy?" I ask, in part because I'm curious and in part to delay talking about my own history.

"Ben. He was much more serious about becoming a lawyer than me. We're still in touch, but he's on to bigger and better things. He got along better with my dad than me, which was kind of a red flag. And he was the last guy I was with, which was months ago. I've been tested since then, just so you know."

I already knew without asking that Beck would have mentioned something if there was something to mention. "I'm negative," I offer, though maybe I should have brought it up earlier. "And I'm on PReP."

"Good to know," he says evenly.

"Why was getting along with your dad a red flag?"

"No more stalling," Beck says, tenting his hands over his bare chest. "Are you the kind of person who stays friends with their exes?"

I want to push back and tell him it's none of his business, but I can't bring myself to be that much of an asshole. Instead, I choose my words carefully. "I really only have one ex. And we decidedly did not stay friends."

Beck frowns. "How is that possible? The only one ex thing?"

I take a deep breath. "The first week of college I met a boy. His name was Aidan, as it happens. He was my first... everything. First kiss. First love, really. I was a dumb kid when we got together, and after four years of being happy, I thought we were going to be together forever. The kind of love that you say Pete and Jack have

—that soulmate kind of love? I thought I had it. Which is why I can tell you it doesn't exist."

"What happened?" Beck asks, voice soft as the pillow under my head.

"We were looking at apartments. We were supposed to move in together, start our lives. I was going to be a great actor, and he was going to become a famous architect. The usual twenty-two-year-old bullshit. And one day he up and tells me he doesn't love me anymore. He doesn't want to be tied down. He wants to be single for a while, he says. But it turns out that was bullshit, too. I found out a little while later that he met someone else, an older guy with tons of money who lived in a penthouse. He moved in with him. They got married like a year later, adopted a couple of kids. He never became an architect. He's living that picture-perfect life that you call relationship goals. And I learned my lesson."

"So that's why you only do casual," Beck says, sounding a little bewildered. "Because your first love dumped you?"

I huff. He makes it sound like I'm overreacting. He wasn't there to see how utterly devastated I was after Aidan left. I could barely get out of bed some days. I loved him so much, and he tossed away four years of happiness like it was a half-eaten bagel. My voice hardens. "I only do casual because I finally grew up and realized that most so-called happy relationships are either bullshit or going to implode in some way."

"You don't really believe that, do you?" Beck looks like I just admitted to kicking puppies and small children.

"Look, maybe the real thing happens once in a while.

Do I want Pete and Jack to be happy? Sure. They deserve it. But it's just too rare to think I have any chance of it. I don't play the lottery, either." Maybe I'm jaded, but it works for me.

Beck looks at me and I force myself to meet his gaze, worried I'm going to find pity there. His face is unreadable, for which I'm grateful, but then he puts a hand on my chest and says quietly, "You deserve it, too, you know."

I open my mouth but say nothing. Apparently, I don't have a comeback for that.

IT'S BEEN a night of revelations, but the biggest one of all is how far out of my comfort zone I'm willing to go when it's Donovan we're talking about. I guess he really is my exception, because instead of letting my heartbreak over his story about his ex ruin both the mood and our night, I realize that maybe the best thing for both of us is to lighten things up.

"Anyway, that's enough sharing and caring for now. You owe me a blow job," I say, my voice brisk.

I thoroughly enjoyed having Donovan's cock in my mouth earlier, but fair is fair, and if he wakes up in the morning and realizes he made a mistake by sleeping with me, I want to get my turn.

He widens his eyes, perhaps surprised that I'm turning the wheel 180 degrees, but then he licks his lips and winks at me. "I do, don't I."

A little belatedly, I realize I'm not exactly daisy fresh after everything we've done tonight. I'm about to offer to shower, but Donovan's already moving, manhandling me to lie flat on the bed, arranging my arms over my head while nudging my legs slightly apart. Being moved around by him already has me plumping up, but then he licks a firm wet stripe from balls to crown and I get most of the way there. When he puts his mouth over the top of my cock and sucks—hard—I moan and clutch at the comforter and harden the rest of the way. Fuck. Looks like he picked up some tricks in his day, too.

It's mostly easy to focus on the pure physical pleasure of bucking my hips into someone's warm and willing mouth instead of on the relentless swirl of emotions that being with Donovan stirs up in me. But then he hums, and I glance down and see the glint in his eyes as he watches me watching him, and I know that as good as this feels, it's only this good because it's with him.

He's not my exception.

He's my rule.

I've done the inevitable and fallen for the one guy who told me he'd never care about me like that—never want from me what I'd be willing to give.

But as my second orgasm whips through me, wringing me out and leaving me empty and sated at the same time, I know it doesn't matter. I'll take what he gives me and at the end of the summer—after he's gone—I'll deal with the fallout on my own. He'll never have to know how I feel about him. We both have our own boundaries, and I'm okay with stepping over mine as long as I keep my eyes open and acknowledge that's what I'm doing.

Later, after Donovan's fallen asleep on top of his comforter, I slip out of his bed, gather my clothes, and turn off his lamp. I tiptoe downstairs naked, consider a shower, then flop into my own bed without bothering. As I fall asleep, exhausted from my huge day, and my improbably glorious night, I tell myself I'm not pathetic for taking the deal Donovan offered me. I'm empowered for grabbing hold of something good, for as long as I can get it.

Right?

I STARTLE AWAKE at Cleo's sharp bark outside my bedroom door. I swear I've only been asleep for a minute, but when I glance at my clock, I find it's an hour later than I'm usually up with her. I scramble into my shorts and fling open the door. Donovan's right there, looking freshly showered, if a little sleepy, and he's putting food in Cleo's bowl.

"Oh. Hey."

"Hey." He smiles and the crinkles at the corners of his eyes have me internally sighing. How is he still so attractive first thing in the morning after we stayed up until all hours trading secrets and orgasms?

"Sorry, I overslept."

"It's okay. I was already up. I can take care of her if you want to go back to sleep." His gaze pinballs from my face to my bare chest to my feet and then back.

I'm suddenly flooded with memories from last night. Kissing on the front steps, hot and urgent, touching each other on his bed. I wonder if it still smells like us in his room. "No, I just need a shower."

"Put on the coffee first?" he asks hopefully before I can escape to my bathroom.

I laugh. "You can learn how to do this, you know." But I walk over to the sink anyway to wash my hands and fill the pot with filtered water from the built-in tap.

"Somehow you have the magic touch," he says. Is there a double entendre in his words?

"It's just that some of us aren't too lazy to grind fresh beans every day." I reach for the grinder to prove my point. A minute later, the scent of freshly ground coffee beans fills the kitchen, perking me up.

I set the machine to brew, then startle at the sensation of a body at my back. Donovan presses into me, pushing my hips against the counter. He kisses the back of my neck, runs his nose through the short soft hairs at my nape.

I turn around, eyebrows raised. "Is this your way of asking for morning sex?"

He puts his hands on the counter on either side of me, boxing me in. He grins lazily. "Not necessarily. I've just wanted to do that for a while. The back of your neck is very distracting."

I stare at him in amazement. I'd assumed this arrangement was about initiating sex when one of us was horny, not tender touches before we've even had our coffee.

While I stare without saying anything, his grin sinks into a grimace. "But maybe I should have asked—"

"It's okay," I interrupt. I've already made peace with myself that I'll take anything he wants to give and give anything he wants to take. I contemplate sinking to my knees and proving just how okay it is, but Cleo lets out another sharp bark.

Donovan glances at her, pulls away. "I'll take her out."

I touch his arm. "Hey, no one's ever told me I had a distracting back of the neck before."

"Really? I get it all the time."

He's playing the moment off with a joke, but I don't miss my opportunity to tell him, "Babe, every part of you is distracting."

I sweep past him and into my room before I can regret the "babe" that just slipped out of me, like my brain wants to sabotage this at every opportunity.

I scrub myself in the shower. I'm objectively dirty after last night, but I'm also looking for a fresh start. I thought I could navigate being Donovan's roommate, friend, and now fuck buddy, but it's tough to keep what few boundaries I have when he's non-sexually touching me. Does he even realize how boyfriend-like he's being? Poor sap probably doesn't. His tale of woe last night cleared up a lot for me. He had his heart broken and he let it break his spirit, too. I'm too smart to believe that through the healing powers of cookies and sex, he'll suddenly want to be in a serious, long-term, monogamous relationship.

But since I haven't lost my hope yet, I guess I'll let myself believe it's not totally impossible.

TWENTY
DONOVAN

AFTER GETTING all sweaty playing with Cleo outside in the rapidly climbing heat, I drink about a gallon of coffee and demolish the breakfast tacos that a newly squeaky-clean Beck somehow whips up in five minutes. I really love his breakfast tacos.

"So, what's on your agenda for this beautifully humid Sunday?" I ask while I'm loading the dishwasher. Part of me wouldn't mind spending the day in bed, since Beck is right here and we have both privacy and a plethora of beds to choose from. Even after scratching my much-delayed itch last night, I'm nowhere near feeling satisfied.

But I know him well enough by now to expect that a lazy Sunday in bed is not Beck's style.

"I was going to head to the farmer's market and get us some fresh produce for the week and see if maybe I can talk to Stacy."

"Stacy?" Is this another member of the Rosedale chapter of the Beck Avery fan club?

"The baker who supplies Hot Brew."

"Ah. Scoping out your competition?" I'm impressed, if a little baffled, by the way Beck's taken to the idea of opening his own bakery twenty-four hours after latching onto the idea in the first place.

"Something like that. Maybe she and I could collaborate instead of compete. Anyway, want to come with?"

"Sure. We could grab some lunch out."

"Sold."

I go up to my room to get my baseball cap and my wallet and my eyes land on my notebook. I have been doing a champion job of avoiding my play most of the week, but Beck's newfound goals are an inspiration, so I take my notebook and pen along. Maybe I can find a place to sit and write a little while Beck's making friends with Stacy.

By unspoken agreement, Beck drives downtown. It takes a few minutes to find a parking space since some of the street is blocked off to traffic for the market. He grabs his reusable bags, and we do a circuit of the fifteen or so booths to check out what's on offer. It's a typical small-town market, but a nice one. There's a local honey purveyor, a table full of jams and jellies, the obligatory fresh produce, even raw milk and cheese.

When we get to the baked goods, Beck pounces on the round, sixty-something woman behind a table piled high with breads, rolls, pies and muffins. "You must be Stacy," he cries. I can tell he has to hold himself back from hugging the stranger.

"That's me," she says pleasantly, inclining her head of gray-streaked black curls.

"I've heard so much about you and I'm so excited to meet you," he says. "I'm Beck Avery. I think you know my cousin Jack and his husband Pete."

"I do know those handsome boys. Nice to meet you, Beck."

Beck launches into a jumbled monologue about loving her stuff and not wanting to step on toes, but he's thinking about opening up some kind of a bakery on Main Street. "Can I buy you lunch one day this week?" he finishes, a little out of breath.

"Oh, you young people and your energy." She laughs and exchanges an amused glance with me.

"Beck is very energetic," I agree, smiling. "And his cookies are incredible."

"Cookies?" Her ears perk up at the word. "You know, cookies are not my speciality. But I hear cookie shops are very popular."

"Me too! What's your favorite kind of cookie?"

I excuse myself quietly to let them bond over baked goods and find a nearby bench to sprawl on. I'm mostly in the shade, but my feet are in the sun. I don't have anywhere particular to be—lunch with Beck is the only thing on my agenda. I haven't felt this relaxed in ages.

For all my complaining about the lack of excitement in small towns, there's something profoundly calming about Rosedale, about the friendly people and their quiet acceptance. I don't feel like I have to prove myself here, a contrast to striving hard for twelve years in the city. Here I can just...be. And being here with Beck is exciting in its own way—his plans and, yes, his energy, can't help but rub off on me. And the fact that we're letting ourselves enjoy each other in other ways adds a little frisson to everything. I'm almost positive I can convince him to take a dip in the pool after lunch. Hopefully naked.

I quickly get out my notebook to keep that train of thought from running away with me. I look at the last thing I wrote—"Julian doesn't want to fall." Julian is the protagonist of the play, such as it is. I have four scenes drafted and a sketchy outline. I owe my agent an update but keep responding to her handful of check-in texts and calls with vague replies. Joan wanted to see a complete draft by mid-July, but that's barely two weeks away; a literal miracle would have to happen to make that deadline.

But for the first time since I got to Rosedale, I don't not want to work on it, if that makes any sense. I remember what intrigued me about my original idea in the first place—Julian has achieved some level of professional accomplishment and now he's wondering what's next. With his whole life stretching out in front of him, does he choose the traditional markers of success—partner, family, home, career—or does he take a different path?

I jot some notes. Maybe he runs into an old friend. They catch up, and the friend seethes with barely repressed jealousy over Julian's rather public success. Then—

Then, what?

I look up and bite the end of my pen. Beck's still talking to Stacy. A guitarist in a peasant dress is setting up a few feet away with a portable mic and a shade umbrella. A woman in cutoffs and a tie-dyed shirt is helping her, but when she sees me watching she stops, says something to the guitarist, then walks over to me.

"Hi, you're Donovan Eastman, right?" She has a low, confident voice.

I get recognized from time to time in the city, but not very often. I definitely didn't expect it here. "Yes."

"I saw you in *Plum Island*. I loved your performance."

"Thank you." It's always nice to hear someone enjoyed your work.

"It was really moving," she says, pushing a hank of long honey-colored hair behind her multi-pierced ear. "In fact, I saw it twice. I teach drama classes at the Rosedale Art Center and I organized a field trip for some of my students to go see it."

I dredge up Pete's mention of the local theater program. "Are you putting on the Shakespeare play this summer?"

She beams. "I am. You don't live in Rosedale, do you? We get a lot of weekenders, but I feel like I would have heard you were in town. I'm Dulcie Martin."

"I'm Van," I say, a bit redundantly, "and I'm just here for the summer. Staying with friends." It's an easier explanation than the real situation.

"Oh wow, that's awesome. I don't suppose I could persuade you to come give a little talk to the students in my summer session?"

The suggestion takes me aback. "What would I talk about?"

"Oh, your experiences in New York theater, maybe give them some insight into what life as an actor is like. Some of them have aspirations, and hearing from someone who's been there would be so valuable. I totally understand if it's not something you're interested in, though. You're probably really busy."

She's giving me a gracious out, but I already know I'll say yes. If nothing else, it would make Pete happy for me to do something for the place where he teaches drawing classes off and on.

And Beck would probably encourage me to do it, too.

"Sure, why not?" I say. "When does your class meet?"

We exchange numbers and plan for me to show up at the Art Center a week from Wednesday.

"So, I know the worst possible question I can ask is what you're doing next," Dulcie says with a wrinkled nose, "but I need to know what shows to start saving up for. Tickets can get pricey."

I laugh lightly. "No shows yet. I'm—" I hesitate, then plunge forward "—I'm writing a play. We'll see what happens with it."

"Hell yeah, that's so cool," she says, rocking back on the heels of her Birkenstocks. "I'm so glad I ran into you. Wait. The friend you're staying with—that wouldn't be Pete Blekitny, would it?"

Internally, I shake my head at the inevitability of small-town connections. "That's right. He's on his honeymoon, so I'm taking care of the dog."

"Now I remember him mentioning he knew you. He is the absolute best," she says.

"He absolutely is."

"Who's absolutely the best?" Beck asks, walking up to Dulcie and me and giving her a curious smile.

"Pete," I say.

"Oh, absolutely," Beck agrees without missing a beat.

I make introductions. "Beck, this is Dulcie. She teaches drama at the Art Center."

"I'm imposing on Van's generosity to get him to come talk to my class," she says.

"I support that one hundred percent," Beck says.

I glance at him and smirk. "I thought you would."

Dulcie's gaze flicks between Beck and me and she gives us a speculative look but doesn't say anything. "Well, I'll let you two enjoy the market. See you soon, Van. And thanks again, really." She sways back to the guitarist, who's playing "Brown Eyed Girl."

"She seems nice. And look at you—doing something for the community."

"You are way too excited about this," I grumble, but only performatively. She does seem nice, and how bad could it be to dredge up some of my horror stories from the Broadway trenches? "What about you? I trust Stacy is your new best friend."

"We have a lunch date for later in the week." He raises two bags filled with bread and other baked goods. "I might have gone a little overboard on the carbs."

I groan. "Remind me to double my workouts."

He pats my stomach and shakes his head sadly. "Yeah, you're really going to seed."

"Shut up," I say, laughing despite myself. "We don't all have your youthful metabolism."

"I know how we can get some more exercise," he says, waggling his eyebrows.

"Oh, yeah?" Now we're talking. "Tell me more."

"Well, after dinner we can...take Cleo on a really long walk."

A joke that weak deserves a response like sticking my tongue out at him, so that's what I do.

He giggles. "Okay, okay. Why don't we go for a swim later? I'll let you put my sunscreen on," he adds in a breathy voice.

"Better."

Later, we do swim, but only after I've touched every inch of Beck's body and made him come with my hands, then emptied myself into his mouth. We lazily swim some laps, then end up having another epic splash fight, Cleo cheering us on with her excited barks from the side of the pool.

We eat dinner on the patio—vegetables and sausages we picked up at the farmer's market, with Stacy's crusty dinner rolls rounding out the meal.

Beck tells me he's going to work on a business plan this week, and I promise myself I'll devote at least a couple of hours each day to my play.

When he starts yawning as he puts some of Stacy's breads in the freezer, I tell him to turn in. I know he didn't get enough sleep last night, and I'm tired, too.

"All right," he says, standing up straight and stretching his arms over his head. There's a suspended moment where I wonder if I should ask him to sleep upstairs with me, which is a wild thought. I rarely share a bed with someone, and it's not like me to want to. He looks like he wants to say something, too, but he just drops his arms to his sides. "Good night, then."

He disappears into his room and it's not until I'm upstairs getting ready to go to sleep in my bed alone that I wonder if what he wanted was a goodnight kiss.

MY DAYS HAVE GONE from relaxed and carefree, where the only thing I had to worry about was making sure I was sending enough photos of Cleo to satisfy Jack and Pete, to busier than I can remember being in a long time. There's so much to do, and I want to do it all right now, but there are still meals to make and Cleo to take care of. And now Donovan to work into my plans.

It's been two weeks since the night at Sparkle when Donovan turned down sex with a stranger to have sex with me. They've been two of the most wonderful, and most confusing, weeks of my life.

I've never been with someone who's as easy to be around as Donovan is most of the time. He's endlessly supportive, giving me notes on my business plan for Beck's Cookie Counter—he's absurdly proud that I'm using his name idea. He's been letting his beard grow a little, and the scruff suits him. I also love the way it feels on my inner thighs and scraping across my tender nipples after he's bitten them to pulsing red dots.

We haven't had sex every single day in the past two weeks, but very nearly. The first time he topped me was the Fourth of July. We went to the town's fireworks show at the high school, then made out in the car in Jack and Pete's driveway until I was about to pass out from lack of oxygen. I took him to my room that night, having prepped for the occasion earlier. He was perfect—slow, then fast—and we did it twice that night. Then again in the morning, despite my ass's protestations. Worth it.

That about sums up the whole situation. Am I confused that the guy I'm not only fucking but *living with* won't consider what we have a real relationship instead of a no-strings summer fling? I might be able to keep my head on straight about it if Donovan didn't start the day with sweet good morning kisses, casually touch me throughout the day, and end the day with whispered "good nights."

I haven't drawn his attention to the incongruity because I don't want him to stop, even though I know we're on borrowed time. If that makes me pathetic, so be it. I'm not giving up what we have just to keep my dignity.

As I mentioned, worth it.

But we're about to face a new hurdle. Kingston's in town for the weekend, and we have plans for a poker night at his place. He said he'd round up a couple of other players since Sergio is back in Seattle permanently. I'm loading the flourless chocolate pecan cookies I made for the occasion into a large container between sheets of parchment paper when my phone dings.

JACK

Checking in. How's everything?

Everything is perfection. How's Cannes?

Already in the rearview. We're in
Venice now.

Which is amazing. We're heading to a
late dinner now.

Everything good with you and Van?

I stare at the phone. What does he mean by that? I haven't said a word about our roommates-with-benefits thing, and I can't imagine Donovan would have mentioned anything, either.

Of course. Why wouldn't it be?

No reason. Great.

I debate before typing my next question, but figure, what the hell?

When you and Pete got together, were you both on the same page about the relationship?

Sort of.

???

I knew I was all in, if that's what you mean. Pete was almost there, but it just took him a little longer. But once he caught on that I was the love of his life, then we were good. Does that answer your question?

Actually, it does. Thanks, cuz. Have a fantastico dinner.

Will do. Take care.

I smile sadly at the phone until it goes dark. I think I get what Jack means—I know I have feelings for Donovan, and if he woke up one day and realized he had feelings for me, then the constant ache in my chest would disappear because we'd both be in this up to our hips. The difference is, I don't have much hope of that actually happening. In fact, I'd be a fool to hope for it.

And I'm already acting as much a fool as I can stomach.

We decide to walk to Kingston's house on Bramble Street. It's only about half a mile away, and that way, neither of us has to be the designated driver. Donovan looks edible in a white short-sleeved button-down shirt that shows off how much sun he's gotten over the past few weeks. He needs a haircut, and his bangs keep flopping into his eyes. I shift my container of cookies to one hand so I can sweep his bangs up.

"Shit, I probably shouldn't do stuff like that at Kingston's, should I?" I say.

"Why?" he asks, adjusting his grip on the bottle of chilled bubbly we're bringing.

"Because Kingston doesn't know we're—" I honestly can't come up with another word besides fucking, and for some reason I don't want to reduce what we have to that.

"Being intimate?" Donovan suggests in a melodramatic voice.

I know he's trying to be funny. "Yes. That."

"Is it a secret?"

That shocks me. "Well, I haven't told anyone. Have you?"

Donovan seems to think. "No. I guess I haven't."

"I don't think it's anyone else's business."

"If that's what you want. You don't want people to know you've stooped to fucking an actor?"

I think he's still being funny, but I answer honestly. "I don't want people to feel sorry for me at the end of the summer."

"Why would they feel sorry for you?" He sounds genuinely perplexed.

"Donovan, if our friends knew we were hooking up, and then you go back to the city while I'm still here, they're going to assume, well, that not hooking up anymore was your idea." I mentally urge him to get my drift so I don't have to explain that not only is that how it'll look, it's how it'll be. So far, he seems to think I'm just as happy with the expiration date stamped on our arrangement as he is.

"That's silly. You're the one who's got big plans. You're going to be the owner of a cookie empire one day. I'm just going back to the grind of auditions."

"That reminds me, how's your audition class coming along?" After he went to speak to Dulcie's class of aspiring thespians at the Art Center, she got him to agree to doing a one-time audition workshop later this summer. For the past few days he's been alternating working on his play, which he says he's made progress on, and the curriculum for the workshop.

"Fine, I guess. I'm not really sure what they're going to want to know, but I have a few ideas. I've never taught anybody anything before," he says, sounding a little nervous.

"You're a natural. If anything, you can just *act* like a teacher, right?" I smile at him encouragingly and he smiles back.

"I don't think that's really how it works, but I'll keep it in mind."

"Dulcie must have thought you could do it or she wouldn't have asked you," I go on. "She doesn't seem like the type to blow smoke."

"No, she's pretty down-to-earth. And the Art Center is paying me, which is actually cool."

I don't know much about Donovan's finances, but if he's been out of acting work for a couple of months already with nothing lined up, I can't imagine some extra cash wouldn't come in handy. I make a mental note to pay for the next round of groceries, even though it's Donovan's turn.

"The point is, we don't have to tell anyone if you don't want to," he says.

There he goes, being nice again. It would be much easier to resent the situation if he were a raging asshole.

"Okay, thanks," I say as we approach 32 Bramble Street, a cute one-story cottage with a gravel driveway and a pleasingly overgrown front yard of pollinator-friendly plants like echinacea and milkweed.

Kingston answers our knock wearing a white tank top undershirt, baggy slacks held up by suspenders, and a paisley handkerchief tied around his locs, keeping them out of his face. "The bad news is my air-conditioning is broken, but I've got every fan in the house on. Ooh, bubbly!" He takes the bottle from Donovan, kisses him on the cheek, and ushers him inside, then repeats the ritual with me after greeting my offering of cookies with an equally enthusiastic exclamation.

The inside of his house is as charming as the outside, miles smaller than Jack and Pete's place, but cozier, with textured rugs and lots of art and books on every surface. He leads us through the living room to a cluttered kitchen where two people in their thirties lean against a small bar with glasses of wine in front of them. The baby-faced man has short sandy brown hair and a pale complexion, while the woman is slight with straight black hair, darker skin, and an air of competence that makes me straighten my posture.

"Beck and Van, I want you to meet two of my very best friends, Reed Bennet and Lani Kalama. They're usually stuck in that paradise called Santa Barbara, but I convinced them to visit us poor east coasters for a bit. And the best news—they have agreed to be trounced by Beck at poker tonight."

"Hey, I agreed to play poker. I didn't agree to lose," Lani says, quirking an eyebrow at Kingston. She waves at Donovan and me. "Nice to meet you."

"I, however, will be happy to lose," Reed says,

offering a handshake to each of us in turn. "I find it's usually best to do whatever Kingston tells me."

"And that is why you are my favorite client," Kingston says, popping the cork on the bottle we brought. "Reed is an author. It's too bad Jack and Pete aren't in town. You three would get along like a house on fire," Kingston says to his friend-slash-client.

"Jack Avery, right? And his illustrator... P.J. Blue?" Reed asks with interest.

"Jack's my cousin," I explain. "I'm... we're," I glance at Donovan, "house-sitting while he and Pete, also known as P.J., are on their honeymoon."

"Your cousin married his illustrator?" Lani asks. She turns to Reed. "I guess it's good you do your own illustrations."

Reed laughs and puts his arm around Lani's waist. I belatedly notice the wedding rings on their fingers. "There are some pretty famous author and illustrator couples, but they usually start out married, then begin working together. But from what I understand, it was the other way around for your cousin."

"Oh, it was a whole mess of secret identities and confusion for a while," Kingston says. "You can't make this stuff up."

"So, you aren't a writer, I guess." I direct my comment to Lani.

She tosses her hair and grins. "No, thank god. I'm a partner in a design firm, Winesap Designs. My partner, Nicole, is the creative side and I'm the business side."

"You're a business owner? I'm actually working on a plan to open a cookie shop here in Rosedale."

"Awesome. Well, if you have any questions, feel free," she offers. "Though I don't know anything about food service."

"How long are you in town? Maybe I could buy you lunch and pick your brain." I've been soaking up knowledge like a sponge, but I haven't hit saturation yet.

"We're here for a few days. I'd be happy to take payment in cookies, actually."

"Her favorite is white chocolate macadamia nut," Reed says. "But I'm partial to oatmeal raisin. Just in case that's relevant," he adds hopefully.

"Two challenging cookies to do well," I muse.

"Good thing you love a challenge," Donovan says with a smile, tipping his glass in my direction.

I smile back. "It's a very good thing."

"Dinner's all set up on the back porch. I got takeout from the new barbecue place because it's too fucking hot to cook," Kingston announces. "Bring your bottles."

Donovan and Reed head outside together, chatting about their favorite kinds of barbecue, while Lani sticks close to my side as I top up my glass. "How long have you and Reed been married?" I ask. Apparently, I'm anxious for relationship and business insights.

She laughs, a bright silvery tinkle. "By some counts a decade, by others, four. It's... complicated. How long have you and Van been together?"

I start with a denial but can't keep it up. "Oh, we're not... well, uh... it's complicated. Kingston doesn't know," I say, hoping that's explanation enough.

She winks at me. "I won't tell."

"Thanks." We go outside while I fret. What am I

doing that makes it so obvious to a stranger that Donovan and I are more than friends? Then Donovan's face lights up when he sees me and he pats the chair next to him, indicating he's saving it for me.

Maybe it's not so much what I'm doing at all.

TWENTY-TWO
DONOVAN

TWO DAYS AFTER POKER NIGHT, in which Kingston's friend Lani indeed walked off with most of the pot and everyone gushed over Beck's chocolate pecan cookies, I make a phone call I've been putting off for weeks.

Beck left an hour ago to meet Lani for lunch downtown, and I procrastinated by throwing the ball for Cleo until my arm was sore and she collapsed at my feet, thoroughly worn out. But now I force myself to page through my contacts and hit the number for Joan Starr, agent extraordinaire. I breathe slowly and channel a confident, successful actor. Wasn't that Beck's advice—to act the part if I don't know what else to do?

The coward in me is hoping she won't pick up, but after three rings, I hear her bark in my ear.

"Van! How's the play coming?"

"I'm fine. How are you, Joan?" I say, because she likes it when I push back at her.

"I might need cataract surgery, but I'm still here so things could be worse. Now you go."

"So the short answer is I don't have a draft for you—yet."

"Yet?"

"I've been working on it," I answer truthfully. "But it's pretty slow."

"What else is there to do in the sticks?" she asks. "You're still in Massachusetts, right?"

"Connecticut."

"You sick of it yet? If you were in the city, I could get you three auditions this week."

"Plays?"

"Commercials, mostly. TV's ramping up, too."

A job is a job. I've done both before and was grateful for the paycheck and the experience. But watching Beck these last few weeks, I'm not sure what I want anymore. He's living on passion. I already hit my goals—I was on Broadway; my show was nominated for Tonys. I paid off my student loans and have worked steadily as an actor for four long years. Now I'm thirty and I have no idea what's next.

"There's a theater group at the local art center here," I say. "I'm teaching a class about auditioning there soon. But it's just a one-off. The play is... going okay. But I don't know..." I stop, frustrated with my inability to articulate what I'm feeling.

"Teaching. Interesting," Joan says. "Look, Van. You're a good actor, you've got some hits under your belt. You might think I want you to write that play so we'd have a great hook for your next part—and we would. You are writing a part for yourself, aren't you?"

I think about Julian, his breezy exterior and his insecure center, and nod, then realize she can't see me. "Of course."

"But I had an ulterior motive for nagging you to write something. I could see you burning out on the grind. Eight shows a week ad nauseam. It gets old, and I could see it happening to you. That's why we decided you should take the summer off, remember? You needed to shake things up. And it sounds like maybe it's working. You're confused. That's a good sign."

"But if I'm not acting..." I stop before finishing my own sentence with the truth—if I'm not acting, I don't know who I am. In New York, I knew who I was, what I wanted. I was Van Eastman, NYU grad, Broadway actor, man-slut, perpetually living with crappy roommates, and always striving for the next audition, hookup, and place to live.

In Rosedale, I'm Donovan. I have stability. I have a house and a dog and—Beck. I didn't think I wanted any of that.

But it's hard to imagine going back to the city now, embarking on the painful chore of looking for an apartment, doing rounds of auditions, trying to find a producer for my play. It sounds exhausting, and I know where I'll be at the end of it—the work will be satisfying, hopefully, but everything else... I guess I'm over it, in a way.

Julian in my play is over it, too. Huh. How about that?

I tune in to what Joan's saying. "...can still act. When

I took you on, I told you I could find you opportunities, but the kind of career you were going to have was up to you. I have clients who only book three jobs a year and they're happy. I have others who aren't happy if they aren't overbooked. And it's okay if you change your mind. I used to be a kindergarten teacher, if you can believe it, when I was young and dumb, until I found my religion—theater. I've been an agent for thirty years. I'll die at this desk, on this phone. But that's me."

"You're amazing," I say, grateful for the millionth time that Joan signed me after my first so-called agent tried to get me to exchange sex for a part.

"I know. But so are you, kiddo." She's a shark when it comes to contracts, but she actually cares. One in a million. "Now, call me when you either have a play for me or you want to book a job. Until then, get some sun, read some books, kiss a boy."

I laugh. "You got it, Joan. Thanks." I hang up, feeling as light as one of Beck's almond meringue cookies. Then I hear a car outside my window; I take a peek and see him climbing out of the GTI. I jog downstairs to meet him in the hall.

"Hey."

"Hey yourself," he answers, his eyes flashing happily when he sees me. "What's got you all bouncy?"

"Had a... reassuring conversation with my agent. How did your lunch go?"

"Amazing. Lani is a force to be reckoned with. She turned her friend Nicole's designs for wallpaper and throw pillows into a seven-figure business in three years. We talked a lot about planning for growth."

"See, I told you, cookie empire."

He grins, pink lips and white teeth, and my gaze fastens on the glimpse I get of his talented tongue when he says, "Maybe so."

"So, you busy right now?" I hadn't exactly intercepted Beck to get him to have sex with me, but now that the idea's in my head, it seems like the best one I've had all day.

His gaze strays in the direction of the kitchen. "I guess I don't have to start dinner for a little while. Why?"

I put my hands on his waist and nuzzle his neck, lightly biting the tendons where his neck meets his shoulder, then soothe the spot with my tongue.

He shivers and laughs and pushes me away. "Right now?"

For a second, I think he's going to turn me down and I experience a flash of doubt. Am I presuming too much? Trading on the convenience of living with someone I'm attracted to—someone I continue to be attracted to, no matter how many times and how many ways we get each other off?

But then he shrugs. "Okay."

That's all the green light I need. I grab Beck around the waist and half carry him down the hall, ducking into the TV room with its conveniently oversized couch. Beck laughs as I lose my balance and we tumble down on the cushions in a pretzel of arms and legs. I kiss the laughter out of his mouth, and he arranges us so he's lying underneath me, his head on a throw pillow. Sex with Beck is always fun. It's all about pleasure, from the small pleasures of the noises he makes when I do something that

makes him feel particularly good, to the overriding pleasure of losing myself in his soft skin, the welcoming heat
of his body when he lets me in. He's been so generous
with me—I want to give him something back. I do a quick
mental inventory to see if what I'm offering is practical,
decide that even though I haven't done any special prep,
it should be okay as long as lots of lube enters the picture.

Between kisses I ask, "Do... you... want... to... top?"

He rears back and squints at me. "Now?"

"Sure. I'm up for it. But we might have to relocate to
a room with lube."

"Surprising that Jack and Pete don't have bottles
stashed all over the house," Beck jokes. "Though they
probably would appreciate it if we didn't fuck on their
couch."

"Your room or mine?"

"Yours, I guess. I feel less guilty about Cleo that
way."

I climb off him and offer him my hand to pull him up.
We race upstairs, and the second we get to my room and
shut the door, I lose my clothes. Beck's faster than me,
and by now he knows where I keep everything, so he's got
condoms and a bottle of lube out on the bedside table by
the time I'm pulling aside the comforter. I climb onto the
mattress and settle on the pillows against the headboard.

"You do this often?" he asks, joining me on the bed
and flicking open the bottle.

"Not a lot," I admit. "But I don't hate it."

"That sounds like a ringing endorsement," he says
dryly. "Donovan, we don't have to."

"I know we don't have to. I want to." That much is

true. I don't usually have sex with the same person more than once or twice. Beck and I have done almost everything but this, and somehow I don't want to miss out on knowing what it feels like to have him inside me the way I've been inside him.

He looks like he's going to say something else, but instead he kisses me, which is a distraction I appreciate—his tongue is in my mouth as his lube-slippery finger breaches my hole. He's had as many as two fingers inside me before, when giving me what I'm not mad to call the best head of my life. But this is different. He opens me up with purpose, shallow but sure strokes that have my cock swelling in anticipation. He doesn't stop kissing me, multitasking like a pro, adding more lube, more fingers, all the while expertly licking into my mouth.

By the time he's up to three fingers, I'm a quivering mess. My lips are throbbing, my hole is stretched but ready for more, my erection, which neither of us has touched, is an angry red. No wonder I'm lightheaded, since all my blood is either in my cock or my kiss-swollen mouth.

"Ready?" he whispers against my temple.

I'm a little overwhelmed already, finding it difficult to summon the words to answer his question. How nonverbal will I be once he actually has his cock in my ass?

"Yeah," I manage to say, which seems to satisfy him because he leaves for a second to wipe his hand on a tissue, then roll on a condom. We discovered we use the same brand, so he has no problem with the ones I keep stocked.

He's between my legs, looking down at where we're about to be joined, but then he seems to change his mind because he stops before he gets farther than soothing my thighs with long brushes of his hands. "Hang on. I think you should get on top."

There's a strange moment of disappointment at not having him like this, and yes, a slight moment of laziness where I don't want to get up from my nest of pillows. He must sense my hesitation because he says, "I really want to see you ride me."

Maybe it's manipulation, but I can't deny him. And I see his point. For our first time like this, it makes sense to give me more of the control. We switch places, Beck lying back and me climbing on top of him. He doesn't make me do all the work, however—he shifts me a little and takes his cock in hand, pointing it toward my hole. The first inch pops in easily enough, but then the thick slide of the rest of him has me grunting as I adjust to the sheer size.

"Okay?" He's biting his lip, and the flush staining his cheeks spreads down almost to his navel. He's holding himself back, so I nod and say, "Go for it." He immediately lifts his hips and, his hands on my waist, slams me down with a snapping motion that has me seeing stars.

"Holy fucking shit," I gasp as the force of our joining jolts through my whole body, pressure and pleasure and the edge of pain mingling together in a potent mix that has me on edge within seconds. It's a good thing he still hasn't touched my cock, because it feels as if the second I get a hand on me, I'll blow.

"That's good?" He checks in with me again and I nod frantically.

"Come on, keep going."

He does, building up a punishing rhythm that feels so good I never want it to end.

"You're fucking tight," he says through gritted teeth. "Opened you up good and you're still so—" His pace stutters and I can tell he's close.

"Yeah, you opened me up so good," I agree. "Opened me up so your big cock could get in there. Feels so good, Beck."

His eyes close, and he stops moving, giving my thighs a break. His hands stroke them, as if he knows how hard they're working. He rubs my pecs, my arms, then pulls me downward, changing the angle and making me moan. He reaches up to kiss me like this—our bodies joined in two places. I can feel the heat coming off him, the sweat on his hairline. I want to lick it off. He's so fucking hot, and I'm in awe that the sweet kid who makes me scrambled eggs and wants to bake cookies so delicious this small town will fall in love with him is also sexy as hell and better in bed than some vastly more experienced sexual partners I've had.

Slowly, he rocks into me while we're still kissing, and all of a sudden, it's too much. Too good. Too... real.

I gasp and yank myself back, holding my seat but grateful for the space between us now. He opens his eyes and questions me with his gaze, but I focus on chasing my orgasm. I might want this to last forever, but that's impossible.

He seems to get what I'm after because he goes all in again, thrusting up with purpose. His hand finds my bare dick that's straining for any kind of friction to take me all the way there. He's somehow gotten his hand lubed up, the magician, and the cool gel on my hot, desperate cock causes what feels like a geyser to erupt from me, stripe upon stripe of come coating Beck's hand, landing on his belly, some getting all the way to his chest as he milks me, never breaking the motion of his hips.

"Oh fuck," he says, letting go of my cock to grab my hips. He's positively jackhammering into me, his stamina kind of eyebrow-raising, but I suppose he did come twice last night. First when we sixty-nined after dinner but before dessert. Following dessert, we rubbed off on each other, our kisses tasting like the vanilla ice cream he'd insisted on making after he discovered an ice cream maker in the pantry.

Finally, when I'm not sure if I'm about to beg for mercy or get hard again, he throws his head back, the tendons in his neck straining beautifully as he comes. I can't feel it through the condom, but I know he's releasing himself into me and I tighten around him sympathetically.

Once I know he's through, I lift myself up so he can slowly slip out of me, holding onto the condom. He rolls over to take care of it quickly, and I gingerly lower myself to the bed. My thighs are burning, my ass is sore, but all in the most delicious way.

"Was that okay?" he asks, almost anxiously.

"Was getting fucked by a sneaky sex god okay? Yeah, it was pretty okay." I have my words, if not my breath, back.

His eyes widen adorably. "Sex god? Oh, my."

"Don't let it go to your head," I grumble, closing my eyes.

I hear him shuffle around me and feel him press a kiss to my nose. I'd protest, but I'm halfway unconscious already. "I'll try not to," he whispers, and a moment later, I'm asleep.

TWENTY-THREE
BECK

I'M SO ROYALLY FUCKED and I have no idea what to do. I can't get anyone's advice because, due to my own stupid insecurity, Donovan and I agreed not to tell anyone about us. Even though Lani guessed, I don't know her well enough to unload my personal problems. I do have some boundaries.

Every time Jack texts me, I overthink my response, lest the fact that I'm fucking my housemate and co-dog-sitter somehow bleed through the updates about Cleo and my business plans.

The cookie shop is the only thing I'm really sure of. I signed the lease on the Main Street space this morning. Donovan wasn't up before I left for the real estate office, so I have to tell him when I get back to the house. I've ordered industrial-sized ovens and mixers and have orders for flour and sugar and vanilla and spices all ready to go from a variety of wholesale providers. My business license and permits are in the works. If everything goes as planned, I'll be soft launching by Labor Day.

There are only two hiccups in my plan. One—I technically don't have anywhere to live once Jack and Pete return in a few short weeks. I'm sure they'd be fine with me staying with them indefinitely, but they're newlyweds. As hard as it'll be to leave behind their lovely house, seeing Cleo every day, and having full reign of their gorgeous kitchen, I'm not going to third wheel my cousin and his new husband.

Unfortunately, the blue house on Turner Street turned out to be a dead end—Noelle was going to try to track down the owner, but she got caught up in red tape at Town Hall, and I don't want to bother her when she's worked so hard to get me a favorable contract for the bakery. Maybe I can find an apartment to rent. It's not as if I'll have much time for housekeeping or fixing up an old house while I'm trying to get my business off the ground, anyway.

The second hiccup is that despite my best efforts not to fall for him like a fifty-pound bag of flour being knocked off a shelf and spilling all over the floor, I'm a complete mess over Donovan.

It's all his fault, too, for being so smiley and perfect. The other day when I came home, and he asked me to fuck him—god, it was so intense. The image of him riding me is the first thing I see when I wake up in the morning and the last thing I picture when I fall asleep.

He has no idea that while he was having hot, gratifying sex with someone he considers a friend, I was having my heart reconfigured, piece by piece. I've been in love before, but not like this. Not where it almost hurts to breathe because the love has wrapped itself around my chest so tightly it feels like it'll never let go.

I worry that love's going to end up shattering me. When Donovan leaves Rosedale, I'll have no choice but to try to let go of the best relationship I never really had.

At least in my inevitable post-Donovan era, I'll have the shop to keep me busy. I'll have Jack and Pete to lean on, I'll even have Kingston, who I now consider a friend. Plus the other new friends I've made, like Stacy the baker and Ariana at the wine shop, who, once I spelled out to her that I was gay, seems happy to be a platonic pal.

I'm building a life here in Rosedale, and I'm proud of the actions I'm taking to get over my fear of choosing the wrong thing yet again. Now I'm simply going after something I care about.

If only Donovan wasn't here all the time, simultaneously within my grasp and laughably out of reach. I walk into the kitchen and watch him grooving to a reggae beat on the speakers. He got a haircut yesterday, though his dark curls still fall luxuriously over the tops of his ears, and his beard's been trimmed back to sexy stubble. He's wearing his swim trunks and nothing else. I try to memorize the muscles of his back as he inspects the contents of the refrigerator.

"You finally got the sound system figured out," I say by way of greeting.

He spins around, a glass container of last night's leftover pasta in his hands. "Hey! Yeah, I did. Turns out it wasn't that hard."

I smirk. "See, I told you I wasn't a genius. I just read directions."

He holds up the pasta. "Want some?"

"Not hungry, but thanks." I walk past him, feeling the sun-warmed heat of his skin as I graze by. He must have just been outside. "I am going to open this, however." I brandish an unopened bottle of Prosecco I pull from the wine shelf in the fridge.

He raises his eyebrows. "What are we celebrating?"

I unwrap the foil. "I signed the lease for Beck's Cookie Counter this morning. I can move in next week." I work the cork out with a pop.

Donovan grabs a champagne glass from the drying rack and hands it to me.

"Join me?"

He hands me a second glass and I pour, then we clink glasses. His gaze meets mine and I smile. I wish I could tell him how I feel—it seems a little dishonest to keep a feeling this big away from the person I'm feeling it about. But I can't be even more reckless with my heart than I've been already. I can only imagine the uncomfortable pity on Donovan's face if I let it slip that this wasn't just a summer fling, at least not to me.

"To Beck's Cookie Counter," I say.

"To Beck's cookie empire," he adds with a smile.

After we sip, he goes about fixing himself a plate of leftovers. "Can I ask you a question?"

I refrain from pointing out that he just did. "Go for it."

"Where are you getting the money to open the Cookie Counter? I was thinking, if you need investors, I could contribute something. Depending on how much you need, I could also ask some of my college friends—the ones who went into finance instead of the arts, obviously."

"Oh." I'm surprised at the offer and touched. "That's so thoughtful. But I'm actually okay." I take a deep breath. My feelings aren't exactly the only thing I've been keeping on the down-low from Donovan. "I'm self-financing it."

"What does that mean?" He takes his plate out of the microwave and sits behind the bar. I lean on the counter across from him and sip my bubbly in an effort to calm my sudden nervousness. It's just that people *always* treat me differently after they find out about my family, and so far I've avoided that particular conversation with Donovan.

"I'm using my own money."

He still looks confused, and I can't blame him. When we met, I was basically living out of my car, with no job, no ambition. "So, back in the olden days, one of my Avery ancestors struck oil on his Texas ranch. Long story short, me and my cousins all have trust funds it would take each of us a lifetime to spend. Opening a cookie shop is within my means—though if I do want to turn it into an empire someday, I'd probably be smart to take on investors at that point." I smile to soften the news that I'm independently wealthy. Strangely, it's ended more than one of my friendships over the years. That and the fact that my dad is—

"So you and Jack are from some rich Texas oil family?" Donovan's brow is wrinkled like a chocolate crinkle cookie. "How come Pete never told me?"

"Probably for the same reason I'm only telling you

now. It makes people think of us differently, which sucks. And by the way, the icing on the cake is that my dad, Jonathan Avery, is—"

"Holy shit. Jonathan Avery—wasn't he just elected to the Senate?"

"Yeah." All of his years in state politics paid off—he and my mom moved to D.C. last year in a blaze of triumph. "Having a gay, non-football-playing son didn't end up hurting him as much politically as he thought it would. I just stay out of the way, which is how we both like it." I sound casual because I've had years to come to terms with the fact that my dad's first love is politics, his second power. His third love is my mother, at least. I may not rate, but he's always been good to her.

"Beck, I really had no idea." Donovan sounds lost. I try to be philosophical, even if my gut churns with the feeling that things are already changing—if I lose him over this, well, it'll just be a little sooner than I would have, anyway.

TWENTY-FOUR
DONOVAN

IT'S BEEN a day since Beck dropped the bomb that not only is he not an itinerant law school dropout living out of his car, but he has a trust fund and a U.S. Senator for a father. I'm trying like hell not to be one of those people he's clearly had experience with that treat him differently after they find out he's got resources the rest of us don't.

But I don't know how good of a job I'm doing.

For one thing, we haven't had sex since before he told me he signed the lease for Beck's Cookie Counter. I had been reading by the pool before he arrived with the news, but once I finished my lunch, lounging the afternoon away suddenly seemed irresponsible. The third act of my play remained unwritten, and after the "wicked success-ful" (Dulcie's words) audition workshop I ran for the Rosedale Art Center, Dulcie booked me to do a class on working with an agent. My little mini-course will teach life skills to aspiring working actors, she says. So instead of going back to the pool or talking Beck into bed, that day I went to my room and hammered out two scenes, plus an outline for the agent workshop, then went to bed early.

Today, Beck is out taking measurements in the shop. I almost offered to help him, but the call of the play was stronger. I actually want to finish it now that I can see the end in sight. The words are coming faster because I know the characters better. Julian's words seem to flow out of my hand onto the page as if we're the same person, which I guess makes sense since he's my avatar in this particular story. He's a man who needs to know what there is to life besides ambition.

Julian might be reaching some understanding, but I'm still floundering. The only thing I know for sure is Jack and Pete return to Rosedale in less than three weeks and I'm supposed to be making plans to go back to the city.

I have a voicemail from Joan, but I haven't called her back because I just don't know what to tell her. As much as I'm happy and excited about certain things in my life— writing the play, for one—I feel strangely ambivalent about living in New York and returning to my bachelor routine.

When Beck finally comes home, my eyes are bleary from staring at words on the page, and Cleo's antsy from being inside all day.

"I'm taking Cleo for a walk," I announce as I gather up her leash.

"Want company?" Beck asks. "I was just thinking about ordering pizza for dinner, anyway."

"Why don't you put in the order and by the time we get back, it'll be here?"

"Good call."

By unspoken agreement, we follow the route from the first night we both took up residence at the house on Wild Rose Lane. The time since then has sped by, a blur of hot and humid days, starry nights, afternoons by the pool, food and friends, poker and Prosecco. And Beck making it all possible, taking what could have been a frustrating and lonely summer and turning it into one of the best of my life. Maybe the best ever.

"What did you do today?" Beck asks as we saunter along, not in any particular hurry. I heard him tell the pizza place to just leave the order on the front step if there was no answer.

"I wrote some more, actually."

"That's great."

"How'd it go at the shop?"

"My head is full of numbers. But it was good. The carpenter I talked to about installing the counter thinks he can get the materials in time for a Labor Day opening. I just have to decide on the finish. And the color. I also reached out to Lani to see if her business partner Nicole would consider doing a quick branding design for me."

"You're quite the networker." Beck can do anything he puts his mind to. I've seen that up close and personal. "So what colors are you thinking?"

"That one," he says, pointing to the empty house he noticed that very first night. "I love that blue so much." He sounds almost sad.

"Blue suits you. Goes with your eyes," I say, my attention focused on Cleo tugging at her lead. I look up to find Beck staring at me. "What?"

"Nothing," he says quickly. "A deep blue would be nice. Soothing. And then a pop of something brighter for contrast. Orange, maybe. Or pink."

"Something with energy," I agree.

"It's really too bad about this house," he says regretfully, staring at it for another moment before turning to go home.

"What do you mean?" I give it another long look. In the summer heat, the front yard has sprouted up even more in the last few weeks. It's a nice-looking house underneath the veneer of disuse. I could see Beck at home there.

I swallow back a lump that suddenly rises in my throat at the image of Beck living in Rosedale, working at his cookie shop, coming home to—what? Cleo isn't his. The house on Wild Rose Lane isn't, either. Will he get a dog of his own? He'll have to find somewhere to live. As usual, I've been a self-centered ass, worried about my own future when Beck has even more to consider and arrange.

"I wanted to see if maybe the owners would sell," Beck says casually. "But Noelle hit a dead end learning who they are, then she got busy with other stuff. I'm going to have to find someplace to rent soon. There are some apartments available, but it's going to be really hard to say goodbye to Jack's kitchen."

I frown. I can't see Beck in some tiny apartment kitchen. He honestly deserves a kitchen out of a Nancy Meyers movie. I wonder if the blue house has a decent kitchen, and why Beck's real estate agent hasn't made any progress with it.

"I'm sure Jack and Pete will let you stay as long as you need to. Is Jack excited that you're sticking around Rosedale?"

"Yeah, actually." Beck's posture perks up. "He's got this weird theory that all his friends should move to Rosedale, that they'd be happier and more well-adjusted or something? Apparently, I'm just following some kind of preordained path that leads all of us here. It's kind of funny. But I like it here. At least for now."

"What do you mean *for now*? You're opening a business. That makes you an honorary local. You fit right in."

"I'm excited about the cookie shop, yes. And I do love Rosedale. Living near my favorite family member is going to be great. And I'll get to see this little furball whenever I want." He bends down and scratches Cleo behind the ears, then straightens and looks right at me. "But I'd be a little more excited if I wasn't afraid I'm going to peter out on it in a few months."

"What are you talking about?"

"I've never stuck with anything I tried after college. You know this. What if I lose interest and all this hard work is for nothing? Or worse, what if the cookie shop is a failure?"

I stop in my tracks. "Beck, believe me when I say the cookie shop is not going to be a failure. I have never for one second believed it wasn't going to be a huge success. It's a home run. You and cookies are a magical pairing, believe me." He smiles a little at that, but I'm not done.

"And if running a cookie shop turns out not to be what you want, well, that's okay. You don't have to do the same thing for the rest of your life, even if it is a success.

You could sell it or hire a manager and do something else. Lots of people are serial entrepreneurs. I wouldn't be so afraid about the future, because if you need a change, you can always pivot."

"Thanks, Donovan. That's good advice." He draws closer and pats my shoulder. "You ever think about pivoting yourself? You could be a killer life coach."

I shake my head at the idea. I'm aware that I stole elements of my own pep talk from Joan, but I decide to play along. "I could do it if all my clients were like you."

He cocks his head. "And what am I like?"

"Smart. Hard-working. Talented." Am I hoping flattery will get me somewhere with Beck? Hell, yes.

His eyes glint. "Talented, huh?"

I look at his mouth, which turns me on by just existing. "Very talented. You're really great at... baking."

He grins. "That reminds me, I have another molasses cookie recipe to try on you tonight."

"Then we better get home," I say.

"Yes, let's go home."

TWENTY-FIVE
BECK

I'M BACK in the kitchen again, grooving to Brazilian samba and making Donovan cookies. I think this is my happy place, because even though my heart still feels on the verge of splintering every time he says something that gives me hope he could have real feelings for me, but then pulls back, I wouldn't be anywhere else.

Donovan's sitting on the other side of the island, writing in his notebook, and I've just put the first batch of my new recipe in the oven. I have a good feeling about this one—I've taken all the notes he's given me from my other attempts at recreating his aunt's recipe, and even if this isn't the one, it's still the best molasses cookie dough I've ever made.

We'll see what the verdict is when they come out of the oven.

"Damn."

I look over and Donovan's frowning down at his notebook.

"What?"

"I'm out of pages. Not a big deal, I'll just—"

"Hang on." I dash to my room, search in the detritus of business notes and color swatches and cash flow projections on my desk. I find the notebook I bought for Donovan weeks ago and run back to the kitchen.

"What's this?" he asks, taking it from my hand when I hold it out.

"I got it in town the other day." I don't specify how long ago I was thinking about him, wanting to do something nice for him.

"This is amazing. Thanks, Beck." He looks up and grabs my wrist lightly, tugs me in, and plants a kiss on my mouth. I kiss back, lightly, mindful of the cookies in the oven. When I pull away, he looks slightly stunned.

"You know, you're really too good to me," he says, cracking open the notebook. "I've got by far the better end of this deal."

"Huh?"

"You cook for me, bake for me, get me useful presents. I'm just a barnacle."

"You give me orgasms," I say before I can overthink it.

"Yeah, but you give me those, too. Sex is a wash."

I know Donovan's not giving himself enough credit. "Remember the first day we met? In Hot Brew?"

"The day you were so hungover, but I wanted to sleep with you, anyway?"

"You make it sound so romantic," I tease, then tense. We're not supposed to be romantic. "Anyway, you saw the state I was in. You made me drink water. You bought me a greasy breakfast sandwich."

"Best cure for a hangover there is," he says.

"My point is, you've been taking care of me since the minute we met. You do more than your share with Cleo. You've been amazing moral support for the shop. You're not a barnacle. You're… amazing." The last word is quiet. Maybe he won't notice what I'm really saying.

"Thanks." He's quiet, too, as if uncomfortable with the praise.

The oven timer goes off, saving me from my own sentimentality. "Okay, in a few minutes, we'll find out how close I got this time." I pull the fragrant tray of cookies out of the oven, put in the next tray I've already prepared.

Donovan scratches away in the new notebook and I take a few pictures of the cookies on the tray to post to the new social feed I set up for the shop. Then I snap a candid photo of him, bent over his work, lock of hair hanging over his forehead, shoulders straining the seams of his olive green tee.

We don't have any pictures of the two of us, I suddenly realize. My phone has become overrun with photos of Cleo, of cookies, of the in-progress shop, some selfies of me by the pool, a few of Donovan, too, because I'm human and am not going to pass up the opportunity to snap a picture of the man without a shirt on—with his okay, of course. But I'm not sure there's a single one of the two of us. The thought makes me oddly sad. I have endless pics of me with my former boyfriends.

But then, Donovan's not my boyfriend.

While I'm scrolling through my photos, he comes to my side and wraps his arms around my middle. Just like a boyfriend would. "Are they cool enough yet?" he practically whines.

"Almost. Want some milk?"

"Just the cookie."

I put down my phone and lean over the counter to test the temperature of one of the big dark brown discs. He leans with me, the solid lines of his body framing mine, surrounding me with his strength and warmth. I hand him a no-longer piping hot cookie, then take a chance. "Can we take a picture?"

"Sure," he says. "Better do it quick, before I take a bite. These smell incredible."

I raise the phone with the camera reversed. It's startling to see myself in the frame beside him, my own face somehow less familiar to me than his after weeks of the privilege of looking at him. He smiles like the pro he is, still pressed against my back. Our intimate position is unmistakable, but that's okay. This photo will just be for me. I smile and click the button.

Over my shoulder, Donovan breaks and takes a comically enormous bite of cookie, and I keep snapping as he makes a silly face, his cheeks bulging out. My own cheeks are stretched wide as I finally set down the phone and turn to face him.

"You goof," I say, laughing. "Don't choke."

"Mrghph," he says with his mouth full.

"I'm getting you that milk." I slip out of his reach, grab the jug from the fridge.

He gratefully takes the glass I hand him, sips, and clears his throat.

"Well?" I'm more than a little nervous about his review.

He takes a much smaller bite, chews, swallows. "How did you do that?"

"Do what?"

"You did it. You made Aunt Sharleen's molasses cookies. It's like *Ratatouille* over here, transporting me back to Christmas in Apple Vale, New York."

I deflect from my relief and delight at his words by saying, "You're from a place called Apple Vale? It sounds adorable."

"You'd love it." He takes another bite and moans. "Oh god, really, Beck. You did it. I love these."

He loves the cookies. Am I greedy for wanting him to love me, too?

I take a cookie of my own and bite into it, savoring the toothsome texture, not too hard or too soft, just the right amount of chewiness. The spice is readily apparent, the heat a subtle undertone.

"How did you get the warm spicy flavor? It's different from the other batches."

"You have a good palate," I say with approval. "It's my secret ingredient. Black pepper."

"No way," he says, looking at the cookie as if he might be able to see the black flecks.

"I also upped the molasses content and changed the ratio of brown sugar to white sugar. No big deal." I shrug modestly and take another bite. They really are delicious.

"Well, I think it is a big deal. Can I get a copy of the recipe to send to my sister? She'd probably like to have it."

"Of course. I'll put together a whole care package for her with some of the cookies and the recipe, too."

"You don't have to do that," Donovan protests, snagging another cookie and knocking my hip with his. "You've already done enough."

Right. That's something a boyfriend would do. God. This is getting confusing. "Okay. Fine. I'll email you the recipe."

"Thanks." Then I'm being kissed, thoroughly, with long sweeps of Donovan's tongue. His mouth tastes like my creation, perfectly spicy-sweet. I open up to the onslaught, hearing him drop his cookie so he can wrap his arms around me, pulling me closer and pressing me into the counter simultaneously. "How else can I thank you?" he asks huskily.

My brain is offline, my body riding high on endorphins and sugar. "Fuck me," I manage to get out.

"Right here?" he asks, slotting his thigh between my legs, letting me press myself against him to relieve some of the ache that's ramping up at lightning speed.

We've never fucked in the kitchen. My flash of guilt at defiling this beautiful space is gone the second Donovan's hand slips under the waistband of my shorts and finds its unerring way to my hole. "C-cleo," I stammer. "L-lube."

"Stay here," he orders. His hand disappears and then he leaves me, panting, clutching the edge of the island. He whistles and herds Cleo into my room, dips inside and comes out, closing the door firmly behind him. He's holding the bottle of lube that had formerly been standing at the ready on my nightstand.

He's back in front of me before I can rethink this. "Turn around," he says, so I do. Easy to follow directions when all I want is for him to be inside me. He lifts my shirt, and I obediently raise my arms so he can take it off. Then he pushes between my shoulder blades until I'm bent so far over that my chest grazes the cold marble countertop. I jerk at the sensation, but his hand holds me firmly in place.

It's arousing as hell to be held there while he stands behind me, unzipping himself one-handed. A moment later I can hear the slap of a hand jerking off a bare, unlubed cock. I imagine him pushing into me like that, dry, and I clench at the imagined sting, the stretch. I know he won't do it, but I'd let him if he wanted to. That's how far gone I am.

He jerks himself while my own cock, full and aching, presses uselessly against the edge of the counter with no real relief. My hands can't find purchase on the smooth surface, the cookie trays and drying racks out of my reach. I spread my fingers wide on the slippery marble as my entire body tenses with anticipation. Finally, his hand still a satisfying weight in the center of my back, he eases my shorts down along with my underwear and at last makes use of the lube by opening the cap one-handed, squirting it straight from the bottle over my crack. His thumb spreads it liberally over my hole, then pushes inside, making me grunt and stick my ass out farther.

"You want more?" he asks rhetorically, but I wiggle my ass in agreement, anyway. He repeats the process, squirting more lube, then stuffing it inside me with the thick, blunt pad of his thumb. The head of my cock bobs under the lip of the counter, in search of something wet and welcoming to sink into.

"More. Your cock," I order desperately when he pushes a third load of lube inside me. "Now."

I feel the tip of him prodding at my hole, but then he stops before giving me what I need. "Shit. I forgot a condom."

I feel the hand at my back start to move away and I bark out, "It's okay. Just—keep going." I don't want to move from this position until we're both so fucked out we can no longer stand. "Please."

He returns his hand to my back, and I practically sigh in relief. I hear the squirt of the lube bottle one more time, and then he's pushing his way inside in one long stroke.

"Fuck," I moan. He's so deep I can feel his pelvic bones against the swell of my ass. Then he starts moving, and it feels so good, but I'm desperate for something around my dick. "Touch me, Donovan. Please," I add, not above begging.

His hand, sticky with lube, reaches around and encases me. I hiss at the pleasure of fucking into his hand while he's fucking my ass, all while he holds me down against the counter, a cold hard contrast to the warm live body blanketed over me, pumping inside me.

"God, you feel good," he grunts. "You're so hot. This ass is so fucking perfect, taking me bare."

Fucking without a condom doesn't feel all that different for me, though it's a little rougher without the barrier to ease the way. I love it.

"Don't stop," I beg, wanting the delicious torture of

being at his mercy while my hands slip and scrabble over the marble countertop to last forever.

"Not gonna stop," he promises, changing the angle of his thrusts to hit my prostate. I jump at the extra sensation, thrusting back as he pushes forward, and he digs just that much deeper.

I swear, loudly and mindlessly, the friction on my dick pushing me dangerously close to coming.

"Are you ready?" he asks. "I'm gonna—"

For the first time, it hits me that he's going to come inside me, not a condom. I'll have his load seeping out of me for hours. "Do it," I grit out as my own orgasm rushes through me and out my dick. I spare a vague worry for the under-island cabinets, hoping Donovan's caught most of my spend. He keeps a hand on me until I'm done, and it's good I have the counter for support because my knees feel loose as homemade jam. He takes his one wet hand and the hand from my back, grabs my hips, and really goes to town, thrusting into me hard, then groans what I've come to know and love as his orgasm noise, a rumble that emanates from the center of his chest.

"Yes, fuck, yes," I babble as he slows and his grip on my hips lessens. "Yes."

"Yes," he agrees. He seems like he's about to pull out, so I reach around with one of my now boneless arms and grope behind me, holding him in place as best I can. He gets the message, I guess, because he stops trying to pull out and instead drapes himself over me. I'm surprised to feel his shirt on my sweaty back, and in my mind's eye I picture us, me naked, my shorts around my ankles, bent ninety degrees over the counter, while Donovan stands behind me, almost fully dressed, his cock still buried inside me.

Eventually he moves, and since I've started to lose feeling in my legs, I let him. His cock slips free in a gush of fluid that immediately starts dripping down my inner thigh. It's gross and hot at the same time. I've done it bare before, but everything with Donovan feels...more.

I push myself upright, crack my back audibly. It's only slightly awkward to reach down and pull up my shorts. I'm a mess, but I'll clean up in a second. For now, I turn around and survey Donovan, whose face is still ruddy from his exertions, and whose shorts are pulled up but not buttoned. He looks at me with a rueful expression. "Are you okay? I think I got carried away."

"That makes two of us," I say, patting the front of his chest reassuringly. "I'm fine." My nose twitches. "But something's not right." The kitchen has been perfumed with the combination of cinnamon, ginger, and the various other spices in Aunt Sharleen's recipe, but now it suddenly smells of burning.

The realization hits me at the same time as Donovan, apparently, because he shouts, "The cookies," as I reach for the oven mitts.

"I forgot to set the timer," I explain as I open the oven door and black smoke pours out. "Open the doors, please."

He throws the French doors wide open to let the noxious smoke escape. The tray of cookies is charred black, and the pan might be a loss, but at least the smoke detector doesn't go off.

The irony of the lost batch hits me. It seems symbolic

of our entire roommates-with-benefits situation. It's all well and good until someone forgets that when time runs out, something gets burned.

It's me. I'm the one who's going to be left a charred husk of myself. And there's nothing I can do to avoid it.

TWENTY-SIX
BECK

I ENTER Hot Brew during a bit of a lull and am able to walk right up to the counter, where Meadow's restocking the pastry case. Ruth's wiping down tables and nods at me shyly when I wave hello.

"Well, if it isn't the competition," Meadow says, eyeing me with one expertly arched, penciled-on black eyebrow.

I know she's just joking, but I still have to tamp down the rush of nerves. I've discussed my plans with her, explaining that the main focus of Beck's Cookie Counter will be, obviously, cookies, and I'm only going to serve cold beverages—milk, water, and soft drinks. After talking with Stacy, she and I decided that if the store finds its footing, I might feature her pies and cakes, which right now are only available from her directly by special order. So there's not actually that much overlap between what I'm offering and the existing businesses in Rosedale.

Meadow, for her part, was pragmatic when I broached the topic. "People love sugar," she said.

"They're either going to come here and get coffee, then go get a cookie, or get a cookie and decide they want coffee. In my book, this is a win-win. Besides, you know I'm just the manager. The owner couldn't care less about a new store, unless it's another coffee shop."

Having both Meadow's and Stacy's support is wonderful. I've been working long days ordering supplies, refining my recipes, and overseeing the installation of the equipment in the shop. Then I go home to Donovan and Cleo, sometimes too tired to do more than flop on my bed and pass out.

"I need the largest coffee you can give me," I tell Meadow. "One of those really big nineties-style mugs would be ideal."

She laughs. "One bowl of coffee coming up. Is that for here or to go?"

"For here, actually. I'm going to do some work if that's okay?"

"Go for it. The Jack Avery table is free," she says, nodding to a small table by the window next to an outlet. "He and Pete will be getting home soon, won't they?"

"Less than a week now," I confirm.

"Well, I'm really glad your temporary stay in Rosedale is becoming more permanent," Meadow says with uncharacteristic warmth.

"Thanks. Me too." And I am. If only I didn't feel the deadline of saying goodbye to Donovan hanging over my head.

I set myself up at what's apparently Jack's regular table. I have to go over the lease agreement for the apartment I'll be moving into. It's a one bedroom in a small building a few blocks from Main Street, and it comes with a parking spot and a gas oven. I can't ask for more right now. I'll even be able to walk to work if I want to.

I laugh when Meadow brings my order to the table—she's filled an actual white ceramic bowl, the kind they use for breakfast bowls and salads, nearly to the brim with coffee. "If I drink all that, I'll vibrate into next week."

"So don't drink all of it," she says acerbically.

The coffee sustains me while I parse the rental contract, which is pretty standard. But when the doorbell jingles and I look up to see Kingston, I'm glad for the distraction.

"Beck, fancy running into you here," Kingston says. "Can I bother you?"

"Please." I gesture to the open chair and he sits, spotting my bowl of coffee and giving me a questioning look.

"It's a joke, sort of. Want some?"

"I already caffeinated, but I wanted to talk to you about throwing a little welcome home party for your cousin and his husband when they get back. What do you think?"

"That's a great idea. How did you know I was here?"

"Van told me. He said you'd either be here or the shop. By the way, I don't know what you're putting in his cookies, but I want some."

"What do you mean?"

"I've never seen the man so relaxed and happy. Figured it was some special ingredient," Kingston says. "Or maybe he just needed a vacation."

"It's been a fun summer," I say, then look down at my

keyboard lest I give something away. I'm glad Kingston thinks Donovan is happy, even if I can't claim credit for it.

"Too bad summer's almost over," Kingston says shrewdly.

What does he mean by that? Does he know—

"I don't want to overstep, but I have been known to stick my nose in other people's business, and I'm too old to change, so I'm just going to say something and then you can tell me to fuck off and I will." He doesn't even wait for me to react before going on. "I've known Van for a long time—almost as long as I've known Pete. We even hooked up once, though maybe he told you about that."

Kingston and Donovan had sex? It fits with the picture I've put together of Donovan's serial hookup life-style. I can't be jealous, because then I'd have to care about all the men he slept with before me, and that's pointless.

"He's had a reputation for going after the next shiny thing and never looking back. But it always seemed a little sad to me, more like a competition with some invisible opponent than something that was really making him happy. But you—you seem to make him happy."

"What are you saying?"

"I'm saying if he makes you happy, too, then you might have to fight for him. He's not going to make it easy for you."

Donovan has been nothing but easy with me, right from the beginning. But maybe I've let things be too easy for him. Maybe I haven't asked for enough.

I haven't asked for anything, now that I think about it.

He's given everything freely, and so have I. I just assumed there were limits to what he'd be willing to share. But what if I'm wrong, and I only have to ask to get what I want?

"Anyway, that's all I wanted to say. Now, the party. My place, the day after the honeymooners return. We'll do it in the afternoon so they aren't too sleepy. You bring the dessert. I'll get the booze. Invite whoever you want, but keep it quiet from Jack and Pete or they'll try to talk us out of it, the antisocial jerks."

I agree to the plan and Kingston leaves as quickly as he arrived. I stare into my bowl of coffee and wonder what exactly I have to lose by telling Donovan how I feel about him.

I can't end up with less than I have now. We're supposed to call it quits soon, anyway. Why don't I go out in a blaze of glory and tell him that I want more?

The traitorous part of my heart that's held out hope from the very beginning urges me to believe there's a chance he'll want more, too.

At least I'll know one way or the other.

I snap my laptop shut, drop the coffee bowl on the counter, and speed walk to my car.

No time like right the fuck now.

TWENTY-SEVEN
DONOVAN

SIX DAYS. Jack and Pete get back from the world's most epic honeymoon in six days, and I have to face the reality of life after Rosedale.

I've put off figuring out what I'm doing next because that would mean summer is over, and this little domestic interlude finished. And that hurts more than I thought it would.

I wrote the last scene in my play this morning and left a message with Joan to call me. She's setting up an audition for a series of commercials and I'm expecting the details any time. It's not a play, but it's a paycheck, if I get it. Maybe between that and my savings, I should bite the bullet and actually buy my own place. It's about time I had a home of my own. It won't be a spacious house, won't have a big backyard or a private pool. But maybe I could get a dog to keep me company. Lots of people have dogs in the city.

There's a life waiting for me back in New York. All I have to do is pack my things and say goodbye to Rosedale.

Which means saying goodbye to Beck.

I briefly consider that the city's only about two hours away. It's not that far for keeping up something long-distance. Hell, I'll be coming up anyway to visit Pete and Jack from time to time.

But I know that's not fair to Beck. He's still looking for what Jack and Pete have, and a long-distance fuck buddy is probably not part of his plan.

So why do I feel sick to my stomach at the idea of never being with him again?

The front door slams and I hear my name being called from downstairs.

"Up here," I call, and a moment later Beck's at my door. "Hey."

"Hey." He looks oddly serious and for a second I'm

terrified Cleo's escaped or something happened with the Cookie Counter lease.

"What's wrong?"

"Um. Nothing. Sort of." He's got splotches of color on his cheeks and my heart starts beating faster, as if my body's going into flight or fight mode. "I just wanted to say that summer's almost over. I mean, technically we have until the fall equinox, and the unofficial end of summer is Labor Day, so there's still some summer left, but Jack and Pete get back in less than a week and that means you'll be leaving so I want you to know that I have feelings for you, and I have since before we started fucking around and even though you say you don't want a boyfriend, you kind of act like you want a boyfriend, like all the time, and so I thought I should let you know that I'd be your boyfriend. For real. If you want. So."

My heart's going triple time now as I listen to Beck's nervous prattle and try to make sense of what he's saying. He has feelings for me. He wants to be my... boyfriend. The idea is hard for me to imagine, let alone conceptualize.

"I don't want a boyfriend," I say. It's my automatic response, the one I've programmed myself to believe for the past eight years.

"Have you been happy this summer?" Beck asks, ignoring my statement. "Have you enjoyed living here with me?"

"You know I have." I can't lie about that. "But that's not the same thing."

"We spend our days together, our nights, too. We take care of each other. We make each other laugh and we help each other when things get hard. We've been co-parenting a dog, for fuck's sake. What else would you call this? Roommates-with-benefits? Roommates don't make love the way we do, Donovan. I told myself it wasn't there, because I didn't want to get hurt, but it is there and I don't want to lie to myself anymore. I don't want you to lie to yourself anymore, either."

He sounds surer of himself now, as if this is all self-evident and I'm just the idiot who didn't realize I was in a relationship until the guy I'm in a relationship with pointed it out to me. But nothing's changed since the night I told Beck I wanted to sleep with him, but that it would be a temporary arrangement.

"No—you're wrong. I enjoyed the hell out of this summer. But what it was—we agreed that's all it could be. So I liked the breakfast tacos and the cookies—those were your idea, not mine. You seduced me with coffee and sugar and great sex."

"I'm a monster, truly," Beck says flatly.

His sarcasm puts me even more on the defensive. "This isn't what I want."

It wasn't, anyway.

"Are you sure, Donovan? Really look around, because it seems like maybe it is. Only you seem dead set on denying it, all because your first idea of happy ever after didn't work out."

"What are you talking about?"

"Don't you think you should stop punishing yourself? Maybe it's time to forgive Aidan for falling in love with someone else."

Hearing his name out of Beck's mouth is like a slap across the face.

"What?"

He shakes his head sadly. "If losing Aidan didn't matter to you anymore, you'd be able to see what we have together."

"You don't know what you're talking about. This isn't about Aidan."

"Fine. Pretend you haven't been sleeping your way through Manhattan to avoid getting hurt again. Pretend you didn't like having me around morning, noon, and night. But don't pretend that I somehow tricked you into playing house with me—all of this has been your choice all along."

He's right, of course, but I need reassurance. "You wanted it, too."

"Yes. I want you. I want this life. I *choose* this life." He looks as if the sight of me makes him want to cry. I hate that I'm hurting him just by being myself, but I don't know what else to do, or how else to be. "The only thing I didn't have a choice about was falling in love with you. That happened despite trying not to, believe me."

"You—" Beck *loves* me?

He stands in silence, letting me process. In the quiet of the afternoon, I can't deny what he's saying. That almost from the beginning, what I told myself was friendliness, or maybe affection, was actually Beck showing love. Am I so oblivious that I didn't notice him falling in love with me?

Or did it not occur to me because his feelings seemed to match my own, so they couldn't possibly be love?

Either way, he's asking for something I'm wholly unequipped to give him.

I channel a stronger person than me, a man who isn't afraid to let down his friend because he knows it's for the best. My chest is a mass of conflicting emotions, so I let my brain take over.

"Look, Beck, it has been a great summer. But this is just a borrowed house. A borrowed dog. A borrowed life. I'm going back to my real life, and that's the way it was always supposed to be."

He nods, but doesn't try to hide the tears forming in his eyes. "You can change your mind about the way it's supposed to be. Just so you know." His voice is thick with emotion.

It's so tantalizing, the idea of change. The idea of a different life.

But I'm too scared of what it would mean to say yes.

So I say, "No."

And Beck leaves, closing the door behind him.

TWENTY-EIGHT
BECK

THE NEXT FEW days pass in a blur. Where before I took joy in simple routines—putting the coffee on, playing with Cleo, making progress on plans for the shop—now everything feels like a monumental effort. The pleasures of a summer spent with Donovan are past, and now it's just work and humidity and trying to reconcile my loneliness with the fact that he's still here.

We're moving around each other because, of course, we still have to share the space. I take care of Cleo in the morning, his does his turn in the evening, the way we arranged it all those weeks ago. I don't try to act like my heart isn't broken, and he doesn't do me the disservice of pretending like nothing has changed. He's polite with me but gives me space. It hurts in its own way, the idea that we might not be able to stay friends the way I have with my other exes. But I guess I didn't feel about them the way I feel about Donovan.

Yeah, friends might be too much to ask of my poor heart.

Cleo seems to notice that the energy has changed. She spends more time lying at my feet when I'm on my computer, or watching me from her bed while I'm working in the kitchen. I try to give her extra cuddles and pets. Not her fault that her temporary minders don't have their shit together.

Now that I've perfected the molasses cookie recipe, I'm working on the white chocolate macadamia one. I'm not sure I'll even have the heart to put molasses cookies on the menu, even though I'm super proud of the recipe. But the memory of Donovan's kisses will be brought to mind every time I mix up a batch, and that won't help if I'm ever going to move on.

Moving on seems like a distant fantasy, however, when my heart still insists on lighting up whenever Donovan walks into the room.

I'm chopping a big bar of white chocolate when he does just that, dressed in jeans and his white button-down that makes his olive skin glow with health. He has his backpack over one shoulder, Pete's keys in hand, and sunglasses pushed up over his head.

"Going somewhere?" I ask.

"Yeah, actually, I have to go to the city."

I drop the knife on the cutting board with a sharp clatter. Jack and Pete get home in two days, and he's cutting and running?

"I have an audition this afternoon. Or a meeting. My agent wasn't very clear. But I have to go, so I was going to ask if you could take care of Cleo tonight?"

"Of course," I answer. Isn't that the whole point of us both doing this job, so if something came up for one of us, the other could take over? Then why does it feel like he's abandoning both me and Cleo?

"I appreciate it. Depending on how the meeting goes, I might stay over in the city tonight. But I'll be back tomorrow. I'm going to park at the station."

I relax minutely. "Don't forget about Jack and Pete's party." I pick up the knife, study the shards of white to judge if I've gotten the size right.

"No, I won't." He stands there for another moment.

"Good luck at your audition-meeting-whatever," I say without looking up.

"Thanks."

Another silence descends, but I don't know how to fix it. I don't know how to get back the easiness between us when he's rejecting everything I can possibly offer him.

"Well, bye," he says finally.

I only look up again when I hear the door to the garage bang shut. I glance at Cleo, who's watching me carefully.

"Don't worry, sweetie," I say, willing myself to believe my own platitudes. "I'll be okay."

TWENTY-NINE
DONOVAN

THE TRAIN to New York is crowded and the air-conditioning is broken in the car I first pick, so I move backward until I find a seat in a cooler car. My nerves are on high alert. Joan told me the casting director for the commercial gig wants to see me, but she wasn't clear if it was an audition or something else. I don't have any script pages to go over and I'm too nervous to read for pleasure. So I stare out the smeared plexiglass window at the ultra-green countryside as it turns into the browns and tans of the suburbs and then the brick and metal and glass buildings of New York City.

I try to keep my mind blank, but I can't help but think about the way Beck looked when I told him I was heading to the city. He was baking—in his element—but he wouldn't meet my eyes. I wonder if he hates me now. I haven't had the courage to ask him, or to leave the house altogether. With Jack and Pete coming home in such a short time, it seems petty to cut out early. Not to mention I still don't have anywhere else to go. My stuff's in storage with a friend who's on Long Island for her summer vacation. Practically everything I own is in the backpack on my back. I'm homeless, as itinerant as Beck was when he showed up in Rosedale. But I don't even have a car.

I sent Joan my play yesterday, but she hasn't read it yet, or if she has read it, she's still figuring out how to tell me she hates it.

This possible job is the only thing I have going for me right now, which is kind of pathetic. Beck's words hover in my mind, making me doubt everything I thought I knew. He said I could change my mind about what my life's supposed to be. For years, I chose my career over a domestic life, telling myself I didn't want both, but when Beck showed me door number three, I was too—what? Scared? Stubborn?—to walk through it.

I emerge from Grand Central and am hit with the unmistakable smell of the city in August—a thick wall of car fumes, damp air, and the exhaled breaths of millions of people. I'm disoriented at first, accidentally start walking in the opposite direction from my destination, which is strange. I've lived in New York for twelve years, and it's one of the easiest cities to navigate. Still, I feel like a visitor in a foreign land.

I'm sweating through my shirt by the time I get to the nondescript office building Joan told me to go to. I take some steadying breaths, put on my audition armor, consisting of my professional smile and my actor's charm. I open the door to the suite and hope for the best.

· · ·

AN HOUR LATER, I'm shaking hands with Phil, the producer of a series of commercials for high-end sunscreen. That's the product I'd be hawking as the star of three commercials—just to start. They want to target gay men with this advertising campaign, and they want to build the campaign around me. It wasn't an audition—it was a pitch. They want to pay me a mind-boggling sum of money to star in ads essentially as myself, only a slightly buffer, sunscreen-wearing version of myself, of course.

I hit it off with the creative team, and they've promised to send Joan the contract by the end of the day. Apparently, they have studio time booked and their first choice fell through at the last minute. I'm not offended to be a replacement, especially when they're saying all the right things.

I leave the building and call Joan.

"You nailed it, baby," she says when she picks up.

"You could have given me more warning," I say lightly.

"It was short notice, and I wasn't even sure you'd want the job, but I'm glad you liked them. Think of me when you're on your yacht."

I laugh. "You know I'm not a boat person. But maybe..." Beck's blue house flashes before my eyes and I blink it away before I can get sidetracked. "Did you read the play?"

"I read it."

"And?" I tell myself it's okay if she doesn't like it. I'm not a real playwright, anyway. It was just a lark. I can stick it in the proverbial drawer and never look at it again.

"It needs some work, but it's dynamite. Julian is...he's

real, Van. And I'm not making any promises, but some day you're going to get to play him and it's going to be magic."

I have to stop in the middle of Park Avenue South and scrub a hand over my face, ignoring the disgruntled pedestrians around me. She liked the play. And playing Julian...that's a dream I can throw my weight behind.

"Thanks, Joan." It's completely inadequate, but I trust she can hear the emotion in my voice.

"Where are you staying at the moment? I want to send you something to celebrate."

I look around, as if I can conjure up a place to live right there. "Ah, I'm currently between addresses. But I'll let you know when I find something permanent."

"Fair enough. I'll be in touch."

"Thanks, again. For everything."

"You got it, baby."

We hang up and I'm about to look up a hotel in this neighborhood when my phone announces a new call. Kingston James.

I slide to answer and realize he's started a video call with me. The screen blurs, then resolves into Kingston's face. I recognize the colors of his Rosedale kitchen behind him. "Kingston? What's up?"

"What is up is what did you do? I called Beck to talk to him about the welcome back party and I thought Cleo was dead he sounded so sad."

"What? Cleo's okay, right?"

"She's fine. But your boy is not. I repeat: what did you do?"

I bristle at the implication, however accurate, that I

did something to Beck. I didn't ask him to fall in love with me. I told him—explicitly—that wasn't something I was capable of. And the fact that I can't stop thinking about him is just an unfortunate byproduct of my bad decisions.

"Not that it's any of your business, but we're disentangling ourselves from our summer arrangement," I say with as much dignity as I can muster while walking in a sea of people toward Union Square Park, sweat gathering under my backpack and soaking through my shirt again.

Kingston grumbles something unintelligible, though I can tell it's not particularly flattering to me. "Hang on, I need reinforcements," he says.

"Huh?" His screen grays out for a few seconds, during which I seriously contemplate hanging up and blaming it on my cell connection. By now I'm in the park, so I take myself out of the flow of traffic and snag a spot on a green New York City park bench.

Kingston returns to the screen, then a second square pops up. It's Pete.

"Pete, where are you?"

My friend grins wide. It's weirdly good to see his smiling, familiar face. "Amsterdam. Where are you? Is everything okay?"

"Rosedale," Kingston answers as I say, "Uh, the city. But just for a minute. And everything is fine," I reassure him before Kingston can start throwing me under the bus, because I have no doubt that's why he brought Pete on the call.

"Oh cool, well, we're mostly all packed. At least I am. Jack's out right now getting another suitcase to take back all his treasures. Can't wait to see you guys."

"Same. Well, we should let you get back to packing," I try, but Kingston interrupts.

"Pete, I wouldn't bother you on your sex vacation, but you've got to back me up. Tell Van that he's being a dumbass about Beck."

"What about Beck? What's going on?" Pete's image is sort of blurry, but his voice comes through loud and clear.

"I don't know what you think is going on, Kingston," I say, "but again, it's none of your—"

"They've been sleeping together all summer," Kingston says with an air of victory.

"How the hell do you know that?" I ask, more curious than upset. "Did Beck—"

"Beck didn't say a word. He didn't have to. Every time you two were in a room together, it was obvious by the heart eyes you were sending each other when you thought no one was looking. And then you both suddenly got way more touchy-feely, and don't even get me started on the vibes—someone way less intelligent than me could see you two were fucking after spending two minutes with you. When Beck started making plans to stay in Rosedale and you were not part of those plans, I could tell we were in for some kind of train wreck. I could see how happy you were, and I couldn't understand why you didn't. I thought maybe you needed a nudge, so I told Beck—"

"You told him to tell me how he felt about me," I say numbly. Without Kingston's interference, would Beck have ever said anything? Would I never have found out that he loves—loved—me?

"I told him I've never seen you this happy before and that if he wanted to keep you, he'd have to fight for it."

I don't have anything to say to that. I *was* happy.

"You and Beck?" Pete asks with his oh-so-carefully soft voice. "Together?"

"We were never together," I say, desperate to explain my side. "It was a summer fling, that's all. This is why I never get involved with roommates. You get it, don't you, Pete? It never ends well. I thought this time we were on the same page because we had an expiration date, but then I went and fell in love with him and ruined everything."

Two pairs of eyes stare at me, shocked, from across the miles and I replay what I just said in my head.

"No! Shit. No—he fell in love with me! That's what I meant to say. Beck fell in love with me. Not the other way around. That was a mistake." The longer I talk, the crazier I feel.

I didn't fall in love with Beck. I don't do love. I haven't since Aidan took my heart, stomped all over it, and returned it in the form of a battered banker's box of stuff I'd left in his dorm room over the years.

"I'm not in love with him," I say again, sounding unhinged to my own ears. "Because—because—" Because if I'm in love with him, that would mean I'd have to face the fact that he was right, about everything. About me treating him in a very boyfriend-y way. About actually wanting the house and the dog and the partner. About wanting the kind of love that Jack and Pete so fearlessly, so gratefully, embody. About wanting a shared future with all of those things in it, and more.

But that means a future where someone could at any minute decide they don't want me anymore and crush me under their foot.

Only I know Beck would never. He's not Aidan. And I'm not the same person I was at twenty-two. I'm not saying I've matured that much, but maybe I've made enough mistakes that I'm able to admit when I've made a colossal one.

"Donovan," Pete says, the use of my whole name getting my attention, "you were a one-man guy. Until you weren't. But I think that's still who you are, deep down. Remember how I said your stubbornness is a strength, but it can also keep you from trying new things? Things that might make you happy? If Beck makes you happy, do you know how stupid you'd have to be not to hang onto him with both hands?"

I look away from the screen and the concerned faces of my friends up to the trees towering over my park bench. I can only just make out the fading blue sky through the leaves. If I was in Rosedale, I could look at the trees with Beck. We could sit outside until bugs threaten to eat us alive, and then we could go in and curl up on the couch watching TV, or talking until we're yawning more than communicating, and then shuffle off to bed, our shared bed. In our shared home. Our shared life.

I'm sick of my own stubbornness. It's time to let go of that old hurt. Time to be honest with myself about what I want. And what I don't want.

I don't want to be in New York a second longer. It no longer feels like home to me. Home is where Beck is.

I tip my head down and glare at the screen. "You two are the most meddlesome busybodies I ever met. You—" I point at Pete "—I'll deal with when you get back from Europe. And you—" I swing my finger to Kingston "—just wait until you fall in love and see how motherfucking meddlesome I can be."

"Does that mean you're coming home?" Kingston asks hopefully.

I'm about to promise to catch the next train, but I hesitate. I don't have anything to offer Beck except the dubious promise that I actually want to be his boyfriend. It seems paltry in comparison to the plethora of skills and assets he's bringing to the relationship.

"I'll be back soon," I say instead. "I've got to take care of some things first."

"Don't be too long," Kingston says. "Beck's not going to wait forever."

"Then help me. Get me the contact info for the real estate agent—what's her name?"

"Noelle." Both of them answer simultaneously.

"That's the one."

"What are you planning?" Pete asks.

"Just a little something to prove to Beck that it's taken me a while to get there, but I finally know exactly what I want."

THIRTY
BECK

DONOVAN TEXTS to let me know he's staying in the city overnight. I sleep poorly, wondering how his audition went. Wondering if being in the city is a relief to him, to be back in his element. To be away from me.

I torture myself with the idea that maybe he picked someone up tonight, that he's having sex with someone new just because he can. Because it's what he does.

I fall asleep way too late and dream I'm lost in Manhattan, trying to find my way to some unknown destination. I ask strangers for help, peer in all the cab windows, but no one can tell me how to get wherever it is I'm supposed to go. I wake up with a headache and to another text from Donovan. He must have gotten up early.

> I'm trying to get back to Rosedale, but I may be delayed. How's Cleo?

I smile at the text against my will. I feel like shit, but I still appreciate his thoughtfulness. I stumble out of bed and into the kitchen, where Cleo's waiting patiently for her breakfast. I take a picture of her and send it to Donovan with a note.

> She's fine and you're worse than Pete.

I'm not expecting a reply but my phone buzzes less than a minute later.

> I guess I get the protective thing more now.

What does that mean? I consider responding, but I have no idea what to say. Besides, as much as I want to be able to simply banter with him, it's too hard right now. As I go about the morning routine of coffee, Cleo, breakfast, I think about how much less satisfying it is to do for one person. Why bother making a whole pot of coffee when I could just grab something at Hot Brew later?

Something else occurs to me. I was afraid that after Jack and Pete came home, I'd never see Donovan again, which itself felt like an icy stab to the heart, but what's worse is that I might actually see him all the time. He's good friends with Pete, and I've seen the way he and Kingston have gone from acquaintances (and apparently onetime fuck buddies) to close friends this summer. Of course he'll come back to Rosedale once in a while.

I'll have to grow a thicker skin and file our summer away under bittersweet memories.

Thank god for the Cookie Counter. I don't have time to ruminate on the unfairness of falling in love with someone unwilling, or unable, to acknowledge how he feels about me.

I have an interview with a prospective employee today, plus about a million other things to do. I'm able to return to the house midday to let Cleo out and grab a quick lunch for myself, but I don't have a second to stop until dinnertime, when I notice that Donovan isn't back yet. He's sent another text, though.

> Looks like I'll be away another night. Are you okay with Cleo? I'm sorry. See you tomorrow.

Tomorrow Jack and Pete get back, and the next day is the party at Kingston's. I have a ton of baking to do. Between Kingston's and my efforts, there are probably going to be thirty people at this small welcome home bash. I can't imagine what's keeping Donovan in the city —or rather, I don't want to. Work? A guy?

My stomach churns and I turn up the angry rock music I unconsciously selected to play while I scarf down some leftovers and get out the ingredients to make my flourless chocolate pecan cookies.

I'll just hold down the home front while he does whatever he wants. Thank goodness baking is my therapy.

I BAKE until well past midnight, then fall asleep on top of my covers with a smear of chocolate on my forehead. Cleo wakes me by barking, which gets my heart racing fast. I take the world's fastest shower, clean the kitchen, and stick the bins of cookies for tomorrow's party in the extra freezer in the garage. Pete's car is still gone, which means Donovan hasn't returned in the night.

The weather is forecasting a heat dome for the next two days, so I brew a huge jug of iced tea and make sure the windows are shut all over the house, so we're not wasting the air conditioning.

I even check the windows in Donovan's room. His stuff is mostly still there—clothes and books and his base-ball cap. He's coming back. Obviously. But it's strange to think about the last time I was in here, in his bed. Naked and happy.

I sigh and glare at my distorted reflection in the windowpane. I'm sick of feeling sorry for myself. So I'm in unrequited love with a great guy whose only flaw seems to be that he doesn't want the same kind of rela-tionship I do. Life goes on, right? Lots of fish in the sea and all that.

An unfamiliar car pulls into the driveway as I'm giving myself the world's saddest pep talk. A stocky guy in a black suit gets out of the driver's door, and then Jack steps out of the back and looks up at the house, catching sight of me through the window. I wave, and he grins.

And then I burst into tears.

"OH, BECK, IT'S OKAY," Jack croons, while I blubber into his shoulder.

"Can we do anything?" Pete asks. "I'm so sorry your summer ended up this way."

They're being so nice to me, which makes me cry harder.

"No, it was an amazing summer," I say as I try to catch my hiccupping breath. "Your house is a dream. Cleo's the best. We had so much fun."

"Yeah, but if I hadn't made you and Van share the house then—"

"It's not your fault," I reassure Pete. "It was me. He told me from the beginning what he didn't want, and I thought I'd be okay with it."

"You're a romantic," Jack says, handing me a tissue from a nearby box. "Like me. It hurts sometimes, but it's who you are."

"And sometimes it just takes time for these things to work themselves out. Some people are slower to understand or act on their feelings," Pete says. "Sometimes they even put up artificial roadblocks even though they want to be on the road they're on. They're just scared."

"Okay. Thanks?" I'm not sure what to do with that. I tried convincing Donovan that he was on the right road—the road I'm on—and he rejected me.

"I think what Pete's saying is you deserve someone who can meet you where you are in a relationship," Jack says, giving Pete an unreadable look.

I blow my nose again and decide that as nice as the attention is, the advice, such as it is, isn't that helpful. "Well, enough about me. I'll be fine." I do believe that, even if it won't be for a while. "How was the flight? Are you exhausted?"

"We slept a little on the plane, but I'm definitely

looking forward to sleeping in my own bed tonight," Jack says.

"Sleep. Yes. Soon," Pete grunts out.

I laugh. "It's barely noon."

"Yeah, we have to try to get on the right time, sweetheart. Can you stay up until at least six?"

"I'll try." Pete yawns. "Is there anything to eat around here?"

"I'll make some lunch," I offer. It's one way to thank the two of them for letting me step into their home and make it my own for two months.

"Why don't you take the bags upstairs and I'll help Beck with lunch?" Jack says, following me into the kitchen.

I get out the ingredients for chicken salad as Jack helps himself to iced tea.

"So I can't wait to show you the shop. The stools are being delivered tomorrow," I say with forced cheer.

"Beck. Stop."

"What?"

"I just want to make sure you're really okay. I feel awful about this. If I'd known what kind of guy Van is, I would never have left you alone with him."

"Jack, seriously, I'm slightly heartbroken, yes. But I'm also an adult, if you hadn't noticed. And Donovan isn't a bad person. He just wants different things out of life. And I guess I thought maybe there was a chance—"

A sound like galloping horses interrupts me, and a second later Pete skids into the kitchen. The noise must have been him tromping down the stairs, such a contrast to Donovan's smooth glide. "I think I forgot my tooth-brush at the hotel."

Then Cleo barks—she's been doing a lot of that today. She yipped and yapped with joy when Jack and Pete first arrived and spent five straight minutes clobbering her with kisses—all while I blubbered out the abbreviated story of my ill-fated fling with Donovan.

"What's up, Cleo?" Three pairs of human eyes and one pair of dog eyes look toward the kitchen entrance as someone comes down the back hall that leads to the garage. Donovan appears a moment later, dressed in the same clothes he left in two days ago.

It hurts to look at him without going over and touching.

"Oh. Hey." He looks at me first, then flicks his gaze over to Jack and Pete. "You guys are back. Great." But his enthusiasm sounds fake.

Cleo bounds up to him, sniffing his knee excitedly.

"Hey, girl," he says, dropping down to kiss her head. "Missed you."

My heart does not melt at that, not even a little bit. I swear.

He rises slowly and we're all still staring, as if we've forgotten how to behave. "Um—Beck, can I talk to you?"

I instantly take half a step forward—it seems my body is willing to act before my mind can tell it why going to Donovan is a bad idea.

Jack, however, gets in my way by stepping right up to Donovan's face. "Maybe he doesn't want to talk to you, you, you—" he seems to struggle to find the word he's looking for. "You rascal!"

Donovan's eyes open wider at the accusation, if that's what it is.

"Jack, honey, I think we should give them some privacy," Pete says.

Cleo barks again.

"I think she needs exercise," I say. "Maybe you two could take her for a walk?"

"No!" The word explodes out of Donovan like a bomb, and I can't help jumping a little.

"Excuse me?" Why is he being so weird?

"Sorry, no, you and I should take her. For a walk. That's a great idea." He crosses the room for her lead, snaps it on Cleo, and then comes around the island to grab my elbow. "Please, take Cleo on a walk with me."

I lose the ability to protest as he stares into my eyes with his bottomless blue ones. "Okay." I don't know why this is so important to him, or what he thinks he's doing, but I can't leave him hanging. Besides, Jack and Pete aren't exactly helping.

I slide into my loafers, snag my hat and keys. "We'll be back soon. Eat, uh, something," I tell Jack before following Donovan outside.

Our summer might be over, but I can't resist taking one more walk with him.

THIRTY-ONE
DONOVAN

"WHICH WAY DO you want to go?" Beck asks when we get to the road.

"This way," I say, turning left with no hesitation. Cleo trots obediently at our sides, seemingly happy to be on her favorite route.

"Is everything okay? How did your audition go?" Beck's making a monumental effort to sound normal and give me the time of day, which is just like him, even though I don't miss the way his eyes are rimmed red and his cheeks are splotchy.

He was crying recently. And it kills me to know it was probably because of me.

"Jack's pretty pissed at me," I say, avoiding his question because if I start telling him about that, I'll have to explain everything, and I'm not quite ready to do that.

"Sorry, when they got home I just sort of—" He looks away from me. "I fell apart for a minute, but I'm good. Really."

I selfishly hope that's not entirely true, but I don't

comment. Instead, I say, "Well, he cares about you, and I was an asshole, so he's got a right." I'm glad that Beck has someone willing to stand up for him.

"You weren't an asshole." Beck's always way too easy on me. Again, my heart leaps with hope.

"We can debate that later," I say. "I'm glad they're home, though."

"Me too. Even if it means the end of my Nancy Meyers kitchen era." He smiles to show he's joking. We're now on Turner Street, and my palms are sweating. Time's running out and I don't know if I have the words for what I need to tell Beck.

There's so much to tell.

"You'll have another one," I say.

"Maybe. I'll be too busy with the shop for a while to worry about anything else."

"Still on track for Labor Day?"

"Yeah, I think so. I hired a baker yesterday, who can also do front of the house things if I need her to."

"That's great."

"Did Joan read your play yet?"

"She did."

"And?" He pokes me in the side, and I startle at the contact. It's almost like it used to be, except the second after he does it, he yanks his hand back like I've got a steel trap under my shirt.

"And she really liked it. She has some notes, of course. But it was nice to hear that she didn't think it was complete garbage. She's going to research some places I can workshop it. Though I was thinking—" Wait. If I tell him about that, I'll be getting ahead of myself.

We're almost to the end of the cul-de-sac, anyway.

I take a breath. Okay, enough stalling.

"So you asked before how the audition went. It went really well—but it wasn't actually an audition. It was an offer for a series of commercials. I signed the contract this morning, as a matter of fact."

"Oh my god, that's incredible. Congratulations!" Beck looks genuinely happy for me. "Is that why you stayed in the city?"

"Partly. I had some business to take care of. And some thinking to do. I didn't want to come back here until I had something to, well, offer you."

"What?"

We're almost to the blue house, which seems like as good a place to stop as any. I pause under the shade of a leafy maple. It already has a few yellowing leaves. Autumn is on its way. Beck turns to face me.

"You are an incredible person," I say, digging deep to find the right words. "And I took you for granted. I also spent most of the summer lying to myself. Look— you were right. I treated you like a boyfriend, without realizing I was craving that kind of relationship. And you made it easy for me to pretend we were just playing around, just in this for the summer. But I don't want that anymore—I don't know that I ever really did. I'm ready to admit that things have changed for me. I still love New York, but I don't need to be there full time. I still love acting, but I like writing and teaching, too. I let being from a small town give me license to scorn them, but it turns out small towns really aren't that bad. And you were right that I was letting what happened with Aidan stop me from growing up."

"Wow, that's a lot of things I was right about," Beck says with a watery smile.

"I'm a stubborn person, but I'd like to think I know when to fold and when to go all in." I take a step closer to Beck. He doesn't move away. "You said once that I was your exception—but I don't want to be your exception. I don't want you to change for me. I want to be yours. Just yours."

I search his face, but he doesn't give anything away.

"And to sweeten the pot, because I know I'd be getting by far the better part of this deal, I have something for you." I point to the blue house, a couple dozen feet behind him. "Noelle was about to call you to tell you she found the owner of the house, but I happened to get her on the phone first. I used my powers of persuasion to get her to work with me. The owner is happy to sell, Beck. Nothing's in writing yet, but Noelle says she thinks a sale will happen. And if it doesn't, I'll find you another house where you can bake and listen to music full blast and get a dog. Cleo needs a cousin."

Cleo's been sitting calmly at our feet and now she wags her tail at the sound of her name. Beck looks over his shoulder at the house and then back at me. "You're giving me a house?"

"Do you still want it?" I swallow and ask the real question. "Do you still want me?"

He closes his eyes, and my heart thumps with panic—one, two, three times—before he opens them again. "Yes."

The panic turns to elation. "Yes—you mean you still love me?"

"Yes, you beautiful idiot." He grins, but then freezes. "Wait. Do you love me?"

"Did I not say that before? Oh god, I am an idiot. Yes, I love you, Beckett Avery. And I know nothing about fixing up houses, but I want to fix this one up with you. I want to do it all with you."

He throws his arms around me, and I cling to him as if he might change his mind at any moment. I hold him hard, relief at having him back where he belongs coursing through my entire body.

His mouth finds mine, and the kiss tastes sweeter than any I've ever had.

"Just to be clear," he says, when our mouths are both red and shiny, "this isn't a transactional relationship. You don't have to buy me a house to get me to be with you."

"And you don't have to cook or bake me cookies to keep me with you," I say, meaning it. "Though of course I will always gladly eat whatever you put in front of me."

"So maybe we should buy the house together," he says. "Fifty-fifty."

"An even split?" I like that idea. My earnings from the commercial gig will cover the down payment, but it would be nice to have something left over for renovations. Between the two of us, we can make it happen.

"I can't believe we're going to live together," Beck says as we slowly walk back to Wild Rose Lane. His hand has found its way to my back pocket, a reassuring weight against my left ass cheek and a promise of celebrating in a more intimate way later. Hopefully, Jack and Pete won't mind if we call it an early night, too.

"I guess we'll need to move into that new apartment anyway while we sort out the house purchase," Beck says. "And who knows what kind of state the interior is in?"

He sounds unconcerned at the amount of work the blue house could end up needing. What the hell. It'll be an adventure.

"Our friends might say we're moving too fast," I warn him.

"We'll just remind them that we moved in together the first day we met, and it worked out okay."

"After I got my act together," I admit.

"And I got brave enough to ask for what I really wanted."

We walk up the driveway and stop on the front steps, the place we had our very first kiss.

"I'm so grateful that what you want is me." And then I kiss my boyfriend with all the love in my heart.

"EPIC PARTY, KINGSTON," I tell our host when I corner him in his kitchen at the surprise welcome home party. "Jack and Pete's expressions were priceless when they realized what we were up to."

"Couldn't have done it without your help, so thank you," he says, raising his glass of bubbly to me in toast. "And everyone's going gaga over your cookies, of course. That cookie shop of yours won't be able to keep up with demand."

"I can only hope." I laugh. "And apparently you deserve a thank you, too, for talking some sense into my boyfriend."

Yes, I say the last word in that sentence with a little smugness. Donovan's also been using it every chance he can get, so I'm not the only one proud of our hard-won label.

Yesterday, after walking through the door hand-in-hand and explaining to Jack and Pete that we'd gotten our shit straightened out, we went up to Donovan's room and talked for hours.

He told me how Kingston and Pete forced him to realize what he should have seen all along—that he'd fallen for me just as hard as I had for him, and the reason he'd been miserable since the day I told him I loved him was that he didn't know how to reconcile the life I represented with the life he'd convinced himself he wanted.

"I'm not saying I'm completely mature enough to handle everything that being in a real relationship means —I'm rusty, but I promise to try," he'd said with so much earnestness that I'd wanted to kiss the tip of his adorable crooked nose.

"I'm not perfect, either," I assured him. "And we just need to promise to figure stuff out together."

"That I can do." And we'd sealed our agreement with a kiss, followed by other stuff that I only felt mildly guilty about engaging in while Jack and Pete were only a few rooms away. I tried to be quiet, but Jack did have a bit of a hard time meeting my gaze over breakfast.

This morning the married couple presented us with thank-you souvenirs from their trip—an early edition of Donovan's favorite play they found in a bookseller's stall along the Seine, and for me a madeleine pan from a famous cookware store in Paris. It took all my self-control not to stop everything and bake madeleines since we had to subtly get Jack and Pete to come with us to Kingston's, where about two dozen of their friends were waiting to give them a warm Rosedale greeting.

An hour into the party, Kingston looks a bit frazzled, but happy. "Well, I could see you and he needed a little nudge to get you on the same page," he says. "Anyone can tell just by looking at you that you're crazy about each other."

"Thanks for helping us." I give him a hug and tell him I'll check in before we leave, then return to Donovan's side and hand him a fresh beer. Dulcie from the Rosedale Art Center is here, and she and Donovan are talking about the best way to workshop his play with the actors and other writers at the Art Center while Pete looks on in shock.

"I didn't know you've been teaching at the Art Center," he says. "I thought you hated community theater."

Donovan blushes scarlet. "Dude, be cool," my boyfriend hisses.

Dulcie just laughs. "Oh, it's okay. I was a snob about it when I first came to Rosedale, too, but the Art Center is a special place."

"Beck, the oatmeal cookies are incredible. They're just like the ones my dad used to make," Meadow says, joining the group, holding hands with Melissa from the bookshop.

I preen a little at the praise.

"We can't wait until the shop opens," Melissa says. "You've put it together so quickly."

"Beck has the gift of being good at anything he puts his hands on," Donovan says.

I'm not sure he means the double entendre, but I ignore the insinuation. "It helps to have the support of the whole community. It honestly feels like a team effort."

"So I hear you're going to be the spokesmodel for some sunscreen company," Meadow says to Donovan.

"The small-town gossip circuit strikes again," he says. "Yes. I'm doing some commercials for a sunscreen company. Should be fun, actually. They're putting me up at a swanky resort for the first round of shooting."

"Wait—your commercial gig is for sunscreen? How did this not come up earlier?" I side-eye Donovan and then let out a gasp as something occurs to me. "Please, please, please tell me they're going to make you wear a Speedo."

He cringes and the blush from before comes back. "I think they mentioned something about trying a few different looks," he says evasively.

"Wow. The man who would not wear a Speedo in his friend's backyard pool might have to appear in a national ad campaign in one." I'm delighted by the poetic justice, but not sure if I'm more proud or jealous of the extent to which the outside world will have access to ogle my boyfriend's hot body.

The group laughs good-naturedly at Donovan's chagrin, then Jack comes over and stands next to his husband.

"What's so funny?" he asks.

Donovan sighs. "Oh, your cousin just thinks it's hilarious that I might have to wear a Speedo in a national ad campaign."

"Speedos? Love those things. Everyone wore them in Europe," Jack says jovially. "Loosen up, man."

"Yeah, loosen up," I echo, sneaking a hand around to pat Donovan on the ass.

He scrunches up his face at me, then kisses me in front of our friends, as if he thinks that might make me be quiet. It's a short kiss, but it still makes me feel things, and wonder how fast we can politely escape the party.

"Wait—am I missing something?" Melissa asks. "I thought you two were just sharing house-sitting duties."

Donovan grins at me, a wide, happy smile that makes my heart turn over in my chest. "We were at first. Just roommates."

"Then I seduced him with cookies and breakfast tacos and beating him at poker," I joke.

"Yeah." He grabs my hand, raises it to his mouth, and kisses the knuckles. "You did."

Instead of melting into a puddle on the floor, I pull myself together enough to say, "So it looks like we're both sticking around Rosedale, at least for now." I don't want to spill the beans about the blue house in case the deal doesn't go through, but even if we end up living in a one-bedroom apartment forever, something tells me it won't be the end of the world, as long as we're there together. "Roommates again."

"The best roommate I ever had," he says softly.

"The best you ever had, period," I add with a saucy wink.

"The very best," he agrees.

EPILOGUE
DONOVAN

MOLLY and I jog down the street, sweat soaking through my shirt and making my hair cling to my neck. It's gotten long again, but Beck likes it that way, so I'm not in a hurry to get a trim.

The multi-colored dog is a relatively new addition to my exercise routine, but a welcome one. A few weeks ago Dulcie called—she had a friend who was moving out of the country and couldn't bring her three-year-old mutt. Beck and I took one look at her and knew we'd found the pup we'd been waiting for. She already had her name, but Beck insists that Molly is short for Molasses—the cookies that brought us together.

She and I were up early to beat the heat. The holiday promises to be a classic New England late summer day—sunny, hot, and humid.

I push open the swinging gate that separates the sidewalk from the path to our front door. Beach roses bloom on either side of me in a profusion of ruby red. Molly pauses to anoint a cone flower that Kingston gave us when we officially moved into the blue house at the end of Turner Street.

That was almost ten months ago, mere weeks after we agreed to buy the house as-is for a low price. Sure, we've had to redo the roof, repaint the outside a fresh coat of the same colonial blue, pull about a million weeds in the front and back yards—and we're still not done with the inside. But as much work as it's been, it's the first place I've been truly able to call home since I went away to college.

I bang through the front door. "Babe, I'm home," I yell.

"I'm in the kitchen," he calls back.

I could have guessed that. Beck's at the Cookie Counter five days a week, but when he's home, he's usually in the kitchen. We renovated it first—which means our bedroom still has seventies-era carpet and a crack in the plaster ceiling—and there are new appliances, cement countertops, recessed lighting, and a heated tile floor. Beck wanted the color scheme to be different from the Cookie Counter's blue and orange, so our kitchen is a clean white with jade green accents.

I kick off my running shoes and head down the hallway. Molly makes a beeline for her water bowl, and I peel off my shirt, tossing it in the general direction of the laundry room. The blue house is bigger than it looks from the outside, with four bedrooms and three bathrooms. Again, things still need work, but the house has good bones, as they say, and it's been surprisingly satisfying to learn how to fix running toilets and patch walls. I even made friends with our contractor, Manny. We play pickleball sometimes on the weekends.

"What are you doing?" I ask my boyfriend when I reach the kitchen.

He looks up with his finger in his mouth, his eyes round with guilt. He pulls his finger out with a pop. "Nothing."

"Nothing? It looks like you're baking." I go around the narrow kitchen island and peer into the bowl attached to the mixer on the counter in front of him. Something that looks suspiciously like chocolate chip cookie dough fills the bowl. I stare at him. "You are. You are baking."

"I know, but we're going to Jack and Pete's later and I thought—"

"It's your day off and you're baking cookies. You're a maniac," I say, enfolding him in a big sweaty hug because I love him so much I can't go another second without touching him.

He wraps his arms around me, not protesting the hug or the sweat. "I know. But you're the one who told me that doing something I love for a job could be rewarding, and you were right. I still love making cookies, even though I do it for work."

"Good thing, because I think if you closed the shop, the fine citizens of Rosedale would revolt and come after you with pitchforks." Beck's Cookie Counter was a hit from day one, growing its revenue every month. Beck almost immediately had to take on more employees. He's made a few missteps, but the kid is a natural business owner, a great boss, and the sky's the limit as far as I'm concerned. Beck's Cookie Empire is truly not out of reach, if he wants it.

"Anyway, I'm almost done. I just have to bake these and then I'm free," he says. "We were going to look at bathroom fixtures, weren't we?"

I groan. "Can we take a break from house stuff for one day?"

"Oh god, yes, please," he says, sagging into me. "We need a break."

I kiss my way from the top of his ear to his mouth, where I lose track of time for a while. "I need a shower," I protest when he starts rubbing against me and giving me ideas about how I'd like to spend the rest of the morning.

"So do I," he murmurs against the pulse in my neck. "Wanna take one together?"

"What about your cookies?"

"The dough needs to rest anyway," he says.

"Awesome."

Together we stumble toward the stairs, kiss at the base of them for a minute, then break apart, laughing a little. Beck's cheeks are flushed and his hair's standing up straight. He looks young, but I know firsthand how much he's taken on. He's impressed me over and over again this past year with his dedication, his creativity, and the fact that even though he's been focused on making his business a success, he always makes time for me, for us. When I got a part in a play with a four-week run in the city over the winter, he rearranged his schedule so he could come and stay with me every single weekend, and he went to every show he could. We even traveled to

Apple Vale to have Christmas with my family, which I haven't done in years. Mom and Dad and my sister loved him, of course, especially after he shared his molasses cookie recipe, making us all feel like Aunt Sharleen was with us.

I thought last summer was amazing, but the past year has been even better.

When we finally get to our bathroom, I strip and get the shower running, but pause before stepping under the spray. "Summer's almost over."

Beck steps out of his underwear, leaving him mouth-wateringly naked. "So it is."

"We've been together for more than a year."

"True."

We celebrated our anniversary not long ago with dinner at the Italian restaurant on Main Street, then came home and fucked slowly on the couch in the dark, Beck grinding down on me, and me feeling like the luckiest man in the world.

"We live together. We own this house together. We have a dog."

"True, true, and true." Beck smiles at me as if he doesn't know where I'm going with this.

"And I love you more every day," I say, because that's true, too.

His smile breaks a little, but I know it's because he feels the same way. "I love you, Donovan."

"So why don't we get married?" I've been wanting to propose since before our anniversary. I can't imagine my life without Beck, and I don't want to.

"What?"

"Why don't we—"

"I heard you, I heard you." And then I have an armful of Beck and the bathroom's filling with steam and I'm laughing because I'm being kissed within an inch of my life, which I think means the man I love wants to marry me, too.

"Is that a yes?" I ask, just to be sure, when Beck's mouth is no longer devouring mine.

"That's the biggest yes. The most yes. A thousand, million yeses."

"I thought so." My heart pulses with joy. Beck is going to be my husband, and we'll both get to live with our favorite roommate for the rest of our lives.

Thank you for reading *Cool for the Summer*!
Want to read about Jack and Pete's wedding (and wedding night 😌)? Sign up for my newsletter at https://ellewatersbooks.substack.com/ and get the free story *Backyard Wedding*, which introduces Donovan and Beck for the very first time!

Keep reading to get Beck's version of Aunt Sharleen's molasses cookie recipe.

Happy reading and happy eating!
xoxo, Elle

AUNT SHARLEEN'S MOLASSES
COOKIE RECIPE

Ingredients

2 cups all-purpose flour

1 teaspoon baking soda

1 tablespoon ground ginger

2 ½ teaspoons cinnamon

¾ teaspoon ground nutmeg

¾ teaspoon ground cloves

½ teaspoon allspice

¼ teaspoon finely ground black pepper

¾ teaspoon salt

12 tablespoons unsalted butter, room temperature

1 cup granulated sugar

¼ cup brown sugar

¼ cup dark molasses

1 large egg

Instructions

Preheat oven to 375 °F. Line two baking sheets with parchment paper.

Stir together flour, baking soda, spices, and salt in a medium bowl and set aside.

Cream the butter and both sugars together for 1 minute until light and fluffy. Add molasses and mix until blended. Add the egg and mix until blended. Scrape the bowl.

Add the flour mixture and blend on low until incorporated, but do not overmix.

Use a 1 ½ inch cookie scoop or a tablespoon to drop the dough 3 inches apart on the baking sheet. Bake until slightly soft, 13-15 minutes.

Best eaten the day they are made, or freeze and bring to room temperature before eating.

Makes about 15 cookies. Enjoy!

ACKNOWLEDGMENTS

My sincere appreciation and gratitude goes out to all my friends sharing in this stimulating, surprising, and wonderful journey that is being an author. Thanks to Taylor Delong, M.E. Montgomery, Arell Rivers, Nicole Locke, Sara Kettler, Isabel Morin, and Annette Nauraine. Thank you to Sara for the amazing copyedit, to Tracy at Amaze Inn Proofreading for the proofread. All mistakes are my own. Thanks to Dar at Wicked Smart Designs for the scorching cover. Thanks to my students and friends at the Westport Writers' Workshop for your enthusiasm and support.

And thanks to you for reading this book, and for asking for more stories set in Rosedale!

xoxo,
Elle

ABOUT THE AUTHOR

Fueled by chocolate and canned wine, Elle Waters writes steamy small town romance with guaranteed happy endings. She lives with her family in Connecticut. Sign up for her newsletter at ellewatersauthor.com to hear about her next release!

Elle loves to hear from readers at elle@ellewatersauthor.com.

facebook.com/ElleWatersAuthor

instagram.com/ellewatersbooks

amazon.com/~/e/B091FZQ4PZ

bookbub.com/authors/elle-waters

www.ingramcontent.com/pod-product-compliance
Lightning Source LLC
Chambersburg PA
CBHW032237310726

48973CB00008B/2173

1

COUPLES ARE THE WORST

Lamb: My legacy? I don't have a legacy. Men have legacies. Women have families.

Interviewer:(laughing) Well, shit. There goes my whole book.

Lamb: Oh, I hadn't thought about that.

Interviewer: Everyone has a legacy, whether they intend to or not.

Excerpt from transcript of interview with Savannah Lamb, recipe blogger

LUCIE

"Couples are the worst." I held up my hands. "There. I said it."

Andrew, who'd been gazing intently at Carly like he could Vulcan mind-meld her into leaving us behind so he could take her home and do couple things like pick out fucking wallpaper, blinked slowly. "No, we're not."

At the same time, Carly said, "What? We're not a couple."

His eyebrows shot up. "That's not what you said last night

when I…" As he whispered the rest in her ear, her cheeks reddened.

Now that they were dating, Andrew regularly joined us at our Wednesday-night happy hours. Boo.

I mean, the guy was okay, but it wasn't the same as when only my three besties and I would hang out. Plus, he was no substitute for Savannah, who hadn't been able to make it down from Sacramento tonight.

"I meant," Carly said, "we're not *that* kind of couple. Like them." She nodded at the booth closest to our high-top where the guy had his tongue down the woman's throat. And possibly his hand up her skirt. I leaned around Tessa to look. Yep, definitely fingering going on.

I straightened. "You're worse," I announced. "Because it's not just hot sex. It's *love.*"

Carly hid her blush against Andrew's soft-looking gray sweater. He stroked her arm, looking like she'd given him a gift he'd been coveting for years.

"You agree with me, right, Tessa?" I swiveled to face her.

Tessa tilted her head, making her long auburn hair cascade down her shoulder. "I find it fascinating how Carly has changed since she's accepted Andrew as part of her life. But I don't need to judge it as better or worse. She's growing, like all of us."

Speaking of Vulcans. "But look at this." I picked up my glass of scotch and pointed at them with it. "They're like a couple of Care Bears—with fucking hearts shooting out of them."

"What are Care Bears?" Andrew's hand had moved from Carly's arm to her hip. They were *snuggling,* at a high top, in the bar.

Carly looked up. "You don't remember them?"

"It's like he grew up on a different planet." Dude was only seven years younger than me, but he seemed so much younger. I sipped my scotch. It burned my throat on the way down, tasting like socks someone had worn to a campout.

"God." Tessa rested her chin on her hand. "I'd forgotten all about Care Bears. I wanted one so badly back in the '80s. Like it would be my passport to social acceptance."

"Did you ever get one?" I asked. Tessa was tighter than a nun's asshole about her past. I could've googled her history, but friends didn't do that. Friends waited for each other to feel comfortable enough to share. And from what she'd shared, which wasn't much, she'd been sheltered. Maybe she'd come from one of those TV-rots-your-brain families.

"No, I didn't." She drained her glass of whiskey and set it down. "Who wants another?"

I raised my hand. All this couple bullshit was stirring up something uncomfortable inside me. Not jealousy exactly but a weird kind of longing. I needed to either drink it away or fuck it away, and from the anemic selection of single people in the bar, it was probably going to be the former.

"Want another glass of sparkling wine?" Andrew murmured. "I'm driving."

Carly smiled at him, her eyes practically matching the string of paper hearts hanging over the table. "Okay."

"Got it. I'll bring you a seltzer, Andrew." Tessa strode to the bar.

A squall came from the booth next to where the couple was making out. A baby reached for the fold-out paper heart hanging over the table and screeched again. Its parents, a couple who looked way too young to be responsible for an entire human, laughed. One dad batted at the heart and set it swinging gently.

The tightness in my chest intensified. I'd never thought of a baby as anything but an annoyance before my thirty-ninth birth-day, half a year ago. That's when the weird feelings had started.

It was FOMO. And I couldn't really fear missing out on having children of my own, could I?

I had a career.

And a book to write.

And great friends. Nothing was lacking in my life.

Right?

"What are you two doing after happy hour?" I asked. "Want to try that new Ethiopian place across the street?"

Carly's lips turned down. "Sorry, we're doing takeout at Andrew's. I have to head down to LA the day after tomorrow, and since it's Valentine's Day..."

"Valentine's Day?" I looked up at the paper hearts. "Guess I lost track of the date." Why did February 14th raise a flag in my brain? It had been a normal day at the paper, and I didn't have any interviews scheduled for my book until March. I lifted my phone.

"Round two," Tessa announced, setting down the four drinks like a pro. She raised her glass. "To...?"

"To love," Carly said, her cheeks turning pink. "I love you all. And Savannah too." She whispered something in Andrew's ear that made him puff out his chest like he'd won an award.

Award.

"Shit!" I plunked down my drink and scraped back in my chair. "Gotta go. I'm late."

"Need us to drive you?" Andrew asked.

That'd be just what I needed, to give my friends a glimpse of my cringeworthy family life. "No, thanks. I'll get a rideshare." I flicked open the app and headed toward the exit.

My friends were happily deluded that I was a moderately successful journalist. I wouldn't reveal what my family never hesitated to toss in my face, that I was a disappointment, destined to be forgotten.

A fact that my next stop was sure to remind me of.

"Looks like they've already started," the driver said as she cruised up the empty circular driveway in front of the campus union hall.

I didn't have to glance at my phone to know how late I was. "Yeah."

"Sorry about the traffic." She waved a hand behind her as if she could still see the snarl we'd fought through on our way from San Francisco.

I shrugged. "It happens." Especially when you leave late because you're drinking with your friends.

One of my dad's many mantras was that we make time for what's important. It was the one he used when he caught me pulling an all-nighter to finish a paper in college and when I said I was busy at work and couldn't make it to whatever university event he wanted to trot me out at like a show pony. But that was before my early promise had faded like old newspaper.

When I stayed in her Tesla, staring at the closed doors of the stucco building, the driver said, "Kind of late for a funeral, isn't it?"

"Funeral?" I tilted my head.

She turned and pointed at my torso. "With that getup..."

I looked down at my black trench coat, which covered my black shirtdress. "Oh. No, it's an award banquet."

Her forehead scrunched, setting the barbell in her eyebrow sparkling in the building's yellow security light. "I hope you're not the one getting the award."

I chuckled. "It's for my father—as usual. Thanks for the ride." I pushed out of the car but paused on the sidewalk to take a deep breath. Then another. Pasting a smile on my face because he expected it, I strode to the door, heaved it open, and flung myself into the lion's den.

The room hummed with conversation, punctuated by the plinks of silverware against china. Round banquet tables filled the ballroom up to a stage at the far end. On the raised platform, a podium stood next to a row of uncomfortable-looking chairs. I smelled coffee and a muddle of foods. Potatoes, maybe? And fish. My stomach rumbled. How long ago was lunch? Oh, right. I'd skipped that, trying to hit my deadline. Maybe I could still scrounge a plate of something.

My father wasn't particularly tall, and he wore a dark suit like all the other men in the room. Yet he had a presence that drew my attention. Everyone's, really. His white hair and beard stood out against his brown skin. He didn't break his perpetually serious expression as he spoke with a colleague, his focus unwavering as I approached.

My mother beamed as I weaved between the tables, her graying strawberry-blond hair glinting in the spotlights from the nearby dais. She usually wore more muted colors, but her dress was the color of one of those heart-shaped candy boxes.

"Lucie! You made it!" Her eyes crinkled, obscuring a few of her freckles.

"Sorry I'm late," I muttered as I kissed her cheek. "Traffic."

I winced as soon as I said it and glanced at Dad, hoping he hadn't heard. My hope died when he turned toward me, jaw set.

"That old story?" he murmured. Louder, he said, "Cal, you remember my daughter, Lucie? She won an award for a seven-part series on human trafficking. How many years ago was that, Lucie?"

My cheeks burned as I shook the older white man's hand. "Fifteen or so."

"She was a brand-new reporter. No idea how she got the assignment, but she made the most of it," Dad said.

I already knew the question was coming before Cal opened his mouth. "And what have you been working on lately?"

"Moldering in the newsroom at the city paper." My father spat out the last two words like he'd said *garbage dump*.

At the same time, I stood to my full height of five foot four and said, "Actually, I'm working on a book. I just signed the deal."

I'd signed it two weeks ago, but I'd wanted to look Dad in the eye when I told him.

His white eyebrow twitched upward.

"Oh, Lucie, we're so proud." Mom squeezed my shoulders.

Cal asked, "What's the book about?"

"It's about legacy. What we intend to leave behind and what we hope we're remembered for."

Cal chuckled. "You going to interview your dad, I assume?"

"It's a book about women's legacies," I said.

"Women's legacies?" Cal asked. "Like motherhood?"

We all glanced at my mother in her red dress and tight smile.

"Women can be more than mothers," I blurted. "I have some interviews lined up. A tech founder, a Hollywood stylist." I left out the facts that they were my best friends, and I hadn't asked them yet. "And—"

"I'll connect you with Dr. Watts," my father said. "The university's first Black female president should have a place in your book."

Cal scratched his gray beard. "Marvin, didn't you speak on a panel recently with Senator Gu? He's got a wife who has... causes, I think."

"That's right," Dad said. "Eleanor. Everyone says their son is on the road to the White House. I'm sure she'll do me a favor and talk to you."

Suddenly, dinner leftovers didn't seem so appetizing.

"I've got it, Dad," I growled.

"All right." He shrugged like he didn't care (he did), then the lights flickered. "Ah. That's my cue." Without another word, he strode to the dais and took his seat next to the university president.

Cal had already disappeared, so I turned to my mother. "Did you save me a seat?"

"You can borrow your father's. He won't need it." She pointed at a chair, then sat in the one next to it. The efficient servers had removed everything edible from the table. I turned the coffee cup over, hoping someone would come to fill it, and I could beg for a leftover dessert.

As the lights dimmed, Mom leaned over to whisper in my ear, "A book deal? We're both so proud of you."

It was a lie. Not an intentional one; my mother was proud of me, and she thought Dad was too. But the only way my father would be proud of me was if I was sitting up on that stage, getting an award for scholarly achievement. He'd been furious the day I'd told him I'd declined my grad school acceptance to go to work for the paper. He'd told me I was throwing my future away. But I'd wanted a different future from his.

It wasn't because Dad's research into the long-term effects of racism on society wasn't valuable. It was. Politicians and activists wore out the cushions of his dining-room chairs as they begged for his advice on how to make the country a better place for citizens.

But I didn't care for the sanitized type of research he did, with statistics and expert interviews. No, I wanted to dig deeper into people's stories and help them share those narratives with a broader audience. Because people connect better with stories than with dry research. I'd blaze my trail and change the world my way.

So, I went to work at the newspaper, where as the new person, I took the assignments no one else wanted: city council meetings, school board meetings, the mayor's press conference announcing the year's budget. Until I was in the right place at the right time, when a reporter called in sick, and I got to cover the bust of a human trafficking ring. Then, I'd convinced the editor to let me do a follow-up piece on some of the victims. Even Dad had noticed when a national news magazine picked it up as a feature.

Too bad I'd done nothing noteworthy in the fifteen years since.

A burst of applause startled me, and I focused on the stage as my father stepped up to the podium. Another plaque for his wall of achievements was displayed on an easel beside him. Was there even space for it? He'd already annexed the wall in my old bedroom, the one that used to be covered in posters of Bono, Jane Goodall, and Nelson Mandela.

The speaker before him must have introduced his work because instead of talking about his research, Dad thanked the university for the honor and launched into a lengthy list of acknowledgments, from his editor at the university press to the graduate students who'd run the statistical analysis.

My eyebrows crept up my forehead. Normally, Dad wasn't big on sharing credit. Some people probably thought he set the type on the printing press himself.

"...and most importantly, I'd like to thank the person who's stood by me through it all, who's supported me, who's encouraged me, who's been my partner in my journey." He paused, still unsmiling.

He usually forgot to acknowledge my mother, but that's what he was winding up to do. I reached for her hand and squeezed. She'd given up everything for him. For us. She'd been forced out of her graduate program when her relationship with my father, who happened to be her adviser, was exposed. Three months later I was born, and she gave up her promising career to become a full-time wife and mother. If anyone deserved his thanks, she did.

"Dr. LaToya Watts," he said. I froze, still gripping my mother's hand. "Without the support of our university president, my research wouldn't have received the exposure it has. Thank you." He lifted the plaque from its easel and posed next to Dr. Watts for photos as the audience applauded.

Had I somehow missed his thanks to her? Judging from the forced smile on her face, I hadn't.

I leaned forward to whisper, "Are you okay?"

Her eyes crinkled at the corners. "Of course I am. This is a major achievement for your father. For us all."

One glance at my father on the stage, shaking hands with the trustees, told me she was wrong. It was an achievement for one person only—him. I hated that he couldn't love me for who I was, but ignoring the person who'd given up everything for him? And what was worse, my mother was fine with going unrecognized yet again. I couldn't sit around and pretend to smile after that.

I kissed her cheek. "Bye, Mom. I've got to go."

She blinked her blue eyes wide. "You're not staying to talk to him after? Come to the house. I'll whip you up a snack."

"No, thanks. Early meeting tomorrow." As much as I longed for one of my mother's meals, listening to my father's pompous speech had ruined my appetite. I needed another drink.

2

WHAT TIME DO YOU GET OFF?

<u>*Valentine's Day Manhattan*</u>
Shake 2 ounces bourbon, 3/4 ounce vanilla liqueur, and a dash of Angostura bitters with ice. Strain into a chilled martini glass. Garnish with a toothpick of Luxardo cherries and a ribbon of orange peel.

DANNY

*H*e was late again. I glanced at my phone, then scanned the Wednesday-night crowd on the other side of the bar. Barb and I had managed so far, but once everyone's desperate Valentine's dates started to tank, people would head back here to Rincon Hill and pile into their neighborhood bar to drink away another lost chance at love.

Believe me, I'd been there.

Every Valentine's Day, I turned into that guy, the one who saw love everywhere. My memories of shoeboxes decorated with red and white construction paper, cheesy puns on the cards, and enough chocolate to put me into a sugar coma always gave me hope that the right person was out there, wanting to be my *significant otter.*

And every Valentine's Day, I was disappointed.

A lime wedge bounced off my forehead. "Look alive, Carbone." Barb nodded at the woman with the sad eyes bellied up to my end of the bar.

"Sorry." I leaped into action, tossing an extra cherry into her Manhattan. She'd need more than that to get through the rest of her date with Bud Light Guy, who couldn't be bothered to fetch their drinks.

I swiped at the bar with a cloth and straightened the garnish tray, plucking a heart-shaped piece of confetti from the olive brine. I squinted at the door like I could make him appear through my power of will.

Barb rolled up beside me and threw the brake on her wheelchair. Her blue eyes crinkled. "Don't worry. He'll show. He's never let us down yet."

"What if there was an accident?" I raked my hands through my hair, then secured it into a low bun with the elastic on my wrist. I'd been looking out for my brother since he was three and his dad had left our mom, so she had to pick up a second job. Poor Mom had never had any luck in love. Not since my father died when I was a year old. Though Leo's dad stayed longer than our sister Giuliana's had.

"Pishposh. It's much more likely he lost track of time in the kitchen than a mishap on the road. Your little brother might be scattered, but he's safe."

"I know." I pulled out my phone. There were plenty of texts in our sibling group chat, but nothing from Leo. "I just—"

"You worry, Mother Hen," she said. "About everything. It's why I trust you with my bar."

A feeling like carbonation bubbled through my stomach. If all went according to plan, it'd be *my* bar this time next year— mine and Leo's.

"Won't you miss this place?" I asked, scanning the polished

wood, the well-worn high-top tables, and the vintage movie posters on the wall.

Barb's gaze fell on her most prized possession in its place of honor next to the bar, the *Breakfast at Tiffany's* poster signed by Audrey Hepburn. "Of course I will. But when I'm on my world cruise looking out at the Sydney Opera House, I don't think I'll be worrying about cockroaches in the dry storage or the rising price of tequila."

I chuckled. "Fair."

"And look." She tipped her head toward the swinging door behind me. "There he is."

My brother barreled into the tight quarters. He was a couple inches taller than me and rounder around the middle, and he always seemed too big for the back bar. He held one of his biodegradable clamshell containers in front of him.

"You have to try this, Danny. And Barb." His round cheeks were pink, either from the February chill or from delight. He opened the box, and a mouthwatering aroma drifted out.

"You were late because of french fries?" I wiped my hands on the towel that hung from my front jeans pocket and reached into the box.

"Be sure to try the garlic aioli." Barb and I both dipped a fry in the sauce and took a bite, then he said, "They're fried in truffle oil. And I shaved a little truffle on top."

I chewed the delicious morsel and swallowed. It was the best thing I'd eaten since our mom's Bolognese last Easter.

"Oh, my stars," Barb said. "My taste buds are singing."

"Good, isn't it?" Leo's tentative smile was full of hope.

"Let me try one, Leo." Walter, one of our regulars, beckoned. Leo held out the box to him.

"Shaved truffle sounds expensive," I grumbled.

"Well, yeah. The truffles cost about fifty an ounce, but there's only a tiny amount on these. And the truffle oil is a little pricey. I paid two hundred for a gallon, but I could probably get a bulk discount."

"Two *hundred?*" My voice rose to an outraged squeak. "You mean it'll cost a *grand* to fill up the fryer? For that kind of money, we could replace the leaky faucet in the ladies' room with the fancy touchless kind."

"I'll try to oven-bake the next batch," he said. "That'll use a lot less oil."

"You gonna eat the rest of those?" Walter said.

Leo handed them over. "They're good, right?"

Walter nodded, his mouth full.

I lowered my voice. "I thought we were saving money, Leo."

"It's for the bar. We'll add them to the menu."

"Walter," I said, "would you pay twenty bucks for those fries?"

He stuffed the last one in his mouth. "Twenty bucks? I could buy a burger and a beer for that. You're not going to charge me, are you?"

I hit Leo with a glare as I poured a fresh glass of water and set it in front of Walter. "The fries were on the house. Thanks for being our guinea pig."

"You boys can do whatever you like with the bar when it's yours," Barb said gently, "but the customers here are middle class. They might have truffle-oil taste, but they've got a peanut-oil budget."

Silently, we scanned the patrons. They were mechanics with grease on their jeans, teachers drinking after a long day with sugared-up kids, landscapers brushing grass clippings out of their hair and onto the sixty-year-old wood-plank floor. My siblings and I had gone to school with some of them. Barb had served them for years. She'd served some of their parents too. It was a place people came to connect with the community and have a little fun after work.

In my eyes, it was perfect.

"I've been thinking," Leo said, "what if we used the kitchen to run a catering business?"

I coughed on a sip of water. "You mean on the side, in addition to the bar food?"

"Yeah. It'd bring in extra cash. I'd manage the whole operation. It'd be my food truck on rails. Well, not literally. But I could make so much more food in a real kitchen. Banquets, weddings, you name it."

I pictured Leo trying to share the tiny space with the cook. Norm had worked with Barb since day one, and I was pretty sure he'd rather quit than bump shoulders with an entire catering staff, including my upstart brother and his fanciful menu.

"Do you really think there's room for a catering business and Norm back there? Installing extra equipment would be—"

"Expensive, I know." Leo sighed. "Maybe we can brainstorm about it later."

"Sure." I'd always humored my little brother's nutty ideas. I'd gone along with my fair share too. But this wouldn't be one of them. "Let's talk tomorrow. You and I are opening."

"Right. Sorry I was late tonight. Time got away from me."

It wasn't the first time. Still, I said, "Don't worry about it. Barb and I had it under control. I'm glad you're here now. Get their drinks?" I pointed at a group of nurses at the far end of the bar.

"On it." He tied an apron around his waist and strode toward them.

Barb, Leo, and I worked like a well-oiled machine that night. There was a rush at eight and another at ten. Barb handled the accessible end of the bar like always while Leo and I took turns serving the rest of it and carrying cases of beer and racks of glasses to the dishwasher and back. We floated and replaced two kegs, and Barb arranged rides for those customers who needed them.

By eleven thirty, the bar was only half full. We'd closed the kitchen. I cut two servers and carried up what I hoped was the last bucket of ice when a tingle raced across my skin. I glanced toward the door.

She'd walked in, cheeks pink and dark curls wild from the wind. She unwound the scarf from her neck, strode to Barb's end of the bar, and sank onto a chair like she owned it.

I couldn't help smiling. Mom had fond memories of an old app where the person who'd visited a particular location the most often was crowned the mayor. If that app were still around, Lucie Knox would be the mayor of Barb's Bar. And she acted like it.

Flashing a queenly smile at another regular, she turned as Barb set her drink on the coaster.

Another scotch night.

After dumping the ice into the bin, I edged closer.

"...total nightmare, as usual," she said. "Hey, Danny."

Whoa. The white flash of her teeth dazzled me. Was she wearing lipstick? I tried to be subtle as I scanned the rest of her. She wore a dress under her black coat. My breath caught at the glimpse of her tan legs, which reminded me of another night when they'd been wrapped around my waist.

She hadn't missed my checking her out. Lucie never missed anything. It was why she was such a talented reporter. She tipped her head. Her dark pupils glittered. "What's up?" And then she glanced pointedly at my crotch.

I took half a step back and bumped into the back wall, rattling a bottle of Tito's.

"H-hi, Lucie." I bent to straighten the bottles in Barb's speed rail so the labels faced out, but that only made more blood rush to my face. Why could I never keep my cool around her?

"Busy night?"

Barb watched us, her eyes glinting.

"Yeah, I guess." I checked the garnish tray. Damn, it was full. "What with the holiday and all…"

"Holiday?" Lucie crinkled her forehead.

I waved at the red and pink streamers hanging from the glass rack. "Valentine's Day."

"Right." Slowly, she nodded, and my heart rate slowed by a few beats. Maybe she wasn't cruising for a post-dating disaster hookup. Maybe she wanted to chat and I wouldn't be faced with the temptation to follow her upstairs, only to have my heart bruised when she inevitably kicked me out without so much as a cuddle.

Because even if Lucie Knox were the kind of woman who was interested in anything more than a hookup, she wouldn't choose me.

She was college educated.

Brilliant.

Had written an amazing piece about human trafficking when I was still in middle school. (Yes, I'd googled her.)

Not to mention confident and gorgeous.

Me? I'd never been to college. I had no deep thoughts about the low value our government put on vulnerable people like women, children, and immigrants. I was a bartender, and I lived in the small apartment upstairs because Barb let me stay there for free.

I'd never be worthy of anything more than an orgasm (or three) to Lucie.

"Hey," she said, her teeth gleaming under that red lipstick, lipstick I was tempted to kiss off her face, "what time do you get off?"

Which, apparently, was exactly what she wanted from me.

3

BLOWING OFF A LITTLE STEAM

My legacy? I hope it's more than my filmography, more than my image on screen. I hope I showed women you can be sexy and serious, tough and compassionate, funny and dramatic. And that because I fought for equal pay and pushed for more female directors in this industry, women see positive role models in films and in life.

Doris Starling, actress in more than sixty films

LUCIE

I stared into his deep brown eyes. The scotch had smoothed some of the sharp corners from my feelings of inadequacy, but as soon as I walked into Barb's and saw Danny's muscular arms flexing as he carried that ice bucket, I knew what I needed. And that was to peel off his ridiculous pink T-shirt—must've been a Valentine's Day thing since Barb and Leo wore them too—and get his veiny forearms wrapped around my thighs.

I knew what they said about not shitting where you eat. Was

it a terrible idea to fuck where I drank? With my downstairs neighbor?

Absolutely. But no one gave me orgasms like Danny Carbone, and I fucking deserved one after tonight's reminder that I wasn't good enough.

I raised my eyebrows after a few seconds of silence. Normally, Danny was a great listener. It made him a fabulous bartender. And a couple months ago, one of the best hookups I'd ever had. But tonight, he either had cotton in his ears, or he was being deliberately obtuse.

I was never one to mince words.

"Want to come to my place when you're done working?" I asked.

With a chuckle, Barb rolled her chair to the far end of the bar.

"I—not tonight, Lucie." His cheeks matched his shirt. He was a couple years younger than me with smooth skin that went blotchy when he blushed.

"Why not tonight?" I leaned forward, letting my arms frame my chest to give him a peek at my cleavage from the button front of my dress. "Do you have a girlfriend now?"

"No, but it's...it's not a good idea." He pulled the rag from the pocket of his low-slung jeans and wiped the beer taps.

"What's wrong with blowing off a little steam? We're good together." At least, I'd thought we were. The couple of times we'd done it, he went slowly and paid attention. He could tell when I'd had enough teasing and needed a release. And when he'd come, his eyes had literally rolled back in his head. Though, after, when I expected him to pull on his pants and go like every other guy I'd hooked up with, he'd gotten a weird expression. Almost sad. Had he not liked it?

I studied his face.

"We *were* good together," he said. With the way he emphasized the word *were,* the knot tightened in my stomach. That expression was back, his pretty lips turned down. A piece of shiny heart-shaped confetti glittered in his dark hair. Hair I wanted to release from that ridiculous bun and run my fingers through. Maybe pull it a little.

"Is it because it's Valentine's Day?" I wanted to flick that confetti. He had the softest hair, like mink. "I swear I'm not one of those people who thinks if we fuck on February 14th it means we're together forever."

"I know, I know." He ran a hand through his hair, and the sparkly heart fell to the floor.

"Then what's the problem? Look." I leaned closer and lowered my voice. "I had a shit night. I'm feeling kind of vulnerable. I'm pretty sure an orgasm will make me feel better."

His lips turned up on one side, then he chuckled. "Hell, Lucie. You don't hold anything back, do you?"

I shrugged. "What's the point of tiptoeing around things? If I tell you what I want, I'm much more likely to get it. Besides, you look like you could use a pick-me-up too."

Barb rolled her chair toward us. "Danny, you opened today, so it's only fair that Leo and I close. Things have gotten pretty slow, so you can go whenever you'd like." She winked at me.

I smiled back. I'd liked Barb since I'd moved into her building two years ago. She was a straight shooter like me. When I looked back at Danny, his gaze was glued to my boobs. Score.

"You coming?" I asked, slowly rising from the chair.

He licked his lips. "Yeah."

I sauntered out of the bar into the vestibule and took the sharp turn into the residents' entrance. After unlocking it, I climbed the first flight of stairs as Danny's heavier footsteps echoed behind me. We passed his floor and continued up the second flight.

I unlocked my door, flicked on the light, and held the door for him. Pausing, he scanned my place as if he were looking for changes since the last time he'd been up here. It was a while ago, around Barb's birthday in December. It had been a wild night in the bar after she shared her plans to retire by her next birthday and announced that Danny and Leo had offered to buy her out.

Danny's face had glowed that night. And even though he never drank anything but water behind the bar, his eyes had been bright and a little unfocused, drunk on joy. He'd come out from behind the bar to catch me up in a dance to "Walking on Sunshine," and when the song ended, our hands stayed on each other's bodies.

Tonight, his eyes were flinty, like he was looking for a reason to walk out. I wasn't about to let him escape. He needed an orgasm as much as I did. Dropping my bag onto the floor, I grasped his hand to pull him inside. I shut the door, locked it, and tossed my coat over the back of a dining chair. Then I stepped in front of him and rested my hands on his broad chest.

"This shirt is ridiculous. It's got to go."

"Shirt? Oh. Yeah. Barb wanted us to look festive."

"You look like Bartender Ken."

It was the wrong thing to say. His eyes narrowed. "I think—"

"Don't think." I ran my hands down his chest to the button of his jeans. "Just relax."

I unbuttoned his jeans and lowered the zipper, dragging my fingertip along the front of his boxers. They weren't the sporty kind but the regular kind with the extra fabric at the butt, cotton in a no-nonsense plaid pattern. He hardened under my touch, tenting the thin fabric. I lowered onto my knees on the rug and dragged his shorts down his legs, then ran my palms up his strong, hairy thighs.

"Oh, uh, you don't have to—"

I licked him from root to tip. Instead of finishing that

sentence, he groaned. Yes, he needed this as much as I did. Briefly, I wondered why before I refocused on my task.

His dick was gorgeous. Veiny like his forearms with a slight upward curve that felt amazing inside me. He was uncut, and the foreskin had already pulled back to reveal the glossy pink head. He was longer than I could comfortably fit in my mouth, so I licked my hand and squeezed the base of his dick while I teased the head with my tongue. I felt, more than saw, the tension leave his shoulders.

I sucked on the head and scratched my short nails down the back of his thigh, feeling the taut skin over his hamstring muscle. Maybe his manual-labor muscles were the secret to the amazing sex. I'd have to remember that the next time I was tempted to hook up with one of the white-collar guys I usually went for.

His muscles tightened, and I sucked harder.

"Lucie, I—"

I dipped my tongue into the divot under the head, and his dick jerked. He let out a shuddering breath as his release filled my mouth. I held on until he finished, then swallowed.

Gently, he touched my hair, then my cheek. "Sorry. I tried to warn you."

"It's fine. As long as you'll be ready to go again in a bit?"

"I can go again right now." He bent and, putting his callused hands under my elbows, lifted me to standing. He dropped to his knees, not bothering to kick off his jeans, and ducked his head under my skirt. "You should wear more skirts. It makes it easier to...oh."

"Oh? Oh my god." I'd forgotten about my shapewear. I'd let Carly, who was a stylist, talk me into it. She'd promised it'd create a better line when I wore dresses. But fuck me if it didn't make me look like a sausage. "Just a sec. I'll roll it down."

"Nuh-uh." His finger traced a line between my legs, and I

shivered even before I felt cool air on my wet skin. "This thing has a fly, like boxers. So you can whip it out?"

His teasing words matched his teasing fingers. I sucked in a breath. "In theory. I tried it once. It was a total failure. Had to go commando the rest of the day. Now I roll them down and wrestle back into them when I'm done. If you'll give me a minute—"

"No need." A gust of hot breath was all the warning I had before his tongue hit my labia.

"Oh god."

He pushed through the gusset with his tongue and lips and a scrape of teeth. I grabbed the back of a dining chair to keep myself upright as pleasure rocketed up my spine.

Yesssss.

I forgot about the spandex holding my belly in and lost myself in the sensation of his sexy lips and talented tongue worshiping me where I stood. Unlike most guys I slept with, he didn't seem to be in a hurry. Instead of shoving a finger into me or going straight for my clit to try to speed things along, he used his thumbs to spread me, feasting on my center. I forgot all about my shit evening, my dad, and my career failures as my world filled with Danny's touch. Pleasure coiled in my belly. My vision grayed at the edges, and my knees shook.

I gripped the chair harder. "More."

I didn't have to say another word. He grabbed my ass with one of his powerful hands and licked up to my clit. One touch of his tongue rocketed me to the roof. And when he closed his lips around it and gently sucked, I soared, squealing, straight on into the stars beyond.

When I opened my eyes, he still kneeled before me. He'd come out from under my skirt and was studying me, a glistening, satisfied smile on his face.

I tapped his shoulder. "Don't look so smug. I was halfway there from the blowjob I gave you."

He smiled even broader. "Sucking me off turned you on?"

I smoothed my skirt. "I'm not going to apologize for being a sexual person who gets turned on both giving and receiving."

"I love that about you."

"Want some water?" I moved toward the kitchen to hide my trembling lips that didn't know whether to smile or cry. It had been a weird night.

"Please."

I filled two glasses from the pitcher in my fridge. When I turned, he'd set his sneakers by the door, his jeans and the ridiculous tee folded on top. He looked relaxed, like it was normal to stand around your neighbor's apartment wearing nothing but a shit-eating grin.

I handed him his glass and waved at his erection. "Holy refractory period. Looks like you're ready for more."

He shrugged. "I also get turned on by giving." He tipped back his head and chugged the water. I sipped mine, pretending not to ogle his throat as it worked. Or his beautiful cock.

He set the glass on the counter. "Want to go again?"

This time, there was no sad bow of his lips, only a nonchalant half-smile despite the heat sparking in his brown eyes. Lust? I could work with that.

"Uh-huh." Grabbing his hand, I carried my water into my bedroom and set it on the coaster on the nightstand. I started to unbutton my dress, but he laid a hand over mine.

"Let me."

"It'll be faster if I—"

"Let me," he repeated.

I rolled my eyes. "Fine."

Smirking, he pushed the button through the hole, then slid his fingers down my chest to the next button. He went slowly and steadily, dragging his fingertips down my front as he went. A tiny line formed between his eyebrows. Like he wasn't thinking about anything else but me.

God, that was hot.

By the time he'd unbuttoned the dress enough that it slipped off my shoulders to the floor, my shapewear was soaked. Vaguely, I wondered if Woolite could save it, but Danny distracted me with a kiss to the valley between my breasts.

"That dress and this bra wrecked me tonight," he muttered as he reached behind me and unfastened the clasps.

I smirked. My big boobs were a pain at work, where they reminded everyone I wasn't one of the guys, but tonight I was grateful they'd reeled in some stress relief. "Glad you liked it."

When my bra joined my dress on the floor, Danny held up my breasts—they fit into his long fingers perfectly—and kissed along the side of my right boob to the tip, which he licked and sucked to a needy peak. He pinched it with his fingers, then kissed along the midline to my left breast and repeated the action.

I rubbed my thighs together, chasing the tingling sensation. "Dan—" Oh god, that had come out as a whine. I cleared my throat. "Danny," I said firmly, "I'm ready."

He nipped my nipple, making me gasp. "But I'm not."

Two could play the teasing game. Reaching between us, I gripped his hard length. "I disagree."

He chuckled. "Physically ready and mentally ready are different. I wanna see if you can come from this." He closed his lips around my nipple and did something I would've told you a second before was physically impossible. He somehow sucked and licked at the same time, while he plucked my other nipple harder.

Wires crossed in my brain, and my sex throbbed. He did it again, and fireworks burst behind my squeezed-shut eyelids as I

made an unintelligible sound. He lapped at my breast and
gentled his touch as aftershocks squeezed my abdomen. "God.
Damn. You're going to have to give me a minute." I flopped onto
my bed.

"Take your time."

I felt another aftershock as he rolled the tight undergarment
off my hips. The covers shifted under me, then the mattress
dipped as he scooted toward me and tucked my back against his
front, his erection hard against my tailbone. He pulled up the
covers, protecting us from the chilly night air. In my lust, I'd
forgotten to turn up the heat.

My body warmed as his hand stroked from my breasts
over my belly, then down my thigh. He reversed direction, his
fingers running up the inside of my thigh, then coming to
rest between my legs, where he petted my clit. I sighed and
stretched my leg over his, opening to his touch. His skillful
fingers danced over me, reminding me of the way he
polished glasses at the bar, his movements gentle but
assured.

When my thighs trembled, I said, "Condoms are in the
bowl."

His fingers stilled, and he let out a short sigh. "I know."

He kissed the spot between my neck and shoulder as he
reached over me and pulled a condom from the bowl. He rolled
away for a moment, then back, his latex-covered cock slipping
between my legs. "This okay?"

"Yeah." I rested my leg on top of his, and he gripped it as he
pushed inside me. I felt a stretch, then delicious friction as I
ground into his lap.

He squeezed my hip. "Wait a sec."

I stilled. "You okay?"

"I don't want to go off too soon."

I laid my hand over his and took a slow breath. "Okay."

He mirrored my breath, then he moved our hands to the center of my chest, over my racing heartbeat.

"What do you think about when you're trying to slow down?" I asked.

"Dunno. Work. Sometimes I think up new drinks."

"What would be in a 'Hookup with My Upstairs Neighbor'?"

"Hmm." He nuzzled my neck. "Something strong as the base. Whiskey, then something spicy and sweet. I'd make a jalapeño and passionfruit syrup and serve it with a cherry garnish."

"Why a cherry?"

"I like spicy and sweet together. And because of how you can tie the stem in a knot with your tongue."

I craned my neck to see his face, but it twinged. "Ow. Shift."

He pulled out, and I rolled over to face him, straddling his leg. "How did you know I can tie a cherry stem with my tongue? I haven't done that since my twenties. Not even on Thanksgiving night, when you had to carry me out of the bar."

"Just a feeling." He grinned. "Not only is your tongue extremely talented, but it seems like the sort of thing teenage Lucie would've practiced until she mastered it."

"Ugh." I buried my face in his chest. He smelled faintly of beer and the sweet bite of whiskey. "Two whole jars of them one weekend when my parents were away at some writers' conference. I'd met a girl who did it as a party trick."

He chuckled. "There's that competitive streak."

"That was a lucky guess. I'm not that obvious."

"Only to someone who pays attention. Here." He guided me to straddle him. "Like this." I sank onto his cock. We both sighed when our hips met.

I rocked forward, and he grunted. "Good?" I asked.

"Very." He licked his thumb, set it on my clit, and rubbed gentle circles over it. "You good?"

I clenched my muscles around him. "Very."

I set the pace, starting with a slow, comfortable rocking motion. As sensation spiraled through me from the combination of his hand on my clit and his dick lighting me up inside, I rose and fell over him. He held my hips as his legs trembled under me and let me take the lead.

Most guys I slept with seemed to feel that it was their duty to direct things in bed. I liked that Danny wasn't like that. He'd let me take charge if that's what I wanted. Even if I wasn't in the mood to lead, he checked in to ensure I was enjoying myself as much as he was.

Tonight, as I ogled his muscular chest and abs, as I admired those pretty lips, parted in a soft smile, as I sought pleasure to erase the pain of inadequacy I'd felt at that terrible banquet, I enjoyed myself immensely.

Danny's thumb grew more insistent, and my body responded. Tingles rocketed through me until I hummed like the office printer before it shot out a toasty-warm page. My release hit in a wave of heat that forced a choking cry from me. Danny thrust up under me, then stilled.

Shaking, I lowered myself across his chest and nestled my nose into his neck. God, he smelled good.

"Wow," I said.

"Uh-huh."

Wetness dribbled down the inside of my thigh. "Huh. I think I might've squirted a little. I thought that only happened in porn."

He huffed out a laugh. "Lucie."

"What?" I propped my chin on his chest. "Am I not allowed to say *porn?* Or admit that I watch it?"

"No, no." He swiped a sweaty tendril of my hair off my forehead and tucked it behind my ear. "Your lack of filter. It's refreshing. A lot of women—"

"You mean the ones your mother introduces you to at

church?" He blinked, so I said, "I've heard Leo asking you about your dates with the 'church girls.'"

He nudged my hips, and I lifted off him. "I'd rather not talk about other women while I'm still inside you. All I'm saying is that a lot of them aren't as frank as you. I like knowing what you're thinking."

I stopped myself from kissing his chest. Hookups didn't do tender things like that. "Mind if I go first in the bathroom? I'm sticky."

"Go ahead."

I cleaned myself up and brushed my teeth, then I put on the robe that hung on the back of my bathroom door. When I emerged, Danny was on the edge of the bed, still naked, elbows on his knees and his hands clasped. His normally olive complexion was white.

"You okay?" I asked.

"I...I don't know. The condom. It broke."

Guess I hadn't squirted after all. "Shit. I didn't think they were expired."

"I checked. They're not. Just a fluke. I got tested at my physical a few months ago. No STIs. And I haven't been with anyone since—except you."

Really? A hot guy like him? "Same. All clear at my physical last month. Wait... It wasn't last month. It was before Christmas..." I ran a calculation in my head. *Shit!* I was overdue for my quarterly shot. I'd missed it to cover a story in LA. "There's a chance my birth control isn't current."

"Want me to run out for Plan B?"

A wave of exhaustion hit me. After a full day at work, the banquet, and two orgasms, all I wanted to do was sleep, not drag myself to the pharmacy—because no way would I let Danny do it for me—and endure whatever side effects I'd experience. As long as I took it within a couple of days, I'd be fine. I shook my head. "Tonight? It's almost two. I'll get it on my lunch break tomorrow."

"You sure you don't want me to go with you?" The shallow crevice was back between his eyebrows.

"No, I'll take care of it. There's a pharmacy around the corner from my office. Speaking of which…" I yawned.

"Right." When he unclasped his hands, they trembled.

I didn't know if it was the post-orgasm hormones or a wave of sympathy for his broken-condom freak-out that made me say, "Why don't you stay?"

"You wouldn't mind?" His brown eyes turned up like a puppy hoping to be allowed on the couch.

"It's late. Lie down." I circled to the other side of the bed, shrugged out of my robe, and slipped under the covers.

After switching off the lamp, he rolled to my side of the bed and tucked me against his chest. "This okay?"

"Yeah, but I usually have trouble sleeping. I might toss and turn for a bit."

"Toss away. I don't mind."

My heavy eyelids closed. The orgasms had done their work — that or his warm breath on the back of my neck. I drifted off into a dreamless sleep.

4
———

JUST ANOTHER HOOKUP

<u>*Blue Hawaiian*</u>
Mix 1 part coconut rum, 1 part blue curaçao, and 2 parts pineapple juice. Shake and pour over ice.

DANNY

I dreamed about Malibu rum. Specifically, I was behind the bar at the White House, making a thousand Blue Hawaiians for a state dinner the female President was hosting for all the female heads of state. I dropped a curl of shaved coconut into a nonalcoholic drink for the Pakistani prime minister when my eyes opened with the smell of coconuts still in my nostrils.

Rumpled sheets and a pillow with a head-sized dent in it met my bleary gaze. I grabbed the pillow and buried my face in it, taking a whiff of Lucie's coconut hair products.

"Hey." It was still dark outside the blinds, but Lucie was dressed in black slacks and a black sweater. "Want a cup of coffee before you go?"

That was Lucie. No "good morning," no "how'd you sleep,"

no "wanna get a drink later," just *get out of my place so I can go to work*. It was fair. She'd surprised me by letting me sleep over.

I sat up. "Want me to make it?"

"No, I've already started a pot. Here's your shirt. Good thing you don't have to go far in it." She tossed the pink T-shirt on the bed next to my boxers and jeans, then walked out of the bedroom.

I had to remind my twinging heart that this had been another hookup, nothing more. I'd gone into this fully aware that *more* was never an option with Lucie. I swung my legs over the side of the bed and slipped on my boxers.

My eyes fell on the wastebasket with the tissue I'd balled up around the condom, and my stomach clenched. I pulled on my jeans and tugged my shirt over my head. "You sure you don't want me to run out for that emergency contraception?" I called. "I can leave it in a bag on your doorknob."

"No, thanks." She came in with two cups of coffee. Hers was already in a travel mug. "I've got it."

"You sure? I bet you've got a busy day at work, and I don't start my shift until four."

"Danny." Her lips were a flat line. "I don't need your help. I'm fully capable of taking care of my body. Go find some little old lady or a child to help. Or, better yet, go live your best life. Don't worry about me."

"I was—"

"Taking care of everyone else instead of yourself. I don't want that. I get plenty of that from my mom. Here's your coffee." She handed me the mug. "You can leave the cup outside my door later."

I set it on her bedside table, toed into my sneakers, and stuffed my socks into my pocket. "I don't need coffee." I had a bitter taste in my mouth.

"Fine. See you later, Danny."

"See you." I strode out of her bedroom and past the spot inside the door where she'd blown me like she cared last night. I closed her door gently but took out my disappointment on the stairs, stomping down to the second floor. After I stepped inside my apartment, I leaned on the door. Why did I do this to myself? Why had I gotten my hopes up? Lucie Knox was way out of my league.

Besides, it was a terrible time for me to date. I needed to focus on getting my finances together to buy the bar and get it running smoothly. Then I'd find some nice woman to settle down with and try to forget all about Lucie.

5

UNENCUMBERED

My legacy is the children who have discovered the magic of books through our foundation. Education is the key to unlocking a child's potential. Fostering a love of reading is one step on that journey. Literacy empowers people, and that's the difference I hope to be remembered for.
Audrey Jones Hayes, Founder of Jasper Jones Literacy Foundation

LUCIE

*B*eing able to walk to work was one of the best things about my apartment. Yesterday's clouds had cleared, the sun peered weakly around the city's skyscrapers, and I was full of energy after a solid seven hours of sleep. It had been decadent falling asleep exhausted from good sex with Danny's arm warming me like a quilt.

Though I hadn't loved the way he'd stomped out of my apartment. I'd only intended to decline his help, but I'd veered too far into brutal honesty by practically calling him a doormat. As my friend Savannah had gently pointed out last week, not everyone wants to hear an honest critique of their life choices.

When I stopped in front of the newspaper building, the ache between my legs reminded me I'd forgotten to stop at the drugstore. I glanced at my phone. Two minutes until the morning meeting. If I walked in late, Mario might give me the sucky story out of spite. I'd go to the drugstore on my way home.

I put my hand on the brass door handle and tugged. I decided to skip the stop at my desk and instead, breezed into the meeting. It hadn't started, but Tad was there, of course, sitting in the prized seat to Mario's right and muttering something to our boss.

"Good morning." I set my bag on the seat to Mario's left.

"Aren't you chipper this morning?" Howard grinned at me with coffee-stained teeth as he set down his mug next to Tad, sloshing a few drops onto the conference table.

"Just full of vitamin D." I grinned back.

He glanced at the pale sun outside the window. "Wait, do you mean—"

"Okay," Mario cut in, "let's get started. City Council meeting today. Who wants it?"

There was silence around the table. "New guy." He pointed at the intern, who'd slunk in. "You're on it. Howard—"

"Still working that piece on the legal situation at Moo-Lah," Howard said.

I glanced at him. How long would he drag that story out? People in San Francisco were used to the ups and downs at tech companies. And Moo-Lah had been around long enough that they'd weather the latest scandal. Did he think he could make a series out of it?

"Okay. We've got the divorce of the founder of ClickClackGo, and this immigration thing to cover," Mario said.

Shit. I usually listened to the news on my walk to work, but I'd been too busy replaying my night with Danny. Apparently,

Tad had missed the story too because he repeated, "Immigration thing?"

"Somebody dumped a planeload of migrants in Sacramento."

My eyes widened. That was a story I could run with. Who'd authorized moving them? Who'd paid for it? Who owned the plane? Would charges be filed? And what would happen to the migrants? How big could the story get?

Tad had his mouth open, but I said, "I'll do it."

"Wait a sec," Tad said. "Celebrity divorce is your beat."

"No, it's not. Why would you say that?"

"It's human interest. Everyone knows you're the best at that." He smirked like he'd made an unassailable point.

"Every story is human interest," I said. "Especially a migrant story."

"You'll turn it into a political statement," Tad said.

I flattened my lips. "I'll run it by the editorial board to ensure it aligns with the paper's editorial values. Would you?"

"Just the facts, ma'am." He looked at Mario.

Ugh. Just the facts, to Tad, meant digging up some petty crime that one of the migrants had committed and portraying them all as a danger to white middle-class society. At least I'd treat these people as humans and not criminals. "A reporter's going to have to go to Sacramento to cover it," I said. "Isn't your wife due any day, Tad?"

He scowled at me. "She is."

Ah, the advantages of being unencumbered by family responsibilities. It was how I'd landed that story on human trafficking years ago. A reporter's kid had gotten sick, and I'd stepped in to cover for her. "Then I'm the best option to write the story. I'm ready to go right now." I stared at Mario.

He glanced at Tad, then back at me. "Tad, you're on the divorce. The migrant story is yours, Lucie. But keep expenses down. I'm not paying for booze, and the word 'suite' better not be anywhere on the hotel bill."

"Got it, boss." I saluted. "See you guys next week." I hadn't unpacked my bag, so I slung it over my shoulder and waved as I walked out. After a quick stop at our admin's desk, I had a flight booked that allowed me enough time to go home and pack before jumping on the train to the airport. Alicia Keys' "Girl on Fire" was the soundtrack on my speed-walk back to my place. I was unstoppable, and I was going to kick ass on my story.

6

SAYING THE QUIET PART OUT LOUD

I hope people remember that I ensured everyone in this state plays by the rules and that I blocked those who would try to exploit vulnerable people for political gain. If they say I left the system a little fairer than I found it, that's enough for me.
Jane Coffey, State Attorney General

LUCIE

*L*ate again, I scanned the restaurant for my friends. Tessa's distinctive red hair was easy to spot, sparkling copper in the March sunlight near the window. I clutched my satchel and traipsed to the table.

"Lucie, there you are." Savannah leaped up to hug me. "I haven't seen you in forever."

I hugged her back. "I've been busy."

"I saw your story in this morning's paper." Tessa patted my shoulder. "Nice work."

I grinned. "Thanks." Sacramento had been worth the trip. Not only had the immigrants' story turned into a piece I was proud of, but the migrants were getting their temporary work visas expedited and had found sponsors to help them settle into their new homes. And the state attorney general had launched an investigation into whether the right-wing organization who'd flown them from El Paso to Sacramento would be charged with kidnapping. *Take that, Tad.* But he'd been on flipping paternity leave, so he'd missed my big-dick-energy at the office.

Carly kissed my cheek. "Sit down. Have a mimosa. You look tired."

"Good tired, though. While I was in Sacramento, the attorney general agreed to let me interview her for my book. After I turned in my story, I did some work on it." I'd ridden that wave of energy from my one excellent night of sleep as far as it would go. I was ready to crash. Though some time with my besties might give me a boost.

"That's fabulous," Savannah said. "I'm so proud of you, and I can't wait to read your book."

"Thanks." I ignored the gnawing sensation in my stomach. I had months before my deadline in November. I'd finish it on time.

Tessa handed me a mimosa. "You look like you could use this."

"I don't look that bad, do I?" I glanced at the window, but my reflection was too ghostly to see properly.

"You're a little pale," Savannah said. "And you've got shadows under your eyes."

I smirked. "Maybe I need a product recommendation, Carly."

"I know just the thing. It's got vitamin C, and it'll perk up your skin like you wouldn't believe. I've got a sample at home."

As Carly extolled the virtues of the cosmetic, I sipped the mimosa. It tasted funny, too acidic. Had the orange juice gone bad? Tessa sipped hers like nothing was wrong, but I set mine down and chugged my water instead.

"Your sales pitch would be more convincing," I interrupted testily, "if we didn't know your glowing skin comes from getting good dick on the regular."

A throat cleared behind me. "Good morning…ladies. Are you ready to order?"

Of course we weren't, so we sent the server away. Savannah hid her red face behind her menu. "Lucie, have you ever considered *not* saying exactly what's on your mind?" she mumbled.

"What's the point? No one looks twice at a man who's direct. If I hid behind nice words, I'd be stuck at the Features desk covering who wore what." I winced. "Shit. Not that that isn't important, Carly."

She waved a hand. "It's not as important as a planeload of kidnapped people. Besides, I do think my skin looks better these days." She whipped out a small mirror to admire her flushed cheeks.

"Are things still going well with Andrew?" Tessa asked.

"We're figuring it out. Like the other day, we were walking along the Embarcadero, and I mentioned the old freeway, then I realized he was born after the '89 quake."

"No!" Savannah said. "Even I remember that, and I lived in Georgia. I was watching the World Series with my dad."

"What about you, Lucie?" Tessa asked. "You're thirty-nine, so you would've been little. What do you remember?"

"Nothing at all." Our house came through fine, and it was just one more memory of my mom sheltering me during a quake. "What about you, Tessa?"

"I was still living out in the Sierra Buttes."

"Why were you—"

She shook her head, and I let it drop. Tessa was the mysterious one. I had a feeling there were layers upon layers of history to unearth, like the archaeological site at Troy. But it was up to her to reveal it to us.

The server returned, and we chose our meals. After the server walked away, I leaned toward Savannah. "How are things with you? Are you okay?"

Her smile was lower wattage than usual. "I'm okay. I started temping to get more recent work experience. But it's boring, you know? I've been stress baking every night. In fact, I've got bags of treats for you all in my car."

I lowered my voice. "Is it only the job that's got you stress baking?"

Her smile wobbled. "I...I moved into the guest bedroom last month," she whispered.

Carly reached across the table and gripped her hand. "I'm so sorry."

"It's okay." When Savannah shook her head, her hair hardly moved. "We're going to go to counseling."

"You think it'll help?" Tessa asked.

"I don't know." Savannah looked down at her lap. "I need him to understand that I want something different now the kids are out of the house."

"Like mutual respect?" I'd never met the guy, but from what Savannah said, he was a dismissive asshole. "Oops, did I say that out loud?"

"And we've come full circle," Carly said, "with Lucie saying the quiet part out loud."

"Hey, it's why you love me. If I hadn't said something at that god-awful seminar, we might all be Stepford Wives, worshiping some jerkoff instead of becoming fabulous goddesses."

"It's true," Savannah said. "We do love you for it."

"Mostly," Carly muttered.

When our food arrived, I dug into my giant waffle. "Mm. I can't get enough carbs these days."

"Really? What's going on?" Tessa asked.

"Do I need a reason?" I mumbled through a mouthful of crispy, sweet waffle. "I'm tired. Not sleeping again."

Savannah frowned. "It's too early for you to be going through menopause, but maybe you've got something hormonal going on."

I rolled my eyes. "Thanks, Mom. I've been successfully *not* sleeping for the past fifteen years. It's nothing new. I'm pretty sure it's because I've been writing like a fiend into the wee hours. And when I get tired, I eat instead of sleep."

"Still," she said, "you should go to the doctor."

Doctor? Shit.

With the story in Sacramento, I'd completely forgotten about that emergency contraception. And now it was too late. Thankfully, my boobs ached, a clear sign I was about to get my period. Defiantly, I stuffed another bite of waffle in my mouth and shook my head.

"You're just like my daughter," Savannah said. "Stubborn as a mule. She's dating this guy, and when she asked what I thought about him, all I said was that he seemed a little...excitable. And now they're inseparable."

"Stubborn and"—I pointed my fork at her—"excitable got me where I am in my career. So I'll eat all the carbs I want, especially when I'm premenstrual."

"You poor woman," Tessa said. "Have my toast too." She handed me the small plate. "Need a Midol?"

"No, it's probably a day or two away. No cramps yet."

"Maybe it's low iron making you pale. Who's got red meat?" Tessa looked around the table. "Savannah, fork over that sausage."

"I'm fine," I said. "Really." But Savannah shoved the sausage link in my face, speared on her fork. "Thanks. And maybe I do need sausage...but the other kind. A good dicking would help me sleep."

A throat cleared again, and I didn't have to look to see that our server had snuck up on us again. "Can I get you all anything else?"

I grimaced at her. "Do you have a hot male friend looking for some no-strings-attached sex?"

Her eyes widened. "S-sorry, not that I can think of."

"Then we're good, thanks."

A balled-up napkin hit me in the face. "Lucie!" Savannah hissed. "Behave."

I wiped a drop of syrup from the corner of my mouth. "Carly, are you going to eat your last pancake? Trade you my cantaloupe for it."

Carly was such a good friend that she traded her pancake for the cantaloupe, even though it smelled off. Strange that my senses of taste and smell had gone funny. Maybe I should visit the doctor like Savannah said.

I'd make time for it. Next week.

7

———

GOOD BONES

<u>Bicicletta</u>

Combine 3 ounces pinot grigio and 2 ounces Campari in a glass. Fill three-quarters with ice, top with chilled club soda, and stir. Garnish with 2 orange wheels.

DANNY

I'd come straight from Mass, but my mom's place was already full of people when I arrived, toting a case of Italian pinot grigio to celebrate the visible signs of spring.

As soon as I set foot on the front walk, cousins clapped me on the back, aunts kissed me, then dragged their thumbs across my cheek to wipe away the lipstick, and small second cousins tackled my legs. I climbed the stairs onto the porch with one, Emma, clinging to my khakis.

Inside the front door, Leo detached the little one and hoisted her onto his hip. "Yo, Nico," he called, "come get this booze."

At the word *booze,* Nico and three other cousins came running. They took the heavy carton from me and carried it to the dining room. I held out my arms for Emma, and Leo handed her over, smelling of anise candy. She smacked my cheek with a sticky kiss.

"There you are," my mother said, bustling up to me and standing on her tiptoes to kiss my cheek. She patted Emma's dark, wispy curls before combing her fingers through my hair. "Come on. I have someone I want you to meet."

"You what?" I shook out my hair. "Ma, we talked about this last Sunday. I'm focused on the bar right now. Leo and I both are."

My brother stared at his loafers. "I'm getting a drink. Want something?"

"Beer," I said.

My mother lifted Emma from my arms and set her on the floor. "There's anginetti in the kitchen," she whispered. Emma beelined to the kitchen.

My mother straightened and narrowed her eyes at me. "Danny, I've known you since you were in my womb. You want a family. And the clock is ticking."

"Ticking?" My voice went squeaky. "I'm only twenty-nine."

"I had three children by the time I was thirty. And the twins when I was thirty-two."

I gulped. "I—I'm not ready for that."

"Come on. There's no harm in meeting a nice young lady. You don't have to propose today, not like your father did with me."

"Is it warm in here? Can I open a window?" I was tempted to pop another button at my collar, but that might send the wrong message to whoever Ma wanted me to meet.

She stepped closer. "I'm telling you, you don't have to do things the way your father and I did. But if you limit yourself to hookups, you'll never meet Ms. Right."

How the hell did my mother know about my hookups? I ran a hand over my face. It was pointless to guess which of my siblings had ratted me out. "It's not like I do it all the time," I muttered. I hadn't hooked up with anyone since Lucie a month ago.

My mother grabbed my hand and held it. "You've always been a caretaker to your younger brothers and sisters. There's an empty place in your heart, and it's waiting for a wife and family of your own."

She wasn't wrong, but... "I've got to buy the bar first. You know every penny I earn is going into my savings account for it."

"You can buy the bar *and* date someone. Anyone who's worth pursuing will go through the lean times with you. It's all about partnership."

"The only partner I want right now is Leo. Once we own the bar, we'll make it a place that ensures anyone in the family can have a good job."

"You're a good boy." She patted my cheek. "Everyone appreciates what you did for Nico, but you're still going to meet Carmela."

"Of course I am," I muttered as she dragged me toward the back porch, where a pretty woman bent over my mother's potted lemon tree. She looked up and smiled when we stepped onto the concrete slab. Her dark hair had waves in it that sparkled in the sunlight, and her eyes were startlingly blue. A gold cross glittered at the hollow between her collarbones.

"Carmela, look who I found! This is my son, Danny." My mother shoved me at Carmela and ducked back inside the house. The screen door slammed shut.

"Classic Carrie Carbone move." I pointed with my thumb at the screen door. "One of her favorite mantras is 'a watched pot never boils.' Nice to meet you."

"We're the simmering pot?" Carmela raised her eyebrows.

"That's what she's hoping." I shook her hand. It was soft in mine.

"Carrie's told me so much about you."

I chuckled. "Don't believe half of it. I'm sure she's made me out to be some kind of saint. But I'm actually a bartender."

"At Barb's Bar? Carrie told me you're planning to take it over. I've never been inside. I'm not much of a drinker, but it looks like a nice place."

"It is. The bar could use some updates, but we've got a healthy crowd of regulars. It's got good bones."

She let her gaze trail over me, from my rust gingham button-down to the polished toes of my brown chukkas. I could see the echo of "good bones" in her appraisal. Lucie would've said it out loud, then jumped them.

I wiped Lucie from my brain. "What do you do, Carmela?"

"I'm a teacher. Second grade."

"You must love kids." No wonder Ma had shoved us together.

"I do. What about you?"

"Yeah." I gazed at the swing set in the backyard. My siblings and I had used it practically every day. Now my young cousins kicked high into the sky. Little Emma climbed the ladder to the slide under the watchful eye of her father.

I let myself imagine pushing a little girl with Carmela's raven hair and blue eyes on the swing while Carmela stood at the bottom of the slide, beckoning a little boy with my long nose to let go and slide down. But it dissolved, and it was just Lucie and me. I was pushing her on the swing, her sable curls flying as she pointed her black combat boots toward the clouds.

I was being ridiculous. Lucie would never come to my mother's house. She wanted exactly one thing from me: my dick. Two things if you counted being served her favorite drink. I needed a nice woman like Carmela to settle down with.

I should've been attracted to her. So, why wasn't I? While I was focused on the bar, I was no good to anyone. Once Leo and I had the deed in our hands, I'd have something to offer a partner. I'd be able to feel something, then I'd let Ma set me up.

I rubbed the back of my neck. "I've got to find my brother. You should grab a plate in the kitchen before my uncles pick it clean. Be sure you try my mother's braciole."

Disappointment tightened Carmela's mouth. "Sure. It was nice meeting you, Danny. Best of luck with the bar. I hope you find what you're looking for."

"Thanks." I slunk back through the door and, avoiding the kitchen where I knew my mother would smack me for ruining her setup, followed the sound of Leo's laugh to the living room, where he stood with Uncle Gio. They both held empty grappa glasses, and the tip of my uncle's nose was red.

"Danny, Danny, Danny. C'mere. Here's your beer," my brother said, holding out a bottle. "Oh, wait, I drank it. I'll get you another one." His unfocused eyes panned over the living room like he'd find a cooler of beers in there.

I slung an arm around his shoulders to steady him. "Don't worry about it. I'm good." I gripped Uncle Gio's shoulder. "How's it going, Zio?"

"Good, good, Danny. I was telling Leo about a space that came available in my neighborhood."

"Space?" I repeated.

Leo put his finger over his lips. "Shh, Zio. We aren't telling Danny, remember?"

"We aren't telling Danny what?" I asked.

"About the kitchen space next to my dry cleaner's," Gio said. "It's only got a couple of tables out front, but the kitchen is—" He kissed his fingertips.

I wrinkled my brow. "Why do we care about a kitchen?"

"For Leo's catering business!"

My brother smacked his hand over his eyes. "Gio—"

"No, no." Gently, I wrestled the glass from my uncle's hand.

"Leo's selling his food truck and buying a bar. With me. Not a kitchen. Isn't that right, Leo?"

"That's the plan." He upended his glass into his mouth, catching the last drops. "I'll get you some water, Uncle Gio." He trudged toward the kitchen.

Gio weaved on his feet. "I could've sworn Leo said he wanted to look at the space."

"I'm sure he was only being polite." I flung my arm around him in a half-hug.

"Or maybe"—his red-rimmed eyes went sharp—"he was only being polite to *you*."

No. Leo and I had talked about buying the bar from practically the day I'd started working there. It was what we both wanted. "I love you, Gio, but you're drunk."

"Maybe I am," he said, "but your brother's never going to be happy running a bar."

It's literally all we've talked about since Barb mentioned retiring five years ago, I didn't say. In my family, you didn't argue with your elders even when they'd had too much grappa and were spouting nonsense.

I wished there were a way for Leo to keep his food truck, but I'd run the numbers a hundred times, and we came up short every time. He had to sell it if we were going to have the money before Barb went on her world cruise in November.

"He'll be happy if we're running it together," I insisted because I believed that. I had to.

8

BETTER THAN A VIBRATOR

I built this place on sweat and bullheadedness. My legacy is the work ethic I instilled in my staff along with the idea that hard work can create something truly great. If our guests have fond memories of their excellent dining experiences here, well, that's all the legacy I need.

Olivia Stein, restaurateur

LUCIE

I dreamed I was asleep. A funny dream, I know. I was aware I was dreaming as I snuggled into a cozy bed with sheets as soft as an old T-shirt and a nest of pillows that felt like a cloud. It definitely wasn't my bed. I was too busy working to buy luxurious bedding. In real life, I had exactly one set of sheets and two pillows, and they were just okay. Nothing like the magnificent bed of my dream.

Dream? Shit!

I startled awake and wiped the drool from my chin with the hand it rested on.

"Hello? Hello?" The tinny words came from my phone's speaker. Thank god I hadn't set this up as a video interview.

"I'm here. Sorry, lost the connection for a second."

"Funny because it sounded like snoring," the city councilwoman said.

I winced as guilt slashed through my stomach. "How strange. I think I caught everything you said though." The recording indicator was still on, so I'd be able to play back the part I missed. I glanced at my bedroom door. If only I slept as well in there. Maybe the dream was my subconscious telling me it was time to upgrade my mattress.

"Good, because the education of our city's children is the most important thing we can do for our future. Don't you agree?"

"Uh, yes." Intellectually, I agreed. Personally? I glanced at the brochure for the fertility clinic I'd picked up months ago, a few days before I'd gotten my book deal. It was shoved under two women's biographies and my most recently filled notebook. I promised to look at it again after I turned in my book. Maybe then I'd be ready to have a kid.

It had never been the right time to have a baby. Certainly not when I was in college and my hookup had begged to put in "just the tip," then came inside me. After that, I'd been so busy trying to be one of the guys at work that it had never made it to my list of priorities. But with forty staring me in the face, I knew my time was running out.

If only I were sure I'd be a good mother. I'd never be like my mother, willing to drop everything for my dad and me. If that meant I'd be bad at it, I shouldn't go back to that fertility clinic.

Like I'd said it out loud, the councilwoman asked, "Are you sure you're the right person to write this story? Should I be talking to your editor instead?"

My face went hot. "No, I'm a senior reporter. And I have what

I need to write the piece. I'll email you with anything I need to confirm or clarify."

"All right..."

"Thank you, Councilwoman. I'll be in touch." I disconnected the call, then rested my forehead on my hand. I needed sleep. I was no good like this. Mario would fire me if he heard I'd fallen asleep during an interview.

I remembered a night I'd slept like a baby. That night I'd let Danny stay over.

I needed an orgasm. Then I'd drift off to sleep on a soporific cocktail of serotonin and oxytocin. Yet my battery-operated boyfriend hadn't helped last night. I mean, my self-administered orgasm had been perfectly adequate, but afterward I tossed and turned until practically three in the morning.

Maybe the magic had been Danny's solid chest at my back. They must sell a pillow like that online, right? Maybe a weighted blanket would feel like his arm, snug around me.

But even one-day shipping would take too long. I needed sleep *now*. Danny usually worked Tuesdays, which meant I could have a nice, greasy burger and a drink while I talked him into coming upstairs at the end of his shift. I'd invite him to stay all night. He'd seemed to like that idea last time.

Even with his puppy-dog eyes guilting me the next morning, he'd be better than a vibrator and a weighted blanket.

I walked into my bathroom to wipe away any traces of drool and apply some lipstick.

I met my gaze in the mirror. I'd get good sleep tonight. Then I'd kick ass at work tomorrow *and* stop neglecting my book.

9

———

SMOOTH MOVE

Negroni
Combine equal parts gin, Campari, and sweet vermouth with ice. Stir,
then strain into a rocks glass over ice. Garnish with an orange peel.

DANNY

*A*round six o'clock, a voice that set my teeth on edge rang out across the bar. "Aunt Barb!"

"Tad, what are you doing here?" She held out her arms, and he flipped up the pass-through to hug her.

I ground my teeth. He didn't belong behind the bar, but I couldn't say anything. He might be a smarmy asshole, but he was still my boss's nephew. He flashed me a shit-eating grin. What was he up to?

Releasing him, Barb said, "I thought my bar was too low-class for you."

"Did I say that?" His eyebrows went high.

"Only about a dozen times," I grumbled, plucking a glass from the rack I'd carried out from the back.

Fuck! Still hot from the dishwasher, it burned my fingertips. I bobbled it and almost dropped it.

"Smooth move, Ex-Lax," Tad crowed.

What the fuck did that mean? Probably some stupid-ass saying from the Stone Age. Regardless, I needed him out of my workspace. I tipped my head toward the other side of the bar. "What can I pour you?"

He sauntered back through the pass-through and bellied up to the bar. "Mojito."

Clenching my jaw, I grabbed a sprig of mint from the shelf where I hid it to discourage people from ordering fussy drinks. That trick didn't work on Tad. I shoved the mint into a glass and crushed it with the muddler.

"What's new, honey?" Barb rolled closer.

Tad leaned on the bar rail and told her about his kids. He had three: a five-year-old, a two-year-old, and a brand-new one who couldn't be more than a month old. What the fuck was he doing at a bar when his wife had to be exhausted at home? I smashed the mint.

Then he shifted into telling his aunt about work. I'll admit it, I eavesdropped. He worked with Lucie, whom I hadn't seen in a while. But he didn't mention her. Instead, he talked about the celebrity divorce he was covering. What a yawn. Lucie wrote about things that mattered. I wondered if Tad was jealous of the article she'd written about the migrants in Sacramento.

I peered into the glass and found I'd muddled the mint into an unrecognizable slurry. I dumped it into the trash and rinsed the glass. I grabbed another sprig and started again.

I set the drink in front of Tad as he said, "So, I was thinking, what if I took the bar off your hands when you retire?"

"Tad, we talked about this when I offered it to you last summer." Barb shot me an apologetic glance and shrugged.

"He's family." Looking back at Tad, she said, "You told me you didn't have the cash to buy me out."

"I'm sure I can beat whatever profit-sharing agreement he offered," Tad said.

I pushed out my chest. "It's a cash offer."

"Cash? Where the hell did you come up with six figures?"

"Hard work. Living cheap." I looked down as I wiped the bar to hide my smug smile. I may have won, but I couldn't act like a douche about it. Not in front of Barb.

His straw gurgled in his empty drink. "Another," he said.

I didn't mind making the next one as much.

An hour later, after I'd put Tad's drunk ass in a cab, I screwed the bottle pourer into a bottle of Bombay and turned back toward the bar only to find *her* there. Lucie. Sitting right in front of me. Wearing...lipstick?

I sucked in a breath. Was she some kind of apparition? Or one of those too-fast vampires from the movies I'd watched when I was in middle school?

"Hey, Danny," she said. Her eyelids drooped, and her skin looked pale. Was she drunk? Couldn't be. It wasn't eight yet, and she'd just gotten here. Was she sick?

"You okay?" I leaned my hands on the bar.

"Yeah." She chuckled. "Just tired. I, um... Could I have a burger and some red wine?"

"Sure." I took in the circles under her eyes as I reached into my back pocket for my order pad. Her gaze landed on the center of my black T-shirt and stuck there as I snagged the pencil tucked into my bun. "You want everything on that?"

"Everything on what?" she said.

"On your burger?"

She blinked her gaze to my face. "Right. No onions, please."

"You got it." I wrote, *HB 86 onions* on the ticket, clipped it to the old-fashioned order wheel in the pass-through, and twirled it to Norm in the kitchen. I grabbed a bottle of Lucie's favorite red and poured it into a glass, then set it in front of her.

She laid her hand on the foot of the glass and swirled it gently.

"You sure you're okay?" I asked.

"Yeah. I..." She cleared her throat. "I haven't been sleeping much lately."

I grunted. I already knew that. I'd heard her marching around again last night. I'd resisted the urge to go up and check on her. She didn't want me. She'd made that clear last month, the morning after Valentine's Day, when she'd booted me from her bed. Besides—I shoved a pint glass into the glass washer with more force than necessary—I couldn't afford to spend my energy mooning over her. My commitments to Barb and Leo were the most important things in my life.

I nodded at Frank, two stools over from Lucie, and pulled another IPA for him. I set his empty into the rack and carried it back to the dishwasher even though it wasn't full yet. Hefting the rack of clean glasses, I returned to the front and started replacing them on the shelves. When I glanced up, Lucie stared at me, her wine seemingly untouched.

"Don't like the wine?"

Blinking, she took a sip and grimaced. "It tastes weird. Is it a different kind?"

"No, it's your usual." I lifted the bottle, uncorked it, and took a sniff. Nothing smelled off. I splashed some into a lowball and sipped it. "Tastes fine to me, but want me to open a fresh bottle?"

"No. I'm sure it's me. A few things have tasted funny to me lately. Maybe I'm coming down with something."

Her pale cheeks and shadowed eyes said she was probably right.

"Order up!" Norm called.

I fetched her burger from the pass-through and placed it in

front of her, along with a bottle of ketchup and the salt and pepper shakers. Then I poured her a tall glass of water. Maybe she was dehydrated. She was probably too busy worrying about vulnerable people like kidnapped migrants and unhoused people to take care of herself like she should.

When I glanced back at her, her mouth was full, and her eyes were closed in satisfaction. She moaned happily, chewed, and swallowed. "Guess I was hungry."

"Did you eat lunch today?"

Shoving a fry into her mouth, she screwed up her face. "Maybe? I think I had a cup of yogurt at some point."

I growled deep in my throat. "You need to take better care of yourself."

Her tired eyes flashed. "I'm a grown-ass woman. I know how to take care of myself."

"Do you?" I stared at her a moment as she chewed angrily, then I headed toward the end of the bar to take care of a couple of new customers. By the time I'd finished shaking their margaritas and returned to check on Frank and Lucie, she'd polished off the burger and most of the fries. She'd drunk half the wine but hadn't touched the water.

Clenching my jaw to keep from reminding her to hydrate, I pulled another beer and set it in front of Frank. He held it up in a toast, then buried his nose in it.

"So, what are you doing tonight?" Lucie dragged a fry through the puddle of ketchup on her plate and popped it into her mouth.

"Me?" I looked around, but Leo was off tonight, and Barb had gone to the back to work on the books.

She snorted. "Yeah, you."

"Working. Is this a trick question?" The smartest person I knew, she was always about a mile in front of me. She'd gone to a fancy college and everything.

"I meant after work. Maybe you'd like to come up to my place?"

My lungs stopped working for a second. Every cell in my body fizzed with joy as I stared at her. But reality crashed back into me. She wanted another hookup, and I was done with that.

Three strides took me to the sink, where I plugged the drain, opened the hot water tap, and squirted dish soap into the sink. "Need a picture hung or something?" Better to give her an easy out, especially with Frank leaning in.

"No." She fluttered her eyelashes. "I've got something that needs pounding, but it's not a nail."

"Hmm?" I stuck my hand into the sink and fished around for something to wash.

"Y'know. My vagina."

Pain sliced into my thumb. "Shit!" I yanked my hand out of the water and grabbed a paper towel to wrap around the blood welling from my thumb.

"You okay?" She peered over the bar top at my hand.

"Yeah, I'm... Don't say shit like that while I'm washing knives."

"You were being deliberately obtuse. Look, I'm exhausted, and I can't sleep. I think I'd sleep better...you know, with a partner."

"I'll be your partner," Frank said, leering.

"Back off, Frank," I snarled.

Lucie rolled her eyes. "So, Danny, you in or what?"

"What? No." I squeezed the paper towel around my thumb.

"No?" Her plush lips curled like she was unfamiliar with the word.

"We want different things. It's not a good idea for us to"—I glanced at Frank—"do that." Again.

"You seemed to enjoy it last time, same as me." She lifted her eyebrows.

"I..." I peered at the door, willing a new customer to come in and save me from this conversation, but it stayed closed. "I'm not interested."

She narrowed her eyes like she could spot the lie on my face. Then she grimaced and pressed her hand into her belly. "Fine."

"You sure you're okay?"

She snorted. "Because I changed my mind about sleeping with you, I must be ill? I mean, the sex was good, Danny—"

I waved my hand to shush her. Frank and every other patron in the bar didn't have to know we'd slept together.

"—but it wasn't so great that I can't take no for an answer," she continued like she didn't care that the entire bar knew our business.

"Good," I growled.

"Good," she echoed.

"I don't mind—" Frank began.

"Shut it, Frank," Lucie and I said at the same time.

I turned my back to the bar and got out the first aid kit. I found a bandage and wrapped it around the cut on my thumb, then I pulled on a black latex glove.

"Hello, Michael Jackson," Lucie said. Frank chuckled.

"What?" I said.

"Michael Jackson," she said. "You remember, he used to wear one glove in his music videos. I danced along to 'Black or White' about a million times. No?"

"We weren't allowed to watch YouTube unsupervised."

"YouTube? Didn't you watch MTV every day after school?" she asked.

"Nope. I had a bunch of little brothers and sisters to watch." Turning back to the sink, I plunged my hands into the soapy water and scrubbed up the knives, more carefully this time. I was cautious not to look at Lucie, though I noticed when she scurried off to the restrooms.

She still hadn't returned by the time I'd dried and put the knives away. I got an unpleasant prickly feeling in the back of my throat when I peered down the hallway to the restrooms. Finally, I asked our dishwasher to man the bar for a minute, then jogged down the hall and stuck my head into the office. "Hey, Barb, can you cover for a minute, please?"

She looked up from the computer screen. "Thank God. I need to look at something that isn't a spreadsheet."

As she wheeled to the bar, I hustled to the restrooms and knocked on the ladies' room door. "Lucie, you in there?"

She coughed. "Yeah." Her voice was hoarse.

"You alone?"

"Yeah." She sounded terrible.

"I'm coming in."

I pushed open the door. A gagging sound came from the first stall.

I was in front of the door in a second. "Lucie, you okay?"

"Not really. I think I puked up a minor organ." The toilet paper roll rattled, then the toilet flushed. When she opened the stall door, her face was green and sweat curled the hair at her temples.

I grabbed her elbow and led her to the sink. I started the cold tap and held her wrists under it.

She swayed, and I braced her with my body behind hers. "Feels nice," she murmured.

"I used to do this with my younger siblings when they were sick to their stomachs. You, uh...you sure that red wine was the only thing you drank today?"

Her red-rimmed eyes flew open. "You think I was day-drinking on a workday?"

I winced. "You don't seem like yourself."

"I'm definitely not. But I'm not drunk either." She pumped the soap and washed her hands, then dried them. "I'm going upstairs to lie down." She looked a second away from passing out.

"I'll walk you up," I said.

She pursed her lips. "Okay. Thanks."

I knew how much that *thanks* had cost independent Lucie. Looping an arm around her waist, I slowly guided her out of the restroom to the back hallway that connected to the residents' rear entrance, then up the stairs.

"Is work going okay?" I asked.

"Work is work, you know?" She squinted up at me.

"I love my work."

"Even when you cut your hand and have to take care of puking customers?"

I huffed out half a laugh. "Cutting my hand was an accident, but I work at Barb's because I love taking care of people."

She glanced at me, then back to the stairs as we continued past the landing to the second floor.

"How's your book coming along?" I asked.

"Ugh, don't ask. I started strong, but I've kind of lost steam lately. I've been feeling uninspired."

"You'll find your groove," I said. "You're so smart. And driven."

"Smarts and drive do zero good when I'm exhausted. I need to fucking sleep."

My stomach clenched. I would *not* sleep with her out of guilt. She'd hate that. I wouldn't sleep with her out of a sense of obligation or even a desire to help her. Judging from what she'd said last time, she'd hate that even more.

The only emotion she wanted from me was lust. And although I definitely felt that, I couldn't follow through. It wasn't worth it if I was going to feel like shit in the morning. And I would when she kicked me out of bed, expecting me to feel nothing but relief that she wasn't one of those clingy women who wanted more. So when we stopped in front of her door and she pulled her key from her pocket, I said gruffly, "You going to be okay?"

She brushed my arm off her waist and stood up, pale and straight. "I'll be fine. Good night, Danny."

"G'night." I trudged back downstairs to the bar, my belly still prickling. Goddamn Catholic guilt. Someday I'd move past it and feel proud for standing up for myself.

But not today.

10

THERE'S NOTHING PLANNED ABOUT THIS

What I want to leave behind is three happy, well-adjusted adults who are kind and resilient. The laughter and silly jokes, the scraped knees I kissed better, the bedtime stories, the love I created in this house. That's what I did.
Savannah Lamb, recipe blogger

LUCIE

Savannah didn't know it, but we'd assigned a schedule of check-ins with her.

Carly was Mondays, Tessa was Wednesdays, and I was Fridays. We gave her the weekends off because that's when her kids usually called or went by for a visit, and that always seemed to cheer her up.

"Hi, honey," I said when she answered my video call.

"Lucie! What a surprise!" She leaned back against her '90s-style oak kitchen cabinets.

I grinned. How had she not figured out it was no accident I'd call her on a Friday? "Just thinking of you on my walk to work."

"Be careful, sweetie. You wouldn't want to trip and fall."

"Don't be such a mom." I glanced down at her face on the screen, then back to the crowded sidewalk. "I've got my eyes on the sidewalk, see?" A guy in a blue suit walked ahead of me. "What are you doing?"

"The banana bread is in the oven, and I was about to start brownies in case the kids come over this weekend."

Uh-oh. Was she stress baking or only regular baking? It was hard to tell with Savannah. I couldn't recall seeing her in any room other than her kitchen on our video chats.

"You feeling okay?" I paused at the don't-walk sign.

"Of course. Baking relaxes me."

I narrowed my eyes. "What do you need relaxing from?"

"Oh, you know... Life. Jason and I had another *conversation* last night. He doesn't understand why I won't move back into the bedroom with him."

"Did you tell him why?"

"I tried. I told him I don't feel like he values me as a person, only as the woman who cooks and cleans and...you know."

"Good for you!" The light turned green, and I stepped into the crosswalk. "What did he say?"

"That of course he values me. That he cares about me. That we've come too far to throw away our marriage."

Huh. Dude had upped his game since their last conversation, when he'd only whined that they needed to reconnect in bed. "Do you believe him?"

"I don't know. Maybe, until he asked if I could make his colonoscopy appointment."

I shook my head. "How's the counseling going?"

"We haven't found a time to go yet. He's so busy..."

Too busy to save his marriage? How could he not try anything he could to stay with her? But Savannah and I had been over this before, and from the look on her face, she was replaying it right now. Time for a distraction. "Are you going to see your kids this weekend?"

"My daughter's coming over this weekend. She's bringing her boyfriend."

"Ooh. Meeting the parents? Think you're going to like him?"

"I've already met him, and he's fine, I guess. But she's too young to get serious."

"How old is she?"

"Twenty-three."

"And how old were you when you got married?"

"Twenty-two. Don't laugh. I was definitely too young to get married. I see that now."

Watching Savannah on my screen, I'd stopped looking where I was going and bumped into blue-suit guy. "Sorry," I muttered through the pain radiating through my chest. He hadn't even noticed, but I had to stop walking and take a minute until the stars cleared my vision.

"Lucie, what's wrong?"

I took in a shallow breath and blew it out. "Wasn't watching where I was going and bumped into someone. I'm PMSing hard, and my boobs are super-tender. It's torture to even put on a bra."

"Weren't you PMSing the last time I saw you?" she asked. "And that was, like, three weeks ago."

"It couldn't have been more than..." No, she was right. They'd just printed the story about the migrants, and I'd written at least three pieces since then.

"You haven't had your period since then?"

"I've always been irregular." I looked at her face, hoping she'd tell me it was fine, and I'd believe it. But deep inside, I knew it wasn't fine. I'd experienced this once before. But I was no terrified college student this time. This time, I could take care of myself. And maybe someone else.

"And there's a... um, reason you might be missing your period?"

I closed my eyes. *Goddamn broken condom.* I nodded.

"Is there a drugstore nearby?" she asked. "I'll stay on while you take the test."

"Really?" I swallowed. "You don't mind?"

"No, sweetie. You shouldn't be alone for this."

"I—okay." Ahead on the left was the drugstore where I'd planned to get Plan B weeks ago before the big story had distracted me. "Hang tight. We're going in."

I marched through the automatic door and found the "Family Planning" aisle. There was nothing planned about this. Ironically, the pregnancy test kits were next to the display of condoms, including a box of the kind that had turned out to be faulty, beside the Plan B I should've bought weeks ago.

"What kind should I get?" I whispered into the phone. "The early result kind?"

"Oh, sugar, it's not early anymore. You can get the regular one. Get the one with two tests because, if I know you, you're going to want to double-check it."

"A broken prophylactic got me into this," I muttered. "Damn right I'm going to verify the results." I bypassed the box with two tests and picked up three single tests from three different brands and marched to the check-out.

Chin high, I glared at the woman who took my card, but she didn't bother looking up as she silently completed the transaction. I shoved the tests into my satchel and strode out.

"Are you going home to do it?" Savannah asked.

"No, I've got to go to work. There's a family-style restroom on the ground floor." It took only a few minutes to walk to the newspaper building and get through the security turnstile. I practically ran to the single-user restroom and flipped the lock.

I turned off my video and set my phone on the counter, then

ripped into the first test. I read the instructions out loud. Same with the second and third tests. They were all pretty similar. Pee on the plastic stick and wait.

My fingers trembled as I ripped the tests from their wrappers and lined them up on the counter. "Okay," I said. "I'm going to do the tests now. Plug your ears if you don't want to hear me pee."

"Let 'er rip," Savannah said.

Taking a deep breath, I sat on the toilet. I'd had a lot of coffee, and it was no problem to take all three tests in succession. I arranged them on a paper towel on the counter.

After washing my hands, I turned my video on. "Now what?"

"You read the instructions. Wait three minutes. Set a timer."

I did. Then I grimaced. "What I really mean is...now what?"

"Oh, sugar." Her lips turned down, and her voice dripped with wisteria and sympathy. "Have you thought about whether you want to...keep it?"

"No. Yes. I don't know. I didn't think I'd be in this position, you know? I...I'd thought about IVF after my last birthday, but I never did anything but the initial consultation. I'm thirty-fuck-ing-nine. I'll be *forty* in August. I thought I'd missed my chance."

Savannah growled. "I wish I could come there and give you a hug."

"It's okay." I leaned against the tile wall. "It means a lot that you're talking me through this."

"You didn't tell us about the IVF. Does that mean you want a child?"

"I...I don't know. I don't know how it'd fit into my life." Mario popped into my brain. He'd freak out when he remembered I wasn't actually one of the guys. He'd hate having to cover my maternity leave. And my book! How would I finish it with a baby?

"What about the father? Do you, um, know who he is?" She winced.

"God, Savannah. I don't have that many hookups. Of course I know who it is. The condom broke, and I forgot to get emergency contraception. Goddammit. How is it fair that this is all on me?"

"It's true that it's your body that will have to carry the baby... if you decide to keep it. But it's not *all* on you. The father has responsibilities and choices too. And you know we're all here for you. You won't be alone."

I grabbed another paper towel and blotted my eyes. "Dammit, Savannah, you're making my mascara run."

"Better get the waterproof. Pregnancy hormones are a bitch. When I was pregnant, I couldn't watch those Sarah McLachlan ASPCA commercials without losing it."

The timer on my phone beeped. "Ready?" she asked.

"No."

"You'll never be ready. Do you want me to look?"

"We'll look together." Taking a deep breath, I turned my phone so she could see while I examined the test sticks. I exhaled.

"Congratulations?" she said.

11

UNICORN PUKE

As the headmistress of an elite school for young men, I inspire them to great achievement. However, I also instill values in them, like charity, responsibility, and respect. I want them to succeed, but I want them to do it in a way that makes them—and us—proud.

Abigail Davidson, Headmistress of St. Bernardino Academy

LUCIE

Holy shit.

I blinked hard, then peered through the glass window in the door to the bar again.

Nope, I was right the first time. Unicorns had puked all over the bar.

There was a rainbow balloon arch over a long table against the far wall. Pastel gift bags sat under the arch like a leprechaun's prize. A giant white-frosted sheet cake dominated one of the four-tops in the middle of the room, and crock pots and chafing dishes took up the tables to the left.

People milled about, smiling. But no smiles were as big as

those of a pair of women holding hands in front of the cake, one of them hugely pregnant.

What the fuck was going on? I'd come down at opening on Saturday to talk to Danny before the bar got busy, but I'd clearly failed at that. Was he even here?

I stuck my face against the glass so I could peer at the bar. He and Leo stood side by side, grinning. Leo pulled a beer, and Danny shook something in a shaker.

When the door opened, I nearly fell on my face. A short woman in her fifties gazed up at me. Silver glinted in her dark curls, and her brown eyes looked familiar. "Are you here for the shower?" she asked.

"Shower?" I repeated.

"I guess not," she said. "The bar opens at two."

She scanned me from head to toe. Was she judging me for peering into a bar at barely noon?

"I'm here to see Danny," I said. "I need to talk to him."

"Oh? What's your name?"

"Lucie. I'm a...a friend of his."

She tipped her head to the side, then took a slower scan of me, lingering on my oversized black wool sweater. "Come in, Lucie. He can take a break."

I hesitated. "I can come back later." I didn't want everyone there to hear what I had to tell Danny, not until we'd figured a few things out.

"Come in, come in. It's no problem. I'll take his place at the bar. How hard can it be?" She patted my upper arm, then tugged me inside.

Fine. I was doing this. It was best to get it over with. As we always said at the newspaper, bad news might sell papers, but it didn't improve with age. The woman towed me toward the bar. When Danny spotted me, his grin faded, and a tiny line formed between his eyebrows.

"Daniel," the woman said. "*Lucie* is here to talk to you." She released my arm and stared at Danny, then at me, like she was deciphering a code.

"Hi," I said. "Could we go somewhere quiet?" The woman narrowed her eyes at me.

"Sure," he said. "Thanks, Ma."

Ma?

He walked to the hallway, but before we got to the restrooms, he opened a door to the right, and I followed him into a tiny office. An ancient metal desk held an old desktop computer and a CRT monitor. Shelves above the desk bowed under the weight of a collection of binders. Metal shelving on the other two walls held an assortment of booze, boxes of napkins, and a giant tub labeled "Christmas Decorations."

I shut the door, squared my shoulders, and faced him.

Danny rolled an armless chair from the corner in front of me, then leaned against the desk. I lowered myself onto the chair. But I hated sitting below him like a misbehaving child, so I stood. "You sit," I said.

The furrow between his eyebrows deepened, but he obeyed. I didn't take his place on the desk. Instead, I paced to the metal shelving, then took a deep breath.

"I'm pregnant."

"Wait. What?" He didn't look shocked, only confused.

"I'm not saying it again."

"But I—but you…"

The tension in my shoulders eased. At least he wasn't going to ask how I knew he was the father. "I forgot, okay? I got busy with work and didn't get the emergency contraception, so here we are."

"Are you okay?" He jumped up. "Sit. Get off your feet."

"I feel fine. It's not like I'm like…like that." I gestured behind me like we could see through the wall to the baby shower beyond. Though, if I carried this through, I would eventually get like that.

Shit. I paced, wishing there was more space in the tiny office. "Who is that, anyway?"

"My cousin Belinda and her wife, Jung-mi. They're expecting twins next month."

"Twins?" Holy shit, what if he'd put twins in me? I put my hand over my racing heart.

"Don't worry," he said like he was reading my mind. "They don't run in my family. Well, I mean, I have siblings who are twins, but there aren't any others in the family. Ma always figured it was their father's genes, but he didn't stick around long enough to find out. Anyway, Belinda's having twins because of the artificial insemination. Do they run in yours?"

"No. Thank god."

There were a few beats of silence as I wiped the image of *two* squalling babies from my brain.

"Do you know what you want to do about it?" he asked.

"I...I don't know. I just found out yesterday. It's a lot, you know?"

"Yeah."

"Look, I know it's a lot for you too. And I'm really sorry I fucked up." I swallowed.

"Hey." He caught my hand, halting my pacing. "I had just as big a part in this as you did. It's okay. And whatever you decide, it'll be okay."

"You want me to decide?"

"It's your body. Your life will change the most, at least over the next seven or eight months."

"I thought you were Catholic. Couldn't you get excommunicated or something?"

He snorted. "I've got a pregnant lesbian cousin. We're not exactly the paragons of traditional Catholicism."

"So do you want me to get an abortion?"

"I didn't say that. I want you to do what's best for you. If that's an abortion, I'll go with you and make sure you're okay. If that's carrying the baby to term, we'll work it out. Together. As co-parents." His Adam's apple bobbed.

"What if...what if I want to keep it?" Saying it made my chest feel lighter, though my stomach was still a pretzel.

He exhaled. "Then that's great."

"I...it might be my last chance, you know? To be a mother."

He scratched his cheek. "You...you wanna get married?"

"What?" I yanked my hand away. "No."

"Okay, then." He nodded. "We'll work out an arrangement. We'll share the responsibilities. And until the baby's born, anything you need, just ask."

"I don't need anything. I'm fine." If I said it often enough, I might believe it. "I've got health insurance, and the paper has a maternity leave policy. It's not great, but it should get me through the early days."

"What about your book?"

I squinted at him. With the bomb I'd just dropped, how had he remembered my book? "I'll finish it before the baby's born."

He smiled, a crooked one that wrinkled up his cheek on one side and made me want to kiss it. "Of course you will."

I wish I had as much confidence in myself as he did.

"So, we're keeping this on the down-low, I assume, for another..." He looked off to the side. "Six weeks?"

"For as long as we can. If my boss finds out, he'll remember I'm a woman, and I'll be working the shit beat."

"Can I tell my family?" he asked. "Not the whole family. Just Leo and my mom."

"That was your mom I met before?"

"Yeah."

"What about your dad?"

"Died when I was little. My siblings all have different dads. None of them stuck around."

"Shit, I'm sorry."

"About my dead dad? That was a long time ago."

"That and...and for not knowing about it." There were so many things I didn't know about Danny. I hadn't thought about all the ways this baby would tie us together. It would have grandparents. I hoped Danny's mother would be better at it than my dad. "Okay, you can tell them. But I don't want"—I gestured through the wall again—"that."

"We can go slow," he said, "until you're sure of what you want."

Heat rose from my chest, up my neck, to my face. "Are you second-guessing me? Because I'm not changing my mind. I know what I want. I might not be into that pastel-rainbow-unicorn bullshit, but I want to be a mother." Until he'd questioned me, until the retort flew out of my mouth, I hadn't known what I wanted to do. But now, as I said it, the truth locked into place.

"Hold on." He put his palms up. "I thought... Never mind. I fucked up. I'm sorry. We can do this however you want. As long as there's room for me in the kid's life."

The word *kid* conjured up an image of Danny running beside a dark-haired boy on a bicycle. Danny walking him up the stairs into a school. Danny tossing a ball with him. All the things my dad never did with me. As I'd pointed out (fine, been an asshole about) that morning after, Danny was all about taking care of people. He'd be a wonderful dad.

"I have some complicated feelings about parents," I said. "I'm sorry. I shouldn't take them out on you."

A tentative smile creased his cheeks. "It's okay. I'm sure we both have a lot of fuckups in our future."

I squinted one eye at him. "For example, did you propose to me in the office of a bar?"

His chuckle came deep from his chest. "It's not the last mistake I'll make, I promise. Let's agree to give each other a little grace?"

"Deal." I held out my hand, and he shook it. "We'll figure it out, together."

12

A GOOD TIME

Whiskey (straight up)
Pour two ounces of Jack Daniels into any glass you can find. Try to keep your hands steady as you drink it. People are depending on you.

DANNY

By the time Leo backed his truck into the driveway of our mother's house in San Bruno, I had so many emotions swirling in my chest that I couldn't tell if my sigh was relief that he was on time (ish) or dread about his reaction to my news. Thrilled or disappointed, in our Italian-American family, the response was sure to be loud.

The door of my ancient Toyota creaked as I got out. I jammed the key into the lock and jiggled it the way my uncle had taught me when he'd sold it to me ten years ago, then I met my brother on the driveway.

"What's up?" he asked. "What couldn't you tell me over the phone?"

I cuffed his shoulder. "You think I'm going to tell you in the front yard where old Mrs. McIntosh might hear? Come inside like a human. I'll tell you and Ma together."

I trudged up the steps, pulled open the door, and walked into the smell of meat sauce. "Ma?"

"In the kitchen. I'm making food."

"Food?" I stepped into the familiar kitchen with its white-painted cabinets. The countertops overflowed with dishes. "It's 10:00 a.m. on a Monday."

She lifted the heavy lasagna pan out of the oven and set it on a folded towel with a grunt. "You said you had news. News goes best with food."

Careful not to let her see my eye roll, I kissed her cheek. "Thanks, Ma. But this is enough food for twenty people."

"Good thing we're here to eat it." My sister Giuliana walked into the kitchen holding a bottle of prosecco in one hand and a bottle of Jack Daniels in the other. "Are we celebrating or commiserating?"

I kissed her cheek. "Ma, I said I wanted to talk to only you and Leo."

"We're family." Ma pulled a foil-wrapped loaf of bread from the oven. "We share news."

I'd promised Lucie I'd keep it quiet for a while. Still, Giuliana didn't know anyone Lucie worked with. Her secret was safe.

"So, which is it?" Giuliana held up the bottles.

Grimacing, I pointed at the prosecco.

She tilted her head. "You sure?"

"No. Can we sit?" I pulled out a chair for my mother at the small, round table that was more often used as extra prep space than a dining space. My mother never hosted fewer than six people for meals, so we usually ate in the dining room at the table she'd inherited from her parents.

The front door slammed. "We're here. What'd we miss?" My

sister Elena bounded into the kitchen, followed by her twin, Tony, who went straight to the pan of lasagna.

"It's not done resting," Ma warned. "You can eat after Danny tells us his news."

"Ma," I said, "the twins? Really?"

"Family, Danny," she reminded me.

"Grab some glasses," Giuliana ordered them.

I sighed. "Ma, sit down."

With a worried look, she sank into the chair. Leo sat on one side of her, and I sat across from her. Giuliana twisted the cage on the bottle of prosecco.

I met each of their gazes, unsure how to start. I wasn't even sure how I felt, much less what they'd think. It had been at this very table that our mother had given Leo and me the talk when we were in middle school. She'd told us to always use condoms and never, ever have sex with someone we wouldn't mind raising a child with. I'd taken it to heart after watching three men abandon her.

I wouldn't mind raising a child with Lucie, but the feeling wasn't mutual.

"So, ah..." I began, "there was an accident—"

"An accident?" Ma leaped from her chair and circled the table to cradle my face and peer into my eyes. "Are you all right?"

"Not that kind of accident, Ma." Gently, I removed her hand from my face and held it. "I got a woman pregnant."

"A baby?" Her concerned expression flashed into joy faster than a grease fire. "You're going to be a father? I'm going to be a grandma?" She tugged me up and hugged me. Even though I was a foot taller than her, it felt as good as the hugs she'd given me when I'd failed a test at school.

"Hey!" Giuliana popped the cork and poured the fizzy wine into the juice glass Tony handed her.

Elena pounded my back. "Danny's gonna be a daddy!"

I winced. "Yeah, I guess? She's decided to keep the baby."

My mother pulled back to scan my face, her eyes narrowing. "Who is she?"

"No one you know. Lucie Knox, my neighbor."

Leo whistled. "Lucie? How'd you manage that? She's way outta your league."

I turned my gaze toward Ma's pampered roses outside the window. "I know."

"Your neighbor is your girlfriend?" Elena asked.

"She's not my girlfriend." A fat bumblebee hovered above the buds as if waiting for them to open. "Like I said, it was an accident."

"Your dick accidentally fell into her vagina?" Tony crowed.

Ma smacked the side of his head. "Don't be crude about my first grandchild. What's done is done. Now there's a baby to think about. When is she due?"

"Due?" I counted on my fingers. "November, I guess?"

"November," Leo said. "But that's when—"

"We have time." Ma squeezed my hand, then returned to her seat. "Giuliana, pass me a glass. Danny, tell me about this girl."

"Girl?" Leo laughed. "Lucie's no girl. She's gotta be, what, late thirties? You met her Saturday, Ma. Remember, she came in during Belinda and Jung-mi's baby shower. Tony, pass me the whiskey."

My mother's glass of prosecco froze, mid-toast. "The older woman in all black?"

I blinked. "Sure, she's older than me, but I wouldn't call her *older*."

"Danny." Ma set down her glass. "How old is she?"

I pulled out my phone and googled her to be sure. "Thirty-nine or forty."

"A baby at forty." Ma slumped back in her chair. "Better pour me some of that." She pointed at the whiskey.

"Ma," I said, "people have babies in their forties all the time."

"Do they? No one I know did. Isn't it dangerous?"

"Dangerous to the mother?" I kept my hands flat on the table to disguise their tremble. What if Lucie died because of that broken condom? I'd never forgive myself.

Leo nudged my hand with a glass of Jack. "Ma, don't be a dinosaur. Just because you popped out five babies before thirty-five doesn't mean that's how people do it these days. Lucie's healthy, and I'm sure she's got health insurance. She'll be fine."

Health insurance? My heart pounded. Lucie had mentioned it when she told me about the pregnancy. The policy Barb offered me was so expensive that I'd bought the state-mandated minimum coverage, which you had to practically sever a limb to make it worth using. How much would this baby cost? I lifted the whiskey and gulped it, grimacing at the burn in my throat.

"I think the bigger question is, what is going to happen between you and Lucie," Leo said. "She's, like, a grown-up with a job."

"Danny has a job," Giuliana said.

"Lucie's got a college degree. She's a journalist," he said. "Didn't you tell me she won some award?"

"Yeah." I cleared my throat. "Plus, she's writing a book."

"But she's not your girlfriend?" my mother said.

"No." I traced a water stain on the table.

"So, you two are..." She tilted her head.

"I don't know," I said, my voice tight.

"Fuck buddies," Tony announced at the same time.

Ma smacked his shoulder.

"Sounds like you need to talk to her, Danny-o," Leo said. "Ask her what she wants."

I ground my molars. I already knew what she wanted. A

good time. I wasn't boyfriend material. Certainly not husband material. We'd never be a traditional family.

"Danny, you look pale," Ma said. "I'll get you some lasagna."

"No, thanks, I'm good." I swallowed the bile rising in my throat.

"I'll eat his." Tony stepped to the counter. "Ma, you hungry? Anyone else?"

Tony made plates of lasagna while I sat in my chair, struggling to breathe through the pressure on my chest. At Belinda and Jung-mi's shower, they'd talked about painting the nursery. My apartment didn't have a second bedroom to use as a nursery. Neither did Lucie's. They'd shown us photos of the crib and the chest of drawers that had a special cushion to use as a changing table. A fancy rocking chair. Not to mention the dozens of things on their baby registry.

How did people afford all that? Every two weeks, I direct-deposited my salary into my savings account for the bar and lived on my tips. Some weeks I lived well. Others, I ate a lot of store-brand peanut-butter sandwiches.

Babies couldn't live like that. I needed to set aside some money for our kid.

We'd never had a lot growing up, and we'd squeezed an adult and five kids into the suburban three-bedroom house my grandparents had left my mother. But we'd always had enough food to grow strong and healthy and enough love to make it through the hard times.

Co-parenting an accidental baby with my neighbor who thought my dick was my only redeeming quality wasn't my idea of a family.

Ma leaned toward me. "Danny, I can see you're worried. Is it money? I don't have a lot extra, but I can help."

I shook myself. "No, I couldn't take your money. I'll work it out."

Her steady gaze was like an x-ray that read the anxious thoughts in my brain. "We've got lots of baby things in the attic. Why don't you look through it and see if there's anything you can use."

"I'll call Tina," Giuliana said. "She got her tubes tied after Emma. I'm sure she's got baby things she could give you. She'll be glad someone can use them."

The tightness in my chest eased a little. It wasn't ideal, but it was a start. I'd show Lucie I was trying to help. Then she might not think I was completely worthless.

"Do you need, like, a real job?" Tony asked. "Working for Aunt Connie's insurance agency isn't the most exciting job, but it's steady. With your people skills, she'd hire you in a second."

I swallowed another gulp of whiskey. Working behind a desk sounded like torture.

"Nah, Tony," Leo said. "Danny's buying the bar. He'll be fine."

"*We're* buying the bar," I corrected him. But his words, combined with the whiskey, warmed up my belly.

He was right. I had to double down on buying the bar. As a bar owner, not just a bartender, I could afford a kid, and I might even be worthy of Lucie Knox.

A WHAT FOR THE WHAT?

It's not only about building a successful company that empowers people to feel beautiful. It's also about showing women they can lead, proving that you can be a strong business-woman and a dedicated mom. I want to inspire others to chase their dreams and find balance in their lives.
Mercy Echegini, CEO of Costus Flower Beauty

LUCIE

I was in the zone. I couldn't feel my body or my fingertips on my keyboard. It was almost like the runner's high Tad droned on about at work. The words appeared on the white page of my word processing program, flowing like magic directly from my brain, or possibly divine inspiration. Words about values and strong women and legacy.

A bang on my door startled me, and my fingers convulsed on the keyboard. A large block of text highlighted briefly, then disappeared.

"Control-Z! Control-Z!" I shouted. But saying it as I banged the keys didn't help. It only deleted another block of text. My hands shot off the keyboard like I'd been shocked.

Another bang. "Fuck," I grumbled. Then louder, "Coming."

I heaved myself out of my chair. *Ouch.* Suddenly, I felt my body again, and my lower back was *not* happy about how long I'd been sitting. I hobbled to the door.

A low, urgent voice came through the door. "Lucie, it's Danny. Can you open up? This is heavy."

I flipped the lock and threw open the door.

"Thank fuck," Leo said, backing through the door. I scrambled out of the way as they carried an old-fashioned crib into my apartment. Inside were two laundry baskets full of tiny sheets, blankets, and clothes smaller than I'd thought possible.

"Where can we put this?" Danny asked. "Do you have a spot picked out for the nursery?"

"A what for the what?" My brain was still half in my book.

Danny's forehead crinkled. "You know, where the baby's going to sleep."

Baby? Sleep?

For the next six months, it would sleep right where Danny's sperm had lodged it in my uterus. I didn't have to worry about that yet. I glanced around my apartment like a second bedroom would magically appear. Danny's and Leo's arms trembled with the weight they held. "I guess...over there?" I gestured at the empty space next to my desk.

There was a stack of books on the floor, so I scurried to shift them out of the way as the two men lumbered toward it with the crib. Grunting, they set it down.

"Um...thanks," I said. I glanced at my computer screen. I could only vaguely remember what I'd been writing before they'd banged on my door, and I was almost positive I could recreate it if I could get my hands back on the keyboard—

"We'll be right back with the rest," Danny said.

"Rest?"

"Yeah," Leo said. "We've got a dresser, a crib mattress, and three more bags of clothes and bottles and other baby shit."

Bottles? Clothes? My breathing quickened like I'd been the one who'd carried a crib up two flights of stairs. "Could you come back later?"

Danny had been wiping sweat from his forehead, but he dropped his hand, his brown eyes wide with hope. "You mean you want me to come back after we've dropped off the baby stuff?"

"No. I mean, can you give me a couple of hours before you bring the rest of the stuff? I'm working."

"Working?" Leo scoffed. "You're on social media." He waved at my second screen, which had Mercy Echegini's Instagram pulled up. My conscience twinged. My father didn't think I did proper work either.

"Lucie's a writer, Leo," Danny said through gritted teeth. "She's doing research." He grabbed Leo's arm. "We'll put the rest of the stuff in my apartment. Let me know when to come back, okay? My shift doesn't start until six."

"Thanks." My gaze drifted back to my screen, and it jogged my cloudy memory about what I'd written earlier. If I could get these two out of my apartment, I was certain I'd be able to recapture it. Without looking, I stepped toward the door and bumped into something hard.

Danny's chest.

His black T-shirt was a little damp, and it smelled...fantastic. I took a deep inhale. He smelled like soap. Faintly floral detergent, plus that cheap green woodsy drugstore soap. And the slight musk of his sweat. I wanted to bury my face in his chest and bring the scent deep into my lungs. Instead, I looked into his eyes, which glittered with an expression I couldn't identify. Didn't want to identify. I stepped back.

"Off you go. Thanks for..." I waved at the crib, which wouldn't be useful as anything but a laundry hamper for months. "Thanks for all this."

Danny's feet stayed planted, crowding me just like that crib. "Sure. Just text when I can bring up the rest of it."

"Okay. You guys can let yourselves out." Because if I followed him to the door, I might not let him leave. I sank into my chair and listened to his sneakers squeak across the hardwoods.

"Bye, Lucie," he said from the door.

I set one hand on the keyboard and raised the other in a dismissive wave. "Bye."

I stared at the screen, but no words came to me.

The zone? I couldn't find it again with a map and a bloodhound.

~

The crib seemed to take up more space as the hours passed. Although it was silent and empty now, its presence reminded me that sooner than I was ready, there'd be another human in my apartment who'd steal my attention more effectively than Danny and his brother had. Every few minutes, my eyes would stray from my screen to the crib. Once, I even thought I heard a baby cry, but it was only a cat down in the alley.

I had plenty of time to prepare for the baby later. What I didn't have time to do was fuck around with my book. My manuscript had to be done by the time the baby came, or I might never finish. I'd end up like my mother, a prisoner to other people's needs, never having time for my own goals. I ripped my gaze from the crib back to my screen. *More words,* I urged myself.

I'd finally started to write again when another knock came at my door.

"Shit, Danny," I muttered. "This baby's going to have more changes of clothes than Beyoncé at a concert."

I made sure to click Save before I hauled myself out of my chair. My toe snagged on something hard, and pain shot up my leg. "Ow!" *Goddamn crib.*

I kicked it with the side of my other foot for good measure, and a pang shot across my instep. I howled again before tossing out a series of curse words.

I hobbled to the door and wrenched it open. "Damn it, Danny, I don't need—"

Savannah stood in the hall, both eyebrows raised. "What don't you need from Danny?"

"Nothing," I grumbled, stepping aside to let her in.

"I tried to call first," she said, "but..."

"I keep my phone off when I'm working," I said.

"Bad time?"

"No." I sighed. "I wasn't getting much writing done anyway, with the interruptions." I gestured at the crib.

"You bought a crib?" She stepped closer to examine it.

"No, Danny and his brother brought it. They have a ton more stuff to bring me, apparently."

Savannah peered at the crib. "How old is this thing?"

"I don't know."

She jiggled the side. "It's clean, but...oh no."

"What's 'oh no'?"

With a clatter, one side of the crib fell. "These things have been illegal for at least ten years," she said. "I mean, I used a drop-side crib for all four of my kids without an issue, but they're banned. You can't use this."

I snorted. "Great. I already thought it was useless, and now it's even more so. Can't the baby just sleep with me for a while?"

Savannah's eyes widened. "No! That's even more dangerous than this crib. You could roll over her, or she could roll out of the bed onto the floor. Or the pillows and blankets could smother her."

"Shit," I said, horrified. "Sometimes I roll onto my stomach in my sleep. Could that hurt the baby?" I rubbed my belly.

"No," she said. "By the time the baby's big enough that sleeping on your stomach could hurt her, you'll be too uncomfortable to sleep that way. Don't worry about it."

"I've got a lot to learn." And when would I have time to learn it? If I was going to finish writing this book before the baby came, I didn't have time to fall into a baby research rabbit hole.

"Well, that's why I brought you this." Savannah reached into her enormous purse and pulled out a small, wrapped package. When I took it from her, I could tell it was a paperback. A thick one.

"What's this?" I untied the bow, then pulled off the wrapping paper.

"It's The Book," she said, and I could tell she thought of it with the same reverence as the Bible. "It's the only one you need."

There was a silhouette of a pregnant woman sitting in a rocking chair on the pink cover. I flipped to the table of contents.

"Everything you need to know is in there. It's an updated version of the one I read when I was pregnant the first time. Of course, you can ask me anything too."

"Thanks." I bit my lip. "First question: do babies really need all this shit?"

She pulled the side of the crib back up, and it locked with a clatter. "They need a safe place to sleep. Diapers. *Tons* of diapers. A few changes of clothes, depending how often you plan to do laundry. Milk—though we won't get into breastfeeding yet—and lots of love. That's really it."

She stepped closer and grabbed my hand. "I'm more worried about what *you* need. Raising a baby is difficult, especially on your own. Remember, you've got me and the rest of the gang to help."

For some reason, my eyes prickled. "Damn hormones," I said, wiping a tear off my cheek. "I'm fine."

That was a lie. I wasn't fine.

"I'll be fine," I amended. I needed a plan to get through the next six months. And then the next eighteen years after that. What if I sucked at it? What if the kid felt neglected because I wasn't at every school pickup and practice like my mom was? "Or will I? Am I doing the right thing by keeping the baby?"

"It's not too late to change your mind," Savannah said. "But you said you were considering IVF. Why did you want to be a mother?"

"I guess...I guess it all happened when I was thinking about this legacy project. I've talked to a lot of brilliant women without kids, including Carly and Tessa. They all seem happy with their professional legacies. But I realized that this book isn't the only thing I want to leave behind. I might not agree with her career decisions, but my mom was a great mother. *Is* a great mother. And when I thought about leaving this earth without raising a child, it seemed...unfulfilling."

"Everyone wants something different out of life," Savannah said. "I'm glad you're being intentional about it."

I flashed her a wry smile. "Getting knocked up while on deadline is probably the least intentional thing I've ever done."

"You know what I mean. Regardless, we're all here to support you in whatever way you need."

The fact that my friend was standing here in my apartment

on a Monday afternoon because she had a feeling I might need her was proof of that. "Thanks," I said. "I'd love some help."

She gathered me into a hug. "Great. Text me the details of your next doctor's appointment, and I'll go with you." Savannah gave the best hugs. No wonder she was such a great mom. But when she stepped back, I noticed her smile wasn't as bright as it usually was.

"Sit." I led her to my couch and sprawled in the corner. "What's going on with you?"

She eased onto the other end of the couch, straightened her tunic over her leggings, then tucked her blond hair back behind her ears.

"I...I found out Jason's cheating on me." She sniffed.

"Oh my god!" I scooted closer to her. "Are you okay?"

"Yes. No. I don't know."

"How'd you find out? Was it a Carly situation? Did the girl-friend show up at your house? Wait, do you need a drink? I've got wine. Or we can go to the bar."

"Wine?" she asked. "When's the last time you had a glass of water? You need to hydrate." She jumped up from the couch and went to my kitchen.

I followed her. "What happened, Savannah?"

She found the pitcher and poured two glasses of water. "It's like he wanted me to find out." She handed me a glass and waited until I took a gulp. "I'd told him I wanted to go see that new rom-com at the movie theater."

"The one with Helen Choi?" I asked. Carly had styled her for the premiere.

"Yes. But he kept putting me off. So, I decided to go by myself on Friday afternoon while he was working. It felt amazing. I got unbuttered popcorn because I hate having greasy fingers. And I sat in the back row. I like to feel like I'm at the movies, you know? Jason always sits in the front because it's more immersive.

"But as I was sitting there, waiting for the movie to start, he walked in with his arm around another woman."

"No!" My face prickled with secondhand humiliation. "What did you do?"

"I tried to enjoy the movie. But I couldn't. I kept watching *them.* So, I walked out."

"And then?" This was better than any rom-com. I grabbed a bag of M&Ms from a cabinet and poured them into a cereal bowl. I held it out to Savannah.

"I shouldn't," she said. I pressed the bowl into her hand. "Okay, fine." She popped one into her mouth. "When he got home, he told me he'd gone to happy hour with a couple of colleagues."

"He did not!" I grabbed a handful of candy.

She took another piece and nodded. "I told him I'd seen him. After a while he...he told me he'd done it because he wasn't getting enough affection at home."

"No!" I said, horrified. "I hope you ripped him a new one."

"No. I—" She took a deep breath. "I asked him if he wanted to stay married. He said yes, but..." She picked up another piece of candy and examined it.

"Is that what you want?"

"I don't know," she said.

I bit my tongue. Literally. Otherwise, I'd tell her she should know what she wanted, and it shouldn't be to stay married to her douche of a husband. Just like I'd tell my mother if she ever asked me. But Savannah wasn't asking me either.

I took a deep breath. "Same thing you said. We're all here to support you in whatever way you need. Though..." I glanced at the crib. "If you need a place to stay, maybe ask Tessa. I think I'm at maximum occupancy here."

"You've got enough going on. I'm sorry I said anything about my troubles."

I gripped her shoulder. "Never apologize for that. I'm always here for you. To listen or help. Whatever you need. That's what best friends do."

A tear spilled onto her cheek. "We'll get through this. We're goddesses, remember?"

"Goddesses," I agreed.

14

THE SITUATIONSHIP

<u>Mojito (shaken)</u>
*In a cocktail shaker, combine a sprig of mint, 2 ounces white rum, 1
ounce lime juice, and 1/2 ounce simple syrup. Lightly muddle. Fill the
shaker halfway with ice. Shake, then strain into a lowball glass. Top
with club soda. Garnish with mint and lime slices.*

DANNY

Tuesday was ladies' night, and I'd hoped Lucie would stop by the bar. She couldn't drink red wine or her favorite negroni or the scotch she forced down when she was feeling insecure, but I'd been experimenting with nonalcoholic drinks I thought she might like. In fact, I was toying with the idea of a whole menu of mocktails.

"Danny-o!" Tad plopped onto a stool at my end of the bar. "Why the long face?"

"Just thinking." I pasted on a fake smile. "The usual?" I grabbed a cocktail shaker and assessed the droopy mint, holding in a sigh. Once the ladies saw me mix up Tad's drink, it'd be nothing but mojitos for the rest of my shift.

"Don't forget I like it in a martini glass."

I gritted my teeth and tossed a few mint leaves into the shaker, then poured in the rum, lime juice, and simple syrup—extra for Tad—and mashed it with a long-handled spoon. I tossed in a few ice cubes, shook it, then strained it into a martini glass. After splashing in club soda, I garnished it with a lime and a sprig of mint.

Carefully, I set it in front of him. "Anything else?"

"You know, in my neighborhood bar, they do a sugar rim."

I winced. "We, uh, don't have too much demand for sugar rims. We're more of a beer and whiskey bar."

"I keep telling Aunt Barb she needs to go more upscale. Maybe when she retires and gives me the bar, I'll rebrand it. Give it a speakeasy vibe, sport coats required, you know?" His gaze lingered on the hem of my T-shirt, where I'd caught it on a dish rack earlier.

I smoothed my hand over the rip. "I'm buying the bar, remember? You were here on Barb's birthday when she announced it."

He leaned closer. "Assuming you and your brother can get the cash together."

My stomach tightened. "We'll get the cash." If only to shove it in Tad's smug face when I told him mojitos were off the menu.

"Sure." His tone gave it about the same probability of a blizzard in hell.

"Tad!" Barb waved from her side of the bar. "Come say hello."

He rolled his eyes as he slipped off the high stool. "I hate that low part of the bar. It's the first thing I'll get rid of."

"It's one of the few wheelchair-accessible bars in Rincon Hill," I said.

He picked up his drink. "People can roll up to tables. No one wants to sit at a table-height bar."

"People who use wheelchairs do." I glanced over at Barb's section. There were two people in wheelchairs bellied up to the bar. "And lots of folks like it." A man had hung his cane on the lip of the bar. His date sat beside him, making flirty eyes.

"Not me." He stalked off toward his aunt.

"Prick," Leo said, grabbing a glass from the rack over my head.

"If things fall through for us, that prick's going to own this bar," I muttered.

He put a comforting hand on my back. "Nothing's gonna fall through. You always figure shit out."

"*We* always figure it out. Together." I surveyed the bar I loved.

Lucie stepped through the door into the foyer. But instead of coming into the bar, she turned up the residents' hall and trudged up the stairs.

"She looks tired, huh?" Leo said. "She okay?"

"I don't know. I haven't talked to her much since we dropped off that baby stuff last week. Just a couple texts. She said she was fine."

"Maybe you should check on her. We'll be good for a while. It's not too busy."

I glanced at the thin crowd. "Okay. I'll ask Norm to make her something to eat."

"Nah, he'll just fry her up a burger."

"She loves burgers," I said.

"I know, but she's eating for two. I'll make her something more nutritious. Give me fifteen minutes." He disappeared into the back.

I made sure there was enough glassware in both sections of the bar and took out the trash. As I washed my hands in the breakroom, Leo presented me with a sack containing two to-go boxes. "Ta-da."

"What is it?" I started to pry open the box on top.

Leo put his hand over the top. "No peeking. Just take it to your lady love."

"She's not my 'lady love,'" I protested.

"Fine. Your baby mama and neighbor-with-benefits situationship."

I didn't correct him about the benefits situation with Lucie. That part of our relationship was, if not completely over, at least on a break while she figured stuff out.

"Thanks for this," I said. "I'll be back to close."

"Sure you will."

What the fuck was it with people? I always followed through on my promises. I'd figure out how to buy the bar and support Lucie and our child. I always found a way.

Upstairs, I tapped on Lucie's door. "Hey, Lucie, it's Danny."

When she opened the door, her computer screen was the only light on in the place. She wore fuzzy socks, leggings, and an oversized sweatshirt. She had on a pair of glasses that made her eyes look extra big, and she blinked up at me. "What are you doing here?"

"I brought you dinner." I held up the sack. "Have you eaten?"

Her stomach rumbled, and she stepped aside to let me in.

I flicked on a light in the entry and walked into the kitchen, where I turned on more lights. I washed my hands, then hunted in her cabinets until I found a couple of plates and some utensils.

"Why don't you make yourself at home," she said wryly.

"Are you drinking enough water?"

She walked to her desk and carried back an almost-full glass of water.

"Good effort," I said. "Be sure you drink that with dinner." I opened the containers. The top one held two chicken breasts nestled into pasta with Leo's special spinach pesto. The bottom one held a salad. How had he found greens and raw veggies in Norm's kitchen? Leo was a culinary magician.

I divided the salad, pasta, and chicken between two plates and carried it to her table. Then I pulled out her chair. "Come sit. Leo made the food, so I'm sure it's good."

She sank into the chair, and I scooted her closer to the table. I went to get myself a glass, filled it from the tap, and joined her across the table.

Lucie already had a mouthful of food.

"How is it?"

She rolled her eyes to the ceiling as she chewed and swallowed. "You're wasting him in that bar, you know. He should run a restaurant."

My shoulders crept up toward my ears.

Deliberately, I lowered them. "He wants to run the bar with me. And he made this downstairs. He and Norm could work something out."

She raised her eyebrows and took a bite of pesto-coated chicken.

"Maybe we can coax Norm into early retirement," I said.

She didn't dignify that with an answer but dug into her dinner. When our plates were clean, we cleared the table.

"You can go back to work." I plugged the sink and started filling it. "I'll clean up."

"Really?" She tipped her head to the side. "Okay." She padded back to her desk.

I washed the dishes and put them away, then I wiped down her counters and table. She was still working, so I swept the kitchen floor too. I refilled her glass from the pitcher in the refrigerator, watching her shoulders hunch as she typed. That couldn't be comfortable.

I imagined what it must be like to have Lucie's job, to work at her desk at the newspaper all day, then return home and work at her desk into the night. Tending bar was hard on my feet, and the hours were shit, but at least I could move all day. I wouldn't trade places with her for the world.

Gently, I rested a hand on her shoulder. "Is this okay?"

The keys clacked under her flying fingers. "Sure, I guess."

With light pressure, I kneaded her shoulders until they eased away from her ears and I didn't feel a knot under my hands. As I worked up the vertebrae at the base of her neck, she groaned. "Feels good."

"Yeah?" I stroked from her neck down between her shoulder blades.

"My shoulders are so tight." She moaned.

My dick stiffened. It remembered another part of her that was tight. Gritting my teeth, I pressed my thumbs into the outsides of her shoulders, then moved them an inch toward her spine and pressed again. I repeated the motion until my thumbs met her backbone. Then, like my physical-therapist sister had taught me, I curled my fingers over the front of her shoulders and pressed my fingertips under her clavicle into the hollow, against her pectoralis major, to counteract her typing hunch.

"More," she said, leaning her head back. Her long eyelashes fanned across her cheeks. I shuffled back half a step. I did *not* want her to lean too far back and figure out I had a hard-on. As I dug my fingers into her muscle, I tried not to imagine letting my hands drift lower to the tops of her breasts. To move over the swell of them and cup them from underneath, to feel their heavy warmth in my hands, to run my thumbs over her nipples and hear her breath catch as pleasure lit her up inside.

I failed. Completely.

I failed so hard that I imagined I heard her gasp. But when I looked into her face, it was relaxed. She wasn't worked up like I was over a G-rated shoulder massage.

Her hands had fallen from her keyboard into her lap. I bet a hand massage would feel great too, so I ran my hand to the cap of her shoulder and opened my mouth to suggest it, but she straightened.

"I'm going to bed," she announced.

I lifted my hands and rolled back her chair. "Good. You look like you could use some sleep."

She stood and arched her brow. "Thanks."

"I didn't mean—I'm sorry. You're gorgeous, even when you're tired."

She tightened her lips. Was she trying to hide a smile? "That's your job, you know. You did this to me, so the least you can do is tell me I look pretty."

"I...I'm sorry?"

"Don't worry about it." She moved her hand toward me like she'd lay it on my arm but snatched it back at the last minute. "I'm joking about it being your fault but not joking about saying I'm pretty."

"You're beautiful," I said. It was true. Despite the shadows underneath, her dark eyes drew me in. I wanted to kiss her more than anything.

Her plush lips kicked up on one side. "Thank you for dinner. And for cleaning up after."

Those lips. I blamed them for the babble I was powerless to stop. "I can come by anytime you like. I could talk to Barb about switching up my schedule. I could come up and make you dinner. I'm no Leo, but I'm a decent cook. And on Saturdays, I don't usually work until after seven, so I could be here all day. I'll clean your place, arrange all the baby stuff—"

"That's sweet," she interrupted me, "but I'm good. My friends have offered to help."

"Okay." My stomach felt heavy like I'd eaten one of Norm's burgers.

"Hey, no pouting," she said with another sexy smile. "I'll let you know if I change my mind, okay?"

I nodded and trudged to the door. Of course she'd accept help from her smart, accomplished friends and not from a bartender.

THE MOST AWKWARD
DOUBLE-DATE EVER

While I'm proud of all the new lives I've helped usher into the world, my legacy extends beyond the delivery room. I've mentored young people who are now doctors. I've supported advancements in women's health. My legacy combines the lives I've touched and the path I've helped pave for a healthier tomorrow.

Dr. Namrita Cheema, OB-GYN

LUCIE

"*I*s there anything more humiliating than wearing a paper poncho while sitting on a roll of paper? I feel like pork loin at a butcher," I said.

"I know you're nervous," Savannah said, folding my shirt and laying it on top of the other clothes she'd placed on the chair in the exam room, "but early exams are no big deal."

"Wait. It gets worse than this?" My voice rose into such a high register that it hurt my throat. I swallowed.

She gave me a flat look. "Honey, everyone at this hospital is going to look at your hoo-hah before this is over. Not to mention —hmm. Plenty of time for that later."

"Not to mention *what*, Savannah?"

"Have you read The Book yet?"

"Not...not yet. I'm still writing mine, remember?"

She squinted at me. "Or are you putting it off, thinking if you don't read it, it might not happen?"

"That's not it." *Quite.* "I'll read The Book and do all the other preparations later, once my manuscript is in a good place. Promise." Was I promising her or myself? Or the fetus lodged in my uterus?

A knock sounded on the door.

"Come in," I said, relieved.

A brown-skinned woman no taller than me bustled in. She flashed me a radiant smile. "Hello, Lucie. I'm Dr. Cheema." When she shook my hand, hers was dry and warm, which made mine feel extra clammy.

Unbothered, she extended her hand to Savannah. "Is this your partner?"

"We're friends. I'm Savannah," she said. "I'll be coming with Lucie to her appointments."

"Ah. And Dad is...?" Dr. Cheema raised her lush eyebrows, making me wish I hadn't overplucked mine back in the '90s.

"Just a...a hookup. And a friend. My neighbor, actually. With benefits. Though that's over now. In fact, I'm actively avoiding him." I cringed. Where had all *that* come from? I certainly hadn't meant to mention the avoiding-him part. But the night he'd brought me dinner and offered to do more haunted my thoughts. His caretaking was dangerous. I couldn't let myself rely on him. I'd gotten myself into this mess, and I'd see it through.

"Is he the kind of friend who might come to your appointments?" Dr. Cheema asked.

"No." Sure, he'd seen me naked, but naked and wearing an oversized envelope was something else entirely. And with all the weird pregnancy hormones, I'd gotten hot and bothered over a flipping *shoulder massage*. It would be too humiliating if I got aroused while I was sitting on a sheet of goddamn paper. "Did you miss the part where I said I'm avoiding him?"

"Okay," she said, making a note on her tablet with a stylus. "Are you planning to invite him into the delivery room?"

Delivery room? I hadn't thought that far ahead. My immediate thought was *no way,* but that didn't seem fair to him, considering we planned to co-parent this baby. Would he want to see his child's birth? "I don't know."

She made another note. "You've got plenty of time to work out your birth plan."

I turned wide eyes on Savannah. "Birth plan?" I mouthed.

"Read The Book," she mouthed back.

Subtly, I gave her the middle finger. She hid her laugh with a cough.

Dr. Cheema looked up. "Do you have questions for me?"

Shit. This felt like a job interview. "Just one. I had a couple sips of wine after I, um...conceived, but before I knew I was pregnant. Do you think the baby's okay?"

The doctor smiled. "I'm sure the baby is fine. But I recommend you don't drink alcohol for the rest of your pregnancy."

"Right." I nodded. It tasted funny now anyway. Though I missed going to the bar. I loved living alone, but living over a bar was like having a family who didn't care if you had a little too much and danced on a table, or if you wanted to drink your goddamn drink in a corner and not say anything.

Dr. Cheema checked her tablet. "Is this your first pregnancy?"

"Second. I had an abortion in college."

"No complications?"

Other than my father's disappointment that I'd almost derailed my career? "No."

"Got it. Are you aware of any genetic conditions in Dad's family?"

I cringed. "No?" I knew nothing at all about Danny's family, except that it was Italian and large.

"Not a problem. Let me know what you find out. Due to gaps in your medical history and your age, would you like to have the screening tests for genetic disorders?"

I must have looked panicked because Savannah mouthed, "The Book."

"I guess?" I shrugged, trying to seem nonchalant while I was sweating through my paper dress. "More information is always better."

Dr. Cheema nodded and made a tick on her tablet. "We'll watch you closely through the pregnancy in case of complications."

"Complications?" Suddenly, keeping the baby didn't seem like such a smart decision.

She set her tablet in her lap and looked into my eyes. "The occurrence of miscarriage, including late miscarriage, increases with age. We'll do the genetic tests for chromosomal abnormalities, and we'll do blood tests to check for gestational diabetes and preeclampsia. You're also at a slightly higher risk for cesarean section, postpartum hemorrhage, and prolonged labor. You should call the office if you experience any spotting."

There wasn't enough air to breathe. Was the ventilation working in the tiny exam room?

Savannah squeezed my hand. "You're going to be fine, honey. You're healthy, and Dr. Cheema and her staff are going to take care of you. Women give birth in their forties all the time."

"I'm thirty-nine," I snapped.

"You'll be forty in August, and that's three months before the baby is born."

"Fuck off." I regretted that instantly. "I mean, you're right."

"Your friend *is* right," Dr. Cheema said. "Starting motherhood in your forties is becoming more and more common. We know so much more now than we did twenty years ago. We'll be well prepared for any complications."

"Okay." I breathed out. My hand steadied under Savannah's. "Okay."

"Okay," Dr. Cheema chirped. "Lie back on the table, and we'll do an ultrasound."

I reclined on the table while Dr. Cheema wheeled over a machine with a weird-looking keyboard and a screen.

"Next time, a technician will do your ultrasound. But I usually like to do the first one. Hearing the baby's heartbeat for the first time never gets old. Feet in the stirrups." She picked up a wand and sheathed it in a condom.

"What?"

As she spread gel over it, she said, "An internal ultrasound gives us a much better picture of the fetus when it's this small."

I glared at Savannah. "You didn't think to warn me about the vaginal probe?"

She winced. "Surprise?"

~

A few weeks after my OB-GYN appointment, on a Thursday in late May, I pulled open the door to welcome Carly and Andrew to my apartment.

I tugged Carly into a hug. "It's good to see you. And you too, Loverboy." I hugged him next, savoring his blush. "Are you treating our girl like the goddess she is?"

"Every chance I can," he said, resting a hand on her lower

back. Carly leaned a little closer to him, fitting into his side like the magnetic cable on my laptop.

Ugh.

As I shut the door behind them, I raised my eyebrows. "Is he?"

"Yes." Now she blushed. "Especially now that award season is over and I'm home most of the time. He treats me like a queen."

"Good." It was what she deserved after the treatment she got from her shitstain of an ex-husband.

"I brought you these." She held up a shopping bag.

I peered inside. "What is it?" It looked like clothes. At least Carly's taste was better than my mother's. She only sent me dresses in the pastel colors she loved but I hated.

"Maternity clothes."

I dropped the bag, and it hit the floor with a bang.

"You won't need them for a while, but Andrew's sister-in-law Alicia was getting rid of them, and they're quality pieces. Work clothes, casual clothes, even an evening gown. Though you might have to have it taken up since she's taller than you." She scanned my face. "Just put them away in your closet for now. In a few months, you'll be glad you have something that fits."

That sounded like a problem for Future Lucie, one I was happy to ignore tonight. I picked up the bag and dumped it into the killer crib. "What's the deal with baby goods? All I have to do is say I'm knocked up, and things show up at my place. Does anyone actually buy new stuff for babies, or have they all been wearing the same ten onesies manufactured in 1982?"

"That stuff is expensive, and kids grow quickly," Carly said. "Accept as many gifts as you can. Growing up, we had a whole program going where the girl down the street would give me her cast-offs, then I'd give them to my younger cousin. Though..." She winked at Andrew. "I don't think everyone shared that experience. I can't imagine Audrey Jones accepting hand-me-downs. Did you ever wear hand-me-downs, sugar?"

"Not really." He brightened. "I had a pair of jeans I wore until they got holes in the knees."

Carly and I exchanged a glance. "That's not the same thing, honey. Anyway, Lucie, if you find you need something else, I know all the good resale shops."

Baby things were already piled to the top of the crib. Anything more, and it'd tower over my desk.

I changed the subject. "Where do you want to go for dinner? There's a good Italian place, a dive where they serve fantastic pizza, and a Thai place, though it hasn't been as great since the original owners sold it and moved to San Diego."

"I heard there's a pop-up supper club near here tonight," Andrew said.

"A what?" Andrew and I might both be millennials, but sometimes he seemed like a different generation entirely.

"A chef sets up a temporary restaurant. Tonight, it's in some place called Barb's Bar. On the map, it looked close to here."

I laughed. "It's downstairs. And I'd bet my last dollar the chef is Leo Carbone. He's, um, Danny's brother." I examined the toe of my high-heeled boot. "His food is excellent. We can go if you want."

"You'll be okay?" Carly asked.

"Yeah." Danny didn't work Thursday nights. Besides, I'd been missing the bar lately. It'd be good to chat with Barb. "Let's go."

Andrew and Carly looked at me funny when I tiptoed past the second-floor landing. It was a habit I'd started since I'd told Danny about the pregnancy. We might be forced into co-parenting, but that didn't mean we had to spend time together before the baby was born. Besides, we both needed time and space to think about our situation. At least I did.

Safely past the landing, Carly told me the story of a starlet she'd styled whose dress had gotten lost in shipment, so Carly had to find a replacement gown at the last minute. Andrew, who must have heard the story before, beamed proudly the whole time she told it.

They were so cute, it was disgusting.

As I pulled open the door to the bar, I said, "Watch out, it's a dive."

But it wasn't.

When we walked in, the place had been transformed. I recognized a few of the Thursday-night regulars looking as confused as I was. They were backed up against the bar, staring at the tables, which had been lined up into two communal rows like at family reunions. White cloths were draped over the stained wooden tables, and fake candles flickered across white china plates alongside silverware that was much nicer than Barb's flimsy, dented service. The long tables were almost full. A delicious aroma of roasted meat and spices filled the air.

Leo carried out a pair of plates from the kitchen and murmured something as he set them in front of a pair of diners. When he straightened, he spotted me. "Lucie!" He spread his arms wide. "You came!"

"I...did?"

"I'm so glad Danny got over himself and invited you. Come on, I've got a private table for friends and family." He winked. "Introduce me to your friends."

I introduced Carly and Andrew to Leo as he guided us to a four-top against the wall. "I'll grab Danny," he said when we were seated.

"You don't have to—" I began, but he'd already hurried off.

Andrew sniffed the air. "It smells incredible in here."

"Remember that place in Milan?" Carly said. "It smells like that."

"That was a fantastic trip," Andrew said.

While they reminisced about it, I started to sweat. Danny hadn't mentioned the supper club. In fact, we hadn't talked for weeks. Not since he'd brought food up to my place. Some of it was because I'd been busy, but a lot of it was because I didn't want him to think I needed him to take care of me. Every time he'd offered to bring me food or help me organize the baby stuff, which I was ashamed to admit was still piled in that damned crib I couldn't use, I'd turned him down. We were in this situation because of me. I'd forgotten the Plan B, and it'd been my choice to keep the baby. He didn't owe me a thing. I could do this on my own.

I hoped he wouldn't think I'd come here looking for him.

I was pleating my napkin in my lap when someone loomed over our table, his woodsy scent cutting through the oregano and fennel that filled the restaurant that night.

"Hey," he said.

His hair was down tonight, curling a bit at his shoulders. He wore a black dress shirt and black trousers, similar to what Leo had on, but Danny's broad shoulders and narrow waist made it look sexier somehow. Not as sexy as his bartender T-shirts, which outlined every muscle on his chest and shoulders. My mouth went dry, remembering what Danny looked like underneath his clothes.

Stop!

I closed my eyes to pull myself together, then I looked up at him. "Hi. These are my friends Carly and Andrew. Andrew suggested that we come down for dinner. I didn't think you'd be here since it's Thursday."

His cheeks turned pink. "I'm working as a favor to Leo. I came over to grab your drink order."

"Oh." My face went hot, and my palms started to sweat.

Andrew stood and held out his hand. "Hi. You must be

Danny. We've heard...nothing about you. Why don't you join us?" He pointed at the empty chair next to me.

"I...but..." He turned dark, helpless eyes on me.

"I insist," Carly said, her eyes glittering.

"I'll, uh, I'll get your drinks first. Wine?" He waited for Carly and Andrew to nod. "Lucie, if you'll come with me, I can mix you up a mocktail."

"I...okay." He was right. We needed to talk before he joined us in what was about to become the most awkward double-date ever.

He pulled out my chair, and I followed him to the bar. He went behind it and selected a bottle of wine from a carton on the floor. As he reached for the glasses on the overhead rack, I tried not to ogle the way the thin fabric of his shirt stretched over his ribs, tracing his obliques, or the way his biceps strained the sleeves as he pulled out the cork.

"I really am sorry," I repeated. "I didn't expect to see you here."

"It's okay," he said gruffly. "It's good to see you. You look good."

"Thanks." I smoothed a hand down my belly. My work pants had started to get tight, so I'd worn a black knee-length skirt with a stretchy waist. That way, I could eat as much as I wanted. My morning sickness was never severe, and it had ended entirely last week. Now I couldn't seem to get enough to eat.

He pulled something out of the refrigerator under the counter and poured it over ice in a highball glass. He spritzed it with club soda and garnished it with a cherry. "Try this," he said.

"Cheers," I said as I picked it up. I sipped it. It was citrusy and bright. Sweet, but not too sweet. "This is delicious," I said before I took a longer swig.

"Glad you like it. I created a mocktail menu, and that's the most popular." His cheeks were red at the tops again as he poured a glass of club soda.

"What do you call it?" I asked.

"The Tell-Tale Tart." The blush cascaded down his neck.

"That's...a great name, actually." I squinted at him. I'd known he was great with drinks, but I hadn't known it extended to words too.

"Are you sure it's okay if I join you and your friends?" he asked. "I don't want to intrude."

"You heard them. Neither of us has a choice in this. She wants to get to know you, I think. She's nice, kind of pushy. And Andrew's a good kid."

"Kid?" He wrinkled his nose. "How old is he?"

"Thirty-three."

He fisted two wineglasses, tucked a bottle of wine under his arm, and lifted his club soda. "Oh."

He stared straight ahead as he walked back to our table, where Carly and Andrew sat with their heads together. When I sat across from her, Carly scooted away from her boyfriend, her cheeks red.

"No canoodling," I said. "Save it for when you get home."

"PDA is allowed on date night," Carly said.

"Remind me to stop joining you on your date nights," I grumbled.

Danny poured wine for Carly and Andrew, then sat down.

Andrew raised his glass. "To new friends."

We echoed him. Was Danny really a friend like I'd told Dr. Cheema? He was a neighbor, and we'd be co-parents soon. It'd probably be easier if he and I were friends. But integrating him into my friend group sounded complicated. Especially when Carly and Andrew shared the kind of intimacy that made me uncomfortable. The kind that required allowing yourself to be vulnerable and imperfect.

"How's your book coming, Lucie?" Andrew asked.

"I had a couple of good phone interviews this week. The premise is coming together." But my writing wasn't. I hadn't been able to tie the interviews together in a way that spoke to me yet. Thinking about how little time I had made my heart race. "I think I can finish the first draft within three months, then revise it before...you know."

It felt like everyone's gaze dropped to my midsection, and I put a hand over it.

Danny cleared his throat. "I'm constantly amazed that Lucie works a full-time job while writing a book. I could never be that smart or organized."

I side-eyed him. He'd never struck me as unintelligent or disorganized. In fact, he seemed to run the bar most nights while Barb chatted up the regulars. But I said nothing.

Carly asked, "You work here at the bar, Danny?"

Before he could answer, Leo strode up to the table. "An amuse-bouche of seared scallops with prosciutto and sage."

He set the plate of four ham-wrapped jumbo scallops in the center of the table.

"Yeah," Danny said, "I've worked here since I was eighteen. I started as a dishwasher. Over the years, Barb's been good to me."

Leo lingered at the table. After a few seconds, he said, "Aren't you going to tell them the rest?"

Danny stared hard at the morsel of food closest to him.

Why was he silent? He hadn't stopped talking about his plans to buy the bar since Barb had announced it last December.

Leo shook his head. "He's buying the place."

"*We're* buying the place," Danny said sharply. "Though..."

"Though what?" I asked.

He kept his eyes on the food. "Now that I have, um, other responsibilities, I'm wondering if my plan still makes sense."

"Wait. You're not talking about *me*, are you?" I leaned over to snag his gaze.

"You and the, um, baby."

"That's my brother," Leo said, a touch of pride in his voice. "Always looking out for family. He was like another parent."

"I don't need your money," I said. "I'm fine. I've got plenty of help." Quickly, I glanced at Carly, who nodded. "It's your dream to own this bar."

"Dreams change," he said. He grabbed the closest scallop and popped it into his mouth. He chewed and swallowed. "Outstanding, Leo."

The rest of us did the same. The scallops were buttery in texture, the taste a perfect mix of salty, herbal, and slightly sweet. "God, Leo, that's amazing," I said.

He glowed at the praise and pulled up a chair. "You like it?"

"Who wouldn't?" I said.

The rest of the meal was just as excellent. As I pushed back my empty panna cotta dish, I said, "When you guys buy the bar, you should serve this."

Leo beamed, but Danny nodded toward the clump of regulars at the bar. A few of them had left, and the ones who remained looked like they'd landed on an alien planet. "I don't think it'll fly with our clientele."

Right. I probably couldn't afford to eat like this every night either. And the types of establishments that served amuse-bouche generally didn't welcome babies. "A supper club would be fun every once in a while though."

"Yeah." Both Carbone brothers seemed to deflate.

"Do you have social media or a website?" Andrew asked. "I'd like to come to your next pop-up. And tell my friends about it."

"Not yet," Leo said. "I wasn't sure if it'd fly."

"It'll fly all right," Andrew said. "Let me know if you need help. I learned how to do promotional posts from my little sister, who's in marketing and public relations. I bet she'd give you a free consult." He pulled one of his Math Nerd cards from his pocket, scrawled his number on the back, and handed it to Leo. "Call me."

"Thanks. Your dinner's on the house."

We protested, and by the time we'd talked Leo into giving us a bill, which Andrew paid, I was yawning.

"I've got to call it a night," I said.

Carly shot me a concerned look. "I've never known you to be the first one to turn in. Are you okay?"

"I know it's no bigger than a lemon, but growing a baby is hard on the body. And I'm not sleeping great either." I covered another yawn.

"We'll walk you up." Carly rose from her chair.

"I can do it," Danny said. He stood and pulled out my chair.

"That's right," Carly said with a knowing smile. "You're her neighbor."

"Fuck you," I murmured as I kissed her cheek.

"Maybe *that's* what you need," she whispered, "to help you sleep?"

Damn it, she had a point. I'd slept so well with Danny. And since he'd already knocked me up, it wasn't like we could get into any more trouble. What was a little sex and a snuggle between co-parents?

Danny and I climbed the stairs in silence. It wasn't until we reached my door that he spoke. "Thanks for coming tonight. It meant a lot to Leo."

"I—I didn't mean to, like, stalk you or anything. I thought you were off on Thursdays."

"Of course I'm going to help Leo out." He narrowed his eyes. "Have you been avoiding me?"

"I'm trying to give you space. And myself. This is a weird situation, right?"

"Yeah." He ran a hand through his hair. "But we don't have to make it weirder by avoiding each other."

I winced. "I'm sorry. I'm glad we came. The food was delicious. I hope it was successful for you guys."

"We had good numbers. I'm hopeful." He leaned against the door, eyelids drooping.

"Tired?" I fit my key into the lock. "Want to come in for a nightcap?" Did that make me sound sultry like Lauren Bacall in a black-and-white movie, or ancient like my grandma?

He stared at me for a long moment, so long that I regretted saying the word *nightcap*. I regretted a lot of things.

"Lucie, what are we? Are we two people in an uncomfortable situation who avoid each other because we don't know how to navigate it, or are we neighbors and friends who could be more?"

"Could we be neighbors and friends who occasionally hook up while navigating an uncomfortable situation? Because an orgasm will help me sleep, and I navigate better when I'm well rested. I write better too."

"You're having a hard time writing your book?"

"Yeah. There's not enough *there* there yet, you know?"

"*There* there?" His dark eyebrows scrunched.

"I'm not done with my interviews. I need one or two big ones and a few regular people. People who've made a difference in their communities but who aren't famous outside them. I want to show people that everyone can have a legacy."

God, the way he listened to me, leaning in, eyes wide, taking in my words, my body language, everything. It was such a turn-on. I stepped closer. "So, want to come in?"

He pushed off the wall. "I don't want to hook up. Not with you." He stomped away, muttering something, but my pulse roared in my ears. Something sharp—shame, probably—lodged in my chest.

"Fuck you," I muttered, "if you don't think I'm good enough for a hookup." I shoved my door open.

Heavy footsteps sounded behind me, and I turned. My breath caught at the smolder in his eyes. Had he changed his mind? Was he going to fuck me against the door again? I shivered.

"I don't want a hookup, Lucie. I want a real relationship. One where we don't play games or avoid each other. One where we act like grown-ups, like people who are going to be parents. Like people who genuinely *like* each other. Because I genuinely like you."

My mouth dropped open, but no words came out. His eyes blazed, and his jaw, I knew, would be hard as granite if I dared to touch it.

"Stop avoiding me, okay?"

I blinked. "I...okay."

"Good." He nodded once, then stalked toward the stairs. This time, I heard his heavy footsteps go all the way down to the first floor to Barb's.

I closed my door. He genuinely liked me? Who the fuck said things like that?

Danny Carbone, that's who.

16

—————

FOR CHRIST'S SAKE

The Tell-Tale Tart
Combine equal parts fresh orange juice, grapefruit juice, and lime juice
in a pitcher. Add a splash of agave nectar. Pour over ice, then top with
club soda. Garnish with a cherry.

DANNY

"*D*anny Carbone, is that you?" a white-haired lady asked as I set the pitcher of margaritas on their table. She'd just joined her friends who, I noticed, wore matching navy skirts and white blouses with a medallion pinned to the pocket.

"Sister Frances!" I said. She stood, and I hugged her.

"How long has it been?" She stepped back and scanned me from head to toe, lingering on my shoulder-length hair.

I pulled it back into a ponytail and secured it with the elastic on my wrist. "I graduated twelve years ago, so that long I guess."

"It doesn't seem possible," she said. "Just the other day, you were the studious boy in my algebra class."

She introduced me around the table to the sisters. They were all younger than Sister Frances. She stepped closer to me, and the women restarted their conversation. More quietly, she said, "I don't suppose you ever made it to college?"

"Nah." I ducked my head. "There wasn't enough money for all five of us to go. Leo and I got jobs, but the younger ones all went. Giuliana is a physical therapist, Tony works at an insurance agency, and Elena is a computer programmer." I straightened my shoulders.

"And what about your cousin Nico?" she asked. "I always worried about him, especially when…"

"He got his GED in prison. And now he works here." Barb had let me hire him when no one else would, even after he'd done his time for stealing those cars.

"You should be very proud." She patted my shoulder. "Of yourself too. Do you manage the bar?"

"More or less. And I'm…" I couldn't keep it inside. I still wanted to impress my favorite teacher. "I'm buying it later this year."

"Really? Then my sisters and I will only have our weekly tipple here from now on." She grinned.

"Tuesday is ladies' night," I teased.

"You think men cruising for ladies could handle all this?" Laughing, she gestured at her friends.

"They wouldn't have a chance, Sister Frances. Can I get you anything…" But a flash of dark, unruly curls had caught my eye.

Lucie paused on the other side of the glass door and waved tentatively. We hadn't seen much of each other in the last couple of weeks since she and her friends had come to Leo's pop-up restaurant, but at least she hadn't seemed to be actively avoiding me. Even though I'd said I genuinely liked her like I was still that fifteen-year-old boy in Sister Frances's class.

But it gave me an idea. When I beckoned her in, she pulled

open the door and strode into the bar. She still looked tired, but her cheeks looked a little fuller and had some color in them.

"Sister Frances, this is Lucie Knox. Lucie is a reporter for the city paper, and she's writing a book. Lucie, Sister Frances taught me math in high school."

The women shook hands, though Lucie looked slightly horrified to be meeting a religious sister. She looked at her hand like it might be singed.

"Lucie's book is about women's legacies," I said. "She's looking for women to interview. Sister Frances, don't you spend your summers volunteering with an organization that builds schools and clinics all over the world?"

"These days, I spend more time teaching and serving in those schools and clinics than building them, but yes."

Lucie's eyes were bright. "Could I interview you, Sister Frances? Not tonight, but sometime? I'd love to hear your story."

"I'm always happy to talk about the mission," Sister Frances said.

I grinned, imagining the battle between these two strong women. Sister Frances would want to talk about the aid group and what they did, but Lucie would tease out the personal details. She'd get Sister Frances to admit she had a legacy.

As they exchanged contact information, I headed to the bar. Lucie grabbed my arm and pulled me around the side to the narrow hallway that led to the restrooms.

She stopped and looked up at me. "Thanks, Danny. That was really thoughtful of you. Sister Frances is exactly the type of person I'm looking to interview."

"Of...of course." I was standing way too close to her. The light from the exit sign glittered red in her hair, and her dark brown eyes seemed to glow, drawing me in. I could smell the coconut in her curls and under that, the musk of her skin. My gaze dropped to her chest, where her black shirt stretched and parted, revealing the deep valley between her breasts. Had her boobs gotten bigger? I wanted to bury my face in them.

Whoa.

I stepped back and dragged my eyes back to her face.

She smirked. "See you around, Danny."

As she slipped past me, her boob grazed my arm. I stilled for a minute until I could walk. Then I went straight to the walk-in cooler in the kitchen and stood there shivering until I got my erection under control. There were nuns in the building, for Christ's sake.

And although my dick was completely on board with Lucie's neighbors-with-benefits plan, my brain knew it was a bad idea. I'd already fallen too far to survive that.

17

ANOTHER PREGNANCY SYMPTOM

Our legacy is more than the clinics and schools we built. Personally, I hope I showed these women, all children of God, they were worthy of love and care, even the forgotten ones. I hope I ignited the fire to fight for themselves and their daughters. If even one of them carries that flame forward to build a better world, that's all the legacy I need.

Sister Frances Pernaska, Catholic Aid Services

LUCIE

I stomped into the office, grumpy and late. Grumpy because none of my pants fit anymore and late because I'd insisted on trying on every pair I owned to confirm it. I'd ended up wearing the same black, stretchy-waist skirt I'd worn every day this week. But the crowning aggravation was that the fitted shirt I'd put on wouldn't button over my growing belly. I'd had to throw on a sweater to hide the gap. And on the third day of an unseasonable-for-June heat wave, I'd sweated all the way to work.

As I poured myself a cup of disgusting decaf in the breakroom, Mario strode in. He grabbed the pot of regular coffee and sloshed it into his mug.

"We missed you at the morning meeting," he said. "I assigned you a piece on the protest at City Hall."

"What are they protesting?" I picked up my phone, trying not to be jealous of his coffee, which must taste fresher than this swill.

"The assault weapons ban."

I tilted my head. "Hasn't that been in effect for decades?"

He shrugged. "Guess they still don't like it. Try to come up with a fresh angle."

"A fresh angle on something that's been law since before the internet?"

"I have faith," he said.

My heart soared at the praise. Until he said the next thing.

"Didn't you wear that skirt yesterday? Laundry machine broken at your place?" His gaze slid down my body, and heat rushed up my neck.

My crankiness dialed up to eleven when Tad sauntered in, looking not at all sweaty but with dark circles under his eyes. He shuffled to the regular coffee pot.

"Howard literally wears the same mustard-yellow shirt every Monday, Wednesday, and Friday," I said. "It's still got the ketchup stain from the hot dog he ate at his desk on Wednesday."

"Really?" My boss wrinkled his nose. "I never noticed."

"Maybe I should write an article on the different fashion expectations for women and men in the workplace."

"Don't get your panties in a twist," Mario said. "I was expressing concern. You don't usually look this sloppy."

"Sloppy?" My face burned. I tugged my black sweater down over the skirt. "I never look sloppy."

His lip curled. "Sitting at a desk all day can be hard on your body. Some time at the gym would make you feel healthier, like Tad here." Mario clapped him on the shoulder. "He and I go to the gym every night after work."

Tad flashed him a smarmy smile. "Good for my body, plus it keeps me out of the house when the kids are at their worst, right before dinner."

"Must be nice," I said, "to stroll into your house, dinner on the table and kids cared for."

"It is," Tad said. "Though you don't have to worry about that. No spouse, no kids. Just freedom."

"And work," Mario added. "People without kids pick up the slack for the rest of us."

"Yeah." I forced a nonchalant smile onto my face, trying not to think about how much Mario was going to hate it when I told him I was going to take maternity leave. After Tad returned from his two weeks of paternity leave, our boss had given him shit assignments for almost a month. Not to mention how he'd act when I came back and had to miss work whenever the kid was sick.

"With all that free time, Lucie, you should try the gym," Mario said. "Firm up that belly." Slapping his taut stomach, he turned and sauntered out.

"Have fun at the rally." Smirking, Tad followed him.

I curled my fingers so tightly around my mug that I thought it might crack. I looked sloppy? *Fuck him. Fuck them both.*

But Mario was my boss, and I needed my health insurance. And, apparently, a pair of pants that fit so I could blend in with the guys. It was time to dig into that bag of scary maternity clothes Carly had brought me.

I poured my decaf down the sink, rinsed out my mug, and headed back to my desk to gather my things. I had a meaning-less protest to cover.

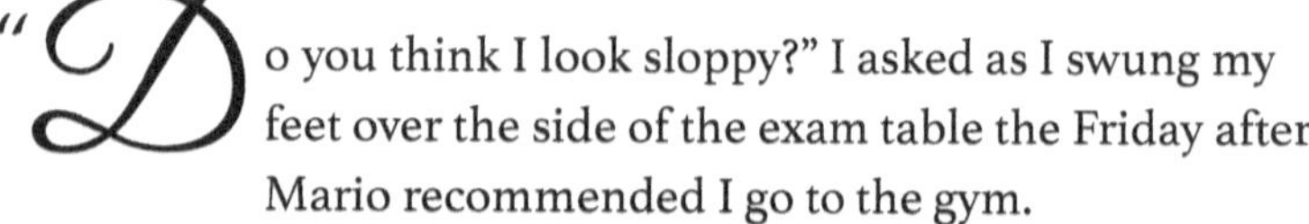

"*D*o you think I look sloppy?" I asked as I swung my feet over the side of the exam table the Friday after Mario recommended I go to the gym.

"Sloppy?" Savannah scrunched her nose. "No. You always look edgy and intentional about what you're wearing, unlike me." She pointed at her pink velour tracksuit and then up at her hair, which was pulled back from her face in a clip. "My grays are awful."

They did look pretty obvious because of the line where her blond hair dye started. I didn't think she wanted me to agree with her, but I wouldn't lie. "You look comfortable. And you work at home, so it doesn't matter what you wear."

"No, I guess it doesn't." She looked down at her white sneakers.

I shifted, crinkling the paper I sat on. "I didn't mean it doesn't matter what you wear. I just mean that no one is judging you for it."

"Are people at work judging you?"

"My boss asked if my washing machine was broken." I pointed at my black skirt folded on the chair next to Savannah's. "That is literally the only thing I don't hate that fits me."

"The in-between time," she said, "when your regular clothes don't fit, but you'd be swimming in maternity clothes, is the worst. Maybe Carly can help you out. I bet she's hidden a baby bump or two."

I smoothed down the paper gown. "Anything Carly picked would make me stand out. I need to blend in with the guys I work with. Whenever my boss remembers I've got a uterus, I get the shit assignments."

"That stinks. What did he say when you told him you were expecting?"

I barked out a bitter laugh. "I'm not saying a word. I'll never get another decent assignment again if he thinks I'm, like, maternal and shit."

She gave me a flat look. "You're going to have to tell him."

"Am I, though? What if I faked an injury and worked remotely until the baby's born?"

"It's kind of hard to get maternity benefits if they don't know you're pregnant."

"Maybe I don't need maternity benefits. If I'm working at home, I can watch the baby and work at the same time."

Savannah shook her head. "I'm not sure you realize how hard childbirth is on your body. Or how much care newborns need. Maybe you need to find a different job."

"Who'd hire a pregnant person?" I asked. "'Please give me a job, and by the way, I'm about to disappear on you for three months.'"

"They can't discriminate against you. It's illegal."

I raised my eyebrows.

"I know, I know, of course they'd get away with it." She sighed.

I examined my toes. "I'll fake some sports injury and say I have to work from home. Though my boss might forget I exist, and I'd be that much easier to let go in the next round of layoffs."

"Layoffs?" Savannah's eyes widened.

"Print media is dying. And don't get me started on generative AI. Of course there'll be layoffs."

She crossed her legs. "I'm sorry. But you've got your book deal. Could you write full time?"

"Not unless it really takes off. My advance was decent, but it's paid out in chunks. I'd have to have a few more books earning royalties to replace my salary."

She flashed me an encouraging smile. "I have confidence in you."

I wish I did.

There was a knock on the door, then it opened and Dr. Cheema bustled in. "Good afternoon, Lucie. How are you feeling today?"

Dr. Cheema didn't want to hear that I felt like crap about my job, so I said, "I'm okay."

"Any morning sickness? Swelling in your ankles? Constipation? Bloating?"

"No. Thank god. That sounds terrible."

Savannah snorted. "Just wait a few months. That's not even the worst of it."

"Wait, what's worse?" I asked.

"Sciatica. Varicose veins. At nine months, I couldn't take a full breath," Savannah said. Then she gasped. "Sorry, I shouldn't have said that. You'll forget all about it when the baby's born."

"Baby brain." Dr. Cheema nodded. "Lie back, and I'll take some measurements."

I lay down on the table.

"Have you been reading The Book?" Savannah asked. "It's all in there. If you're curious."

I'd stacked two biographies and a thriller on top of it on my bedside table. "Not yet."

"Read it. It'll help."

"Your friend is right," Dr. Cheema said, laying a very unscientific-looking tape measure across my baby bump. "More information is always better."

My head was ready to burst with all the interviews I'd done for my book. I couldn't squeeze in an entire baby book. Not until I was done with mine. So I changed the subject. "Thanks for the *external* ultrasound this time."

She pocketed her measuring tape. "Your baby's big enough

that we can scan it from the outside." She flicked on the screen, and we all peered at it. "Your baby looks healthy. Development is on track, heartbeat is in the normal range. Blood flow looks good, and the placenta and amniotic fluid are normal."

On the screen was a black-and-white profile of a baby. Its head was huge and its little body was curled up. I thought I could make out a bent leg and possibly— "Are those its fingers?"

"Good eye. Baby's hand is up in front of its face, and those are its fingertips. Here, there's sound too." Dr. Cheema clicked a button, and a rhythmic whooshing sound started. It reminded me of when I was a little girl, and I'd lie on the couch with my mom, listening to her heartbeat.

Hearing the baby's heart beating and seeing those five tiny bright points on the screen made something slot into place. There was an actual baby inside me. It had fingers and, I assumed, toes. It had a face. And a heartbeat that proved it was alive.

I couldn't distinguish any features. It looked like a generic baby. But it might have my father's nose. Or my mother's. My brown eyes. Danny's firm jaw.

"Do you want to know the baby's sex?" Dr. Cheema asked.

"You can tell?" I asked.

"Baby cooperated, so I'm fairly certain."

I exchanged a glance with Savannah. She'd been so supportive through this. She'd been a wonderful friend, but she wasn't the baby's parent. It didn't seem right to share the knowledge with her first. Especially after Danny had done me such a huge favor by introducing me to Sister Frances. Her interview had been gold.

"Could you write it on a piece of paper for me? I'd like to, um, share it with the father first."

"Aw." Savannah clapped softly. "I love that. We can seal it in an envelope with some of the screenshots, and you can have a little moment together."

"It's not a *moment*," I grumbled. "It's a reveal of what type of genitalia the baby has. It says nothing about what sort of person they'll grow into."

"Still…" She gave me a sidelong glance. "I think it's adorable that you want to find out together. But you'll tell me after? I want to get you an annoyingly gendered gift."

"Of course you do," I said. "And yes, I will." I reached out a hand, and she clasped it. "Thank you for coming to my appointments with me."

"…but now you want to ask Danny if he wants to come with you." She nodded. "I'm glad. But if he can't make it, call me, okay?"

"Yeah. God, my eyes are burning. I think it must be the low light in here."

Dr. Cheema and Savannah exchanged a glance. "Pregnancy symptom," they said at the same time.

"Your hormone levels are fluctuating," my doctor said, handing me a tissue. "You'll probably experience more emotional shifts than usual."

I blotted my eyes. "Goddammit."

18

I BUY INTO A SOCIAL CONSTRUCT

The Taming of the Blue
*Fill a highball glass with ice. Pour over ¼ cup blueberry syrup,
squeeze in a lemon wedge, and top with club soda. Garnish with blueberries and a lemon wheel.*

DANNY

Friday nights during the summer, especially when the Giants played, we were always slammed. I'd been pulling beers since the after-work crowd started trickling in at four. The crowd was rowdy by the bottom of the third inning when our first baseman hit a solo home run. I cheered along with the rest, then I turned away from the TV screen to see who needed refills. Lucie appeared in the seat directly in front of me.

She bit her lip and set a manila envelope on the bar. "Hi, Danny."

"Hey. It's been a minute." I could've kicked myself for saying it. Why had I said anything about how little I'd seen of her in the month since I'd introduced her to Sister Frances? Why couldn't I have said I was glad to see her? Because I was. She looked good. Her skin glowed, and her eyes were bright. I might have been seeing what I wanted, but I thought there was a curve to her belly under the oversized black top she wore over a long black skirt.

"Yeah. Um, got a second? Or like ten minutes?"

I glanced around at my thirsty patrons. "Give me a few to take care of everyone and then I'll take a break. You want something to drink?"

"I'd love a club soda."

"I can do better than that." I mixed up the simplest of my new mocktails, a club soda with a splash of lemon and my homemade blueberry syrup. I tossed in a few blueberries. The vitamin C would be good for Lucie and the baby.

I slid the drink in front of her, then I moved on to refilling beers and sodas. There was a burger up in the window, so I served that and took an order for chicken wings.

When everyone was happy, I turned back to Lucie. She was sucking down the last of her drink, the straw making a rattling slurp at the bottom of the glass.

"Want another?" I asked, grinning.

"Yes, please." She scooted the glass toward me. "I need to drink more fluids, and that was delicious."

"Are you hungry? Want me to put in your usual order?"

She clutched her stomach. "I already had dinner, but I'm hungry again. Would you, please?"

"You bet." I put in the food order, then I mixed her another mocktail. After one last check of everyone's drink levels, I told Nico I was going on break for a few, and I opened the hatch and walked out.

Lucie tipped her head toward an empty booth far away from

the televisions, and I followed her to it. I set her drink in front of her, then sat on the other side.

"What's up? You doing okay?" I asked.

"I'm fine. It's just..." She looked down at the manila envelope. "I don't feel I've been fair to you. This is...this is your baby too, and we've agreed to co-parent. I went to the doctor today, and she gave me some pictures. I wanted to share them with you." She slid the envelope toward me.

I started to pick it up, but she pinned it down with a fingertip. "I asked her to write the baby's sex on a slip of paper. I don't know it yet."

I yanked my hands off the envelope. "So this is, like, a gender reveal?"

She wrinkled her nose. "Gender is a social construct, at least until the child decides how they identify. But the doctor made an assumption based on the genitalia and wrote that down and sealed it in here."

I couldn't help but smile. Lucie was so smart. I usually went along with social conventions, but Lucie deeply thought about things, like whether our baby wanted to be assigned a gender before they even knew what that meant.

Still, years of social conditioning meant I'd bought into this particular social construct. It meant something to me. Lucie knew it, and she was letting me into this moment. Like a gift.

"You want to open it?" I asked.

"No, I want you to do it. Then tell me."

Taking a deep breath, I tugged on the envelope. Lucie let it slip under her fingers. I pried open the brad and pulled out a few photos. It was dark in the booth, so I grabbed my phone from my pocket and turned on the flashlight.

They were ultrasound photos, like the ones I'd seen at Belinda's baby shower. But this time, the baby was mine. The baby was curled up in Lucie's womb, and its tiny hand floated close to its face like it was about to suck its thumb. Remembering what Ma had said about pregnancy at Lucie's age, I asked, "It's healthy?"

She shot me a wry smile. "So far, so good. The genetic tests all came back negative."

"And you're feeling okay?"

"Yeah. I don't have any of the symptoms my doctor asked about. I'm good. Except I'm hungry all the time." She put a hand over her stomach.

"Good thing you live over a bar," I said right as Nico brought over Lucie's burger. Lucie thanked him and he walked away. "My kitchen is pretty well stocked. You could come down if you ever need a snack."

"Yeah, right." She didn't touch her burger. Instead, she fixed her gaze on the envelope. "You gonna look?"

I nodded. Taking a deep breath, I upended the envelope. A slip of paper fluttered onto the table. I lifted it. "Girl."

Lucie slumped back against the cracked vinyl cushion. "Girl."

"What, you wanted a boy?"

"No. I just hadn't thought about her gender being, you know, real. She's going to have to fight for everything she gets in this world. I'm going to have to talk to her about periods and the pink tax. She's going to have to carry a whistle or pepper spray, take self-defense classes, call someone when she's walking alone at night—"

Lucie's eyes were getting big and wild, so I interrupted her. "But there are great things about girls too. I have two sisters. I used to braid their hair. And when I had a few extra bucks, I'd buy them the fruit-scented lip gloss they liked. And one day, she could be a mother too." Thinking about my mother, I added, "Women are strong."

"We have to be." She cut her burger in half and shoved one half into her mouth. She rolled her eyes to the ceiling and muttered, "'om make a goo bur'er."

"Norm's the best," I agreed.

She chewed and swallowed. "So, my friend Savannah has been going with me to my doctor visits. And she's happy to do it. But if you, like, wanted to go with me, that'd be okay."

"You're inviting me to your doctor appointments?" My mind raced ahead. "Do you think I could be in the delivery room too?"

Lucie's shoulders tensed toward her ears. I was afraid I'd gone too far, too fast. She pulled a few napkins from the dispenser and wiped her hands. "If you want. You're the baby's father. I think you should be among the first to meet it—her."

"I'd love that. All of it. The doctor's appointments and the delivery room. Let me know when, and I'll get someone to cover my shifts. When the baby comes, I'll drive you to the hospital." We were doing this. We'd be partners. Not strangers who shared custody. Not a couple, but two people who'd share some aspects of our lives with each other because we shared responsibility for another human. There was pressure on my fingers, and I looked down. Somehow, I was clutching her hand.

She squeezed my hand again. "Okay."

When I looked up into her eyes, something strange happened. There was a swoop in my belly like the time Leo and I pretended we were superheroes and jumped from the garage roof. Words bubbled to my lips that I couldn't have stopped if I'd tried.

"My aunt and uncle's anniversary party is tomorrow. Come with me and meet my family?" The second the words flew out of my mouth, I wanted to hide my face. She'd never want to go to a party and meet a hundred nosy, loud Italian Americans. Not in a million—

"Okay."

"Okay?" I searched her face. Was she caught up in the moment too? Would she regret it later? Probably. And I'd let her out of it if she did. But she'd agreed to go with me.

The customers at the bar whooped. The Giants must have scored again. But it felt like they were cheering for me.

19

THIRTY-WHAT?

I'll never be the kind of person who gets awards or headlines.
My legacy is my kids' security, their happiness, and the strength
I show them every day. I proved you can be a mother, a provider,
and a fighter all at once. That's what I hope they remember
about me.

Carrie Carbone, dental assistant and mother of five

LUCIE

I stared through the window of Danny's Toyota at the giant cross on top of the modern building. "You brought me to church?"

"We aren't going to Mass," he said. "The church has a hall we rent for family gatherings. It's bigger than my aunt and uncle's place."

I got out of the car. Why had I thought meeting his family was a good idea? "I'm an atheist."

"Then you'll probably flame up as you cross the threshold," he said dryly.

"I'm serious," I said. "Are you religious?"

"Not really. My family is, though, so the church has always been a part of my life." When he circled to my side of the car, he held out his hand.

I didn't take it. "Are they going to have a problem when our child isn't baptized?"

"Maybe?" But his expression said *definitely.* "But I'll deal with that."

No way was I going to raise a child Catholic. Not after that story I'd done on how a local church—thankfully, not this one—had covered up decades of molestation by its priest. I'd learned the regional leadership protected all kinds of bad people in the name of religion. But a bubble of guilt about denying Danny something that mattered to him lodged in my belly, right next to our banana-sized fetus. "Are *you* going to have a problem with it?"

Pressing a hand to my back, Danny guided me through the parking lot toward the fellowship hall. He didn't answer until we stepped onto the sidewalk next to the sign that read, "CONNIE AND RANGI'S SILVER ANNIVERSARY PARTY THIS WAY." Tied to it were a bunch of balloons that danced in the breeze. He grabbed the strings to keep them from blowing in my face.

Finally, he said, "You still believe in birthdays, right?"

I chuckled. "I'm an atheist, not a monster."

"So, my family could host a big bash for our kid's birthday?" he asked. "Or we could take her to one of those awful pizza joints with the creepy animatronics?"

I grimaced. "I think there could be some negotiation around the animatronics."

"Then I don't care about the religion shit. But will it be okay if I tell her I believe in God, even if you don't? And would it be okay if we all went to my mom's place for Easter and Christmas?"

We all made it sound like he wanted to be something more

than co-parents. I might be meeting his family, but I wasn't ready for more. Not yet. Maybe not ever. I sidestepped that sinkhole by saying, "We can engage in dialogue around religion when the kid's an appropriate age. And I don't have any dispute with holidays, especially if it's a mostly secular celebration."

He grinned. "You've always gotta use those big, smart words. But I get it." He opened the door to the hall. "I think we'll be good."

I should've told him what weighed on my mind. That coming here was a step I wasn't sure I was ready to make. That he might read more into it than I intended for this concession I was making out of remorse for cutting him out of the pregnancy. But it was too late to turn back. Squaring my shoulders, I walked through the door.

"Danny!" A small child ran at Danny, and he swung her up onto his hip. My breath caught in my chest. God, it was sexy seeing him holding that little girl. One of my ovaries might have exploded. Good thing I was already pregnant.

Then I shook my head. A man showing care for a child shouldn't be anything special. Women did it all the time. *Stupid internalized patriarchy.*

The girl smacked a kiss on his cheek. "Nonna gave me almonds. Want one?" She held out a netting bag of pastel Jordan almonds. The candy coating had melted on her palm in colorful smears.

"Sure, put it here." He opened his mouth, and she dropped one in.

No, that wasn't adorable. It was disgusting.

"Really?" I said.

He shrugged. "Candy's candy. Want one?"

"I'll pass."

"That's cool," he said. "There's going to be a lot of great food. You'll need to pace yourself. Isn't that right, Emma?"

"'Cept the anise cookies." She shuddered. "They taste like black licorice. Yuck."

"More for me," he said.

"There you are." A dark-haired woman with Danny's olive skin clacked up to us in a pair of platform sandals. She stretched up to kiss his cheek, then wiped away her red lipstick print with her thumb. "She's got a special radar for her favorite cousin."

Acid reflux was burning in my gut, not jealousy that made me want to put my own lipstick print on Danny's cheek—if I were wearing lipstick.

"How's it going?" he asked her.

"Nuts, as usual. The boys have baseball games this afternoon, so we've got to hustle out of here in a minute. But first I want to meet your date." She cut her gaze to me.

Date?

"So, you didn't come over here to talk to me?" he said. "Lucie, meet my cousin Tina and her daughter, Emma. Tina, this is my upstairs neighbor, Lucie Knox. Lucie's a journalist for the city paper."

"A neighbor? Not your girlfriend?" she asked. When she looked at me, her gaze seemed to linger on my belly. I crossed an arm protectively over it. I thought I'd hidden my bump pretty well with my A-line dress.

"Christ, Tina," he muttered.

She shot me an apologetic expression I was sure was fake. "I'm an optimist. Sue me."

"We're friends and neighbors," I said. "That's all."

Danny seemed to stiffen.

"Hmm." Tina's glittering gaze ping-ponged between us. "I'm sorry I can't stay and talk, but the coach is, like, *intense* about being on time. I'll call you this week, Danny." She leaned in and kissed his cheek again. Then she shot me a sly smirk like she could sense the acid boiling in my belly.

Emma grabbed Danny's ears and planted a sticky kiss on the tip of his nose. "Bye, Danny. Lucie, don't eat the anise cookies, 'kay?"

"Got it," I said. "Nice meeting you."

He set Emma on the floor, and she trotted off with her mother.

"Hungry?" he asked.

"Starving. I don't like anise, but talking about cookies is making my stomach growl."

"No one goes hungry at an Italian party," he said. "I've gotta introduce you to the guests of honor and then I promise I'll feed you. Come on."

He led me to a couple who looked a few years older than us. The woman was about my height and shared Danny's dark hair and brown eyes. The man's skin was darker than hers, about the same shade as mine. He was taller and broader than Danny, with high cheekbones.

When the group they were talking to wandered toward the open doors that led to the courtyard and buffet tables, Danny stepped up and hugged them. "Aunt Connie, Uncle Rangi, let me introduce my friend Lucie Knox."

Connie leaned toward me as if she'd hug me, but I held out my hand for a shake. "Happy anniversary," I said.

She shook my hand, narrowing her eyes. "Only a friend? I think you're more than that." Unsubtly, she stared at my stomach. "Or you will be in a few months."

"Ma told you?" Danny asked. "She promised she wouldn't!"

Could she see I was pregnant? I sucked in a breath and pressed a hand on my belly as if I could flatten it.

"Of course she did." Rangi rolled his eyes. "There's no secrets between sisters. Congratulations, you two."

"But I—" Danny sighed. "Sorry, Lucie. I know you aren't ready for it to be public knowledge."

I rubbed my chest where my heart was beating too fast. "It's okay. As long as it doesn't get back to my boss."

"Promise." He traced an X over his breastbone. Then he turned to his aunt and uncle. "We're friends who're going to co-parent our...our daughter." A slow smile spread over his face.

I pressed my hand against my chest. Hearing him say "our daughter" like that wasn't sexy. Nope.

"Do you two have kids?" I asked. I hoped they had a dozen, and we could talk about all of them instead of the tiny human growing inside me—and my relationship with her father.

"No. I was almost forty when we met," Connie said. "I wasn't interested in kids. And twenty-five years ago, it wasn't as popular to start a family in your forties."

"Wait," I said. "How old are you?"

"Lucie," Danny chided gently.

Connie laughed. "It's all right. I take it as a compliment. I just turned sixty-three. And my groom is fifty-five, though he doesn't look a day over forty." She slipped her arm around his waist, and his big hand went around her shoulders.

It was true. He could've been our age. Though Danny didn't have smile lines like his uncle's, I was pretty sure I had a few. And Connie looked fabulous. "Your family has great genes," I said.

"It's all the red wine we drink," she said. "But speaking of my maturity, Danny, I'll be ready to retire in a few years, and I'm looking for someone to take over my insurance agency. Tony said you might be interested, considering your situation." She shot another pointed look at my belly.

"Oh, no." I wanted to step in front of Danny and shield him. I couldn't imagine him sitting in an office all day. "Danny and his brother are going to buy the bar where they work."

"Ah," Connie said. "Then I must have misheard about Leo going to see a kitchen space with Gio."

Danny's posture stiffened. "Leo wouldn't do that."

"Sure, Danny. But if anything changes, let me know. It's a solid business. You'd sell a lot of insurance with that face." She reached up and patted his cheek.

"Connie," Rangi said. "He said he wasn't interested."

She tilted her head. "*Lucie* said he wasn't interested."

When I glanced at Danny, he rubbed his hand over his mouth. I sighed. He was such a people-pleaser that he couldn't tell his aunt no. I'd already done what I could, so I waited for him to say the right thing.

He glanced at my midsection. "I'll call you if I change my mind, okay?"

That wasn't the right thing. I glared at him.

Connie's smile was broad. "Okay."

"We need to get Lucie some food," he said.

"It was nice meeting you both," I said. "Happy anniversary again."

"Thank you," Rangi said. "Good luck with the..." Another look at my belly.

Connie's glittering smile was calculating. "Talk to you soon, Danny."

As we walked through the doorway to the grassy courtyard, I wanted to put my arm around him. But what would I be protecting him from? His inability to say no to people? That was a problem he needed to solve himself.

"You're not seriously considering working at an insurance agency," I said.

"No." But that "no" sounded uncertain.

"You'd hate sitting behind a desk and wearing a tie." He wasn't wearing a tie today. He wore a soft-looking button-down in a green checked pattern that brought out the lighter streaks in his brown eyes. He'd rolled up the sleeves to show off his muscular forearms, sunlight sparkling on the dark hair. I swallowed and looked straight ahead at the tables of food.

"Maybe," he said. "I'm not the only person I have to think about."

I stroked my belly. "The baby will be fine. I've got health insurance."

"Doctor's visits aren't the only cost when you have a child," he said gently. "Daycare is expensive. So is college."

"Daycare." My head felt light. "I hadn't thought of that yet."

Like he could sense me wobbling, he threaded my arm through his. "I can switch up my schedule so I can take care of her while you're at work. My family can cover for us in an emergency, like if you have to travel."

The ground steadied. "That sounds good."

"We'll be fine. We've got some time. Now, what do you want to eat?"

I stared at the table loaded with food. "Everything."

Danny wouldn't let me try any of the cured meats or soft cheeses, but there were plenty of other things to eat. When we'd filled our plates, he led me to a table headed up by his mother. I recognized her from the baby shower I'd walked in on when I'd told him about the pregnancy. That seemed so long ago.

I sat next to Leo, and Danny sat on my other side, next to his mother. Across the table were a dark-haired man and woman and a blond woman, all in their twenties.

"Ma, you remember Lucie," Danny said. "Lucie, this is my mother, Carrie. You know Leo. And these are my other siblings. Elena and Tony—they're twins—and Giuliana."

"Hi." I nodded at them. Did they all know about the baby? They must, right? I didn't have any siblings, but if Carrie had told her sister, Danny must have told his siblings.

"I'm so glad you came." Carrie beamed. "I'm sorry I didn't

properly welcome you when we met at the bar. But welcome to the family. We're so excited. The very first grandchild!"

That answered *that* question. "Thank you." I speared a bite of sausage and popped it into my mouth. *Delicious.* Briefly, I closed my eyes to enjoy the savory, spicy flavor.

"Danny tells us you're a journalist," Carrie said.

"And you're writing a book!" Elena interjected. "Is it fiction or nonfiction?"

"Nonfiction," I said. "I'm interviewing women about their legacies."

"Like, politicians and philanthropists?" Elena asked.

"Some. And, also, regular women. Danny introduced me to Sister Frances."

"What a good idea," Danny's mother said, patting his hand. "She's helped so many people all over the world."

"And right here," I said. "In schools, shaping young minds."

"Young minds like Danny's," Giuliana said, raising her eyebrows.

Danny growled, "Watch it, Giuliana."

I glanced between them.

Leo nudged my elbow. "Try the mushroom ravioli."

I picked up a square of pasta with my fork and bit into it. Umami, thyme, garlic, and gooey cheese burst over my tongue. The buttery sauce tasted like comfort, like a warm blanket and a fire on a wintry day. I hummed in pleasure. "One of your recipes, Leo?"

"I made the pasta myself," he said proudly. "If you like it, I'll make you a to-go container."

"Yes, please," I said, spearing another square.

"Lucie, my sister and brothers and I want to throw you guys a baby shower," Elena said.

"A baby shower?" I repeated.

"You know," Tony said, "a party with tons of presents and embarrassing games."

"And food," Leo said. "I'll make a cream cake."

I glanced at Giuliana. Her blond eyebrows pinched together as her gaze hopped between Danny and me. Did she not want to host the party? Or was she concerned about something else?

The others were waiting for me to say something. They'd offered me a kindness I should accept because I wasn't an asshole. "Thank you. I'd..." I cleared my throat. I might not be an asshole, but I wouldn't lie and tell them I'd love it. Embarrassing games sounded awful. "Let's do it."

Elena jumped up and circled the table to hug me. Leo squeezed my shoulder. On my other side, Danny's grin stretched his cheeks.

Across the table, Giuliana's long blond hair hid her face like a curtain as she whispered something to Tony that made him frown. He glanced at Danny, then at me. When he saw me watching them, he dropped his gaze to his plate and mumbled something.

Giuliana's smile was feral when she looked across the table at her brother. "Speaking of celebrations, what are you planning to do for your birthday, Danny?"

"Piantagrane," Leo muttered beside me.

"What?" I asked.

He shook his head. "She's stirring up trouble."

Danny's cheeks went red as he set down the slice of garlic bread he'd lifted to his lips. "I don't know. I don't have plans."

I bumped his shoulder with mine. "I didn't know your birthday was coming up."

"Birthdays aren't a big deal for me." He picked up his fork and moved some food around on his plate.

He'd asked about celebrating birthdays earlier. Why would he say he didn't want to celebrate his? "We could do something,"

I whispered. Were those mind-altering mushrooms in Leo's ravioli? Had I just offered to do something couple-y with him?

"Really?" he asked, just as softly. Those gold-brown eyes of his sucked me in.

"Yeah," I murmured. Were mushrooms an aphrodisiac? Something strange was going on here. I swayed closer to him.

"Of course your birthday is a big deal," his mother said. "You'll come to the house. We'll have a party. Prosecco, cake, and music. It's not every day you turn thirty."

The happy haze cleared from my brain.

"Thirty...what?" I asked.

20

A HOT MESS

It's a tough job. Heartbreaking, sometimes. But I do it for the wins. Like the mom who stays clean for her kids. Or the guy who educates himself and rebuilds his life. Guiding these folks to become more than the mistakes they made, that's my legacy. Seeing that transformation, that fight to be better...that's what keeps me going.

Consuela Nova, parole officer

LUCIE

*W*ere auditory hallucinations another pregnancy symptom? I stared at Danny's mom, hoping she'd add another number to the thirty. Preferably a number bigger than five.

Giuliana's brutal smile broadened. "My big brother's turning thirty next week. Why? How old are you?"

My heart thundered in my chest. Danny seemed so mature, so in control. He had freaking *goals.* I hadn't had a clue about life when I was twenty-nine—which was *ten years* ago. I stood so fast my folding chair thumped to the ground.

"I—I need air."

Danny stood and righted my chair. "We're already outside. Are you okay?"

"No." I looked up into his unlined face. Fuck! I'd seen what I wanted to see. Anyone who paid attention would know it wasn't good genes that made his skin so flawless. Or kept his stomach so flat and his hair so lush. It was the fact that he was in his goddamn *twenties!* "I'm leaving. I'll call a rideshare."

I turned and jogged away as quickly as I could, considering the sway of my upsized pregnancy boobs. I'd just reached the open doors into the hall when I felt a touch on my arm.

"No." Knowing it was Danny, I shook my head. But I slowed to a brisk walk now that I was inside.

"Lucie, it doesn't matter."

I spun to face him. "You knew I thought you were older! Because I'd never...I wouldn't..." But I had. Not only had I slept with a man in his twenties, but I'd let him get me pregnant. I'd saddled a man ten years younger than me with a child.

"I...figured you thought I was older. Most people do. Since I was a kid, and my mom needed help with my younger siblings, I've always acted like I was older. More responsible." He glanced around us. "Let's go outside."

Shaking off his hand, I stomped out of the hall to the parking lot. The sun broke out from behind the clouds and blazed down on me, soaking into my black dress and heating my skin uncomfortably.

"You aren't ready for this." I gestured at my slightly rounded belly. "I wasn't when I was in my twenties. How could you fucking not tell me you're only *twenty-nine*? Did you know I'm ten years older than you? I'll be forty in August."

"How could I not tell you?" He flipped his palms up to the sky. "Because all you want to do with me is fuck. We don't talk."

"Talk? What do you want to talk about? We have nothing in common."

He looked like I'd slapped him. "Because I didn't go to college, because I work in a bar—"

"That's not it," I cut in. "My life was totally different when I was in my twenties. I was still finding my way, figuring shit out."

He raised an eyebrow. "And now you've got it all figured out?"

Sweat trickled between my boobs. I was a hot mess. And by *hot,* I didn't mean attractive. And he'd called me on my bullshit. "Fuck you." I pulled my phone from my dress pocket and pulled up a rideshare app.

He covered the screen with his big hand. "How can we be partners when you don't talk to me? When every time you don't like something, you storm off and give me the silent treatment?"

My hackles rose. "Okay. Fine. You want to talk? Let's talk. When I was in my twenties, I had an abortion. I wasn't ready to be a mother. Just like you aren't ready to be a father."

His eyes widened, and he shot a quick glance at the church. "Let's go sit in my car. I'll turn on the air conditioning."

"I don't want to sit in your car," I said. Steam was probably rising from my head. "I want to go home. *Alone.* While you stay here. Or go out. A guy your age should be partying with your friends on a Saturday. Or sitting at a baseball game, drinking a beer." God, a beer sounded fantastic. But I'd have to settle for a big, cathartic cry by myself in my apartment.

"God—fucking—damn it, Lucie!" He ran a hand through his hair. "Why can't you see that I'm exactly where I want to be? I want to be here, at the goddamn church, with my nosy, trouble-making family, and *you.*"

The sun had fried my brain. That was it. It made me halluci-nate. I sank to the hot concrete curb.

Danny was next to me in a moment. "Lucie, are you okay?

Do you need to go to the hospital? I can get Giuliana. She's trained in first aid."

"No," I mumbled. "I...I thought I heard you say you wanted to be here with me."

"That's what I said." He rubbed a circle on my back, and it felt nice. "Lucie, I don't give a shit about our age difference. I like you. A lot. And I'm ready to be your partner in this."

"How?" I looked up from the pavement. "How can we do this?"

He made a slower circle. "Any way we want. I don't care what anyone else thinks or how anyone else would do it. I want us to figure it out. Together."

I let my temple fall to his shoulder. I was still warm, but I wasn't ready to claw out of my dress, out of my skin, anymore. "I don't think Giuliana likes me."

His chin settled on my forehead. "She thinks she's protecting me. She's a lot like you. She can't imagine I'd want a baby. A family. Because she doesn't."

"Why do you want a family?" I asked, hypnotized by those circles he made on my back.

He paused. "I've always been surrounded by family. Even though I didn't have what most people think of as a traditional family. You know we all have different fathers? Except for the twins, of course."

I lifted my head from his shoulder to look at him. He didn't seem upset or embarrassed about it. "Tell me more."

Gently, he encouraged me to snuggle back into him with my head on his shoulder. "My mom and dad were married. He was older than her by about ten years."

"There seems to be a theme here," I said.

"Maybe." He shrugged. "He died of a heart attack when I was one."

"Wow. So young."

"You can have a heart attack, even in your thirties."

That could be a reason he didn't want to wait to have kids. "So, your mom remarried?"

"Nah. I think she didn't want to go through that heartbreak again. But she still liked sex, so..."

I hid my face in his shirt. I knew exactly what that *so* meant. Carrie and I had something in common.

"What about you?" he asked. "Why did you decide you were ready for a family now?"

"I figured it was my last chance. I'd been thinking about IVF, so when fate offered a free pregnancy, I...I kept it." My story felt a lot more selfish than Danny's.

"And what about your family?" he asked softly.

I considered telling him how pregnancy had shattered my mother's dreams. How my father had selfishly stayed in the program that ejected her. How my brilliant mother had set everything aside to be less than she could've been.

I shrugged. "Just your typical family. Nothing special."

"Hey." He eased out from under me and set two fingers under my chin. "Everything about you is special. Don't ever forget it." Then he kissed me.

I wasn't worthy of his high opinion of me, or of his care, or even of his big, loud family, but I kissed him back.

And just like Danny had promised, I burst into flame.

21

———

LADY LOVE OR BABY MAMA?

<u>Hope Is the Thing with Pomegranates</u>
In a pitcher filled with ice, combine equal parts verjus and pome-
granate juice. Stir. Strain into a champagne flute until half full. Top
with sparkling water and stir again. Garnish with raspberries.

DANNY

When Leo fiddled with the dial on my stove for the hundredth time, I finally asked, "What's wrong?"

"Nervous?" He shot me an evil smile. "Because your baby mama's coming for your birthday?"

"Yeah, I'm fucking nervous." I scanned the salad. Were there enough croutons? Or too many? Had I put them in too early? Would they be soggy by the time Lucie got here? "I'm asking if you are too."

"I hate your shitty stove," he said. "There's gas downstairs. Why didn't they run the fucking line up here?"

I shrugged and tossed a few more croutons into the salad.

"If we'd done your birthday dinner at my place, like usual, I wouldn't have to stress about whether the braciole's going to be raw or burned."

"If we'd done it at your place, it'd be harder for Lucie to come."

"You think if she had to do more than walk down a flight of stairs, she wouldn't come to your *birthday party?*"

"Fuck off," I said. I hated how well my brother knew me.

He cranked the stove dial down. "How's the risotto coming?"

"My arm's sore from all this stirring," Lizbeth whined.

Leo checked her pot. "Just a little more, baby. It's almost done."

"Yeah? I've still got a little more broth," she said.

"Pour it in, then when it's incorporated, kill the heat and stir in the cheese. Five more minutes, tops," he said.

"I'm going to need a shoulder massage later," she said.

He kissed the tip of her nose. "I got you."

I wasn't sure if I was jealous or revolted. Leo and Lizbeth had been dating about a month, since she started working at his favorite tomato stand at the farmer's market. They interacted so easily. I'd given Lucie only one shoulder massage, three months ago, and I hadn't been in her apartment since. She'd never, *ever* let me kiss her nose.

Lizbeth glanced at me over her shoulder. "So, this woman isn't your girlfriend?"

"Not really, no." I picked a crouton out of the salad and crunched into it.

"Do you have a girlfriend?" she asked.

I grimaced. "God, no."

"Danny's staying faithful to a woman who doesn't give a shit if he's fucking anyone else," Leo said, summing it up.

"Fuck you," I said. She might care. A little. I hadn't told Leo about kissing her in front of the church last week. She'd kissed me back. Though physical affection had never been a problem for us. It was the rest of her, her head and her heart, that I couldn't break through to. She'd made that obvious when I'd asked her about her family, and she'd called it "typical." No one's family was typical. She just wouldn't let me see all the weird, wonderful ways it was different.

The knock at my door made me jump, and I dropped the bag of Leo's homemade croutons. They bounced off the counter onto the floor, and crunchy bread cubes spilled everywhere.

"Shit!" I muttered. "Lizbeth, can you answer the door while I sweep up?"

"Nah, I've got it," Leo said. "Go kiss your lady love."

"Shh! She's not my *lady love*. Please don't say the word *love* tonight. Or *baby mama*. Or—"

"Answer the door," Leo said, "before she changes her mind."

"Go to hell." Stepping carefully over the mess, I jogged to the door and flung it open.

Lucie cradled a bottle of wine. She wore the same knee-length black dress she'd worn to the anniversary party last weekend. It looked comfortable, like an oversized T-shirt. Her tan legs were bare down to her black combat boots.

"You came." Something inside me slotted into place. My heart hammered at my ribs, but I felt like I could take a full breath for the first time in hours. When I did, I got a whiff of the coconut product she used on her hair. It smelled amazing.

She held out the wine. "Happy birthday."

"Thank you." I took it.

"It's not so bad," she said.

I checked the label on the wine. "It's pretty good, actually. Barb's too cheap to serve this."

"I meant your thirties." She scratched her arm. "When I turned thirty, I thought it was the end of my youth. And it kind of was, but there are good things about being in your thirties."

"Like?" I stood aside so she could come in.

She bent to take off her boots and set them next to the pile of Leo's and Lizbeth's sneakers. "Like, I'm surer of myself than I was in my twenties. I sure as hell don't know everything, but I know what's important to me and what I want."

"I guess that's the one thing I'm ahead on. I already know all that."

"Huh. I wish I'd had my head together when I was your age. Maybe my career would've taken off."

I stared at her, hard. "Your career is amazing. You write incredible pieces all the time. The one about the assault weapons protest made me truly understand what those people were trying to say."

"Oh, god. You don't agree with them, do you?"

"No, of course not. But you made them seem like real people and not nutjobs."

"Thanks." She sniffed the air. "It smells amazing in here."

"It's Leo's famous braciole. Don't tell my ma, but it's better than hers. You'll love it." At least I hoped she would. I hoped spending time with my family would help her see that we could be a family too. That despite how we began, we could find a way to love each other. That someday we could pull a highchair up to the table and have a special meal with all the people we cared most about.

I led her into the kitchen. "You already know Leo, and this is his girlfriend, Lizbeth."

"I'm not really his girlfriend." Lizbeth stuck out her hand. "We're just fucking. Who wants to settle down? But I couldn't pass up the chance to try Leo's braciole."

I widened my eyes at my brother. He shrugged. "I'm a superstar in both the kitchen and the sack. Sue me."

No, no, no. This was exactly the wrong message to give Lucie. *Family, not fuck-buddies.* I should've invited Giuliana instead. At least she wouldn't have brought a casual hookup to my birthday party. Probably.

"Who wants a drink?" I asked, going to the refrigerator. "I mixed up some nonalcoholic negroni sbagliatos, Lucie."

"Yes, please," Lucie said. "I'll open the wine for the rest of you."

I set the pitcher on the counter and passed her two wineglasses and the bottle opener. "I'll drink the phony negronis," I said. The pomegranate juice had given it a gorgeous red color like the real thing.

When Lucie stepped to the counter, I heard a crunch.

"Ow. What was that?" She looked down.

"Crouton. Sorry." Stepping on a crouton had to be almost as bad as stepping on one of my cousins' LEGO bricks. Without thinking, I bent and scooped her into my arms.

She squealed, a very un-Lucie-like sound, but her arm went around my neck as I carried her to the table. "What the fuck, Danny?"

"I, um, didn't want you to hurt your feet." I set her in a chair at the table.

"On a goddamn crouton?"

Leo set her glass in front of her. "If you haven't figured it out yet, my brother's always saving someone. Even if it's only from croutons."

My cheeks burned, and I turned away to open the wine.

Fortunately, dinner was amazing, and Lucie forgot to yell at me about picking her up without her consent as she devoured the beef, risotto, and salad. Leo and Lizbeth finished off Lucie's bottle of wine, and I'd stood to open another bottle when Lucie asked Leo about his food truck.

"It's incredible," Lizbeth gushed. "He gets more requests to show up in front of office buildings and events than he can physically do. He's thinking about getting a second truck."

I jammed the corkscrew into the cork. "No, he's not. He's going to sell his truck so we can buy the bar." I figured he'd have told Lizbeth that much, even if they were only fuck-buddies.

When Leo said nothing, I glanced at him over my shoulder while I twisted the screw into the cork. "Right, Leo?"

"Oh, yeah. It was just an idea I was tossing around. If I had a commercial kitchen, I could run two trucks. You know, in case you changed your mind about the bar."

I set the wine bottle on the counter harder than I meant to, and it made a clanging sound. "In case *I* changed *my* mind about the bar? This is *our* dream. We both want this. Not just for ourselves, but for the whole family."

"Why would Leo want that?" Lizbeth asked, her eyes narrowed in a challenge. "His food truck is hella successful. He could have a whole fleet. *And* his own catering kitchen."

Ignoring Lizbeth, his not-girlfriend, I stared at my brother. "When we buy the bar, he will have his own kitchen."

Leo stared at his plate and nodded.

"Is that what you want, Leo?" Lucie asked. "The kitchen downstairs is hardly bigger than this one. And it comes with Norm."

"I know," he said. "But it's what Danny and I have always said we'd do when we got the cash. And Danny's given up so much for me, for all of us, it's the least I can do."

"Giving up your dream is the least you can do?" Lucie asked. "That seems like a lot to give up for someone else's dream."

"Wait," I said. "You don't want to buy the bar with me?"

"Sure, I do," he said, standing and picking up the empty plates. He still wouldn't look at me. "It's what we've always talked about."

"See?" I glared at Lizbeth. "It's what he wants."

She rolled her eyes. "Sure."

"It is!"

"Lizbeth," Leo called, "where'd you put the candles?"

With another eye roll, she stood and went to the kitchen.

"Need some help, Leo?" I asked.

"Nah, it's your birthday. We've got it."

But sitting while others worked made me nuts. "Want another drink? Or some decaf?"

Lucie stared at Leo as he sprinkled powdered sugar on slices of lemon ricotta cake. "I'll take a water, please."

As I poured her some from the pitcher in the fridge, I tried not to listen to Leo and Lizbeth's whispered argument. Still, I caught Lizbeth's angry, "Tell him," and Leo's muttered, "Don't want to—"

I thunked the pitcher on the counter. "You don't want to *what,* Leo?"

He looked up from the slice of cake with the candle in it, his eyes round with guilt. "I don't wanna have this argument here." He tipped his chin toward the table, where Lucie didn't bother to pretend she wasn't listening. "Not on your birthday."

"I'll go." Lucie stood. "You guys need to talk."

"Don't go," I said.

"You haven't even had cake," Leo said.

But Lucie was already jamming her feet into her boots at the door. "Thanks for dinner, Leo. It was delicious."

"I'll walk you up." I grabbed a plate of cake, slipped on my shoes, and followed her out.

We climbed the stairs in silence. When we reached the third floor, she said, "I hope I didn't spoil your birthday."

"Nah, it's fine." Though it wasn't, not really. Finding out my brother was having second thoughts about something we'd promised each other for years wasn't great. Especially not on my thirtieth birthday, when my life was supposed to be settling into place. And definitely not in front of my baby mama who I was trying to woo.

She put her key into the lock, and something clenched in my chest.

"Can I come in?" I asked. "Leo's cake is the best. We can share it."

She pushed open the door, then looked up at me. Her brown eyes shimmered with kindness, and I almost stumbled back in surprise. Lucie was driven and sexy and upstanding. I'd never seen such a soft expression on her face. "You and your brother need to talk." She put a hand on mine. "You can't hide from him up here."

I growled, "I'm not hiding. I'd much rather spend time with you on my birthday." I bent and hovered my lips over hers for a second, then I brushed her lips, a question.

She curled her fingers around the back of my neck and buried them in my hair, pulling me to her, answering. With the hand that wasn't holding the cake, I clutched the back of her dress, then I licked inside her mouth, tasting spice and garlic and *her*. She slipped her tongue against mine, a caress softer than any she'd given me before. This was way better than last weekend's kiss in front of the church.

A hungry sound escaped me. I imagined waking up to her touch with a glide of her smooth hand down my chest or a gentle kiss on my shoulder. Silky bedsheets and a pillow that smelled like coconut. Sliding my hand down to the delectable curve of her ass, I tugged her closer so she could feel my arousal against her belly.

When she pulled away, her pupils had swallowed her irises. She looked a second away from pulling me through the door. "Happy birthday," she murmured.

"I'll show you how happy I am," I rumbled.

She shook her head slowly, and the lust faded from her gaze. "You need to talk things over with your brother."

I had a brother? "Now?"

"Tell me how it goes. Goodnight." After taking the plate of cake from my hand, she closed the door gently—in my face.

I stood there for a moment. She was probably right. I needed to talk to Leo about our plan, our dream. Or maybe it was only my dream. But I didn't want to have that conversation on my fucking thirtieth birthday, so I did something I never did.

I jogged down the two flights of stairs to the bar to get drunk.

22

NOT THAT KIND OF FRIEND

My legacy is that I fostered a culture of innovation and inclusivity, where students could thrive regardless of background. The breakthroughs sparked in our labs, the voices that found confidence on our stage, and the engaged citizens who walked out our doors are a testament to the potential unlocked by a vibrant university community. That's the lasting impact I strive for: an institution that ignites potential and shapes a more equitable future.

Dr. LaToya Watts, president, NorCal University

LUCIE

Early had found the perfect dress style for me at six months pregnant. It had something she called an empire waist, and it hugged my oh-my-god-when-are-they-going-to-stop-expanding boobs at the top but swung out over my belly in a flare that made it almost look like I still had a waist.

What had made me late was choosing shoes to go with it. I'd

stood in front of the mirror in my favorite combat boots for a full five minutes, trying to convince myself I could get away with it. But in the end, I couldn't. I'd dug through the bottom of my closet for a pair of black flats that wouldn't make my mother cluck her tongue.

Smoothing down the soft black fabric of my skirt, I grabbed the door handle to the fancy restaurant my parents had chosen when I asked them to meet me for brunch.

Taking a deep breath, I strode inside. La Colombe Bleue wasn't the kind of place where they let you wander around looking for your party, so I allowed the host to guide me to my parents' table near the window. They looked the same as they had in February. My mother's hair was strawberry blond down to its roots, and my father's suit was impeccably pressed as always.

Mom spotted me first. Smiling, she stood and held out her arms. I fell into her embrace. She gave the best hugs, and I needed one after hanging out with way-too-young Danny, his brother, and his not-girlfriend who made me feel like the kind of woman who started sentences with, "Back in my day…"

Hanging with Danny's family at the anniversary party and then with his brother on his birthday two weekends ago had made me realize that I probably owed it to my family to tell them the news that seemed to spread faster than wildfire. Even if they wouldn't be nearly as pleased about it as Danny's family.

After a few seconds, she released me and looked down my body. Could she feel my firm belly?

"That's a pretty dress," she said. "Does it come in a brighter color?"

My lip curled. "I wouldn't know. I only care if it comes in black. Hi, Dad."

His hug was much briefer. "Good morning. I'm glad you

called. We haven't seen you in months, and your mother misses you."

Aaaaand he'd delivered me a plate of guilt before I'd even looked at the menu. At the square table, I chose the chair next to my father, across from my mother.

The waiter bustled over with a pitcher. "Mimosa?"

God, this was going to be difficult without the pleasant buzz of alcohol. "No, thank you. Could I have sparkling water, please?"

That earned me another searching gaze from my mother.

My father lifted his champagne flute and sipped. "We missed you at our cocktail party. Your mother put on an impressive event, as usual."

"It's so easy these days," she said. "All I have to do is put out half a dozen charcuterie boards, and everyone's happy. I don't even bother with hot hors d'oeuvres anymore."

"It was a friend's birthday," I said. "I couldn't miss it." Though I'd been glad of the excuse not to be apologized for in front of Dad's colleagues.

The waiter brought my sparkling water, and since my parents were ready to order, I chose hurriedly and handed him the menu folio.

"What are you working on?" Dad asked.

"You know, whatever the news is that day. And my book."

"You shouldn't still be a staff reporter," he said. "You should be a managing editor by now."

"Managing editors don't have any fun." Suddenly, I was a surly fifteen-year-old again. "They stay in the office all day. They don't get to go outside and cover authentic stories."

"But managing editors can share their opinions," he said. "Those opinions have weight in the community. People listen to them. Instead of writing about what happened at a gun rights rally, you could have written a piece about how dangerous assault weapons are and how they've been used in so many tragic shootings. Or how the right policies could prevent needless suffering."

"I-I'd rather report the facts and let people draw their own conclusions," I lied. He knew me too well to believe that.

He speared me with a flinty stare before lifting his glass. "Then I suppose you're in the right place."

I felt like one of his grad students who'd submitted an essay riddled with typos. But I lifted my chin. "I am."

"How is your book going, honey?" Mom asked.

"Well," I lied. Again. "I have several interviews lined up."

"Interviews?" Dad asked. "Shouldn't you have completed your research? You sold the book eight months ago."

"I...I'm still looking for the star interview. The one that's going to turn the book from good to great," I admitted.

"Did you talk to Dr. Watts?" he asked. "She's one of the most notable Black female presidents of a major university."

"Yes, we talked last week. Thank you for connecting us." Thankfully, the server arrived with our meals, and I didn't have to defend myself for a while as we started to eat.

But after we'd been eating for a few minutes, my mother set down her fork. "Lucie, how are you? Aside from work?" She'd taken only a few bites of her meal, and she eyed my almost-empty plate.

Reluctantly, I set down my fork. The blueberry pancakes I'd ordered were delicious, and my little tapeworm of a fetus wanted more. It was time to tell them about the pregnancy.

"I'm doing well, but—" I cleared my throat. "And I'm pregnant."

Three seconds of silence ticked by. Then my father burst out laughing. "Good one, Lucie."

My mother didn't crack a smile. "Marvin, I don't think she's joking."

"What?" He wiped his eyes.

"It's true," I said. My cheeks burned. "I'm due in November."

"Who's the father?" he demanded as my mother asked, "How are you feeling?"

"I'm feeling fine," I said. "The father is a...a friend of mine. It was unplanned."

"And this is what you want?" My mother pressed her lips together. "Motherhood is a massive responsibility, especially with a demanding career and...alone."

"I won't be alone," I said. "My friend, Danny, wants to co-parent. He works nights, so we plan to divide childcare." That sounded so responsible, even to me.

"Tell me more about this *friend,*" my father said, his white eyebrows already arched in judgment.

"He's just a friend," I said. I'd been so good, sending him away the night of his birthday instead of inviting him in like I'd wanted to do. "He's kind and caring and generous. He'll be a good co-parent."

"And what about his prospects?" Dad clenched his fork. "Can he support you financially? Where did he go to college?"

"He...he didn't." I stared at my plate. What was left of my pancakes was broken down into a slurry of bread and syrup.

"He didn't *go to college?*" he demanded in the same tone of voice he'd ask about a crime.

I glared at him. "He still has time. He's young." Fuck, why had I said that?

"How young, Lucie?" Mom asked. Dad's face had gone purple as the smashed blueberries on my plate.

"Thirty."

My father closed his eyes and shook his head. I was twelve years old, and he'd caught me toilet-papering the house of a girl who'd made fun of me after class. "I can't believe you were so careless."

"Marvin." My mother sent him a stern look. "Lucie, you should bring him to dinner this week."

I grimaced. "He's not that kind of friend." The kind who'd put up with an interrogation about his age and the balance in his savings account and his career aspirations. Who'd smile while my father put him down. No. Even sweet, kindhearted Danny would run away screaming.

"But he's the kind of friend you had unprotected sex with?" my father said, loud enough that heads turned at the next table.

"Marvin." Mom put her hand over his.

"You've made a lot of ridiculous decisions, Lucie," he said, a little more quietly, "but this is the goddamn cherry on top of a steaming pile of cow manure. What about your book? I hope you have a clause that lets you out of it by only paying back the advance."

I lifted my chin. "I don't need out of it. I'm going to finish it."

"Better ask for an extension," he said.

"I don't need a goddamn extension," I growled, standing.

"Lucie, be reasonable," my mother said. "Of course you'll need more time. You're growing a baby. You'll be exhausted by the time November rolls around."

My lungs felt like the baby had punched through the wall of my uterus and grabbed them. I'd expected Dad's criticism, but I'd hoped my mother would be sympathetic since she'd been through something similar once upon a time. Fuck it. I didn't need their approval or their support.

"I'll be fine," I said and tossed my napkin over what remained of those delicious blueberry pancakes. Later, I'd be sad about not finishing them, but asking for a doggy bag would have ruined my dramatic exit. "Mom, Dad, thanks for breakfast. I'm leaving."

I turned on the toe of my ballet slipper, which, as it turned out, was much better for the maneuver than my combat boots would have been, and stalked out of the restaurant.

I'd done what I intended to do. I'd told them. I didn't need their approval. Which was fortunate because no matter what I did, I'd never earn it.

23

———

PREGNANCY HORMONES
ARE THE WORST

My legacy is the confidence and sense of self-worth I inspired in my clients. I hope people see all the different body types I've styled and realize that they are beautiful and can express their personal aesthetic in whatever body they inhabit.
Carly Rose, celebrity stylist

LUCIE

*W*hen it buzzed, I glanced down at my phone. Another text from my mother. This one began, *Sweetie, I'm so sorry about that day at brunch...*

I swiped the notification away. Tonight was about my girls, not my mother's fake apologies. She'd been trying for a month to restore our family's peace. Fuck peace. I didn't need it.

My stomach swooped at the knock on my door even though I was expecting my friends.

"Calm down," I muttered as if it was the baby who wanted to see Danny. Danny was working tonight like he did every Saturday night. I stroked my belly. It felt hard and tight. I rubbed a circle on it as I walked to the door and opened it.

Carly was on the other side, an expression of elation on her face and bags weighing down both shoulders.

"Hey." I stepped aside so she could enter. "What's in the bags?"

"A surprise," she said, clutching the one over her right shoulder. It had a mesh panel in the front like the bag Danny carried to the gym. I doubted Carly's surprise was a pair of stinky sneakers.

"Damn, I was hoping it was dinner," I said.

"You don't want me to be responsible for food. Savannah's bringing that."

"I know, babe." I kissed her cheek. "Though I trust you to order takeout."

"Hold the door," Tessa called. She carried a couple of reusable grocery bags into my apartment.

"What did you bring?" I asked.

"Drinks. I'm going to set them up in the kitchen."

I sighed. "Got it." I missed our Wednesday happy hours. "I've got seltzer in the fridge." Danny had kindly brought me my favorite flavors, but none of them compared to a margarita.

I peered into the hallway. "Where's Savannah?"

"I'm sure she'll be here soon," Tessa said.

I checked my phone. No texts from her. "Traffic from Sacramento can be a bitch."

Tessa set her bags on my counter and started opening cabinets. "I wish she'd move here. I'm worried about her."

After one last scan of the hallway, I shut the door. "Why? What's going on?"

"She hasn't said anything, but things aren't great with her husband." Tessa slammed a cabinet door closed. "Jason." Her lip curled when she said his name.

"Ugh," I agreed. "I hate him more than any other person I've never met."

"Right?" Carly said. She dropped one of her bags on the floor next to the couch. She gracefully lowered herself to sit—as a former model, she did almost everything with style—and gently settled the other bag onto her lap.

"What's the surprise?" I asked, flopping into my favorite chair, ungracefully.

"Ah-ah. Not until we're all here."

"I hate surprises," Tessa said, still hunting through my cabinets.

"This is a good one," Carly said. "I promise."

"No such thing," Tessa grumbled. "I give up. Where are your wineglasses?"

"Danny moved them since I wouldn't be needing them for a while." I waved at the coat closet. "They're in a box on the top shelf."

She arched an auburn eyebrow. "Removing temptation?"

"Making room for 'healthy snacks.'" I made air quotes. "He filled my cabinets with dried fruit and granola bars and shit. So far, I've only eaten the chocolate-covered ones."

She opened the closet door and, with her Amazonian height, pulled down the box. "What else is he keeping at your place? A change of clothes? A toothbrush?"

My face burned. "It's not like that." Though I almost wished it was. With my stomach making it more and more obvious every day that this was really happening, my brain was busy when it should have been sleeping. I'd been thinking about what I was going to do about that death crib, where my daughter would sleep when she was too big for a crib, and where I was going to come up with a college fund. Not to mention that damn end-of-November book deadline looming over me like a guillotine's blade. The couple of times I'd slept with Danny, his arms around me were like a lead blanket protecting me from my racing thoughts. I needed that comfort.

"You're sure it's not like that?" Carly asked.

"No! We're just friends. And co-parents to be. Sure, we had some fun, but we want different things."

"What kind of different things?" Tessa asked, handing me a wineglass of something that looked like sangria. Sliced oranges and berries floated on top of a sparkling red liquid. She handed another glass to Carly, then sat in the chair next to mine, listening.

"He's supposed to be buying the bar downstairs, but his brother's not all in on it. He comes from a big family, and he probably wants to buy a house next door to his mom in the suburbs and raise a half-dozen kids. Which is exactly what I *don't* want. I want to focus on my career." Even though at least once a week, Mario shot a suspicious look at my belly. I was going to have to tell him about the pregnancy soon, but I knew once I did, I'd get all the shitty fluff-pieces.

"Danny's so young," I added. "He's still figuring his shit out. And once he does, he probably won't want to live downstairs from a woman who's ten years older than he is with a kid."

"You mean the woman who's the mother of *his* kid?" Tessa asked.

"It was a mistake. I made a ton of mistakes in my twenties that I regret. Mistakes I'm glad aren't holding me back from what I want to be in my forties."

"How do you know that's how he'll feel?" Carly asked. "Just because he's young doesn't mean he doesn't know what he wants. Andrew does."

"God, if I were Andrew, I'd know what I wanted, too, and that's you," I said with a smirk.

Carly blushed.

"Besides, your man's a few years older than Danny," I said. "He went to college. He's fully baked."

"Don't be elitist," Tessa said. "Just because he didn't go to college doesn't mean he's incapable of determining his life path."

"You're right." I gazed into my drink. "I sound like my dad."

Tessa flashed me a rueful smile. "We all sound a little like our dads." She stood and got her glass from the kitchen. "A toast. To being smarter than our parents and giving people a chance."

I sipped the nonalcoholic sangria. It burned my mouth, and not in a good way. It was like I'd bitten into a raw cranberry. My mouth puckered. I choked it down when I really wanted to spray the drink across the room. "This is cranberry juice!"

"What'd you think I was giving you? Wine?" Tessa took another cautious sip. "At least it's pretty."

Danny would never serve me swill like that. "Come on, hand it over." I gathered up the glasses and carried them into the kitchen. I strained out the disgusting mock sangria and refilled the glasses with orange-flavored seltzer.

I handed the drinks back to my friends. "Still pretty, and less cranberry."

We drank, and although there was a little tartness left over from the cranberry juice, the drink was inoffensive.

"We need to plan your birthday party, Lucie," Carly said.

"Ugh, forty," I groaned.

"Remember, you'll never be this young again," she said.

"Is that supposed to make me feel better?"

"We should do something fun like ziplining," Tessa said, "or a trip!"

"She's pregnant, remember?" Carly said. "She can't go ziplining. And is she even allowed to travel?" They stared at me, eyebrows raised.

"Travel's okay until the last month. But I'd prefer something low-key. Maybe a party at Barb's?"

"You and that bar." Tessa rolled her eyes. "It's like you're that guy from *Cheers*."

"It's true. Everybody does know my name." And if we had it down there, it wouldn't be weird to invite Danny. Plus, my parents would be unlikely to show up. Two points for Barb's.

"Do you think we could get Danny's brother to cater?" Carly asked. "His food is to die for."

"Maybe. I'll ask," I said.

"Okay," Tessa said. "When Savannah gets here, we'll schedule it."

A tap sounded on the door. "Perfect timing," Tessa said. I rocked my weight forward, readying myself to stand. "Sit down. I've got it." She walked to the door and opened it.

"There you are," she said, hugging Savannah. "We were worried."

"I, um, I got a late start," Savannah said.

"Everything okay?" Tessa asked.

"Not really."

With effort, I hauled myself off the chair. "Sit down. Need a little vodka in your seltzer?"

"No, thanks. I'll drink whatever you're having." She hugged Carly, then flopped onto the sofa next to her. "What's in the bag?"

"A surprise," Carly said. "I was saving it until you got here, but it can wait until you tell us what's going on."

I brought in a seltzer topped with the remaining fruit and handed it to Savannah. Then I slumped into my chair and waited.

"Surprise first," she said. "Maybe it'll help."

Carly dragged the bigger bag in front of her feet. "First surprise..." She pulled out a pink makeup case. "It's makeover night! I've got nail polish, facial masks, hair dye, and makeup, of course."

Savannah's dull expression brightened. "That sounds fun."

"What's the other surprise?" I asked.

She zipped open the bag with the mesh side and lifted out something reddish brown and white—and furry. "Andrew and I got a dog. Ladies, meet Chanel."

The dog had long ears and sad-looking eyes. She was clipped short all over, and her tail, which didn't even wag, looked scraggly. She shivered in Carly's arms. But she had two jaunty blue bows perched on top of her ears.

Savannah cooed while Carly held the dog protectively. "She's a rescue, and she's a little fearful of strangers. We'll give her a minute to adjust and then you can pet her if you like."

Savannah shoved her hands under her thighs as if to stop herself from touching the dog. "She's adorable."

"What's up with her fur?" I asked.

"Poor thing." Carly stroked her side. "We rescued her from a puppy mill. She'd been used for breeding. Her fur was all matted, and her tail was just unspeakable. It all had to go. But it ought to grow back, and with a good diet and lots of brushing, she'll be gorgeous. Though she's already beautiful, aren't you, Chanel?" She kissed the dog's white blaze.

Savannah gave Carly a wry smile, then held out her palm for the dog to sniff. When the dog licked her thumb, Savannah scratched her under her chin. "Sounds like a familiar story. I'm an old, used-up mother too."

We all protested, but Tessa was loudest. "Don't say that. Don't even think that. You are beautiful and valuable."

"We all love you, Savannah," Carly said. "What's going on?"

She took a few seconds to formulate her words. "Remember how Jason cheated on me? Well, he...he's still doing it."

"He's what?" I burst out. "What the fuck?"

"He's been using a dating app," she said.

"He's married. Why the hell is he on an app?" Tessa said through a tight jaw.

"He...he called it a plea for attention."

"Attention?" I snorted. "More like a plea for a divorce."

"He didn't even bother hiding it." Savannah looked down into her lap. "He used his regular credit card, the one I pay with all the other bills. To, you know, buy the subscription and pay for..." She took a shuddering breath. "Dates."

Carly plopped the dog onto Savannah's lap. "What did he say when you confronted him?"

Savannah stroked Chanel's ears. "Same stuff as before. That I wasn't giving him enough...affection. Sex, basically. Menopause has been rough on me, and I haven't felt...sexy, you know?"

Only Carly had started perimenopause, but we all rushed to say something, anything, to comfort her. "Not being able to trust your partner zaps libido too," was my contribution.

Carly put a hand on her shoulder. "What are you going to do?"

"Divorce him," I said, "obviously."

Carly gave me a warning look. "It's not that simple. Marriages can be complicated and messy. Savannah might not want that."

"Or she might," Tessa said.

"I want to think about it for a minute," Savannah said. "He promised to go to counseling this time."

"If you decide to end it," Carly said, "I can refer you to my divorce lawyer."

"No offense," Tessa said, "but your lawyer sucked if she couldn't get you out of that awful prenup. I know someone."

"You're probably right," Carly said. "Though it turned out fine in the end. I'm free of my ex, and I'm doing great. Whatever you decide, you'll be fine too, Savannah."

"And we're here for you," I said. "Whatever you need."

"Thank you," she whispered, finally looking up. Her eyes were red and puddled with tears. "You three are the best. I'm so glad we found each other."

Tessa reached across and gripped Savannah's hand. "So am I."

"Me too." Carly squeezed her shoulder.

"God-fucking-dammit," I said, wiping tears off my cheeks. "I'm glad too, but stop making me cry. What the hell is wrong with me?"

"Pregnancy hormones," Savannah said. "They're the worst. Have you had any new symptoms?"

I blinked and sniffled. "Stop worrying about me. Worry about yourself and what you need."

"You should read The Book," she said.

"Yeah, yeah." My stomach tensed. But it wasn't my stomach. It was lower, and when I touched it, my belly felt as hard as stone. Maybe I should read that damned book.

"Looks like Lucie's hungry," Tessa said.

"Darn it, I was supposed to bring dinner, wasn't I?" Savannah said. "I forgot with everything going on."

"Don't worry about it," Tessa said. "I'll order delivery. How does pasta sound?"

"Carbs won't solve anything," Savannah said, "but they'll make me feel better."

"With a salad, please," Carly said.

"And garlic breadsticks. I don't care about the indigestion," I added. "Carly, in the meantime, it's time to make us gorgeous."

"We're already gorgeous," she said. "But this is going to be fun."

And it was. Getting support from my besties, and giving it right back, was just what I needed to convince myself everything was going to be okay.

24

IT'S MY PARTY, AND I'LL
DITCH IF I WANT TO

Wright: I don't want to talk about my legacy.
Interviewer: Carly and Savannah talked to me. I even got
Andrew's mother.
Wright: Well, I won't.
Interviewer: Come on, Tessa. I know you're sitting on a pile of
cash from god-knows-what. And you've given some significant
donations to women's health organizations. I want to hear what
you have to say.
Wright: I have two words for you: Fuck. Off. Go enjoy your party.
Transcript from interview with Tessa Wright, mysteriously wealthy
person

LUCIE

I only realized it was a fucking terrible idea to have my
fortieth birthday party in a bar when I walked in the
door and saw Tad sitting on a barstool. I needed a whiskey to
dull the sharp edges of my irritation. But, sadly, being a responsible forty-year-old mom-to-be meant no whiskey for me. But
then an evil idea fluttered into my sober brain.

I marched up to him. "Hey, Tad, what's going on?"

He kept his gaze on the television. "Enjoying some late-season baseball and an after-work drink." He tapped his martini glass. "Hey, Nico, can I get another?"

"You must have missed the sign on the door," I said. "The bar closes at seven for a private party. And it's five to seven, so you missed your last call."

"Private party?" He looked away from the game. "I practically own the...whoa."

His gaze settled on my seven-months-pregnant belly, which no longer looked like weight gain but like I'd strapped on a soccer ball. Instantly, I recognized I'd screwed this up. Tad would go running to Mario on Monday morning and spring the news on him. The news I'd hidden by (truthfully) claiming a sore back as an excuse to work from home. *Shit.*

"So that's why you haven't been in the office," he said unnecessarily.

"My personal health conditions are none of your business," I said through clenched teeth. I guessed now I'd be forced to reveal that I planned to take leave in a couple of months. Leave that federal and state law entitled me to.

"Sure they are," he said, "when I'll be forced to pick up the slack at the office. When are you due, anyway? It's got to be soon."

"November."

"Really? With that belly, it must be fucking twins at least. Fertility treatments?"

I sucked in air through my nose. If I said what I wanted to say, he'd probably get so angry he wouldn't wait for Monday to tell Mario. "I'm going to call you a rideshare, Tad. You can go drink somewhere else or go home. You can't stay here."

"I think my aunt Barb will have something to say about that," he said. Then he leaned closer. "Though between you and me, when I take over this bar—and that's a *when*, not an *if*—it's going to get an upgrade. Think molecular mixology and haute cuisine." His gaze took a leisurely tour from my clipped-up curls to my hand-me-down maternity dress to my combat boots, then back up to my face. "With a dress code. I'm not sure you'll feel... comfortable here when that happens."

My face and chest ignited. I filled my lungs to tell him off, but before I opened my mouth, a big hand squeezed my shoulder.

"Hey, Lucie. Tad." Tad's name was a growl in Danny's chest. "Sorry, man, but the private party is starting, and you're not on the guest list."

"You can't make me leave," Tad said. "Aunt Barb will let me stay."

"I don't think she will," Danny said. "Plus, none of the bartenders will serve you, so you might as well go."

Tad narrowed his eyes at Danny, then at me. "There are ten better bars within walking distance."

"Then you should walk to one of those better bars," Danny said. "Be safe, Tad."

With one last, mulish glare, Tad slipped off the stool and stalked out.

"Fucking asshole," Danny muttered. He reached for his wallet and put a twenty on the bar. "Who the fuck doesn't tip their bartender, especially when they drink for free?"

"Tad, that's who," I said. My racing heart slowed. Danny was more effective than my weighted blanket at muffling stress.

"Happy birthday." He squeezed my shoulder again and released it, stepping away.

I missed his touch, but I stood my ground. *You're ten years older. Don't tie him down.* "Thank you."

The door opened, and my three besties exploded into the

bar. Andrew followed, clutching gift bags in one hand and an enormous bunch of balloons in the other.

"I'll check on Leo," Danny said.

"Stay." I grabbed his hand. "Meet my friends."

The slow smile that spread over his face was like the moon rising over mountains. "Okay."

A second later, I was engulfed in hugs and squeals of "Happy birthday!"

"Sorry, we meant to get here earlier to help decorate," Savannah said, "but I asked Carly if she could zhuzh me up, and it took a minute." Her dress hugged her figure, and her gray roots were gone.

"You look fantastic," I said. Her skin was poreless. Though no amount of makeup could disguise the dullness in her eyes from her struggles with her terrible husband. Thank goodness I'd never be in that situation. I clasped her hand.

"Thank you." Her glossy lips turned up in a grin, not as wide as usual, but she was trying.

"Let me introduce you to Danny," I said. "Danny, meet my friends Savannah and Tessa. You've already met Carly and Andrew."

"It's so nice to meet you." Savannah released my hand to enthusiastically pump Danny's.

"You're even yummier than Lucie said," Tessa purred, letting her gaze linger on his broad chest.

Pain in my jaw made me realize I was grinding my teeth. "I never called him that."

"Interesting," Tessa said. "Did you see how she stepped in front of him, Carly?"

Carly chuckled. "I did."

"Did no—" But then I felt his chest at my back. "Screw you," I said.

"I think I'll leave that to him." Tessa's smirk was pure evil.

"Danny, where would I find a stepladder? Savannah says we need to put up streamers." She lifted the box she was holding to show us the rainbow of crepe paper inside.

"I'll hang them," he said. "I don't think our insurance covers guests on ladders."

Tessa handed him the box, and he disappeared down the back hall.

"That wasn't very nice," Savannah chided Tessa.

"It was an experiment," Tessa said. "And we all saw the results. You *like* him, Lucie."

Feeling like a cornered animal, I lifted my chin. "We're friends."

"Friends with combustible sexual chemistry," Tessa said.

"Which we're not doing anything about. Anymore," I amended. "I told you he's ten years younger. It'd be irresponsible of me to confuse him and let him think anything permanent could happen between us."

"You're worried about ten years?" Tessa rolled her eyes. "Ask Carly how her thirteen-year age gap is going."

"I don't have to ask," I muttered, carefully not looking at Carly's glowing skin that I knew was caused by love and good sex on the regular, not by expensive cosmetics. "But it's different with the baby. I don't want him to feel trapped for the rest of his life because of a mistake." Guilt panged in my abdomen. Why hadn't I gotten that Plan B like I'd said I would?

"Fucking hell," Tessa said. "Did your dress just *move?*"

"Is the baby kicking?" Savannah asked, her palm hovering over my belly. "Can I touch you?"

"Sure." So what if it was the baby and not guilt that had kicked me in the gut? I still wouldn't trap Danny into a relationship at only thirty years old.

Savannah laughed. "Right here! Come on, you two, she's kicking my hand!"

Carly set her hand where Savannah's had been. She grinned up at me. "That's so exciting! We're going to be aunts to a pro soccer player! Come on, Tessa, you want in on this?"

Tessa edged back. "I'm not going to touch Lucie's stomach. I wouldn't have done it before she was pregnant, and I'm not doing it now."

I frowned at her. "It's okay. I hate it when the cashier at the bodega rubs my belly, but I don't mind when my friends do, especially if you ask first."

She crossed her arms. "It's a boundary thing. I don't like people touching my body. So I'll refrain from touching yours."

Interesting. I'd have to try again to get an interview with Tessa. She never talked about her money or her past, which I found wildly intriguing. I'd refrained from unleashing my investigative journalism skills to dig up her story since it felt creepy to do that to a friend. Maybe if I plied her with Danny's potent cocktails, she'd open up.

Danny emerged from the back with the stepladder, and Tessa went to supervise the decorations. Savannah, Carly, and I got drinks at the bar, and the room filled with friends and Danny's family. What? So I'd asked Danny to invite them. They were sweet, even his cousin Tina with her lipstick kiss on Danny's cheek. And they each brought me a little something: a bouquet of flowers or a tin of homemade cookies or a box of chocolates.

I wasn't where I'd dreamed I'd be at forty, with a less-than-stellar career and an unplanned baby on the way, but I was... happy. I couldn't blame booze for the warm, bubbly feeling in my chest. I was surrounded by people I liked on my birthday, people who hugged me and complimented me and told interesting stories.

I felt a prickle on the back of my neck. Danny was standing next to me, and we were laughing at something his uncle Rangi had said when I glanced over my shoulder and saw the last two people I'd ever expected to show up at Barb's dive bar: my parents.

My father frowned like he'd entered a classroom of unruly freshmen. My mother wrinkled her nose. Shit! I'd texted her about the party out of a sense of obligation, but I hadn't thought they'd actually come.

"Excuse me," I muttered. I strode toward my parents, not sure if I wanted to protect them from the other guests or protect the other guests from them.

"Mom. Dad." I kissed their cheeks. "What a surprise."

"Of course we came to see you on your birthday," my mother said. "We're on our way to another party, but we had to stop by. Didn't we, Marvin?"

"Who are all these people?" he asked, eyeing Uncle Gio, who'd had more than his share of prosecco and was doing some kind of kicking dance with a scarf tied around his expansive belly.

"They're my friends," I said. "And...family."

My heart rate slowed when I sensed Danny's solid shape at my side again. When I looked up at him, he was grinning.

He stuck out his hand. "You must be Lucie's father. It's nice to meet you, Dr. Knox. I'm Danny Carbone."

When my dad shook Danny's hand, I released the breath I'd been holding. Until he opened his mouth.

"So, you're the one who did this to poor Lucie." He skewered Danny with a glare.

"I, um—" Danny began.

"No, Dad," I said. "He didn't do anything to me. I fully participated. And I was the one who decided to keep the baby. Danny stepped up when I needed him. He's brought me all kinds of baby things, and he makes sure I have enough to eat, and he's going to my appointments with me. He's a good guy, just like I told you at brunch."

"You sound like a lovely young man, Danny," my mother said. "Can I give you a hug?"

I noticed when Danny pulled his hand from my father's, he shook it out a little. But then he embraced my mother, and seeing the two sweetest people I knew together made my eyes prickle.

Goddamn pregnancy hormones.

"We're so glad Lucie's found someone like you," Mom said.

I didn't know if it was pregnancy exhaustion, or the rebellion against my father that was hard coded into me, or one of those fucks Carly was always talking about flying away, but I didn't bother to correct her. And when Danny stepped back from their hug and slipped his arm around my waist like it belonged there, I let him gather me closer.

"I'm glad too," he said.

I glanced up at him. He'd had a couple of beers, enough to brighten his eyes. His lips were pink and plush, and I remembered all too well what he could do with them. I smiled at the memory, and he grinned back.

"Well, I don't like it," my father grumbled. "She's ruining her chances at a successful career."

A chill raced over my skin. I was sixteen again, and he was chiding me for missing the dean's list one semester, telling me that brown women couldn't make a mistake if they wanted to succeed in life. But then I remembered my research and stood straighter, like all those successful women were propping me up.

"I've interviewed a lot of women for my book. Many of them are mothers who also thrive in their careers. It's possible to do both."

"Possible, but challenging," my mother said softly.

I looked away. I could never hope to live up to either of their ideals: the renowned university professor and author, or the perfect mother.

"If anyone can do it, Lucie can," Danny said. He pulled me tighter.

"She's going to need a lot of help." Dad narrowed his eyes like Danny was a student who'd asked for an extension on a paper.

"I'll be there for her. For them both. I promise."

I shivered. His sexy lips tilted up, and his restless fingers rubbed circles on my hip. God, that was sexy. If we hadn't been standing in a crowded bar, I'd have climbed him like a tree. I bit my lip to keep from saying something I'd regret in front of my parents.

"I like you, Danny," Mom said. "I hope we'll be seeing more of you in the future."

My dad cleared his throat. "We should go, Ellen, or we'll be late."

"All right." As she leaned in to kiss my cheek, she whispered, "It's good to see you so happy."

Happy? Was that what I was feeling? I shouldn't be. I was desperately behind on my manuscript with an unplanned baby on the way. But the warm sensation behind my breastbone kind of felt like happiness.

Dad leaned forward and kissed my forehead. "If you need to ask for more time, let me know. I know some people at your publisher."

My smile turned over. "I won't need more time. I've got this."

"Okay." But I could tell he didn't believe me. "Call your mother every once in a while."

When they walked away, I sagged into Danny. "I'm sorry."

"Don't be." He kissed the top of my head. "I'm glad you introduced me to them."

"Really?" I looked up at him, searching his eyes for the truth. "They can be kind of intense."

"I like intense." He brushed a curl off my cheek, his thumb lingering on my cheekbone.

My skin zinged. "What else do you like?" I brushed my lips over his palm.

His pupils dilated. "Your smarts. Your sense of humor. This ass." He cupped it. "Your tits. They look amazing in that dress. And your smile, especially when it's for me." He tilted his head down and pressed his lips to mine.

My head spun like someone had slipped vodka into my mocktails. But it wasn't alcohol that fuzzed my brain. It was Danny. His arms around me made me feel safe. His scent had become familiar and comforting. And his words acknowledged both my brain and the parts that craved his touch.

"Want to get out of here?" I asked.

"Yeah. Wait, no. This is your birthday party. You can't just leave."

"Can't I?" I fluttered my eyelashes. "It's my party, and I'll ditch if I want to."

"After you tell everyone goodbye. That's how we Italians do it."

I sighed. "Fine. But the longer this takes, the longer it's going to be before I can suck your cock."

His jaw steeled. "Let's get started."

25

THE ITALIAN EXIT

<u>*Italian Exit*</u>

Combine equal parts dry and sweet vermouth with a splash of Fernet-Branca in a cocktail shaker with ice. Stir to chill. Strain into a chilled coupe glass and garnish with orange peel.

DANNY

By the time Lucie had made her goodbye rounds to everyone at the party, I was hard as a rock. Not only had she planted in my brain the image of her lush lips around my dick, but every time she touched me—nothing X-rated, just my wrist, my arm, my shoulder—my skin warmed until I felt like I was wearing a heated blanket of her handprints. I couldn't stop imagining her fingers on my naked skin. And mine on hers.

I stood behind her as she hugged her friends. Standing behind her lush ass in that swingy skirt did nothing to erase the vision of bending her over a chair, but it was the best way I could think of to hide the ridge in my jeans.

Carly's fiancé, Andrew, sidled up to me. "Hey, man."

I blinked away the fantasy of her glowing, naked skin and

glanced at him. He was my height and around my age, but he'd been to college, he came from money, and he looked like it in his button-down and khakis that I knew hadn't come from the Gap.

"Hey," I said.

"I'm glad you two are working your stuff out. She looks happy."

Were we working our stuff out? I'd thought we were, until she'd found out my age. But in the months since, I'd been nudging my way into her life through a slow campaign of doctor's visits, healthy snack drop-offs, and a steadily growing selection of literary-themed mocktails. I glanced at her, catching her profile. Her cheeks were rosy, and her plush lips curved up into a smile. "She does."

"I'm really sorry I have to say this because I like you a lot, but if you hurt Lucie, especially with the baby and her book, I'm going to have to—"

"Beat me up," I interrupted him. "I get it. I have sisters."

"Actually, no, I'm getting too old for that, and Carly likes my face the way it is," he said, smirking. "I will ruin you. Financially. I know people who could get this place shut down in a heartbeat. So, treat her right."

I shuddered to think of what Andrew Jones could do to me and my family. His family had a flipping hospital named after them. But thinking I'd ever do anything to hurt Lucie was jacked up.

"Look, man," I muttered, "I care about her. Hurting her would be like ripping my heart out of my chest."

He glared at me for a second before a slow grin spread over his face. "Having another guy in the group is going to be amazing."

"Like having someone who can shoot the shit about baseball and cars while they talk about shoes and old-school boy bands?" I hadn't pegged Andrew for a guy who looked down on women. I'd much rather hang with Lucie than some basic-ass dude.

With a perfectly straight face, he said, "No. To help them carry out their plans for world domination."

I was still wondering if he was serious when Lucie turned to face me. Her belly brushed against the front of my jeans, and I sucked in a breath. All thoughts of Andrew and anyone else flew right out of my brain.

"I'm ready to go," she said. "I've said goodbye to everyone. Some of them twice."

"Then you've done it right," I said. "You're an honorary Italian now."

She shot me an expression I couldn't decipher. Her lips were tipped up like she was happy, but her brow furrowed. I'd never minded everything that came with being Italian—the big family, the constant ribbing, the carbs—but she might.

She took my hand and walked to the door. "Let's go upstairs. I've been a good girl all night. I deserve a reward."

"I have a present for you." I strode ahead of her to open the door. "It's in my apartment."

She breezed through it into the vestibule and pulled out her key to unlock the door to the residents' stairs. "You mean it will be, when you dick me down in your bed."

I let out a short, shocked laugh. She always managed to surprise me. "No. I have an actual gift. In a gift bag."

She raised her eyebrows. "Sure you do." Then she turned and walked up the stairs, giving me a glorious view of the curve of her ass in that swingy dress. My hard-on had eased while I was talking to Andrew, but now it raged back. After adjusting myself so I could walk, I followed her up.

Inside my apartment, I snatched the shiny red gift bag from my kitchen table. "Happy birthday, Lucie," I said, not at all smugly. Okay, I was super-smug about it.

She stared at it. "You seriously got me a gift? I didn't get you a gift on your birthday."

"You brought wine," I said. "And coming to dinner was a gift."

"You didn't even drink the wine. Damn it, Danny." She jammed her hand into the bag and pulled out a wad of tissue paper. She peered inside. "A notebook. And a pen."

I shoved a hand through my hair, but I forgot I'd put it in a bun. My fingers tangled and stuck. "I'm sorry it's not much. I'm saving everything I can for the bar."

"Danny." When she looked up, her eyes glistened. Were those...tears? "This is exactly the kind of notebook I use in my favorite color, black, which, by the way, is hard to find. And you got me the fancy pen I don't like to buy because it costs three dollars more than the next-best one. Thank you."

"You're welcome. But are you okay?" I'd never seen her cry before, not even when she told me about the pregnancy.

"I'm fine. In fact, I'm really happy. It's these stupid hormones." She set the gift on my table and stepped closer. "Now I want the other part of my gift."

I'd kissed her on my birthday, but that was two months ago. She was a different shape now, her belly rounded and firm between us. But I was determined to make this good. I leaned forward and curled my arms around her back. An inch from her lips, I murmured, "Is this okay?"

She grabbed my head. "Kiss me, and it'll be better than okay." She tugged me down until our lips met.

Her lips were as lush as I remembered. When I ran my tongue across her lower lip, I tasted the blueberry syrup from her favorite mocktail. She opened to me and slid her tongue along mine, lighting up every nerve in my body.

"Mmm," she purred. "You taste like beer."

"Sorry." I kissed along her jaw to her ear. "I meant to stick to nonalcoholic like you, but my brothers kept bringing me pints, so I drank a couple."

"I don't mind." She yanked at the elastic in my hair. The tug on my roots hurt, but it was a good kind of pain, the kind that danced down my spine. "I miss it. Next time, drink a whiskey so I can have a little taste."

I stroked my hands down her back to the curve of her ass. I liked the sound of *next time*. Meanwhile, she'd worked the elastic out of my hair, and the release of the steady tug on my roots was an almost sexual relief. She trailed her fingers along my scalp, then combed through the strands.

"I love your hair," she said.

Goose bumps erupted on my forearms. I knew she hadn't said she loved *me,* but my dumbass heart said it was close enough. I buried my face in her neck so she wouldn't see my goofy expression. Between kisses on her golden skin, I said, "You could pull it later."

She gave an experimental tug. "You don't mind?"

My dick strained in my jeans. "God, no."

"Noted," she said, tugging again.

"That's it." I curled my hands under her thighs to lift her. "Time for your other present."

She squealed and clutched my neck as I carried her to the couch and set her down. I untied her boots and pulled them off, setting them to the side. Then I pulled off her socks and set them inside one of her boots. Kneeling between her legs, I put my hands on her knees and slowly slid them up her thighs and under her skirt. "This okay?"

"Danny." Her eyes blazed. "I hereby give you blanket permission to touch every part of me with the aim of making me come on my birthday. Got it?"

"You don't have to be sassy about it." I grabbed her panties and yanked them off. I reached for the hem of her skirt to lift it, but she put a hand on mine.

"Look," she said, "it's hard to shave these days. I've been too busy with work and my book to make a waxing appointment. So things might be a little wild down there."

I quirked one side of my mouth. "I'm counting on it."

I flipped up her skirt and sat back on my heels. I'd been so focused on her pussy that I'd almost forgotten about everything else. Seeing her belly under her clothes was one thing but seeing it bare was something else. It was round with purplish lines spidering across the golden skin on the sides.

As much as I wanted to admire her, I wasn't here to make her uncomfortable. "Lie back," I said.

She reclined toward the arm of the couch, keeping one leg hooked around my back so her legs were spread for me.

"Comfortable?" I asked.

She grasped my shoulder to pull herself up and repositioned a pillow under her back. "Now I am."

"Good." I drew my hands up the insides of her thighs until they met at her center. I watched her face as I explored her swollen labia and smeared her wetness over them. "Tell me if anything doesn't feel good."

She flung an arm over her eyes. "So far, so good."

I continued caressing her, occasionally dipping a fingertip inside, teasing her until I had her squirming. "Danny," she growled, "I need your dick."

My dick was fully on board with that, straining in my jeans. "Not yet," I said. I plunged my fingers inside her, curling them up and stroking her until I found the spot that made her legs stiffen, then I leaned forward and pressed my tongue to her clit.

She shouted my name, and her leg trembled on my shoulder. I stroked and licked her through it, soaking myself in her scent and taste, until she pressed my forehead.

"Enough," she said, her voice rough.

I pulled out my fingers and sucked them clean. She tasted saltier than I remembered. But a lot of things were different now. Not only her swollen belly, but also how I felt about her. Sure, I'd totally crushed on her as someone sexy and unattainable, but now that I knew her better, my feelings had deepened. I wanted to stay beside her, supporting her, always.

I loved her. But did she feel the same?

I watched her heaving chest like I could see inside to her beating heart. She'd defended me to her parents tonight. She'd come to my family's celebration and then to my birthday party. I knew she was conflicted about our age difference. But after spending her birthday with her, in front of her friends and my family, I suspected that this sex was different for her too, like it meant something to her. Even if it wasn't love yet, she might be nudging closer to it.

I'd run with that. If my dick could make her happy in bed, maybe she'd discover she couldn't live without the rest of me as well.

"I think we should move this to the bedroom," I said, ducking under her leg and gently laying it on the couch. "You ready?" I held out a hand.

She grasped it. "My joints are all wonky these days. I think it'll be easier for me to suck you off from on top than kneeling on the floor."

I stood and supported her as she levered off the couch. "This isn't an exchange. You've been on your feet all night, and you're tired. If it's okay with you, I'd rather fuck, then go to sleep." I made it sound careless on purpose, like it was only about the fucking and not about the feelings straining in my chest. *She isn't ready.*

I could almost see the struggle on her face to let go of her idea of fairness. Finally, she nodded. "That sounds fantastic."

I led her to the bathroom in the hallway. "Need to stop here first?"

"Always." She slipped into the bathroom and shut the door.

I washed my hands and face at the sink in the kitchen, then went into my bedroom and pulled back the sheets. I tugged off my shirt and tossed it into the hamper, then followed it with my jeans, socks, and underwear. Grabbing my dick, I gave it a rough stroke to relieve some of the building pressure.

"Fuck, that's sexy," Lucie said, leaning in the doorway.

"Yeah?" I did it again, squeezing at the base to keep myself from going off under her admiring gaze.

"Yeah. Don't let this go to your head, but you have a pretty dick."

"Pretty?" I looked down at it. It was just a dick, bigger than some, but not the biggest. Not as straight as others I'd seen.

She walked to me, bent at the waist, and kissed the head, slipping in a little tongue. My eyes rolled back. I forced myself to step backward. I wanted to save my release for later, when I held her in my arms.

"Can I help you with the zipper?" I asked.

"Okay." She turned her back to me. Her hair was still clipped up, and I brushed a few stray curls out of the way. Then I grasped the zipper and tugged it down, following the curve of her spine, all the way to the top of her ass. I pushed the dress off her shoulders, then bent to pick it up off the floor as she carefully stepped out. She kept her back to me as I lay her dress on the dresser. "Unhook my bra?"

I did, my fingers trembling. She pulled it off from the front and tossed it on top of her dress. "One more thing," I said. Gently, I pinched the clip in her hair to release it. I used my fingers to disentangle it from her curls, trying not to pull any strands. I set it on top of her bra.

She reached up to tousle her hair, groaning in pleasure. Then she turned to face me.

Her tits were heavier than the last time I'd seen them, and her tan nipples had darkened to a rosy brown. I'd seen the bottom of her abdomen before when I flipped up her skirt, but now I saw all of her. The baby sat low, giving her a pear shape.

She was indescribably gorgeous.

One of my hands was already reaching toward her. "Can I—"

"Blanket permission, remember?" she said.

I started with a brush of my hand on the side of her breast and worked my way forward. I licked her nipple first, then smoothed my thumb across the peak. She pressed closer. I repeated the action with her other breast, gazing into her eyes as my thumbs circled her pointed nipples. I caught the scent of her arousal and licked my lips.

A sly spark lit her eyes as she reached down and grasped my dick. It was already leaking, and her thumb slipped across the head, making me shiver. "Let's lie down," she said.

"What's comfortable?" I asked as she sat on the bed and scooted toward the middle.

"I'm not supposed to lie on my stomach, and my back hurts if I lie on it for too long. Maybe doggy style?"

No way was I going to look at her ass, delectable as it was, while I fucked her. Not while this felt more like making love than fucking, no matter what I'd said. "Try on your side? I have an idea."

"A dirty idea, I hope," she said, smirking.

"Sex isn't dirty," I said, kneeling on the bed. "It's natural and beautiful, especially with someone you lo—care about." I cleared my throat. *Condom.* I leaned over to pull out the bedside table drawer.

Her fingers wrapped around my wrist. "It's not like I can get more pregnant. And I haven't been with anyone since you."

I swallowed. "Neither have I. You're sure?" I'd never been bare with anyone before.

"Yeah." She licked her lips.

I planted my hands on the mattress to hide their tremble and sat back on my heels. "Lift your top leg."

She did, and I straddled her bottom leg, scooting up to her thigh. I rested her raised leg on my shoulder. "This okay?"

"Yeah."

I took a second to admire the contrast of her dark hair against the white pillowcase and the smooth curve of her flushed cheek. I kissed her ankle, then ran my hand down the inside of her thigh to her center. I swiped across her lips. They were slick and swollen, ready for me. Grabbing my aching dick, I rubbed it across her. She hummed, her eyelids drooping.

Mindful that she hadn't had partnered sex in a while and things might feel different, I pushed inside her slowly. She moaned as I filled her, and so did I. It was so good—the squeeze of her around me, the friction, the warm wetness. I wanted to stay like that for hours, or the rest of my life.

But then she contracted around me, and I gripped her leg like a rudder, like it was the only thing keeping me from going off after less than ten seconds inside her.

"My clit, Danny," she said.

The fog cleared a little. "Right, sorry."

"Don't be sorry," she said. "Rub my clit. I'm so close."

I swiped my thumb where we were connected to gather her wetness, then I set it on her clit, strumming gently as I pulled back and thrust forward.

She gave an incoherent moan, so I kept doing it. When the sensations around my dick got to be too much, the best kind of pain from holding myself back, I rested my forehead against her leg and breathed in the scent of her skin. Feeling her muscles tense against my chest, I thrummed her faster.

Letting out a choked cry, she stiffened, and I let myself go. I thrust into her once, twice, then relief and pleasure flooded me. I was shaking, and my lips trembled as I brushed a lingering kiss against her ankle. "Christ, I..."

"I know, honey," she said, laying her hand on my chest.

The pet name, her hand on my heart, the pulses that still massaged my dick, all of it broke me. "I love you, Lucie."

The words hung in the air between us for a second as I simultaneously wished I could call them back—*she's not ready, dumbass*—and desperately searched her face for a reaction.

At last, she patted my chest. "Sure you do, honey. Now get up. I've got to pee."

A ROUNDHOUSE KICK IN THE HEART

If these walls could talk, my dear. My legacy is in the first dates that became true love. In the after-work celebrations and World Series cheers. Even in the breakups, the times people came to drown their sorrows, the losses. Because I made a safe place for all that. A shoulder to cry on, a beefy guy to break up a fight, an extra shot in their glass to help numb the pain, and a ride home after. Those special moments? I was here for all of them.
Barbara McMahon, bar owner

LUCIE

The warmth at my back was gone, but the sheets were still toasty, and they held the scent of his skin. I buried my nose in the pillow. If I hadn't seen the sun coming up, I could've pretended it wasn't morning yet.

There was a clatter followed by a muttered, "Oh shit." I raised my head to look.

Danny stood in the doorway, trying to hold a tray one-handed and blot something on it with the other. He wore pajama pants and a faded Giants T-shirt, and he smelled like...

"Coffee?" I said hopefully.

"Decaf, and I spilled some."

"It's okay. Bring it here."

He set the tray on the bed. There was toast, two bananas, two mugs of coffee, and a newspaper.

I picked up a mug and sipped, then I nodded at the paper. "Where'd you get one of those?"

"I get it delivered, same as you." He blotted at the coffee stain on the newspaper.

"If I didn't work there, I wouldn't get a physical paper. I'd get a digital subscription. Most people my age—and certainly *your* age—wouldn't even do that."

"The delivery person is already delivering to your place, so it's easy to deliver to mine." He picked up the folded paper and blotted under it.

"But...do you actually read it?"

"Of course I do. Especially when you have a piece in it." His cheeks went pink. "Besides, I like to stay informed so I can talk with our customers about what's going on in the world."

"Every other millennial I know gets their news from social media."

He shrugged. "I don't. Eat some toast."

"I'm not going to eat toast in your bed. I don't want crumbs poking me in the ass when you're dicking me down."

His face went crimson. "Christ, Lucie. The things you say."

"I only say what's true." I picked up a banana.

"I'll wash the sheets."

"What if I want one more for the road? Now?" I peeled back the skin of the banana and licked the tip suggestively.

"We don't have time for that. You've got to eat and go to work."

I bit off the tip of the banana. "Spoilsport," I said, my mouth full.

"You're usually the one sprinting out of here in the morning. This is the first morning for two weeks, since the day after your birthday, that I've had time to make you coffee before you ran off." He narrowed his eyes. "Is something wrong?"

I swallowed the bite of banana. "I told my boss, Mario, about the pregnancy on Friday. He didn't take it well." That was an understatement. He'd ranted about having to cover for me on short notice. And he had a point. I should have told him earlier, but I'd been afraid he'd find an excuse to fire me. I'd been careful with my book advance, and if I had to, I could live on that, assuming I could deliver the book on time. But it was more than a paycheck I was afraid to lose. It was the difference I made, the good I did in the world through my reporting, that I'd miss if I lost my job.

"Shit, Lucie, I'm sorry," he said, leaning forward to kiss my temple. "What can I do to help?"

I clutched at him. "Make me late for work?" I whispered in his ear.

He shivered. "I'd love to, but that sounds like it might hurt your relationship with your boss."

"I don't give a shit." The baby kicked my side like she'd heard me lie. I sucked in a breath.

Danny leaned back. "Are you okay?"

"Yeah. Your goddamned progeny just roundhouse-kicked me."

"Yeah?" He stared at my belly through my shirt. Well, his shirt. I'd stolen it to sleep in.

"Want to feel?"

The look on his face was like Oprah had given him a new car. "Can I?"

I rucked up his shirt to expose my abdomen. Grabbing his hand, I held it to my side. A second later, she did it again.

His mouth dropped open. "That's her?"

"That or there's something seriously wrong in my large intestine," I joked.

"That's...that's amazing."

"Sometimes I forget there's a baby in there, doing baby things, like stretching and sleeping and sucking her thumb. Then she reminds me by stomping on my bladder."

He chuckled, then his expression went serious. "Thank you for sharing it with me."

I nodded, afraid I'd say something too vulnerable. Too encouraging.

On my birthday, he'd told me he loved me. He hadn't meant it. He'd been caught up in the moment. And even though I was the one carrying the baby, I likely wasn't the only one whose hormones were fucked up about it.

Even if he had meant it, I couldn't let this develop into more. A dozen years from now, when I was in my fifties and in a menopausal rage and our kid was exactly the kind of bitchy, hormonal adolescent I'd been, he'd regret letting me trap him into a relationship during this pregnancy.

"Thanks for the coffee," I said. "Mind if I take my toast to go?"

"Yeah." He grinned. "The ace reporter's got scandals to uncover and wrongs to right."

God, I wished I were half the person he thought I was.

He set the tray aside and held out a hand. I pulled on the stretchy maternity pants I'd worn here last night and grabbed my tunic off the floor.

"It's, um, it's Monday," he said, rubbing the back of his neck. "I'll be working late. Want a key so you can let yourself in tonight? You can make yourself at home and go to sleep here if you want. You did say you sleep better in my bed."

I hated to saddle him with that responsibility. Knowing him, he'd think it was his job to be my body pillow, but I was too weak to resist.

"Yeah, that'd be nice," I said. "Promise you'll wake me up when you get here?"

He put his arms around me and nuzzled my neck. "Promise."

27

——————

SOMETHING NEEDS DRILLING

<u>*A Pepper in the Sun*</u>
Rim a copper mug with chili salt and fill with crushed ice. Add 2 ounces jalapeño syrup and 1 ounce fresh lime juice. Top with nonalcoholic ginger beer and stir. Garnish with jalapeño slices.

DANNY

I wiped a bead of sweat from my temple before I knocked on Lucie's door. The hallway was stifling, like the rest of the building. Even the central air conditioning in the bar downstairs didn't cut it in this heat wave. We'd thrown open the doors and windows to welcome in the nonexistent breeze, and Leo and I had bought the last fans the hardware store had to cool off Norm in the kitchen. It was a lot for freaking September.

The upper floors were unairconditioned though I knew Lucie had two AC window units. The one in her bedroom dripped condensation onto my window unit with an incessant pinging sound.

Were they enough in this heat?

The hardware store didn't have any left, but I'd haul my unit up for her if she needed it. Tina said she always ran hot when she was pregnant.

When Lucie opened the door, the first thing I noticed was her hair. The curls weren't round and bouncy like usual. They were wiry and frizzy, standing out from her head like a lion's mane. Her forehead glistened.

"What do you want?" she snarled.

"I'm just checking on you. Are you doing okay? It's pretty hot out."

"I'm fine. I'm busy." She stood in the door, blocking me, which was weird because we'd slept together most nights since her birthday party last month. I'd spent almost as much time at her place as at mine. Though she'd been heads-down in her book project after work all week, and the only time I'd seen her was Wednesday when I'd carried up a case of seltzer. She'd had her friends with her that night, so I hadn't stayed.

"Can I come in?" I asked. "I want to check if your apartment is cool enough."

"It's fine. Or it would be if I could sit still for a minute."

"Then you should sit down. What can I do to help?"

"Help?" Her nose crinkled. "Nothing."

"Let me get you some ice water, then you can rest for a minute. I could give you a shoulder massage."

She rolled her shoulder, then grumbled, "It's too hot for a massage. I don't want to be touched."

I held up my hands. "Okay. No touching. How about some water, and I'll look at your AC unit?"

She walked into her living room and flopped onto her couch. I went to her kitchen and poured her favorite seltzer in a highball glass over ice. I handed it to her and walked to the window unit. It was blowing cold air like a champ. The perspiration dried on my temples, and I tugged my T-shirt away from my sweaty chest.

When I turned to face her, I found her gaze on me. Specifically, on my loose basketball shorts. I cleared my throat, and her attention rocketed up to my face. Her cheeks pinked. "Are you cool enough?" I asked.

"As long as I sit down, I'm fine. But I was…" She waved her hand at her desk. "Doing stuff."

I glanced at her monitor, but it was turned off. Then I noticed the hammer on the desk.

"What were you doing?"

"Trying to fix the crib."

I walked over to check it out. "What's wrong with it?"

"When Savannah was here this week, she reminded me I can't use that crib because of the drop side. It's dangerous."

"Oh, right. Tina said something about that when I picked it up. But with, you know…" I waved my hand in the air like she could see all my mixed-up emotions from being in love with a woman who didn't love me back. "With everything, I forgot."

"I found instructions on YouTube for fixing it, but it was a lot." She wiped a trickle of sweat from her temple. "When you go, could you take it with you? I'll order a new one."

It felt like she'd reached into my chest and grasped my heart. "Why didn't you ask? I can fix it."

"You can?"

I gave her a rueful smile. "When you grow up with more siblings than money, you learn how to fix things. I'll get my tools and take care of it."

"I—" She swallowed. "Okay." She set her water on the coffee table next to a pink book with an illustration of a pregnant woman on the cover. "I'll move some of that stuff."

"No. Sit there and rest. Want me to make you a snack?"

"A burger from Barb's?" Her eyes lit up.

"It's only eleven. The heat's making Norm especially cranky, and he'd kill us both if I asked him to make you a burger before noon. How about some dried fruit and almonds, then when I'm done, we can go down for lunch?"

She crossed her arms. "Fine." Her breasts pushed out over them, and the scoop neck of her dress pulled down, exposing the valley in between. I swallowed hard. I loved her breasts before, but they were amazing now. I'd spent a lot of time with them over the past month, and I could practically taste her—

She cleared her throat and tugged up her dress to cover that enticing hollow.

"Wh-what?" My brain was full of static.

"You were going to get me a snack. And then tools. But I can get my own snack if you need a minute to reboot." She smirked.

"No." I shook my head. "No, I've got it." *Get it together, Carbone.* I trudged into her kitchen. I had a job to do. Besides, whether or not we were sleeping together, ogling her was disrespectful. I grabbed the giant container of trail mix I'd picked up at the warehouse store and shook some into a bowl. Careful not to look at her again, I set the bowl on her coffee table. "Be right back," I muttered.

I returned with my tools and a clearer head. She'd put away all the stuff that had been piled in the crib, probably in the secondhand dresser my siblings had gifted her at the shower. "Did you need me to run any of those new baby clothes through the wash?" I asked as I assessed the crib. "Tina says we need to use that special baby detergent."

When she didn't answer, I glanced over my shoulder. "Lucie?"

She was ogling me.

"I'll do the laundry after," I said.

"We'll do it after," she murmured, eyes glued to my ass.

I couldn't help smiling—or flexing—as I bent to pick up my cordless drill. "I'm gonna sink a couple of screws in here," I said.

She swallowed. "Uh-huh."

I drilled a recess for the head of the screw so it would sit below the surface of the wood, then I switched bits and drilled a longer pilot hole for the shaft. After repeating the steps on the right side, I sank the screws in, securing the side to the ends of the crib. I rattled the side experimentally, but it didn't budge.

"See?" I said, dropping my drill into its bag. "Now the side butts up against the corners. It's not going anywhere."

I turned to see her response, but she was right in front of me. She put her hands on the side of the crib, caging me in. "It's not?"

"No." I lowered my eyebrows. Was she talking about the crib or me? Regardless, the answer was the same. "It's not."

"Guess I'm stuck with it then." She pressed closer, and her glorious breasts brushed my chest.

I sucked in a breath as all the blood rushed from my brain to my other head. "Stuck with me," I echoed nonsensically.

"Look," she said, "you can't come in here acting out some thin porno plotline and not fuck me."

"I...I can't?" My brain had gone offline.

She reached up to the back of my neck and tugged out the pony-tail holder securing my hair. The pull at my scalp made the hairs rise on my arms. When she tunneled her fingers into my hair, I couldn't help it. My hands naturally fit themselves to the curve of her lower back. One wandered down to explore the succulent curve of her ass. She pressed her hips to me, pinning my erection against her belly.

"No, your line is, 'I think something else needs drilling,'" she murmured. Her lips looked plush. The sweet scent of the almonds she'd eaten wafted up to me. I lowered my head, seeking her kiss.

When our lips met, it was electric. Like I'd stuck a screwdriver in a wall socket, heat licked up my spine. I bent to touch, to taste her. She was soft and delicious and hungry, opening to me, licking inside my mouth, lighting up every nerve as she fused her body to mine. My scalp tingled as she scratched her short nails through my hair.

Her other hand clamped onto my ass. I groaned, rubbing myself against her firm belly. My thin shorts let me feel every curve of her, curves I wanted to explore and map.

She broke the kiss, panting. "Want to take this someplace more comfortable?"

"Yeah." I took her hand and followed her to her bedroom like I was actually a porno handyman.

It was cooler in here, and I took a moment to savor the sensation of sweat drying on my skin. The anticipation of touching Lucie's skin, of folding her into my arms, of hearing her heart beat.

Then I heard rustling.

I opened my eyes to find her picking up clothing off the comforter and tossing it into a suitcase on the bed.

"You're packing?"

"Yeah, I've got a trip tomorrow." She bent to pick up the suitcase.

"Let me." I lifted it from the bed and set it on the floor. "But you can't go on a trip tomorrow. You're practically eight months pregnant. Will they even let you on a plane?"

"Of course they will. I can fly up to a month before my due date."

"Which is in *six weeks,*" I said.

"Exactly." She lifted a pile of clothes and tossed them into the suitcase.

"But should you? What if you have a complication like…" I

searched my brain for the title of one of the pamphlets in her doctor's office. "Gestational diabetes? Or preeclampsia?"

"Then I'll deal with it. There are hospitals in DC too."

"DC?" My jaw clenched. "You're going to the East Coast? That's, like, an eight-hour flight! You can't sit on a plane that long. You'll get blood clots."

She stepped closer to me and put a hand on my chest. "It's only five hours. And I'll get up at least once an hour and walk around. Now, where were we?" She trailed her hand lower.

I took a giant step back and bumped into her dresser. "You can't go. Your boss can't make you."

Frowning, she put her hands on her hips. "Yes, I can. And it's not for my boss. I have an opportunity to do an interview with a subject for my book."

I didn't want to stand in the way of her research. Writing that book was her dream. "Then I'll go with you."

"You'll go...with me?" She narrowed her eyes.

"Sure. I'll take a few days off. I'll carry your bag. Make sure you're hydrated." So what if I'd never been on a plane before. Or been farther from home than Vegas. How hard could it be? "You'll need help."

It was the wrong thing to say. Her eyes blazed. "I do *not* need help. I especially don't need it from someone who won't get paid to do a job he can't work when he's in a different state."

My head snapped back. "You won't accept my help because I'm paid hourly?"

"No, goddammit." Her voice rose. "I won't accept your help because I don't fucking need help!"

"Christ, Lucie, everyone needs help!" My voice strained from the effort it took not to yell at her. Everything in the room had a red haze to it except for her. She blazed bright like a floodlight.

I don't know which of us moved first, but the next thing I knew, I had my hands on her and I was kissing her. Maybe *kiss* was too nice a word for it. Our mouths pressed together, our teeth clacked, and our tongues wrestled like a pair of beefy guys in spandex trunks and kneepads.

My brain couldn't have been more fried if Lucie had hit me over the head with a folding chair. Nothing rational was left, only the gaping wound she'd left when she'd said I wasn't worthy of helping her and the blinding need to prove I could take care of her in every way she needed.

She yanked down my shorts and underwear, and I hissed when her cool hand squeezed my hot, angry dick. I was too close to the edge, but there was no way I was going off in her hand. I broke the kiss. "No. Hands up here." I put her hands on my shoulders.

"Like this?" She twirled her fingers in my hair and gave a vicious yank that made my scalp erupt in pain. My dick jumped.

"Yeah," I grunted. I rucked up her skirt. Not bothering to pull off her panties, I tugged the crotch aside and buried my fingers in her wet heat, tracing her swollen lips.

She gasped and bit my shoulder.

"Ow!" But some ancient part of me flickered to life like a flame igniting from embers. I shoved two fingers inside her and flicked her clit with my thumb.

She stiffened, then let out a high-pitched moan as I pulled my fingers out and thrust them back in. I tapped her clit again. She pressed her body into my hand. "More," she demanded.

I gave it to her. Because I wanted to. She rippled around me as I moved my hand faster, deeper, as I kept my thumb on her clit as an anchor. Her fingers tightened on my shoulders, digging into the muscle, until her whole body clenched. Her muscles locked around my fingers, holding them in place. Finally, she shivered and relaxed.

"Thank you," she said, "I—"

"You think you're done?" I gritted out. I pulled my fingers out of her and wiped them on my T-shirt before I pulled it off. "Panties off. Hands and knees on the bed."

I would have found the control to stop if she'd protested. But she didn't. Her pupils were blown, and her lips parted when she scanned my face. Then she reached down and shimmied her underwear to the floor. Keeping her gaze on my face, she kneeled on the bed, then turned away and flicked her dress up over her ass.

One step brought me behind her. I bent and licked her glistening pussy. She flinched in surprise, then moaned when I gripped her ass cheeks and buried my face in her.

She'd hardly come down from her last orgasm, and soon she was shuddering and shouting my name. I sucked her one more time and then brushed my dripping chin against her haunch. "Who just made you come twice?"

"You did, Danny," she said hoarsely.

"And who's about to make you come again with my dick?"

"You are, Danny. You."

"You need me," I said, lining myself up at her entrance.

She didn't respond to that except with a grunt as I slid inside. "You need me," I repeated as I reversed and thrust back in, gripping her hips.

She let out a wordless cry, pushing back against me. And the fact that she refused to admit she needed me only made me angrier. I pulled out and ground back in as far as I could go.

"Danny!" she screamed. "Yes!"

I kept up a brutal rhythm until my vision hazed and everything drew up tight. I was so focused on the sensation of her tight squeeze around me that I couldn't tell if she'd come again or not, so I reached around and tweaked her clit. Her back bowed, and that was it. I emptied myself inside her, groaning her name. When my knees wobbled, I pulled out and collapsed onto the bed beside her.

She flopped to her side. "So much for not wanting to be touched."

A chill raced across my skin. "Shit, Lucie. Did I go too far?"

"No." She sat up and put a hand on my arm. "I wanted that. Needed it."

"Needed *it?*" Something pinged in my chest. I should've known better than to hope Lucie Knox would ever say she needed *me*.

"Yes. Now, give me a minute and then we can take a nap." She pushed herself off the bed and went inside the bathroom.

But I didn't wait. I tugged on my clothes. My face flamed when I realized I hadn't bothered to take off my shoes. Then I picked up my tool bag and left.

28

I'LL BE WATCHING YOU

Legacy isn't only what you achieve yourself. For me, it's about raising a generation that feels the call to serve. My son is in politics and serves our country. My daughters serve too—one healing the sick, the other bringing relief to those in need. They walk their own paths, but seeing them use their gifts to make a difference, that's my greatest pride.

Eleanor Gu, former librarian and wife to Senator William Gu

LUCIE

Somewhere over Nebraska, I finally admitted what was keeping me from preparing for my interview, reading the thriller I'd picked up at the airport bookstore, or watching that Sandra Bullock movie Savannah had raved about.

I rubbed my chest where it felt raw. It didn't feel great to be the one left behind.

I'd done it dozens of times, or maybe hundreds, in twenty years of no-strings relationships. I'd always figured getting dressed and leaving was the right thing to do. That way, I could sleep in my bed, and we didn't have to have the awkward morning-after conversation with the empty, "I'll text you" or "Let's do this again soon." No lies, no guilt.

And after a hookup at my place, I encouraged them to put on their pants and go. Skip the awkward dance about who'd go first in the bathroom and the apologies for not keeping stevia or oat milk or whatever millennial bullshit they put in their coffee.

Over the last month, I'd let that rule lapse. Danny knew how I liked my coffee—black, and, sadly, decaf—and he drank it that way too. We were already tied together not only as neighbors but with this baby, so there was no escaping him even if I'd wanted to. Plus, it had been kind of nice to wake up with him cuddled around me.

So, when I came out of the bathroom yesterday afternoon and found my bed empty, something tightened in my belly. And it wasn't Braxton Hicks contractions, which I'd learned so much about when I couldn't sleep and finally picked up The Book.

Maybe it had a chapter on what to do when pregnancy hormones made you think you were starting to feel feelings for the man you'd just had angry sex with. Who was also your baby daddy. Because the tension in my gut, the heaviness that made it hard to drag myself out of bed this morning, that little skip in my heart whenever I thought of Danny, all of it had to be caused by the weird hormones flowing through my body.

Besides, who the fuck cared about what I was feeling? Danny was a great person, but he was way too young to want to be tied to a washed-up journalist who couldn't even finish the book she'd dreamed about writing for years. He should save his kindness and hot handyman muscles and that glorious cock for one of the Nice Church Girls his mom wanted him to marry. He must've realized it, too, and that's why he'd fled my place.

I reached under the seat in front of me. Or tried to. My body didn't bend in the same way it used to.

"Excuse me," I said to the woman in the aisle seat. "Can you reach that book in my bag?"

"Sure!" She bent down and pulled the book from the outside pocket of my messenger bag. She glanced at the cover. "Oh my god! You're pregnant?"

My cheeks went hot. Wasn't it obvious? "Uh-huh."

"Isn't this the best book ever? I mean, not only does it tell you everything you need to know, but it makes you feel better about yourself at the same time. I read it before I had each of my kids, and I got something new out of it every time."

"Really?" The woman had not a strand of gray in her dark brown hair. She had to be younger than me. "How many kids do you have?"

"Four. I know, I know. I was young and clueless when I started. But The Book helped. How many do you have?"

"This is my first." *And only,* I didn't add.

Her eyes rounded. "Wow. Good for you. Be sure to read the chapter on pregnancy later in life. It helped me with my last one. And, um..." She glanced at my left hand. "There's a chapter on single parenting. One of my girlfriends said it was fantastic."

Last night, when I couldn't sleep, I'd skipped right to the chapter about symptoms during the eighth month of pregnancy, where I'd learned what the tightening of my stomach muscles was about. I'd been planning to read about the ninth month because that was right around the corner, but maybe I should check out the table of contents. "Thanks."

"So, what's on your birth plan?" she asked, turning fully toward me. "I've tried it all. Epidural, natural, even a water birth —though you wouldn't believe how fast I got out of that tub once the real contractions hit. Do you have a doula?"

"A what?"

And for the next two hours, a woman five years younger than me schooled me in everything I didn't know about childbirth, which, for a know-it-all like me, felt worse than being left after a hookup with someone you cared about more than you should.

~

*H*ours later, as I wrapped up my interview with Eleanor Gu, the heavy feeling lingered. Mrs. Gu was a champion for literacy, a senator's wife, and the mother of a man everyone called a future president. Her thoughts on legacy were supposed to be a highlight of my book. From the slight furrow between her brows, I feared I'd fucked up because I couldn't seem to follow the thread of our conversation. Only the recording would tell if I'd done the interview justice.

I tapped my phone to end the recording. "Thanks for your time today. I'll send you the transcript as we discussed."

"Good luck with your book," she said. "I'll be watching."

"Oh, you don't have to watch out for it." I closed my notebook and slipped it into my bag. "I'll send you an advance copy as soon as I get them from the publisher."

"No." She waited until I met her piercing, dark gaze. "I'll be watching *you.*"

"Me?" I rubbed my forehead. It had been throbbing for hours.

"I think you've got more than this one book in you. I'm interested to see where you go from here."

I dropped my hand from my face. "But—but your life is so full, between your work for libraries and schools, your family, and the campaigning you do for the senator and your son, the congressman. And your daughters. How do you have time to pay attention to anything else?"

"Ms. Knox. You should have learned by now that you make time for what's important. And you, my dear, are important."

"I...I..." I swallowed. Few people had the power to steal my words, but Mrs. Gu had done it.

"Just say, thank you, dear." She stood.

"Thank you." But when I rose to my feet, spots danced in my vision. I blinked to clear them, but they only grew until everything faded from view.

"Ms. Knox!"

My knees buckled, and I sprawled onto the hard sofa. "I'm okay. I just need a minute."

"John," she called, "get Mindy."

"No, really, I'm fine." Now that I was sitting, my vision cleared. I tugged my skirt down from where it had ridden up on my thighs.

"You're pregnant, aren't you?" Mrs. Gu was sitting next to me, cradling my hand with two fingers on my wrist.

"Yes."

"Then we're getting you checked out. Fainting could be a sign of something serious."

"I was only lightheaded for a minute." I squinted in the sunshine streaming through the window, which stabbed directly into my brain. "Besides, I need to get to the airport or I'm going to be late for my flight."

"My assistant will rebook you. Your health can't wait. I don't like how rapid your pulse is."

"I thought your daughter was the doctor," I joked, closing my eyes for a minute.

"I was a school librarian for years. I'm still first-aid certified. It comes in handy."

"Hi there," an unfamiliar voice said. "What's going on?"

I opened my eyes to find a young woman sitting in front of me. She didn't wear scrubs or a white coat, but she pulled a stethoscope from her bag.

"You're not old enough to be a doctor," I said as she put the metal piece over my heart.

Mrs. Gu cackled. "I remember the first time I thought that. My kids' pediatrician retired, and the new doctor seemed so young! Now it's you, Mindy."

"My name is Dr. Gu, and I'm fully qualified." The young woman pulled out a blood pressure cuff. "Do you need to look up my medical license before I treat you?"

Holy shit. I'd insulted my interviewee's daughter. "No, sorry, I...I've got this headache. I don't usually have much of a filter, but I think it's fried."

She inflated the cuff and listened, then removed it from my arm. "A headache. When's the last time you drank something?"

"Like booze? Months. Since I, y'know." I pointed at my belly.

Her lips pursed like she was holding in a smile. "No, I mean water. Juice. A soda."

"I had some water on the plane and decaf at the airport before my flight."

"You need to drink more water," she said. "You should carry a water bottle at all times and aim to empty it every hour."

"That's what my boy—my friend. That's what he says too. He's always bringing me seltzer and making me mocktails."

"That's a good start, but you need to drink plain water too, and lots of it."

I laughed, thinking of that trend where all the influencers had to have the silly insulated cup with the handle. But the doctor didn't laugh.

"Wait, you're serious?" I said.

"Serious as a collapse due to dehydration. I'm going to call the hospital and have them give you some IV fluids. Meanwhile, drink this." She pulled a bottle of an electrolyte drink from her bag and handed it to me.

I cracked open the lid and took a swig. "I bet this will fix me right up. No need to go to the hospital. My flight home is in a couple of hours."

"You need more fluids than you can drink right now," Dr. Gu said. "And the dry cabin air on the airplane will make it worse. You don't want to be that person who has a medical emergency at thirty thousand feet." Her gaze dropped to my baby bump. "Hydration is essential for your developing fetus. There are serious impacts to sustained dehydration during pregnancy."

"Goddammit," I muttered. "I'll go."

"Good choice," Mrs. Gu said. "John will drive you to the hospital. I'd go with you, but I've got to get on a flight myself."

"I'll go with her," Dr. Gu said. "My shift starts in a couple of hours anyway. I'll keep you updated, Mom."

"Thank you, dear. And Ms. Knox, I hope you remember to take care of yourself. Your child is going to depend on you, and you can't take care of her if you're sick."

"I understand," I said. An icy chill raced through my veins. I hadn't thought of it like that before. I didn't envy the poor kid who relied on me as a mother. I had to get my shit together.

And that meant spending an hour at a DC hospital hooked up to an IV, taking a later flight home, and dragging my exhausted body back to my building right at Barb's closing time. When there was a hundred percent chance Danny would notice.

29

BORING, RESPECTABLE, AND STABLE

Banana-Spinach Smoothie
Combine a frozen banana, 1 cup fresh spinach, 1/2 cup Greek yogurt, a
dollop of almond butter, 1/2 cup almond milk, and a drizzle of honey
in a blender. Blend until smooth. Pour into a glass and drink your
goddamn electrolytes, Lucie.

DANNY

When I flicked on the overhead lights, Frank and Walter squinted and grumbled. "Go on home, guys," I said. "Need me to call you a ride?"

"I've got them," Leo said. "And Nico and I'll take care of the cleanup. You should worry about that." He tipped his chin at something behind me.

I turned and spotted Lucie in the residents' hallway. She shuffled like a zombie, and she looked just as pale. What was she doing out this late? Had something happened?

I curbed my urge to run to her and took a breath. "You sure you'll be okay?" I asked.

"Yeah, yeah. We've got this. But..." He looked down at his

kitchen clogs. "Could you meet me tomorrow morning? I've got something I want to show you."

"Everything all right?" He'd been weird tonight, switching between wild-eyed excitement and quiet, almost guilty introspection.

"Yeah, it's good. I just had an idea I wanted to talk to you about, but it can wait until tomorrow."

"If you're sure…" But I was already moving toward the hall that led to the stairs. I felt a tug in my gut like Lucie was a magnet and I was a nail.

I caught up with her on the second-floor landing. "Hey."

"Hey, Danny." She didn't even try to smile. She looked dead on her feet.

"Let me take your bag." I lifted the messenger bag from her shoulder. She shook out her arm, and that's when I noticed the bandage, the bruise, and the hospital bracelet. "Jesus Christ! What happened?"

She slapped her other hand over her wrist. "Nothing. I mean, yeah, I had to go to the hospital, but it was only dehydration. They pumped me full of electrolytes and let me come home. They said I had to keep the bracelet on for twenty-four hours, though, in case anything else happened."

I tugged her into my arms and held her like I could protect her from whatever "anything else" meant. And she let me. She didn't push me away. Instead, she relaxed into my arms. I never wanted to let her go.

But she needed her bed. "Can I carry you up?"

"Carry me?" she scoffed. "There's nothing wrong with me that twelve hours of sleep won't cure." She pushed away and slowly ascended the stairs. Then she looked back. "Come on."

Joy filled me up and threatened to overflow. I bounded up the stairs after her, her bag bumping against my hip. "How'd the interview go?"

"Okay, I hope. I started to feel a little out of it toward the end, so I don't know if I asked the right questions." She handed me her key, and I fit it into the lock. "I'll listen to the recording tomorrow."

I pushed the door open and flicked on the light. Not bothering to take off her shoes, she went straight to her bedroom while I took a moment to bolt the door and slip off my sneakers. On the way to her bedroom, I set her satchel in her desk chair.

She'd flopped onto her side on the bed, her feet sticking out over the edge. I unlaced her boots and pulled off her thick socks. "These must've been a bitch at airport security."

"God, yes," she said, her voice muffled by the comforter.

"Want me to find you some pajamas?"

"Pajamas? Like anything fits. Can you do the zipper?"

I lowered the back zipper of her dress and averted my eyes. This was no time to ogle her. She was exhausted after a long day of airports, airplanes, and interviews. I wanted to shake her for going on the trip in the first place, examine every part of her to be sure she was okay, lick her pussy until she admitted she belonged here with me, and hold her forever so she'd never leave the state again.

But that was my lizard brain trying to take charge. Lucie always thought with the rational part of her brain, and none of that would make any sense to her. Finally, an idea appeared that would satisfy my caveman urge to claim her without being creepy. "I could bring you some of my T-shirts. They'd probably fit you."

"That would be amazing." She pushed herself up to sit. "How about that one?" She stared at my black Barb's Bar tee.

"Yeah, I've got one like it downstairs." I stood.

"Don't go," she said. "That one's fine."

"I just worked a ten-hour shift in this. It smells like sweat and beer."

She shrugged. "Keep it then." She let her dress fall from her shoulders and reached back to undo her bra.

As on edge as I was, I'd combust if I saw her bare breasts. There was no way I could keep my hands off her, and she needed rest. I ripped off the shirt and handed it to her. "Here. If you want it."

She smiled, victorious, and slipped it over her head. It fell to the tops of her thighs, and there was just enough room in it for her rounded belly. It skimmed her breasts as she did a complicated shimmy to take off her bra underneath it. She sighed as she tugged the bra out of the armhole and dropped it on the floor. "Much better."

She rose to her knees to tug back the covers, and I averted my eyes from the tantalizing glimpse of her panties and the backs of her thighs. It reminded me of yesterday's angry sex and the blinding pleasure when I'd come inside her.

I'd been right about the trip. It had been too much. But there was no comfort in being right. She settled in bed, her curls fanning across her silk pillowcase. "You going to join me?"

"I, um, I don't think I should." Sex was the last thing she needed when she was this exhausted.

"You don't want to stay, or you don't think I want you to stay? Because I do. I want you to stay." She met my gaze, and hers was unguarded, revealing her need. "No funny business. I promise."

"I can't do anything about this." I gestured at the bulge in my jeans.

"Sure you can. You can jack off in my shower if you need to."

"Jesus, Lucie!"

"Look, I need to go to sleep. And I'll sleep better with you. So will you stay? Please?"

"Yeah." Because what else could I say? "I'll stay." I shucked off my jeans and socks and crawled into bed beside her. "You've got to be the big spoon, though." I turned my back to her.

"No problem." When her arms came around me, the plastic bracelet scratched my chest.

I put my hand over it and the bandage on her forearm, snugging her arm tightly against my chest. Her belly pressed into my back, and I was thankful for the layer of cotton between us that let me pretend it was an extra-firm pillow and not the sexiest woman I'd ever met cuddling me. "Night, Lucie."

"G'night." Her exhale tickled the back of my neck, and in less than a minute, her breathing evened out. I stayed awake a while longer, waiting for my erection to soften and wishing I could fall asleep like this every night for the rest of my life.

~

The next morning, I left a big insulated cup of water and a spinach-banana smoothie on Lucie's counter while she slept. It was unappetizingly green, but I'd dosed it liberally with honey, so I hoped she'd drink it to replenish her electrolytes.

I didn't want to leave her, but I'd promised to meet Leo. The address he'd texted me turned out to be an empty storefront next to a dry cleaner's. On the dingy front window, I could make out the faint outline of the word DELI.

"Hey!" Leo bounced out of the front door like he'd had a full eight hours of sleep and not five or six. "Come in!"

"What are you doing in there?" I looked up and down the street, my gaze lingering on the business next door, which looked way more reputable than this one. "Is this a drug house?" I whispered. "Are you huffing dry cleaning chemicals?"

"What the fuck?" he said. "I don't do shit like that anymore. Come inside."

Inside was no better. The linoleum floor was so faded that I couldn't distinguish the pattern. There was wood paneling halfway up the walls, and more of the dated panels covered the small counter to the left. Behind that were ancient refrigerated display cases. Everything looked like it had been installed at least a decade before I was born. To the right was a picture frame, but it didn't hold a long-expired certificate from the health department. It showcased a bullet hole in the wall.

"Cool, yeah?" Leo's eyebrows had lifted practically to his hairline, and he wore the same expression as when we used to go to the arcade as kids and he saw the neon-lit dance pad of his favorite game.

"Ugh, not unless you're a cockroach."

His smile dipped, but then it broadened. "I haven't shown you the best part."

He went through a set of double doors in the back. I followed him into the darkened space.

"The lights are still off, but...ta-da!" He flicked on his phone's flashlight and illuminated a stainless steel kitchen. In the center was a long prep counter. In back was a stove with a griddle. On the left side side were a couple of refrigerators, and a dish-washing station was on the right. It was easily twice as big as the kitchen at Barb's. Though I shuddered to think of what it looked like with the lights on. Or how many insects might be hiding inside the walls.

"Impressive, huh?" he asked.

"Impressive," I echoed, "that it hasn't been condemned and torn down."

"So the storefront's a little dated. All this stuff is perfectly serviceable. Or I bet it is once we turn on the power and gas."

"Who's *we*? *We* don't need this. We're six weeks away from buying Barb's."

"That's not what Tad said. He said he was taking it over."

I clenched my fists. "Tad's a fucking liar."

"Oh." I couldn't see his expression in the dark, but I heard the disappointment in his voice. "You always said you wanted to raise kids in the suburbs, in a place with a yard. I figured it was your idea to let Barb sell to Tad instead so you could use the cash for a down payment on a house."

"No." I tried to keep my voice steady. "I promised you we'd buy the bar together, and I keep my promises. I'd have talked to you if I was thinking of changing my mind."

"This is me offering you an out, then. Uncle Gio said he'd be my silent partner in a catering business. This place is perfect, right?"

"I never said I wanted an out. This place would be a lot of work. And it's next to a fucking dry cleaner. It could be a Superfund site."

"Come on." He led me out into the front where there was light. "Do you really want to follow through on buying the bar? You've always wanted stability. A house. A fucking minivan. Are you sure you want to raise a kid over a bar? 'Cause that kind of sounds like how we grew up before Ma inherited Nonna's place."

"Look, I...I don't know." Buying Barb's had been my dream for so long, and I hadn't stopped to think about how being a father might change that. Months ago, Lucie had said she didn't want to get married. But we'd grown closer, and things between us had shifted. She might've changed her mind. And how amazing would it be to become a real family with Lucie and our daughter? I could take Aunt Connie up on her offer to take over her insurance business. That would be the kind of job that meant I'd qualify for a mortgage and would be home in time to make dinner every night. Boring, respectable, and stable. All the things I'd imagined when I was a kid.

My brother drew himself up. "Well, I know what I want. And it's not buying Barb's. It's buying a kitchen big enough to run a catering business."

"What?" I pushed my hair behind my ears. Maybe I hadn't heard him right. "But we've always wanted to run the bar together."

"No." He looked down. "*You* wanted the bar. And I wanted to give something back to my big brother who was always there for me, who was kind of a dad to me, who made time for me when no one else did. But now I've realized that isn't a good enough reason. We'll be happier if we each do what we love."

Do what we love? But we'd agreed to do this together. "Jesus fucking Christ! When were you going to tell me this?" I roared.

"Today, Danny. I'm telling you today." His voice was as quiet as mine was loud.

I pushed the door so hard it banged against the exterior wall.

Not caring where I went, I turned right and walked along the street, seeing nothing. It was a good thing it was Sunday morning and traffic was light. On a weekday, I'd have walked out into a busy street and probably been hit by a commuter.

I wouldn't have cared.

My brother had betrayed me. After all we'd been through together, after all the times I'd fucking saved him from himself, after working at Barb's for years, planning and saving for the day when it'd be ours, he'd dropped this bomb on me.

Without Leo, I didn't have enough cash to buy Barb's. And if Gio was funding Leo, he wouldn't have any extra to help me out. I had a fleeting thought of asking for a loan at the bank, but who'd give a business loan to a bartender who'd never gone to college, who had no business experience, who owned nothing but a crappy old Toyota? Who had a child to support?

Maybe Leo was right. Maybe I'd be better off focusing on my daughter. The money I'd saved for the bar would buy a good chunk of a nice little house in the suburbs.

I realized I'd been walking next to a park, and at the next break in the hedge, I stepped inside. Stretching before me was an expanse of wood chips with a play structure. It had a few swings, a slide, and one of those towers that kids could climb. I sank onto a bench.

It'd be a pain in the ass to share custody if I lived in the suburbs and Lucie still lived in the city. What about when the kid was old enough to go to school? Would Lucie let her live with me, or would I be a weekends-only dad?

That thought left me cold. As loving as my mom was, I'd watched her struggle on her own. I'd always wished I had two parents. That's what I wanted for my kid.

A little girl ran to one of the swings, and her dad followed. She clambered into the seat, and he pulled her back and let her fly forward. Tucking her feet, she swung back, and he pushed her. "Higher!" she squealed, kicking her feet out in front and leaning back.

"Not too high," her mother called from the bench behind them.

Could that be us someday, Lucie, me, and our daughter? Lucie'd be the one pushing, of course, and I'd be the one worrying about her flying too high and falling. But could we be a family?

She might not admit it to herself, but Lucie needed me. That trip had been a bad idea, like I'd said. And who had she needed after? Me. She had to see that. We were stronger together.

Jesus Christ. Was she waiting for me to say it? To tell her I loved her and that we belonged together as a family?

To propose for real this time?

30

I DON'T WANT A NICE WOMAN

<u>*The Color Purple*</u>
*In a cocktail shaker, combine 1/2 ounce blue curaçao syrup and 1
ounce grape juice and shake. Pour into a lowball glass filled with ice.
Top off the glass with black cherry seltzer. Garnish with blackberries
and blueberries.*

DANNY

"What are you so dressed up for?" Lucie asked when she opened her door.

"Our date." I wasn't exactly dressed up, but I'd ironed my jeans, and I had on the dark gray wool sweater Ma had gotten me for Christmas last year. Giuliana said it made my eyes look like topaz.

Lucie didn't know it, but we were getting photographed. I wanted to show our daughter the pictures from today and be proud of how I looked. Smiling, I extended the bouquet of daisies.

She didn't take them. "You said we were going for a walk. I spent ten minutes trying to tie my damn boots." She held up a foot. "Do you have any idea how hard it is to put on shoes when there's a beach ball strapped to your middle?"

I grimaced. "Sorry. You should have waited. I'd have helped you."

"I don't need help." She tugged down her black tunic so it covered the stretchy panel in her black maternity pants. "And why would I need flowers for a walk?"

That was the problem with dating a journalist. She asked an awful lot of questions. "You don't *need* them. I wanted to give them to you to show you I care about you."

She fisted the front of my sweater and pulled me down for a kiss. It was rough and needy and demanding, like I hadn't left her apartment an hour ago. Like we hadn't slept together in her bed every night for the last week since she'd come home from her trip. At last, she pulled back. "We don't need to go for a fucking walk for you to show me that. We can stay here and you can do that thing with your tongue. Though I'm going to need help getting my shoes off."

Tempting as her offer was, I smoothed my sweater. "We have plans. We'll go for a walk, and when we come back, I'll fuck you senseless. I promise."

"Senseless sounds amazing." She pressed up against me, and I felt a jab against my hip. "See, even she likes the idea."

I stepped back. "The thought of our daughter wanting me to fuck you is really confusing for my libido, you know."

"Okay, I can understand that. But she's excited about something. Feel this." She took my hand and held it to the side of her belly. Something hard poked my palm. After a second, it happened again.

"What is that?" I asked.

"Foot? Or an elbow, maybe? I'm guessing it's getting pretty tight in there, and she's trying to make more room. Gotta say, I much prefer her kicking that direction than toward my bladder. Speaking of which, I'd better pee before we go."

"I'll put these in water." I waved the bouquet.

In her kitchen, I pulled the vase from the top of her refrigerator. I knew she wouldn't love the idea of moving out to the suburbs, but the kitchens out there were so much better. She'd have enough cabinets for more than one vase. There would be room for healthy snacks and her collection of barware. But the best part was that there'd be a room for the baby, with a separate office to write her books. And I'd take care of it all, from finding a place to handling the movers to ensuring everything was freshly painted and clean. All Lucie would have to do would be show up at our new home and sit down at her desk to write.

It would be great for all three of us.

I filled the vase with water, snipped the ends of the stems, and stuck them into the vase. I took a minute to wash the plate and cup in her sink and put them away. Yes, living together would be the best situation for all of us.

Lucie appeared in the doorway. "Let's go before I have to pee again."

My heart flipped. It was almost time for the big event. I clasped her hand. "Let's go."

The drive to Golden Gate Park didn't take long on a Saturday, although parking was a bitch. Fortunately, there was a restroom at the main entrance, and we were running only a little behind schedule by the time we set off toward the far side of the park.

I should've been prepared for how slowly Lucie walked these days. I supposed I'd amble too if I were carrying an almost full-grown infant and my joints were loosening to prepare for childbirth. Yeah, I'd been reading *Dr. Dunne's Guide to Pregnancy* too. I already knew a lot from watching Ma's pregnancies, and my cousins', but Dr. Dorothy Dunne explained everything I'd observed so clearly.

Still, it was hard to be patient with the buzzes coming from the phone in my pocket. My heart raced as we plodded along the path around the conifer lawn.

"Let's sit." Lucie beelined toward a bench. "Then we can turn back."

"Turn back?" That would ruin my plan. I paced next to the bench, too wound up to sit. "We'll rest, then we'll go a little farther. There's something I want to show you."

"You can show me whatever it is next time. My hips are aching." She rubbed the side of her stretchy maternity pants.

That hit me right in the chest. I'd pushed her too far. Why hadn't I tried harder to find parking at the north entrance?

"What if I carry you?" I asked.

She looked like I'd proposed she join the Polar Bear Club and jump into the Pacific in January. "Excuse me, did you just offer to carry me?"

"Umm...yeah? There's a really pretty pond with a platform that extends into the middle of it." Where my family was waiting for the big moment. "It's not far. You could ride piggyback."

"Absolutely not. Now help me up, and we'll turn back."

"Hold on, hold on." I could salvage my plan. I whipped my phone out of my pocket and texted the group, *Come meet us at the conifer lawn. Hurry!*

"We can rest here a little longer." I sat next to her on the bench. "I'll rub your feet."

"You can do that at home," she said. "Let's go."

Home slowed my heartbeat. Soon, we'd have a home together, all three of us. I scanned the tree line. I could do this without witnesses. The thing that mattered most was that she knew how I felt and that we were together, always.

"Lucie, I have a question." I slipped off the bench and

kneeled at her feet. "This last month since your birthday, we've grown so much closer. I love taking care of you. In fact"—I took a deep breath—"I love you, and I want us to be together. Not just as co-parents, but as partners. I want you to marry me." Digging in my pocket, I found the velvet box. I opened it, then I looked up into her face.

She had that same look of horror as when I'd proposed to carry her.

She needed more convincing.

"I'm going to get us a house in the suburbs. Something near my mom's. It's a good neighborhood for kids, and we won't need to put the baby into daycare because my family will babysit. She can grow up with my little cousins." I pushed the ring closer to her. The diamond was tiny, since I wanted to put as large a down payment as I could on the house. But it was high quality, like Lucie.

"Stop." She held up her hands, and that's when I heard the click of a shutter. Elena, always the fastest runner, had reached us with her Nikon to capture the moment. "You're buying a house?"

"It'll be better for us to live together while we raise the baby. I'll take care of both of you."

"What about the bar? What about your dream?"

I rubbed the sore spot in my chest. "It's not my dream anymore. You and our family are my dream now."

"Oh, Danny." Her expression turned from horror to pity. "I can't be your dream. You're so young. You're caught up in this pregnancy, and it's confused you about what you want."

There was another click, and Lucie turned her head and spotted Elena crouching nearby. "Is that your sister?"

"Yeah." My face went hot.

"Hey, Elena. Could you cool it with the photos, please?"

"Sure, Lucie." She put her camera down but stared at us like she was at Shakespeare in the Park.

This scene was starting to feel like I was the butt of a joke in a comedy. My blood heated. "Just because I'm a few years younger than you doesn't mean I don't know what I want. I'm an adult. I've taken care of all four of my younger siblings and a bunch of my cousins. I'm good at it. You'll see."

She shook her head. "No, Danny, I won't. My mother gave up her life, her career, and her dreams for my dad and me, and I—"

"But I'm not asking you to give up anything," I insisted. The rest of my family had arrived, and they were loitering nearby, pretending to mind their own business but listening to every word. "I'm offering to help you achieve your dreams. When we're married and living together, it'll be easy for me to care for the baby while you're off saving the world."

"Let me finish," she said. "I won't let you do what my mom did. My dreams aren't the only ones that are important. I didn't want to saddle you with a baby, much less a mortgage. You can't give up your plans for the bar, not even for the baby. And certainly not for me."

She heaved herself off the bench and started walking back the way we'd come.

I snapped the box shut and shoved it back into my pocket. When I looked up, all four of my siblings and my mom stared at me as they held up their phones. *Fuck!* They'd recorded the whole humiliating spectacle. Because I'd asked them to.

I sprang after Lucie.

She was walking fast, but she was still tired and pregnant. I caught her in a minute. "Look, let's take some time to think about it. We'll talk. You'll tell me what you want, and we'll find a middle ground."

She planted her feet and jammed her hands onto her hips. "We don't have to talk through it. Here's what I want: I want to live in the city so I can do my job. I want this child to grow up seeing her mother as a strong, independent woman who doesn't have to compromise between motherhood and a career.

"And here's what I don't want: I don't want to ruin your life by making you give up what you want for some family fantasy I can't—I won't—give you."

She waved back to where my family stood in a circle around that bench, sneaking looks at us. "I can't give you that. This baby is it for me. Someday, you'll find one of those nice women at church who can give you five more kids and who wants to live out in the fucking suburbs. But that's not me." She strode off down the path.

I jogged to catch up. "I don't want a nice woman. I want you." Then I played back what I'd said and winced. "I mean—"

She gazed straight ahead. "You're very sweet, Danny. But you're young, and you have no idea what you want."

I grabbed her hand and pulled her to a stop. "Goddammit! I'm thirty fucking years old! I know what I want, and it's you!"

"No, Danny, it's not." Her eyes glistened with tears. "You want the dream. That's not me."

I tugged her into my arms. "You're right about a lot of things, Lucie Knox, but you're wrong about this." I kissed the top of her head. "Come on. I'll take you home, then I'll go to work. We can talk about it in the morning."

"No." She pulled out of my arms. "I already texted Carly. She's going to pick me up. I need space."

"Okay. We can talk after I get off work tonight."

She shook her head. "I need more space than that. I'll find you when I'm ready to talk."

"But when—"

She turned and walked away, and I knew better than to follow. I wasn't sure I could, anyway, with my heart shattered in pieces there on the path.

WE BAT-SIGNAL THE GODDESS GANG

I put dinner on the table so Marvin could do research that changed the world. I made sure our home was a haven where your mind could soar. When you were frustrated, which was a lot when you were young, I'd remind you to use your words. Now, you use your words to hold those in power accountable. His legacy and yours, the good work you do for others, is mine too.

Ellen Knox, homemaker

LUCIE

When I got into her car, Carly asked if I was okay, and I said I was. After that, my brain was too busy to speak. Why had Danny thought I'd accept a marriage proposal just because I was growing a child who shared my DNA and his? What indication had I given that I wanted that, especially in front of witnesses? And why the fuck did he think that at thirty he had any idea what he wanted?

Carly and Andrew's new place wasn't far from the park, but I counted seventeen worried glances during the drive. Finally, as she pulled into her driveway, she said, "I hope you don't mind, but after you called, I texted Tessa and Savannah. This seemed like an all-hands-on-deck situation."

There was a dull pang in my gut. I had hated having to call Carly, and I didn't want to be the one who bat-signaled the whole Goddess Gang. But I had to admit it, I needed my girls.

"Thank you."

An SUV whipped into the driveway as Carly pulled her sedan into the garage. Tessa. Her unmistakable mane of red hair glowed through the tinted windshield. When I hauled myself out of the car, Savannah was there to steady me.

"Where'd you come from?" I asked.

"I was with Tessa when we got Carly's text." Her face was pale, and her eyes were red, but she flashed me a grin. "I'm glad I was already in the city. I wouldn't miss this for the world."

"Miss what?" I asked. How much had Carly told them? I'd only told Carly I needed a ride and a place to stay for a few days.

"A Goddess Gang sleepover, obviously. Carly said we're helping you through a crisis, with manicures."

"I wouldn't call it a crisis," I grumbled.

Tessa slipped off her sunglasses to give me a piercing stare with those eerie green eyes of hers. "It's not a crisis when the unflappable Lucie Knox needs an extraction from one of the most romantic spots in the city?"

Busted. It sucked having a genius as a bestie.

"Come inside," Carly said. "We'll settle in, find out what's going on, and make a plan."

Carly loved plans. Her job as a stylist was to ensure that everything appeared perfect, which, as it turned out, required a ton of preparation and effort. Carly's notebook wasn't full of gifts from her muse. It was packed with to-do lists.

"I don't think this is something you can fix," I said as I

walked into her white kitchen. I didn't want her to treat my catastrophe like a job or as her problem to solve.

"Maybe not, but the right self-care might make it feel better. We'll get some snacks and mocktails and do some facial masks or mani-pedis." She opened the refrigerator and assessed its contents.

"Could one of you massage my lower back?" I asked. "I did a lot of walking today, and there's this massage Dan—" Nope, I wasn't ready to say his name yet. "A massage I read about in The Book that works really well on my sore back."

"I know the one," Savannah said. She dropped her big purse on the counter. "Fists on the sides of your spine, right?"

"Yes." I would *not* think about how the last time Danny had done it, he'd ended up entering me from behind while he fingered my clit and whispered dirty, dirty things in my ear.

"I'm on mocktails," Tessa announced. "Do you have fresh mint and seltzer? I can make my no-jitos."

"Plain seltzer is good for me." Mocktails would only make me miss Danny's superior bartending skills. I walked from the kitchen toward the living room and almost bumped into Andrew, who carried their dog in his arms. She looked up at him with the same besotted expression Carly often did. "Hey there, Loverboy."

"Hi, Lucie. Doing okay?"

"Not really." I wished I could get Danny out of my head, but it seemed everything made me think of him.

"Go sit on the couch, and I'll put Chanel in your lap. She makes everything better."

I stroked the silky white blaze on top of her head. "That sounds nice." I walked into their living room and sank onto the couch.

Andrew eyed the narrow space between my belly and my knees. "I'll just set her here."

He placed her next to me on the cushion. She looked up at me with her big brown eyes and rested her chin on my knee. I stroked her from the top of her head to her tail and sighed.

"Almost as good as therapy." He winked, then went to the kitchen where he wrapped his arms around Carly and murmured in her ear as she scanned the contents of her refrigerator. She turned in his arms and kissed him. I had to look away.

Savannah carried a kitchen chair into the living room and set it next to the couch. She leaned against it, her back to the kitchen. In a too-bright tone, she said, "Hungry? How about some raw veggies with ranch dip?"

"How about pizza? Or pasta?" Pasta made me think of Leo's homemade ravioli. Still, it sounded comforting and filling, which was what I needed. "And ice cream. Definitely chocolate. Though maybe something salty too? Like pretzels."

She frowned. "You should watch your salt intake. But if you promise to eat some veggies, you can have ice cream."

"What am I, six?" I asked. "I'll eat your damn veggies, but not because you're dangling a treat in front of me."

"Sorry. Old habits. I'm not sure they ever go away. You'll see."

Tessa walked in with a pad of paper. "Andrew's making a supply run. What do we need?"

"Pizza and a crudités platter." Savannah glanced at me. "Plus, ice cream. The kind that's chocolate with the salted caramel ribbon through it. And pretzels."

"Make it a pepperoni pizza," I said. "And baked ziti if they have it."

"Make it a veggie pizza," Savannah said. "Cured meats aren't great for the baby. And garlic knots."

My mouth watered. Garlic knots would almost make up for the lack of pepperoni. "Fine. Can Andrew pick up my laptop from my place? I need it, but I don't want to go back there right now."

"Sure. Keys?" Tessa asked.

"Carly has one," I said.

"Great." She turned and handed the list to Andrew. "Thanks for doing this."

He smiled. "It's my pleasure. I feel like Nick Fury taking care of the Avengers." Turning with a squeak of his sneaker, he planted another kiss on Carly's lips, then strode out the door.

"Here. Switch with me." Savannah held out a hand and pulled me up. She guided me to sit facing the back of the chair with my arms folded on top to cradle my head. She sat on the couch and started the massage with long, gentle strokes down my back. The tension drained out of me, and I understood why Chanel liked being petted so much.

Tessa's voice came from the other side of the coffee table. "Tell us what happened."

"We were taking a walk in the botanical garden, and when we sat down to rest, Danny proposed. He had a ring and everything."

Savannah's hands froze on my back, and she squealed. "Did he get down on one knee?"

I snorted. "Yeah. Why the hell would he think I wanted that?"

"You mean the knee or the proposal?" Tessa asked.

"Either. We've got a perfectly good thing going. There's no reason to change it. And no one wants a house in the suburbs. No offense," I added, looking back at Savannah.

"Suburban life isn't for everyone," she said.

"Wait, he wants you to move to the suburbs?" Tessa asked.

"He wants to use the money he was saving up to buy Barb's to buy a house for the baby. I don't want that. The baby doesn't want that. A few years from now, he'll wake up and discover he doesn't want it either. He'll regret giving up his dreams for it."

"Will he?" Carly spoke up for the first time. "He's in love with you."

"In love with me? What the fuck does he know at thirty? Of course he'll regret it. I've seen it firsthand. My mother gave up everything for my father—and me—and what does she have to show for it? Not even a fucking thank you when he wins yet another award."

"She has you to show for it." Savannah rubbed the spot where my shoulder met my neck. "She's so proud of you."

I sat up and shook off her hand. "But she could've had a career. She could've been winning awards. That's why I decided not to have a baby when I was twenty."

"And that was the right choice for you. But it might not have been the right choice for her. People are different. Is your mother more like you or like Danny?"

Danny had skipped college and given the money to his sister. He'd wanted to buy Barb's so he could employ Nico and any of his other family members who needed a job. And he'd offered to give up his dream so I could have a fucking home office to write in. He didn't want to live in the spotlight. Instead, he wanted to be the one who helped everyone else achieve what they wanted. "Damn it. He's exactly like my mom."

"You're writing about legacies," Tessa said. "You're your mom's legacy. And so is at least part of your dad's work."

"But she should want something with her name on it," I said. "And so should Danny."

"Should they?" Carly asked. "Just because you want that doesn't mean they do."

"But...but he's so young." I straightened and rolled my shoulders. "I don't want him to give up his future for me. He could meet someone else and have more kids. He comes from a big family. He probably wants that."

"Not necessarily," Carly said. "He might've had enough child-rearing already."

"Exactly!" I raised a finger. "He's only thirty. Why would he want to be saddled with an oops-wife-and-kid for the rest of his life?"

Savannah stroked my back. "Because he's a good guy. Because he loves you and that kid, regardless of whether or not he planned it."

"Well, I'm sorry," I said, "but I won't let him ruin his life like that. And I'm not moving to any fucking suburb."

"Fair," Tessa said. "What you want matters too. And if that's not Danny, that's okay."

"Exactly." I leaned into the chair and let Savannah do the thing with her fists on my lower back. I didn't want Danny. "All I want is someone who can share the parenting load so I can write my damn book."

Savannah stopped moving her hands. "And if that's all you want, then it's not fair to Danny to take him up on his offer."

I turned my head to look at her. "That's what I—oh, shit. Why are you crying?"

She waved a hand in front of her face. "Don't mind me."

"Savannah," Tessa said. "Tell them."

She rubbed a tear off her face with the back of her hand. "Tonight's about Lucie and her problems."

"I don't have a problem," I said. "I already did the right thing. What's going on with you?"

"I—" She sniffed, then her face crumpled. She hid it behind her hands.

"She asked for a divorce from her unappreciative, cheating husband," Tessa said.

"I thought you were going to couples therapy," I said.

Savannah wiped her eyes. "We did. And it made me realize we've been growing apart since the kids left the house. And before that. Our marriage had become kind of...two-dimensional. We did all the things we were supposed to, but there was nothing behind it. No passion. Maybe not even any love. It seemed like we were only sharing space. He'd go to work, and I'd deal with the house and the kids. We've been living separate lives, really. And I deserve more than that. I *want* more. And if he's not willing to...to..."

"Treat you like a goddess?" Carly prompted.

"To treat me like a valuable human being," Savannah said, "then I'd rather be alone."

"You won't be alone," Carly said. "You have us."

"And so do you, Lucie," Tessa said.

"Thank you," Savannah whispered.

"Goddamn fucking hormones." I scrubbed a tear off my cheek.

32

I'VE GOT IT IN THE BAG

Broken Heart
Combine 2 parts vodka, 1 part pomegranate juice, and 1/2 part Cointreau in a shaker with ice. Shake well. Strain into a chilled martini glass. Garnish with pomegranate seeds.

DANNY

A flash of dark hair made me look up from the beer I was pouring. Of course it wasn't her. She hadn't been to the bar in over two weeks, not since I'd offered her my heart at the botanical garden only for her to stomp all over it in her combat boots.

Something ice-cold flowed over my hand. "Damn it," I muttered, pushing back the handle to close the beer tap.

"You okay, Danny?" Barb asked. She'd wheeled herself to my side.

"Sorry, I'll clean this up." I set the beer in front of Frank and tugged the rag from my pocket.

"What's wrong?" she said.

I scrubbed at the spill. "Wrong? Nothing." Nothing I wanted to tell her about. Not until I'd talked it over with Leo.

"Something happen with Lucie?" she asked. "She hasn't been around in a while."

"Yeah, we…" I couldn't say we'd broken up since we'd never really been together. It had been nothing but a one-sided fantasy. "We aren't seeing much of each other these days. I think she's working on her book."

Andrew had come by the other night and picked up a bag from her place. And then the whole gang had brought her back a couple days later, walking as a phalanx with Lucie in the center. The message was clear: stay away, Danny. After that, I'd heard her door open and close a few times, mostly around meal-times. She was probably getting delivery. The sticky note I'd put on her door, *Let me know if you need anything,* had disappeared the following day. No response.

She didn't want anything. Not from me. And that hurt more than anything she'd said at the park.

"Why don't you take a break?" Barb said. "Leo looks like he wants to talk." She tipped her chin toward the corner booth, where Leo sat alone, nursing a beer.

I supposed we needed to talk. I'd given Leo the silent treatment for almost a month, since the day he'd shown me that crappy kitchen. "You sure?"

"Yeah. Nico and I can manage for a bit."

"Okay. Thanks." I missed my brother, and it was time to act like the grown-up I was.

I poured myself an ice water and took it to Leo's table. "Mind if I sit?"

He watched me warily. "Go ahead."

I slid into the booth. "Listen—"

At the same time, he said, "Look, Danny—"

We chuckled. "Go ahead," he said. "You first."

I sipped my water, then set it down. "I'm sorry I was a dick about that restaurant space. I was disappointed about my plans for the bar. But you're allowed to have different dreams and plans than mine. You should buy that space if it's still available."

His eyes lit with a hopeful expression, then he looked down at the table. "That's not fair to you. I said I'd buy the bar with you, and I'm a man of my word. I'll do it. And we'll be so successful that in a few years, I'll have enough money saved that I can buy an even better space and run the catering business as a side hustle."

I flashed him a wry smile. "While I appreciate your confidence, that might take a while. And by then, you might have other goals, like a family. I don't want you to miss out on this chance."

"But what about you?"

"I'll figure it out. I made appointments with a few banks on Monday. One of them will approve a loan for me to make up the difference, I'm sure." My words were confident, but my stomach twisted. Why would a bank lend money to me? I'd done the research and found that restaurants and bars had one of the highest failure rates of any type of small business. Any banker worth his shiny loafers would tell me margins were thinner than a slice of prosciutto. But why tell Leo that? We expressed our love through food and drink. Neither of us could imagine doing anything different.

"You think?" Leo's smile was tentative. "I bet Uncle Gio and Aunt Connie would write you letters of recommendation. The bank would be nuts not to lend you money to buy this bar."

"A loan?" Tad slithered up to our table. "You think a bank will lend *you* money?" He ticked off points on his fingers. "No college degree. No collateral. And your nobody aunt and uncle to vouch for you. Hmm, sounds like you've got it in the bag."

"Fuck off, Tad," Leo growled.

"Oh, I'm sorry," Tad said. "I meant *I've* got it in the bag. Barb's retiring at the end of November. If you don't have the cash, she'll have no choice but to sell to me. And by then, she'll be desperate enough to give me the family discount." He turned to assess the bar. "I think I'll bring a contractor by on Monday to take some measurements."

Leo's hand balled into a fist. I set my palm over it. Tad had said what I already knew. Best not to piss him off if he was going to be my boss in a few weeks.

Like he could read the thought on my face, Tad smirked and sauntered off toward the bar. I hoped the mint for his mojito had wilted.

"You can't let him have it," Leo muttered. "We can't let him ruin what Barb built. Where will Frank go? And Walter? What about Norm and Nico? Nico can't get another job with his rap sheet, and Norm flipped burgers for the dinosaurs. No one else is gonna hire him." He scrubbed the back of his neck. "I'll sell my food truck if I have to. Whatever it takes to keep Tad's manicured fingers out of this place. How much can you get for a kidney?"

"Keep your kidney. It won't come to that," I said with more confidence than I felt.

A toddler ran past our table, followed closely by his dad. He grabbed the kid under the armpits and swung him up in the air. The boy laughed and laughed. "Come on," the dad said, "let's eat some french fries to soak up that Shirley Temple." Clutching his kid, he walked back to the table where his partner sat, a loving grin on his face.

"Hey," Leo said softly. "You look like you dropped your ice cream cone. What's wrong?"

"Nothing's wrong." I took another sip of water.

He glanced at the family, now struggling to get the buzzing

child into the highchair. "Ma, uh, she told me about your proposal. Are you okay?"

My cheeks burned with shame. "I made a bad call. I thought Lucie and I wanted the same thing. But we don't. I wanted more. She wants things to stay the same."

He snorted. "Nothing's going to be the same once that baby comes. Remember when the twins were born? It took all four of us to manage them. Poor Giuliana ate cereal three meals a day for weeks. Lucie's gonna need you."

"I know she will. And I'll be there when she does. But I was kind of hoping to be more than a babysitter, you know?"

"Either way, you'll be more than that. You'll love that kid so hard. But just because things didn't work out with Lucie doesn't mean you can't find Ms. Right. Once your life settles down, I'll help you build a dating profile. We'll find you a woman to settle down with. A stepmom for the little bambina. You'll get the family you've always wanted."

"Look, I appreciate it, but I don't think I'll ever be ready to look for love on apps."

"Okay. We'll canvas every Catholic congregation in the city until we find you the nice woman you're looking for."

But it wasn't a nice woman I wanted. Lucie Knox was it for me.

Still, I smiled and nodded.

One of us should get what we wanted, though I knew it'd never be me.

33

T MINUS FIVE DAYS

I've listened to the pregnancy and delivery stories of people from all over the world. I've heard about their anxieties, their tragedies, their triumphs. Many have told me they felt empowered to enter this experience with the knowledge I helped provide. I'm happy to have been a small part of their journey to bring their own legacies into the world.
Dr. Dorothy Dunne, OB-GYN and bestselling author of Dr. Dunne's Guide to Pregnancy

LUCIE

I trudged up the steps to the fancy hotel where Dr. Dorothy Dunne was staying. Pregnancy books must bring in the dough. Though, I supposed, with over three million babies born in the US each year, her book had a solid market.

But I was concerned about my book. Specifically, that I'd been heads-down writing it for three weeks, ever since I'd returned from Carly's, and it still wasn't right. I took breaks only for meals and, y'know, my job—though I did that from home now, having finally given up on the pretense that I could walk a mile and a half to the office at almost nine months pregnant—but no amount of brute force could make it come together into a coherent message about women's legacies.

Every evening, I devoured The Book. Dr. Dunne reassured me that everything I was going through, from swollen ankles to Braxton Hicks contractions to the purplish stretch marks spidering across my belly, was perfectly normal. But there was another message in the book that fascinated me. It was that I was enough and that I could do this with or without a partner. And that even though millions of women around the world were pregnant and gave birth every day, I was doing something special and worthy.

How the hell did she do it?

Thanking the doorman, I passed into the lobby and headed for the elevator. Fortunately, Dorothy Dunne was doing a tour for the new edition of her book, and she had a stop in San Francisco. This close to my due date, no airline would allow me on a plane.

I stepped into the elevator and carefully wedged my expansive belly into the available space. By now, I was used to the skeptical looks and personal comments.

"You look about ready to pop," a woman said. "When's your due date?"

"In five days." I'd tried jokes and snarky comments but found it was better to give a straight answer to even the rudest, most personal questions.

"You're not going to have it in here, are you?" The man next to her gave a nervous chuckle.

I rolled my eyes. "Not planning on it, but I'll let you know."

And there it was. The judgy expression that said, *I feel sorry for your kid.*

Fuck him. I stared at the numbers illuminating on the panel.

Fortunately, the next stop was mine, and I lumbered out of the elevator.

"Good luck, honey," the woman said.

I trudged down the hall to Dorothy Dunne's suite and knocked on the door. When an assistant answered, I gave my name, and she ushered me in.

Dr. Dunne sat on a small sofa facing a view of the San Francisco skyline. She sipped coffee from a china cup with the hotel's logo on it. God, coffee smelled good. *Just another week,* I told myself. I'd drink gallons of it. My OB-GYN had said that coffee was okay while breastfeeding, and in chapter fifty-two, Dorothy Dunne agreed.

"Good morning, Dr. Dunne," I said, extending my hand. "I'm Lucie Knox. I reached out through your publicist. I'm writing a book about women's legacies, and I'm interested in yours."

She rose and shook my hand. "Call me Dottie." She gestured to the straight-backed chair next to her. "It might be easier to get in and out of that. But if you'd prefer to sit on the sofa, I'll call in my assistant, and we'll heave you out of it, I promise."

I let out a shocked bark of a laugh. "Thanks. The chair is good." I sank into it, wincing at the dull ache in my back that had started this morning. I propped my notebook on the arm and got out my phone. "Mind if I record our conversation?"

"Not at all." She settled back onto the sofa. Her mostly white hair had short natural curls. Her brown skin was lightly wrinkled around her eyes and neck, with a sprinkling of darker freckles across her cheeks. She wore a comfortable-looking purple caftan with white leggings underneath and a pair of red slides. I wished I could get away with wearing a caftan. That flowy garment would've solved at least eighty percent of my pregnancy wardrobe problems.

But I wasn't here to covet her outfit. I had an hour—make

that fifty-five minutes—to get Dr. Dunne's perspective on women's legacies.

"Dr. Dunne—"

"Dottie," she reminded me gently.

She'd forced a smile out of me. "Dottie. What's your legacy?"

"Am I limited to only one?" She chuckled.

"I suppose not. Though I've talked to a lot of women who've focused their efforts on one thing. Politics, business, family. Some of them have said they make more progress when they're working on a singular thing than if they try to advance multiple interests."

"Respectfully, I have to disagree with those women. I'm many things: a scholar, a teacher, an author, a mother, a grandmother, an auntie, a friend. I plan to leave behind many things. My scholarly research. My book." She waved at the copy poking out of my bag. "My children. And many memories, I hope."

"But your book," I argued. "Over forty million copies have been sold. That's a massive legacy."

"It's true," she said. "I hope my book has helped those mothers feel better about themselves. That they've gone on to be the best parents and grandparents they can be as well as the best workers and volunteers and professionals they can be. You see" —she leaned in closer—"women can be more than one thing. I know, I know..." She waved a hand. "Men like to be known for one thing: their careers. They think the rest of their lives are irrelevant."

That was what my dad thought. He focused all his energies on his research and publishing. He never talked publicly about being a husband or father. Though, I supposed, whether he talked about it or not, it was part of his identity. And whether or not he was proud of me, I was part of his legacy.

"But," she continued, "being a parent is anything but irrelevant. That's why, when a father takes paternity leave or shows up in his work clothes to his kid's soccer game or makes a video about doing his daughter's hair, he's a hero. Whereas a woman who does the same things is only doing what's expected of her."

I thought of all the times I'd taken my mother for granted. When she'd sat for an hour in the car line to pick me up from school. When she'd been the cookie mom for my Girl Scout troop. When she'd shown up not only to the big things like graduations and award ceremonies and band concerts but to the small things like elementary school pancake breakfasts, pediatrician visits, and days I was home with a cold or incapacitating menstrual cramps. It was what I'd thought she'd been forced to do.

Or was it? I'd always assumed she resented giving up her scholarly career because I would have. But I'd never asked how she felt about it. If she'd asked my father to give up anything. If she'd done exactly what she wanted in life...or not.

"Here's why I wrote my book." She paused until I looked up from my notebook. "I wanted to give women the confidence, and the permission—not that they need it, but in case they do—to be a mother. To set aside that time, whether it be a few minutes a day or years of their lives, to create that special legacy in their children. Do you have fond memories of your mother?"

"I...I do." The times she'd stroked my back and held my hair back when I'd had stomach flu. Her proud smile when I'd bounced up to her at my graduation, utterly failing at looking cocky and cool. The old-school scrapbook she'd made with yellowing newspaper clippings of my work. Although I'd acted like I didn't care, I did. She'd made me feel loved. Like I was enough. Like I was worth the sacrifice.

But was I? I would never be a mother like her. If I devoted one hundred percent of my life to this baby, to anyone, the spark that made me *me* would dim a little more each day until there was nothing left.

"What if..." I cleared my throat. "What if I'm the one who shows up mid-soccer game? What if I'm the kind of mother who doesn't know how to do her daughter's hair? What if I yell sometimes? And what if I toss out my kid's finger paintings? Will I be a terrible mother?"

"There are some people out there who aren't good parents. Who can never care for another person because they're too wrapped up in themselves. But you don't seem like that kind of person. You care about people. You're writing a book about other women's legacies. You're asking the right questions. I think you'll be an excellent mother."

I relaxed back into the chair, but my back twinged, so I sat up straighter. "Is that your legacy, a lifetime of helping people become better parents?"

"I suppose if I had to narrow it down to a single legacy, that's what it would be. To borrow from Mr. Whitman, people, including parents, contain multitudes. Parenting can be a thankless job. And whether or not a person is employed outside the home, mothering is also a full-time job. We should celebrate it however we can. If my book helps people realize how miraculous, how beautiful motherhood can be—no matter if a mother chooses to pursue other interests or not, whether they do it alone or with a partner or rely on friends, family, or staff—then I consider it a success.

"Now," she continued, "tell me about your book. How's it going?"

"Not great." My voice cracked. How could she lay truth on me like that and expect me to talk about my sorry excuse for a book, which would never touch as many people as hers?

"Give yourself some grace. You've got time." She sipped her coffee like she had all the time in the world.

The unfairness of it all walloped me like the winter wind. "Time? I don't have the luxury of time. I'm at T minus five days."

I pointed at my belly. "If I don't finish this book by then, I'll never finish it."

"Won't you?" Her gaze speared me. "You don't seem like a quitter. The baby will change your life, but it won't change who you are inside. You're dedicated to your work. You'll finish."

My eyes itched and burned, and when I rubbed them, my fingers came away wet. "Goddamn pregnancy hormones," I muttered.

"They help you get in touch with who you really are, Lucie. To care. And that's what mothering is about." She held out a tissue.

When I reached for it, my back twinged again. I rubbed it, then blotted my eyes.

"Is your back hurting?" Dr. Dunne asked.

"A little. Off and on."

"That's a sign of labor. Read Chapter—"

"Thirty-seven. I know. But I'm not due for another week. My back's sore from supporting this bowling ball." I patted my belly, and the baby kicked at my hand.

"A call to your doctor's office wouldn't be a bad idea," she said.

"Yeah, okay." But I knew I wouldn't bother. Just like I hadn't bothered to mention my backache at my appointment the day before yesterday. I had five more days to finish my manuscript.

Besides, there was someone else I needed to talk to.

34

DEATH AND LOVE

DANNY

The Lucie Poem
Add 1/2 ounce blue curaçao syrup to a hurricane glass filled with ice.
Fill halfway with lemonade, and top with club soda. Stir. Garnish
with a pick of fresh blueberries.

My heart was lodged somewhere in my stomach when I found Barb in the tiny office off the hallway to the restrooms. She sat in front of the ancient computer, a web page about the Taj Mahal pulled up. I hated to ruin her mood, but I couldn't put it off any longer. It was only a few weeks before she planned to leave on her world cruise. "Hey, Barb, can we talk?"

She turned her head to look at me. "Who died?"

I smoothed my tie. "Oh, um, nobody. I had some appointments at a few banks."

"Yeah? You finally buying that place in the suburbs?"

"No. Not exactly. Mind if I sit down?"

She tipped her chin at the rickety chair I used whenever I

worked on the books or ordered supplies. I sank into it and waited while she maneuvered her chair to face me.

"I can't think of a good way to tell you, so I'm just going to say it. I can't buy the bar."

Her eyes widened, but I rushed on. "Leo's dream kitchen came on the market, and I told him he should buy it. He's finally going to start that catering business he's always wanted."

"Good for him!" She beamed.

"But that means I don't have the cash to buy the bar. No one I know has that kind of money available, and every bank I talked to turned me down. It seems that a bartender who never went to college, who never took a business class, isn't a good risk."

Her smile dimmed. Then she nodded. "We'll figure it out. I can finance you. Pay me what you can now as a down payment, and we can work out a schedule for the rest."

The white dome on the screen was impossibly beautiful. And expensive looking. "World cruises don't come cheap. And neither do the renovations I want to make to the bar. Plus, I'll be supporting a kid soon. What would you do if I paid late or not at all one month? This is your retirement we're talking about. It wouldn't feel right if you took that risk. Besides, you have another buyer."

She sighed. "Tad wants to turn this place into a hipster hangout. Our regulars can't afford thirty-dollar martinis with caviar-stuffed olives. They want a beer and a burger in a place they can bring their kids."

"Maybe Tad's right. Maybe the smarter business decision is to fancy up the place. Find a new clientele." She tried to interrupt me, but I plowed on. "Regardless, you should let him buy it. Because I...I can't."

My throat clogged, and pressure built behind my eyelids. I was letting everyone down—Barb, Norm, Nico, and all our regulars. All the folks from the neighborhood who came here for a drink they could pronounce and food that was more filling than fancy. Lucie would hate having her nemesis own the bar she loved. Every time she came home, she'd have to look at Tad's smug face as she passed the door to a bar she used to love but now couldn't afford.

But most of all, I was letting down myself.

I loved working at Barb's, but there was no way I could work for Tad, even if he'd let someone like me in the door. And if I quit my job at the bar, I'd have to move out of my apartment. Taking care of our baby would be more complicated if I didn't live downstairs from her. But what else could I do? I couldn't force Leo to give up his dream for the sake of mine, and I couldn't ask Barb to give up her dream either.

She patted my hand. "It'll be okay. Let's give it a week. Maybe a solution will come to us by then."

That was Barb, always an optimist. But I didn't believe in manifesting or attracting positive energy. I'd gained what I had through hard work. Even that wouldn't save this situation.

I gave her a tight smile. "I'm going to put my jacket and tie in my locker, then start my shift."

"I believe in us, Danny. We'll get through this."

I wished I could believe it too.

~

I'd just flipped off the blender when a throat cleared behind me. "Excuse me."

I held up a finger. "One sec." I poured out the frozen margaritas for the Monday-night bunco club and garnished them with lime wheels.

Turning, I said, "I've got to drop off this tray, but I'll be right..."

My words died when I saw the last person I'd ever expected

to walk into this bar again—Lucie's mother. She wore a pink cardigan and matching blouse over a black skirt and heels. She looked like she'd gotten lost on her way to the theater district.

"Mrs. Knox. Hi." I bobbled the tray but kept most of the drinks in their glasses.

"Do you have a minute to talk? After you take care of that?" She nodded at my tray.

"Um, sure. Yeah." I carried the drinks out to the ladies' table while my mind spun. What was Lucie's mother doing here? Was Lucie all right? I hadn't seen her in a couple of days, though I'd heard the occasional scrape of her office chair against my ceiling.

When I returned to my post behind the bar, Mrs. Knox sat on a barstool, carefully not touching the bar top. I passed a damp rag over it and washed my hands. "What can I get you?"

"Do you have wine?"

I lifted a bottle. "This is what Lucie drinks. Or what she used to drink. It's not terrible. Want to try it?"

"Thank you."

I checked that the glass was clean, then poured the wine and set it in front of her. "Is Lucie okay?"

"I think so. She called me, and I'm on my way to see her. But first I wanted to talk to you." She sipped the wine. "Lucie drinks this?"

"Yeah, when she's not choking back scotch. But I started a mock-tail menu, and she likes those now. Well, she did." I'd picked up one of the laminated menus as if to hand it to her, but I set it back down. Lucie didn't come here anymore. Because I'd fucked everything up.

Placing two fingers on the menu, Mrs. Knox slid it toward herself and scanned it. "The Lucie Poem? Is that a reference to Wordsworth's Lucy poems?" She raised her eyebrows in a way that reminded me of Lucie.

"Yeah." I scrubbed at a sticky spot on the bar.

"You know those poems are all about death, right?"

"And love," I insisted. "Anyway, Lucie's popular around here. And the mocktails...I made them for her."

She cleared her throat and pushed away the glass of wine. "I came here to apologize for my behavior—mine and my husband's—at Lucie's birthday party. Lucie had led us to believe...or we wanted to believe... We didn't think you two were serious about a relationship. Clearly, we were wrong."

"Oh." My face went hot. "We're not anymore. Except as, you know, co-parents. She doesn't want more."

"Doesn't she?" She tipped her head exactly the way Lucie did when she asked a hard question. "Let me tell you something about my daughter. Her father is a very driven man. Driven not only to succeed but also to do what is right. Lucie picked that up at an early age. She's always had a clear view of right and wrong and strives to stay on the side of right."

"Sure." I set down the rag. "That's why she's a journalist. So she can explore issues, figure out her view of events, and tell the story. Writing about that gun rights rally with a neutral viewpoint really pissed her off."

"Exactly. It irks her father too. He thought she should have gone into academia. But that wasn't what she wanted. She had opinions about what academia had done to me."

"Oh, right. They kicked you out because you, um, you got pregnant."

"What Lucie didn't understand was that, although that university closed the door on me, it wasn't my only option. I decided to leave my academic career to raise her and support Marvin's career."

"And what a career it's been," I said. "I bet he couldn't have done it without you."

She chuckled. "He can't find matching socks without me, much less win a Pulitzer."

Damn, I liked her. I'd been so nervous meeting Lucie's parents at the party that I hadn't been able to see how alike they were. I'd been too focused on my hurt feelings. But now I realized that some of what I loved about Lucie—her humor, her intelligence, her idealism—came from her parents.

"Lucie's like her father," Mrs. Knox said. "She needs someone to support her so she can be her best self."

The warm feeling evaporated. "She's done pretty damn well on her own for the past twenty or so years. She supports herself just fine."

"No, no." She reached across the bar to put a hand over mine. "That's not what I mean. Of course our Lucie is independent. Stubborn. Driven to champion her causes. But she's also afraid of doing the wrong thing. Of being wrong. Of messing up."

"She won't," I insisted. "She'll do motherhood the same way she does everything else, by throwing her whole self into it and trying her best."

"You know she'll be a wonderful mother. So do I. But sometimes Lucie can't see past her fear. Fear that she won't be enough. Fear that she'll fail."

I slipped my hand out from under hers. "What can I do? She didn't want me."

"Is that what she said?"

"I proposed. She turned me down." I reached down to the speed rail and turned each bottle so the labels faced me.

"For Lucie, marriage and a baby mean losing part of oneself. Giving up one's dreams. That's not how I saw my experience, but it's the story she created."

I froze with my hand on the bottle of Jack Daniels. I'd come in hot with the ring, the engagement photos, the house in the suburbs. It was what I wanted, not what she wanted. She'd have had to file off a huge chunk of herself to fit into the space I offered. How could I have asked her to do that when I loved every part of her just the way she was?

"Have you told her this?" I asked.

She traced the rim of her wineglass. "We don't talk as much as I'd like."

I stood up straight. "So what do I do to support her in the way she needs?"

She smiled. "I think you already know. Tell her how extraordinary, how talented and capable she is. Show her she's worthy by meeting her where she is."

I scratched my neck. "But...but I'm just a bartender. My plans to buy the bar fell through. Am I what she needs? Maybe I should stay out of her way."

"Did Lucie say she only liked you because you were buying the bar?"

"No, but...but she deserves so much more."

"Don't you think it's up to her to decide what she deserves? What she wants?"

"She already decided." I stared down at my sneakers. "It wasn't me."

"I wouldn't be so sure. I think her decision was more about herself than about you. Be there for her, okay? Even if she says she doesn't need anything. Knowing you're there will be a comfort to her."

Would it? Hanging around waiting for the woman I loved to need me wasn't what I'd imagined when I'd thought about fatherhood and my future. But when the woman I loved was Lucie Knox, I couldn't imagine living my life in any other way.

35

MY BINGO CARD IS FULL

What I've learned from writing and revising a book about pregnancy is that there's no "typical" pregnancy and no "typical" delivery. Pregnancy and childbirth aren't only a physical process. They're emotional and intellectual too, and that makes them unique. Every mother's relationship with their child is different. And as long as that relationship benefits them both, when it's respectful and safe, we should celebrate it.
Dr. Dorothy Dunne, OB-GYN and bestselling author of Dr. Dunne's Guide to Pregnancy

LUCIE

Something inside me lightened when I heard the knock at my door. *Mom's here.* It was like the time I was eight years old, sitting on the curb, my bike crumpled beside me and my knee sliced open. She showed up with a wet wipe and a Mulan bandage and made everything better.

But this time the stakes were a lot higher. I had days before a whole-ass human was about to become my responsibility. A responsibility I wasn't prepared for. Maybe not even suited for. Not like she was.

When I heaved myself out of my office chair, pain shot across my abdomen, all the way around to my back. The Braxton Hicks contractions were cute three months ago, but now they were obnoxious. I rubbed my belly with one hand and kneaded my back with the other as I hobbled to the door.

I opened it to find my mom beaming at me. I threw myself at her and hugged her as hard as I could.

She stroked my hair. "It's good to see you. Thanks for inviting me over."

After one last squeeze, I released her. "Thanks for coming." I led her into my apartment. "Can I get you a drink? Water? Seltzer? I don't have much else."

"I'm here to take care of you," she said. "Why don't you sit down?"

My euphoria fizzled out. "I didn't ask you here to take care of me," I grumbled. "I can take care of myself."

"Okay," she said carefully. "Still, you should sit. One thing I learned as a mother is to follow Winston Churchill's advice: you should never stand when you can sit, and never sit when you can lie down."

"I can't believe you're citing Winston Churchill," I huffed. "Though lying down sounds amazing." I lowered myself to the sofa. "I've still got to finish reading through my draft later tonight." I pointed at the laptop where I'd left it on the coffee table.

"Your book?" She joined me on the sofa. "You have a draft?"

I nodded.

"That's fantastic, honey."

"Yeah, I think if I work on it for another couple days, it'll be good enough to send to my editor." Good enough wasn't what I wanted. I wanted it to be perfect, but I was out of time. I'd make it perfect in revisions.

Mom hummed her approval, then glanced at the corner of the living room I used as an office. "Is that where the baby's going to sleep?"

"I...I guess?" After that one brief flurry of putting the baby things away, right before Danny had fixed the crib, I'd forced myself to focus on my book. The mattress was still propped on its side, and the sheet was draped over the top of it. "I was hoping to get everything set up after I send my draft to my editor."

"I can do that while we chat. Wouldn't you rather have the crib in your bedroom so you don't have to come all the way out here to feed her in the middle of the night? You can work out here while she sleeps during the day. Of course, you should sleep while she sleeps, if you can. You're going to be tired as your body heals."

Anger flared hot inside me. I hated being wrong about *anything,* including where to put the damned crib. But Dr. Dunne said the same thing about resting in The Book. How did my mom naturally know these things? Dr. Dunne might know a lot about pregnancy, but she was wrong about me. I was going to be a crap mother.

As much as I hated it, I could admit when I'd been wrong. "That sounds like a good idea. Why don't we move it to the bedroom?" I reached for one end, but a twinge seized me, and I hissed, holding my back where the worst of it hit.

"Are you all right?" My mother steadied me under my elbow.

"Yeah, yeah. My back has been hurting for a few days. You think it might be sciatica? I read about that in The Book." I pointed to the worn tome on my desk.

"Is it in your back and legs, or does it go all the way around to your stomach?" she asked.

I chuckled, stroking my belly. "The Braxton Hicks contractions want to get in on it too. They join the party when they can."

Her smile disappeared. "Are you saying you're having contractions with back pain?"

"It's another fun symptom of pregnancy. I've almost blacked out my bingo card: swollen feet, stretch marks, forgetfulness, giant boobs—"

"Lucie. That isn't a pregnancy symptom. It's a labor symptom. How far apart are the contractions?" She pulled her phone from her skirt pocket.

My heart pounded in my ears. "This isn't labor. I'm not due for three more days. I have *three more days* to turn in my book!" My voice had gone shrill, but maybe it was time to be shrill. I stared at the bare crib mattress. I needed more time.

Shaking her head, my mother gripped my elbow and led me to the couch. "That's not how babies work. They come when they're ready, whether you are or not."

I sank onto the couch. "That hardly seems fair. It's my body. I should have some say in it."

"You'll get to make a lot of decisions on your child's behalf before she's eighteen. But this isn't one of them. Drink some water."

I reached for my bottle of water. So far, so good. At my visit last week, Dr. Cheema had told me not to come to the hospital until the contractions were a minute long, five minutes apart, for an hour. She'd also told me a lot of things about making a plan to get to the hospital, packing a bag, and turning in that birth plan I'd been meaning to work on for months. "Can you hand me my notebook, please?" I pointed at my desk.

My mother went to the desk and returned with my notebook and a pen. "For recording the contraction times?"

"First I need to finish my birth plan." I flipped through it to find where I'd started it. At least, I'd hoped I'd started it. "Goddammit!" The pain seized me without warning, radiating from my back to my front.

My mother gripped my hand and gave me her most encouraging smile, the same one she'd flashed me when she'd dropped me off for my first day of middle school. When it was over, she tapped her phone and said, "By my best guess, that's about four minutes from the last one. Where's your go bag?"

"I—" Shit. Was this really happening?

"It's okay. I'll pack some things for you. Where do you keep your luggage?"

"Under the bed." When she got up, I pointed to my desk. "Could you hand me that book?"

She walked back to the desk and picked up The Book. "This one?"

"Yes, it's got a packing list."

She handed it to me. "I'll put in some toiletries and a change of clothes for you and the baby."

"Clothes...for the baby?" Shit, I hadn't thought ahead to walking out of the hospital with a baby. Who needed clothes.

"Are you keeping her things in here?" She walked to the dresser, and without waiting for my answer, pulled open the top drawer. She pulled out a pink onesie. "See? It's going to be okay. I'll just pack some things for you." She strode into my bedroom.

"Will it be okay?" I stroked my belly and murmured, "You sure you can't wait three more days? Five would be better."

From my closet, Mom called, "What about a car seat?"

I snorted. "Mom. I don't own a car."

She appeared in the doorway with my small suitcase. "Do you plan to walk back from the hospital holding the baby?"

"Fuck!"

"It's fine," she said. "I'll ask Danny to run out for one."

"Danny?" I blinked. "But you hate him."

"I don't hate him. I just didn't know how much you two cared about each other. He'll forgive your father and me for how we acted. We had a chat before I came up here. Why don't you text him and tell him we're heading to the hospital in a few minutes?"

My body went numb. I'd hidden from him since that terrible day at the botanical garden. But I'd committed to allowing him to witness the birth of his daughter. I supposed it was time to come out of hiding.

I wished I hadn't fucked everything up so badly. I'd fully intended to have everything set up for her, to have a safe and welcoming space for the baby. To have turned in my book so I could focus on mothering. To have my shit together.

I'd utterly failed. My mother had seen it, and Danny was going to judge me.

"I'm already the worst mother ever," I groaned.

"No, you're not. Why would you say that?"

"Because I don't know what I'm doing. I'm already fucking everything up." I sniffled.

"Honey." She peered into my eyes. "Everyone makes mistakes. That doesn't make them poor parents. It means they're learning."

When the contraction eased, I said, "You don't make mistakes."

She snorted. "Of course I do. In your closet, I saw the rack full of dresses I've given you with the tags still on. It wasn't until I saw all those pastels next to all the black that I realized I was asking you to wear something you hate. I thought I was doing something nice for you, but all I was doing was trying to make you seem happy. I should know you're happiest in monochrome. Like Wednesday Addams."

"I'm no—" Lightning seared across my belly, so acute that it stole my breath.

"Another contraction?" Mom asked.

"Yeah," I gritted out, my molars clenched.

She picked up my hand, and I squeezed back, closing my eyes. When I thought the pain would go on forever, it eased.

"Still four minutes," she said. "We should go soon. But I want to tell you something first."

"The secret to motherhood?" My fingers itched for my notebook.

"I wish I knew it. Maybe then, I wouldn't have been too scared to continue my career and be a wife and mother at the same time. I admire you so much." Her voice cracked, but she cleared it. "You're so strong, and you're going to be a fantastic mother."

My heart gave a hopeful skip. "You think so?"

"I know so. You're confident, fearless, smart. You know what you want."

But did I? I wanted to do what was right for the baby, myself, and Danny. And that was to handle all this motherhood stuff and let Danny live his life. But every time I thought about him, my heart ached. I missed him. But missing him had no place in my plan to do right by him.

"Maybe," I said.

"Definitely." She nodded. "I'm going to grab your toiletries from the bathroom. Call Danny. Remember, he's part of this too. You can rely on him and share the burden."

I snorted. "Like you did with Dad?"

"No," she said. "That was another of my failings. After I gave up on my career, I poured one hundred percent of myself into being the best wife and mother I could be. If I'd let your father share some of the work, maybe you'd have a better relationship with him. And with me."

"I'm sorry." Why was this the first time we'd talked about

this? I'd been so focused on judging her, never asking her how she really felt.

"We'll work on it. We've got time." She stood. "Now, call Danny."

But I wasn't ready for him to hear my panicked voice. Instead, I texted him, *In labor. Heading to the hospital. Want to come with?*

I stared at my phone for a minute, but there was no response. It was Monday night, so he was working. He might not have even felt the buzz in his pocket. Or he had, and he was so angry with me that he didn't want to come to the hospital anymore.

Fair.

The next contraction was miserable enough to make me groan. But when it ended, my mother stood in front of me with my suitcase. "If there's anything I've forgotten, I'll come back for it. You've got your phone? I'll grab your keys. Let's go." She held out her hand.

"I'll need this." I handed her my laptop. "And this." I handed her The Book.

"Book, yes," she said. "Laptop, no. You won't have the energy to write. And what if something happens to it? You could lose your work."

"Goddammit, you're right again." My eyes prickled as she set the laptop on the coffee table.

"How about we take your notebook? If you're inspired, you can write in that," she said.

I handed it to her, then took her hand to heave myself from the couch.

We made it to the top of the stairs before another contraction gripped me. I leaned against the wall and squeezed my mother's hand so tightly I heard her knuckles crack. "Sorry," I muttered.

"It's fine," she said. "Ready?"

"Yeah."

The next contraction hit almost at the bottom of the stairwell. "This sucks," I grunted.

"They can give you something to ease the pain at the hospital," she said.

"Thank god."

I started toward the exit door, but Mom held me back. "Don't forget Danny."

"He...fine." He might not have seen the text. And even if he had and had chosen to ignore it, I deserved whatever humiliation I was in for. It might not even be the worst embarrassment I'd experience through this childbirth.

I let her tug me through the door into the bar. "Danny!" She waved the arm that wasn't clutching me. "It's time."

My gaze went straight to where he stood behind the bar. He had on a black T-shirt that revealed his muscular arms as he poured a beer. His loose hair flopped over his face, but when he lifted his head, our eyes met. His widened. "Time?"

"If...if you want to go with me. With us," I said.

There was a crash and a splatter. "Shit!" He looked down.

"I've got it." Leo bounded up to him. "Go."

Danny looked up again, his face pale. Was that terror? Irritation? Shock?

Another contraction hit, and this time, I felt a gush of wetness down my leg. "What the fuck?" I mumbled. When I lifted my boot, the shaft was wet.

"Looks like your water broke," my mother said. "Good thing I thought to pack a towel."

"I've got that, too, Luce!" Leo said, louder than he needed to. "Better head out."

Great. I'd lost my fucking amniotic fluid in my favorite bar.

I was never coming back here.

36

THE BRAVEST THING

Emergency Cocktail
Go to the hospital vending machine. Pay $8 for two Cokes. Each take a chug off the top, then pour in Jack Daniels from Marvin's flask. Good luck getting your hands to stop shaking.

DANNY

I remembered three things from that night:

Terror that made my heart beat so fast spots flashed across my vision.

Lucie's glowing face as she did the bravest thing I'd ever seen anyone do.

Our tiny daughter's fierce squall when the nurse set her on Lucie's chest.

Everything else was a blur of people in scrubs, machines beeping, and antiseptic smells. I ignored my buzzing phone and focused on Lucie, holding her hand, praising her, and encouraging her—not that she needed it. I'd never remember what I said, but some of it made her snarl at me, and some of it made her smile between contractions. But mostly, she focused on what she was doing like the star she was, and at 4:18 a.m., she gave birth to our healthy baby girl.

After they fixed her up and made her comfortable, after Lucie cuddled our daughter for an hour or so, gazing at her with wonder, I got to hold her at last.

She was the most beautiful human I'd ever seen, even with her red skin and her dark hair sticking up from her scalp.

I handed her off to Marvin and Ellen for a while. After the nurse came to check on Lucie, both Lucie and the baby passed out. Lucie's parents tiptoed out, promising to come back after a few hours of sleep.

But I was too wired to sleep.

I wheeled the sleeping baby to the nursery in her bassinet to let Lucie rest, knowing it might be her last chance for a while. I walked the hall, then I stared through the glass at the handful of newborns in their plastic bassinets. They were all so little, so helpless. But with love and care, they'd grow up. They'd ride bikes and take spelling tests and make fools of themselves on social media. They'd get minimum-wage jobs and go to prom and fall in love. They might go to college. They'd start careers and bring home paychecks. And someday, one of them might stand at a window like this, looking at their own infant.

I hoped for all of these things for them, especially the one in the pink cap with *Baby Girl Knox* scrawled on the label at the foot of her bassinet. Lucie had promised I'd be a part of our daughter's life. But that wasn't everything I wanted. I wanted to be beside Lucie for all of it, just like I had been tonight. I wanted to be part of her life, not only our daughter's.

I'd been overjoyed—and shocked—when she and her mom had grabbed me on the way to the hospital. I'd been afraid that her weeks of silence meant she'd take back her offer of letting me participate in the birth. But she hadn't taken it back. Instead, she'd used my hand as a stress ball and let me ramble at her.

Her body had been pumped full of hormones and painkillers. I shouldn't read anything into it.

I eyed the hard vinyl couch in the waiting room. I could stretch out for a few hours. But then I wouldn't be there if Lucie needed something. So, quietly, I let myself back into her room.

Her hair was pulled up into a loose bun on the top of her head, wispy curls popping out around her face. She wore the hospital's gown, white with a print of ugly flowers on it. She'd wanted to change into her oversized, faded black T-shirt and loose pajama pants, but the nurses had made her try to feed the baby, and it was easier to do it with the hospital gown that tied at the front.

The breastfeeding had sounded frustrating, with lots of discussion about latching on and letting down and a fuck-ton of terms I didn't understand. Standing outside her room in the hall and listening to her voice getting wearier and more irritated, I'd felt useless. And I hated it.

Now, even as she slept, Lucie's forehead was furrowed. I wished I could do something to take away her pain.

I also wished I could give her the space she wanted and not watch her sleep like a creeper—she'd really hate it if she knew—but I couldn't stand the idea of leaving her and our baby here alone.

So I eased myself into the chair by the side of her bed and gazed at her, my gorgeous, exhausted goddess. I wondered if she regretted any of it now: our hookup or deciding to keep the baby. Or when we'd briefly felt like we could be a family.

Probably.

I didn't regret a thing. Except the part where I'd tried to force her into my vision of what an ideal family looked like. I should've known, having grown up in an odd-shaped family myself, that it didn't matter if the parents lived together or even if there were two parents. As long as there was love, everything would be okay.

And with that hopeful thought, I drifted off to sleep.

37

___

GOOD MOTHERS DON'T
SHOW THEIR ASSES

Author's note: When I decided to write this book, I thought it would be my legacy. But what I've discovered after talking with all these inspiring women is that we don't have a singular legacy. The best of us leave behind a hole that can't be filled, or even many small holes that someday, someone encounters and thinks, Oh, that's what she did.

I hope when you read this book, you recognize someone's lasting impact on you. I know I did.
- Lucie Knox

LUCIE

When I woke up, everything hurt. The bruise on my back where they'd given me the epidural. The searing sting on my vagina where they'd stitched me up. A dull ache in my abdomen. Even my teeth hurt from when I'd clenched during each contraction.

But it was over.

When I glanced to the side of the bed, panic flashed through me. The baby was gone. Her bassinet was missing too. They must have taken her to the nursery. She couldn't go far since her little bracelet had a sensor that would set off an alarm if she left the maternity floor.

A sigh from the other side of the bed made me turn my head. Danny was draped across the vinyl armchair in a position that made my neck hurt in sympathy.

He'd stayed beside me all night.

My memories were muddled because of the pain my brain was already trying to forget, but I knew it hadn't been pretty. Not only had I shoved a baby through a too-small channel and produced fluids and odors that I'd rather not remember, but I'd said things. Snapped. Shouted. About pain and exhaustion and the goddamn patriarchy even though the birth of a child was one thing the patriarchy, no matter how much it tried, couldn't ruin.

I was sure good mothers didn't show their asses—in the metaphorical sense—during childbirth. They took it in stride and appreciated the miracle of birth and the support of their partner, which was *not* what I'd done.

Yet Danny was still here.

He'd done his duty. He'd watched our child being born. He could be sleeping in that fabulous, cozy bed of his. Instead, he was here, waiting for me to wake up.

I shifted to face him and curled my legs up to minimize the pressure on my bladder. That first trip to the bathroom was going to suck.

Why had he stayed?

I couldn't delude myself any longer. I knew why he'd stayed. Why he'd come in the first place even though I'd pushed him away and ignored him for weeks.

He loved me. For all that I was, the good and the bad. He saw it all, and he loved me anyway. I couldn't repress the smile that curled my lips. I loved him too.

He was hardworking and principled and caring. He cared so much about everyone. Not in the way that I did, standing up for what was right in an abstract sense. No, Danny cared about individual people. Once he let you into his circle of people, he'd go to the ends of the earth for you. That was why he cared so much about the bar, and Barb, and his family.

And me.

I didn't even have to prove myself worthy because he already thought I was.

But I wanted to prove it anyway.

I reached for the controls on the bed and raised the head so I could sit up, then I scooted to the edge and dropped my feet over the side. A pungent odor hit my nostrils.

Thanks, pregnancy hormones.

"Why the *fuck* does it smell like a bar in here?"

38

EASIEST THING I'VE EVER DONE

<u>*Truth Serum*</u>
Pour a shot of vodka, a shot of triple sec, a shot of Midori, a shot of blue curaçao into a highball glass with ice. Add a dash of absinthe. Top up the glass with lemonade and stir.

DANNY

"**W**hy the *fuck* does it smell like a bar in here?"

I cracked open a bleary eye. Lucie was sitting up on the bed, her bare legs dangling over the side. It had to be early morning because although it was still dark outside the window, I could hear a jay calling from the tree on the other side of the glass. When she set her toes on the floor, I jumped to my feet.

"What are you doing?" I asked, putting out a hand to steady her but stopping short of touching her. "The nurse said to call before you get up."

"I can make it to the bathroom by myself. And it's you who smells like beer." She wrinkled her nose.

I supported her as she shuffled toward the tiny bathroom. "I dropped one on myself, remember?"

"You haven't been home?" she glanced up at me.

"I didn't want to leave you here alone."

She continued her slow steps. "I feel like I got hit by a car."

"You pushed a seven-pound, five-ounce human out of your body. That's a pretty traumatic experience."

She paused at the doorway. "You were traumatized?"

"No, no. Of course not. I meant, it had to be hard on your body. I was glad to be here. Thank you for including me."

She stared down at the linoleum. "Ugh!" She wiped under her eyes. "These hormones are killing me." She closed the door.

I waited outside while she used the bathroom, listening for any sounds of distress. She groaned and cursed but didn't call for help. After a while, she emerged, smelling like toothpaste. I offered her my arm, and she took it as she scuffed back to the bed.

"Good morning." A new nurse wheeled in the bassinet with our baby in it. The tiny thing squeezed her eyes shut, making a breathless, huffing cry. "Someone's hungry. Want to try feeding her?"

"Okay," Lucie said warily, easing herself back into the bed. The top of it was already raised, and she leaned back and untied the top of the gown.

"Want me to wait outside?" I asked.

"You don't have to. It's nothing you haven't seen before."

She was wrong. I remembered my mother breastfeeding the twins, and Giuliana before that, but watching Lucie feed our child was like nothing I'd ever seen. She approached it with the same intensity I'd seen her use when working on her book. Lucie strived to be the best at everything, including breastfeeding. After some work with the nurse positioning the baby and after a few frustrated curses, Lucie stilled.

"You've got it." The nurse made some notes on a tablet. "I'll wait until you're done to check your vitals."

"That's...weird," Lucie said, looking down at our daughter, who'd finally quieted.

"Are you okay?" I asked.

"Yeah. It's a strange feeling."

"It's been a few months of strange feelings, I bet."

She chuckled. "A hundred percent."

"Are you hungry?" I asked. "You should eat too."

"Food service will come by soon," the nurse said. "Be sure to ask for a tray for Dad too."

Dad. The name sent a happy shiver through me. I reached out to touch our daughter's foot through the blanket that covered her.

After the nurse walked out, Lucie said, "You can go home, you know, and get some rest. We'll be fine here. There's plenty of people to look after me."

A chill replaced the warmth from a moment earlier. "You don't want me here?"

"I don't want you to feel like you have to stay. I've been an ass to you. I don't want you to stay out of a sense of obligation."

"It's not obligation. There's no place I'd rather be right now." The baby kicked my hand. I held on to her toes.

"I don't think I'll be doing this again." She tipped her chin at the baby. "I'm one and done."

"Okay."

"And I'm going to keep working. I...I finished my book. I'll send it to my editor when I get home. And when my maternity leave is up, I'm going back to work at the paper."

"That's excellent news about your book." Pride swelled inside me, but I wouldn't dream of telling her I was proud of her. I didn't want her to think I was diminishing her achievement by taking any credit for it. Not like her dad did. "And you shouldn't give up your work. It's too important."

"I like living where we live. I love Barb's. I hate the suburbs."

"Understood." Where was she going with this? I opened my mouth to ask, but there was a commotion in the hallway. Leo walked in with a sack from Dolci Momenti. The buttery, sweet aroma of pastry instantly covered the stale beer, sweat, and anti-septic smells in the room.

He took one look at Lucie and clapped his hand over his eyes. "Sorry!"

My mother bumped into his back, then shoved him aside. "Don't be childish. Everyone in a five-mile radius is going to see Lucie's boobs. Baby's got to eat. How are you, Lucie?"

"I'm okay." She tried to arrange her gown to hide her breast and failed. "Even more in awe of you now. You pushed out *five* of these?"

"Not all at once." Mom winked. "The secret is pregnancy amnesia. You'll forget how terrible it is by this time next year."

Lucie shuddered. "I don't think I will."

Giuliana came around to the side of the bed where I was standing and peered at the baby. "Who does she look like?"

I exchanged a mystified look with Lucie. "I don't know," I said. "She looks like herself."

Tony hip-checked me to the side. "I hope she looks like Lucie. Everyone knows I'm the good-looking one in this family." He leaned over the bed to stare too.

"What's going on in here?" The nurse stood in the doorway, hands on her hips. "Only three visitors are allowed at a time."

"We're family!" my mother said.

"It's true," Lucie said, shocking the hell out of me. "I don't mind."

"It's hospital policy," the nurse insisted.

Tony shot her his dazzling smile. "We'll work out shifts. Just give us a minute, okay?"

She blinked. "I'll be back in five to check."

"Looking forward to it." He winked.

Knowing none of my family would leave the room voluntarily, I pulled him and Giuliana away from the bed. "Give Lucie some space. You can ogle the baby later."

"She's asleep," Lucie said. "Mrs. Carbone, would you like to hold her?"

Faster than I'd have thought possible, the baby was in my mother's arms. She gazed down at her. "She has Lucie's nose and mouth. We'll have to wait for her to wake up to see her eyes."

"They both have magnificent hair," Elena said. She peeled back the baby's pink cap. "And so does she. What's her name?"

Cold prickles erupted in my belly. "I...I don't know. We haven't talked about it. Lucie, do you know what you want to call her?"

Her eyebrows scrunched together. "No. But we'll figure it out."

My lips curled up in a tentative smile. I liked that *we*.

"Can you come here?" Lucie asked.

I shuffled past Giuliana and Tony to get to her side. She held out her hand, and I stared at it, shocked, for a moment. Then I took it.

"Danny, I've made a lot of mistakes over the past nine months."

My chest felt tight. We were here because of one of those mistakes. Was she regretting it all? "I'm sor—"

"Let me finish. Please. What I'm trying to say is that I'm going to keep making mistakes. And goddammit, I'm going to hate it every time I do. However. I'm learning to accept that I'm never going to be the world's best mother. I can only try to be the best mother I can be. The best *person* I can be."

"You're already a great person," I said.

She snorted. "Even at forty years old, I'm a work in progress. But I...I love that you're so confident in me. That you accept me for who I am. That you're fucking *here* for me. I—"

"Oh, wow, I didn't expect a party." Lucie's friend Savannah squeezed in with a gigantic bouquet of sunflowers. Carly and Tessa followed. They beelined to Lucie and hugged her. When they jostled me out of the way, I lost contact with Lucie's hand.

It was okay. She'd want her friends. I took the vase of flowers from Savannah and set them on the windowsill. I wished I'd thought to get her flowers. I could slip out and run downstairs to the hospital gift shop. No one would even notice I was gone in all the noise. I edged behind Savannah and Giuliana, but the nurse barred my way.

"More people?" she thundered. "Here. At least wear these." She held out a fistful of surgical masks.

I took them from her. "Sorry, we've got a lot of family. I'll step out for a minute."

"No. Stop." Lucie's voice rang out clear over the others. "Danny, come here. I'm not done. Tessa, scoot over and let him through."

Not done? Shit, what was she going to say? My feet didn't want to move, but my siblings' hands pushed me to her bedside. Someone snatched the masks from me. Smirking, Tessa grabbed my shoulders and shoved me to sit on the bed beside Lucie.

"Sorry, I—" I tried to stand, but Lucie grabbed my hand and pinned me in place. This close, I could see the shadows under her eyes. She needed rest, not a million people squeezed into her tiny hospital room. When she kicked me out, I'd take my family with me and make them wait until the baby was home from the hospital to visit.

Her hand was cold and a little dry, so I rubbed warmth into it.

"Danny." She squeezed my hand. "What I'm trying to say is—"

"Lucie," a voice boomed. "Who are all these people?"

Rolling her eyes, she muttered, "Fucking wonderful." Then louder, "Hi, Dad. Hi, Mom. These are my friends. And family."

Despite the Jack and Coke we'd shared last night, Marvin's—Dr. Knox's—presence prickled at my back. I could feel his judgment and indignation that Lucie had claimed my undereducated, lower-class family for her child.

But she carried on. "Carrie's got the baby. You can hold her in a minute. Put on a mask first. I have something I need to say to Danny."

Her brown eyes blazed. "Danny, what I've been trying to say is that I appreciate you. All the things you do for me. How you keep coming back, no matter how hard I try to push you away. That you still like me even though I'm far from perfect."

"No one's perfect," I said, "but you're pretty close."

She rolled her eyes. "That's what I'm talking about. You willingly delude yourself about me, and I don't understand why."

One corner of my mouth quirked up. "You're the smartest person I know. You know why. It's because I love you. I see all the good parts of you, even the ones you can't."

"Goddammit, Danny. Why is that so easy for you?"

"What, falling for you? Easiest thing I've ever done."

"No. Saying it." She took a deep breath and held my hand tighter. "I love you too, Danny Carbone."

My head swam like the crowd of people had sucked all the oxygen from the room. "You...you do?"

"Yes." She lifted her other hand to my cheek. It was cool enough to steady me. "And I want us to be a family."

My gaze caught on her plastic hospital bracelet. "Is this the hormones talking, or do you really want that?"

"It's true, my hormones are super fucked-up right now. But I can't imagine living the rest of my life without you in it. I'm a better person with you than I am without you. I want to be my best self for you, and for her."

"Jesus Christ." I surged forward. My mom tutted at my curse, but I didn't care. I hugged Lucie and kissed her temple.

"Come on," she murmured in my ear. "I may be a mother now, but I'm not *your* mother. You can do better than that."

I pulled back far enough that I could kiss her lips. Gently, since there were still a dozen people in the room and she'd just been through a grueling physical ordeal. But she didn't want gentle. She tunneled her hands into my hair and yanked, then crushed me to her. I deepened the kiss, no longer caring about our audience. I shoved my hands between her back and the rough hospital sheets and gathered her to my chest.

Leo's whistle, muffled behind his mask, broke into my focus. Reluctantly, I pulled away and stared into her eyes. "Really? You want me? I've still got the ring back at my place."

"I want you," she said. "No ring, no wedding, no house in the suburbs. Just you, me, and...Mia. What do you think?"

The muttering in the room stopped. Behind me, Savannah sucked in a breath.

My heart swelled in my chest. "It's a beautiful name. Almost as beautiful as she is."

Savannah whooshed out a breath.

My mother announced, "A good Italian name. Now, what about a middle name? My mother's name was Paulina, but maybe you have a family name you'd like to use, Ellen and Marvin?"

They could argue about her middle name all they wanted. I didn't care. All I cared about was that Lucie wanted me. Loved me. Wanted to be with me. Forever.

EPILOGUE 1
TESSA'S LEGACY

TESSA

"Come on, y'all." When Savannah grasped my wrist and pulled me from Lucie's hospital room, I flinched. I trusted Savannah, but unexpected touches always sent a kick through my nervous system.

"Where are we going?" Carly asked as Savannah led us toward the elevator bank. "I wanted to hold the baby."

My lip curled. I'd come to check on my friend, but I didn't need to hold her baby. And I'd rather not have witnessed Lucie's sappy declaration to Danny, who I guessed was her boyfriend now. All that emotion made me itchy. I tugged my wrist from Savannah's grip and scratched it.

She pressed the call button. "Lucie's mother mentioned they don't have a car seat. So we're going shopping." When the elevator doors slid open, she stepped in and beamed. "It's going to be so much fun!"

Carly stepped inside and tapped on her phone. "There's a boutique, Le Petit Bébé, about twenty minutes away. I used to shop there for baby shower gifts." She flipped her phone around to show us a photo of a store decorated in shades of white.

"Looks expensive," Savannah grumbled, hitching up her tracksuit pants.

"Or..." I pulled out my phone. "We could order a car seat to be delivered to their door. No muss, no fuss. I can have it there by this afternoon."

"No." Savannah put her hand over my phone screen. "No impersonal online ordering." She glared at Carly. "No pricey boutiques. There's a Target five minutes from here. They have everything we need."

She was right about the distance. It took longer to find my car in the hospital parking deck than to drive to the discount store. Savannah marched inside, leading the way like she was a determined mother duck and Carly and I were her fluffy, clueless ducklings.

When the automatic door whooshed shut behind me, I froze. The store was huge, even more gigantic than it had looked from the outside. And open. My black Converse squeaked on the vinyl tiles. When I checked the ceiling out of habit, it was covered in security cameras. The back of my neck prickled, and my chest tightened.

"You okay, Tessa?" Savannah's voice interrupted the one in my head that told me to get out of there.

I shook it off. There was nothing to fear. It wasn't even my voice in my head, warning me to get the hell out; it was my dad's, and we hardly talked anymore. "I'm fine."

"Then let's go!" She yanked a huge red plastic cart from a tangle of them. She also scanned the ceiling, then pointed toward the far wall. "Baby section is that way."

The space was too big, too bright, too full of people. Plus, Red Rover shoppers came here all the time. *It's been fifteen years,* I reminded myself. *None of the associates who knew you then are still working for them. No one will recognize you.* Still, I kept my head down as I followed my friends. The last thing we needed was for someone to call me out. Or spit on me. That had only happened once, right after everything went to shit. But once was sufficient.

"Keep up, Carly," Savannah said.

Our friend had stopped in front of a display of mannequins wearing sweaters and scarves. There was even a plastic dog wearing a tiny green plaid sweater. "How adorable! Chanel needs a sweater, and that emerald one would be gorgeous on her."

"Why does a dog need a sweater?" I asked. "She's covered in fur."

Carly shuffled through the rack. "She likes to look well dressed, just like her mama."

I doubted that. None of my cats had ever expressed an interest in fashion. Though they left the house even more infrequently than I did. We had dogs growing up, and they had jobs, not clothes. But Carly's dog's job seemed to be warming her lap, and maybe that required a sweater.

She laid the garment in Savannah's cart. "Okay, baby section next."

But we had to stop two more times, once at a Christmas display so Savannah could cluck that it was too early to think about Christmas (while my dad's rant about the manufactured waste of capitalism played in my head), and once in the toy section when Carly spotted a mesh bag of marbles.

"Andrew and Oliver need these." She plucked the bag from the hook.

I snorted. "Because they lost theirs?" Andrew was a math nerd, and his friend Oliver was a science nerd who always seemed to be staring, sad-eyed, off into space, except when he was watching me in a way that made me uncomfortably aware of exactly how public my life had been fifteen years ago. And of the fact that, if he were ten years older, that solemn intensity would've made him my type. So, as usual, I covered it with snark. "Sorry, couldn't resist."

Carly lifted her chin. "They're doing a video on Newton's laws of motion. Those videos may be ridiculous, but now they've got some interest from a streaming television service, they could be laughing all the way to the bank."

"Wait, aren't they rich already?" I asked. Both Andrew and his friend moved through the world with that elegant carelessness I'd observed in those who'd been born with money. Like they never panicked, however briefly, when presented with a menu with no prices on it. Like they didn't hyperventilate when they authorized a mid-five-figure wire transfer to buy a car.

"They've got trust funds," Carly said, "but they prefer to earn their own money. Andrew relies on the channel for his income now. Oliver still works for the biotech startup he founded. They're very driven, you know."

At their age, I'd already sold my business and lost my drive. I'd lost my way, too, though I hadn't known it then.

"It's so cute how tongue-tied Oliver gets around you, Tessa." Savannah smirked as she pushed the cart past a display of children's footie pajamas.

"Tongue-tied? More like stuck up," I said, careful not to meet her gaze.

"Oh, no, honey," Carly said. "Oliver talks all the time, except when he's thinking up something brilliant in that big brain of his. You intimidate him."

"Good." Because he intimidated me, too, with that intelligent gaze that saw too much.

"Here we are," Savannah sang out as she turned down an aisle and halted in front of a display of car seats.

Perfect. I needed a problem to solve. There had to be twenty to choose from. "Which one do we need?"

"The kind for infants." Savannah pointed to the ones on the right.

"Those look like snail shells," I said. "How do you even fit the baby inside? You couldn't squeeze even your purse dog in there, Carly."

"Didn't you see how tiny Mia is?" Savannah said, tugging at the straps on a display model. "She'll fit in here with room to spare. See? This one has a teeny bolster for her widdle head."

"Isn't she the cutest?" Carly cooed. "I wanted to eat her up."

I rolled my eyes to the ceiling, but when I spotted the security camera, I ducked my head. Were those two women standing at the endcap staring at us?

I was being paranoid. No one was paying us any attention. Besides Carly's haute couture, nothing about us stood out. I was wearing a goddamned hoodie like half the people in San Francisco, for Christ's sake.

Drawing my hood up over my head, I glanced back at the demonstration unit. Babies had never interested me, even before I learned I'd never have one. But I saw something that drew my attention: data. I stepped closer to peer at the tag, but the print blurred.

I patted my hip. I hadn't brought my bag. "Glasses. Anyone have a pair of readers?"

"I've got you." Savannah dug through her enormous tote and pulled out a pair.

"Thanks." I slipped them onto my nose. Savannah's prescription was stronger than mine, but if I squinted, the data came into focus.

"Andrew showed me the coolest thing the other day," Carly said. "There's an app for your phone that can magnify. It even lights up so I can read menus in dim lighting. Total game-changer."

I tuned out Savannah's answer as I tapped on my phone to analyze the data. In a few minutes, I pointed. "That one."

Savannah scrunched her nose. "Why that one?"

I ticked off the facts on my fingers. "Five point safety harness. Industry-leading side-impact protection. Anti-rebound bar. Plus LATCH connections and a tether system. It has a five-star crash-test rating from a consumer safety group. It's the safest."

Carly caressed the one next to it. "But that one's hideous. This one comes in shades of gray and black. Lucie's color scheme."

"This is her goddamn *baby* we're talking about," I said, "not a couch or a pair of boots. We go with what's safest." A tingle shot down my spine. Authority. Power. Like when I used to run meetings and make billion-dollar decisions. Well, one billion-dollar decision, and the world knew how that had turned out. But I was confident about this one. I stood up straighter, towering over my friends.

"Tessa's right," Savannah said, laying her hand on Carly's arm. "It might be ugly, but we want the safest one."

"What's so ugly about it?" I asked.

"Boat print fabric?" Carly curled her lip. "Don't even get me started."

I hovered my thumb over my phone. "I could special-order it in all black."

"No." Savannah reached her other hand to cover my phone. "No special orders. We walk out with this one, slap a bow on it, and give it to Lucie and Danny. In person."

"Fine," Carly huffed.

I grabbed the box from under the display and heaved it into the cart. "Anything else?"

Jutting out her chin, Carly picked up a pair of zebra-striped booties with bells on the toes. "These. They're adorable."

Savannah shook her head. "Those bells are a choking hazard. Try these." She plucked a different pair from the display. They were black-and-white striped with enormous plush ladybugs on the toes.

Carly's nostrils flared, but she nodded. "Also cute."

Savannah tossed them into the cart and turned it toward the front of the store. But now it was evident that the two women were staring at me. One of them stepped in front of our cart.

Her eyes glinted dangerously. "You're Tessa Wright."

I breathed in deep and straightened my shoulders. "I am."

"My big sister drove for Red Rover," she said. "She had breast cancer and needed the health insurance."

"I'm sor—"

"Then you took it away. You walked away with a billion dollars. But without her insurance, my sister couldn't afford her treatments or even her routine checkups. And by the time we found out and made her see her doctor, it was too late. She died seven years ago."

"I'm sorry," I said. So, so sorry. Sorry I'd ever let Harry talk me into that deal. Sorry I'd gone to ground instead of standing up. Sorry I hadn't done enough soon enough.

"Sorry doesn't bring her back," the woman spat.

"I know it doesn't. Can I..." But I didn't know what I could do. My foundation for Red Rover employees might help her family recover financially, but there were wounds my money couldn't heal.

"You can crawl back into your hole," she said, curling her lip.

"Hey, now." Carly stepped between us. "That's our friend you're talking to."

Savannah marched up beside Carly, acting as a barrier

between the stranger and me. "I don't know what you think she's done, but you're out of line."

Savannah was wrong. I'd done exactly what she said I had, and it wasn't out of line to call me on it. I set my hands on my friends' shoulders. "It's okay. I'll talk to her."

The woman held her head high. "I don't want to talk to you. Come on." Linking arms with her friend, she pivoted on her heel and walked away.

After a beat, Carly turned to me. "What the hell was that about?"

I stared up at the convex eye of the security system. "That, my friends, is my legacy."

EPILOGUE 2
CLOSE TO PERFECT

One Year Later

Interviewer: So, what's your legacy?

Carbone: I thought this book wasn't about legacy.

Interviewer: I'm the author here. I can ask whatever the fuck I want.

Carbone: You need a snack.

Interviewer: Don't fucking tell me what I need! Well, actually, yeah, some trail mix would be good. The kind with the little peanut butter cups. Thank you.

Interviewer: God, I was hungry. Now. Your legacy.

Carbone: I don't need a legacy. You've got enough for both of us.

Interviewer: Goddammit, Danny. Of course you have a legacy. It's your bar that makes so many people happy. Your family who couldn't survive without you. Including Mia and me.

Carbone: If you know, why'd you ask me?

Interviewer: Because you needed to hear it.

Transcript from untitled manuscript about parenthood

LUCIE

"*D*on't you think it's a little much for a one-year-old's birthday party?"

Standing on the stepstool, Danny pivoted from the streamer he was hanging to face me. "What's too much?"

The streamers. The full-sheet cake. The signature cocktails. Fifty guests. But I didn't say any of that. Because his question was rhetorical. For Danny, there was no such thing as too much for those he loved.

"Never mind, babe. In fact, keep going." I crossed my arms and put one finger on my lips. "Your ass looks great from this angle."

And it did. His faded Levis put his taut glutes on display, and I could fully appreciate them from a few feet below him. Actually, if he turned and came down one step, I could unbutton his jeans, pull out his glorious cock, and—

"Oh, no," he said. "We don't have time to satisfy that gleam in your eye. The grandparents will be here any minute, and Mia's waking up." He nodded at the video monitor, where our one-year-old daughter stretched her little arms over her head in her crib.

"I was the one who did all the work a year ago. I should get a present too." I pouted.

He ripped the streamer so it dangled from the wall, then descended from the stool. His arms wrapped around me, and his familiar scent surrounded me. "I promise you'll get yours tonight." His hand wandered down to my ass and squeezed.

I cheated. I tunneled my hand inside his jeans, under the waistband of his boxers, and cupped his butt. He hardened against my belly.

"No fair," he grumbled, ducking his head to kiss my neck in

the spot under my ear that made me shiver. "Now I'm going to have a hard-on when I open the door for your mother."

"Or..." I stretched my neck and let my fingers wander toward his hips on their way to the promised land. "We could have a quickie on the couch in my office."

"I don't want quick," he said, kissing down to the base of my neck. "I want slow. Leisurely. All." He kissed my lips. "Night." He pressed his hips closer, preventing my hands from squeezing between us.

There was a tap at the door.

"Damn it," I muttered. "There goes our quickie."

He stepped away and adjusted his jeans. "I was never on board with the quickie proposal."

I stared pointedly at the bulge in his pants. "Sure you weren't."

"Da-da." Our daughter's voice burbled from the monitor.

"Duty calls." With a wink, he turned toward the spiral staircase we'd installed to connect our apartments into a single unit.

With Barb's permission, we'd converted my apartment upstairs into a large bedroom for Danny and me and a smaller bedroom for Mia, plus a combination family room and playroom. Danny's former apartment housed the main kitchen and dining area, plus my office, where I now worked full-time, thanks to the income from the bar and the advance for my second book. Dropping my resignation letter on Mario's desk and watching his expression crumble was one of the most satisfying moments of my life.

Danny had built bookshelves on two walls and made me promise to reserve one shelf for books I'd written. I'd slid the first copies of my book about legacies onto that shelf last month.

At the second sharp rap on the door, I strode toward it. "Coming!"

"You wish," Danny teased, already halfway up the stairs.

"You'll pay for that later," I called back.

"And I'll enjoy every minute."

I threw open the door to find Leo there with two assistants holding heavy insulated bags of food.

"I should charge you extra for the stairs," he grumbled as he entered.

"Hello to you, too," I said. "As I recall, you refused when we offered to pay you."

"I can't charge you to cater my niece's birthday party," he said, unpacking a stack of foil trays that smelled like oregano and heaven. "Especially since you and Danny provide liquor for my events at cost."

"That's how family works," I said. It was a lesson I'd learned over the past year as part of the Carbone family. Everyone did favors for everyone else. And everyone was accepted for exactly who they were. Including me.

"Bar was busy downstairs," Leo said.

We'd made a lot of changes since I'd pooled my book advance with Danny's savings to buy the bar from Barb. But not the kind of changes Tad had envisioned. (He hadn't been back since Danny had taken over.) "Saturdays are family days. After cake, we'll take all the kids down there to see the balloon artist."

He shuddered. "As long as I can stay up here, put my feet up, and have a beer, I'm good." He turned on the two ovens and stacked the foil trays inside.

"You know Mia's going to want her favorite uncle with her." I stole a pepper from the antipasto tray his assistant had unwrapped.

"She'll be so hopped up on cake she won't even notice me enjoying a little peace and quiet away from the kiddos," Leo said. "Besides, she has an entire fan club."

"Hello!" Carly called from the doorway. "I'm letting myself in."

"See what I mean?" Leo said as Tessa and Savannah followed Carly inside.

I rushed to hug my friends. "Where are the guys?"

"They stopped at the bar to watch the end of the game since we're early." The tray Savannah carried bumped my stomach as I leaned in to kiss her cheek.

"What'd you bring?" I asked, my mouth watering at the savory scent.

"Just some spinach dip and homemade crackers," she said. "If there's room in the oven, I'll keep it warm."

"Check with Leo. If not, we've still got the oven upstairs," I said.

Danny's heavy steps sounded on the spiral staircase. "Look who's up," he sang out.

Savannah shoved the tray into my hands. "Mia, my love!" She rushed to greet my daughter, Carly right on her heels.

Tessa hung back beside me. "You doing all right, Luce?"

I watched Danny smooth down the skirt of Mia's rust-orange party dress. He'd even managed to wrestle her into leggings and a pair of soft, grippy booties that helped her take her toddling steps, provided anyone would let her feet touch the floor today. Her face lit up when she saw my friends. She reached for Savannah first, curling her fingers into her pink hair. Fortunately, Savannah didn't mind. Danny stood by proudly, hands on his hips.

"Yeah," I said. "I'm excellent."

"Still one-and-done?" she asked.

"Not you too." I glared at her. "Danny made his family promise not to ask me that anymore."

"Hey." She held up her hands. "You know I'm not into kids. I'm just saying, your man could make anyone burst an ovary."

"True. But I promise to keep my wits about me, despite his ovary-exploding powers. Our family is perfect as is."

"Hello!" My mother's voice rang out behind me. "We came early to help."

"Just what I need," I muttered.

"Need me to run interference?" Tessa asked. "I can ask your dad about his research. That's good for an hour-long conversation."

"I'll let you know. Code word is *mayday*."

She snorted, then headed off to greet Mia and Danny. I turned to face my parents.

My mother hugged me. "How's the proud mama?" she asked.

"Doing fine, thanks."

"We watched Danny's video of Mia's first steps a dozen times, didn't we, Marvin?" she said.

"We did. And how many words does she have?"

"Dad," I warned. "Don't start."

"What? I'm asking about my granddaughter's development."

I raised my eyebrows. "You're testing her."

"Why would I do that? She's a baby."

Because that's what you did to me, I didn't say. "We talked about this, Dad."

"I know. But there's no harm in trying to teach her to say 'Grandpa,' is there?" He rubbed his hands together.

"I guess not. And she'd love it if you'd read her a book."

"It's excellent that you're instilling a love of reading in her," he said.

I blinked at his praise. "Thank you."

My mother nudged him, and he cleared his throat. "I read your book."

"You did?" My heart pounded. "The—the whole thing?"

"The whole book. Your mother and I read it together." He didn't let any expression cross his stoic face.

"And..." It was hard to squeeze the words out past the constriction in my throat. "What did you think?"

My mother squeezed my father's arm. "Stop teasing her, Marvin."

He smiled. "We loved it. I loved it. You conveyed the complexity of being a woman in today's challenging times. I'm so proud, Lucie."

"Proud?" My fingertips tingled, and I shook the feeling back into them. "Thank you."

"Now I'm going to say hello to my granddaughter and Danny. I have to thank him for the videos." He strode toward Mia, who was now perched on Carly's hip.

My mother lingered for a moment. "He's trying, you know."

I rolled my eyes. "Could've fooled me."

"He realizes he didn't do the best job parenting you. He's trying to do better at grandparenting. He loves you both, and he's striving to show it."

I took a deep breath and sighed it out. I was trying to be less hard on myself. I should extend that grace to my father too. "Okay."

"I'll make sure he doesn't try too hard with the 'Grandpa' thing," she said, following my father.

I stayed back. He was proud of me. They both were. At forty-one years old, I shouldn't care. But I did. I felt warm inside.

"Hey." Danny put an arm around my shoulders. "You all right?"

"Yeah." I smiled up at him. "You?"

"You, me, and our family on Mia's first birthday? I can't imagine being happier."

I rose on my tiptoes to kiss his cheek. "Me neither."

❧

Thank you so much for reading *Books and Hookups*. Please consider posting a review on your favorite retailer's site, BookBub, or Goodreads.

Members of my free VIP Reader List get a free bonus epilogue showing how Lucie and Danny flip a marriage proposal on its head. Go to michellemccraw.com/BAHBonus or scan the code below to grab it!

Tessa's story is next. When secretive billionaire Tessa resolves to create her own legacy to erase the one that's been thrust on her, she must partner up with a brilliant scientist who demands what she can't give: her trust. Be sure to get your copy of *Conspiracies and Chemistry,* available at all retailers.

ACKNOWLEDGMENTS

First, I'd like to thank you, my readers, for spending your time with Danny and Lucie and the rest of the Goddess Gang. Your support means the world to me.

Thanks also to my beta readers and writing besties, Carla Luna and Ofelia Martinez. Your feedback made this book so much better. And talking with you about writing and publishing makes the grind more fun.

Thanks to Melanie Rose Clarke for getting up early to write with me. Your encouragement and accountability mean the world to me.

Finally, writing a book with a pregnancy plot tied my brain in knots. It is only because of my fabulous editor, Brittany Ortega, that Lucie's pregnancy wasn't eleven months long and that she received up-to-date maternal care. Brittany, thanks for your research, your attention to detail, and your patience with my fucked-up timeline. I'm so glad I found you.

ABOUT MICHELLE

Michelle McCraw loves reading kissing books and working in tech. One day, she decided to combine her two interests, and now she writes steamy, nerdy contemporary romance that just might make you laugh. Her books feature characters who unashamedly love science, engineering, and technology.

A native Texan, Michelle has shoveled snow during nor'easters and knows the proper response when someone yells, "O-H." She now calls Georgia home, where she doesn't miss snow AT ALL. She enjoys reading, travel, drinking bourbon, and spoiling her extraordinarily ill-behaved but adorable dog. She has been a finalist in the RWA Vivian Contest, the Contemporary Romance Writers' Stiletto Contest, and the Windy City Romance Writers' Four Seasons Contest.

For updates about upcoming books and more free reads—plus guaranteed puppy pics—subscribe to Michelle's newsletter at michellemccraw.com. You can also follow the author on Facebook and Instagram.

facebook.com/MichelleMcCrawAuthor

instagram.com/MMOWriter

amazon.com/author/michellemccraw

goodreads.com/MichelleMcCraw

bookbub.com/authors/michelle-mccraw

BOOKS IN THE 40 AND FABULOUS SERIES

Fashion and Passion

After a disastrous self-help seminar, Carly finds friendship,
empowerment, and maybe love with a younger admirer. Get swept
away by sparkling banter, new besties, and spicy seduction, perfect for a
bubbly escape.

Frenemies and Lovers

When Carly needs a date to her ex's wedding, she agrees to a deal with
Andrew, a devilishly handsome younger man. Her frenemy's son. Who
happens to be her one-night stand. What could go wrong? Who says
you can't be fabulous over forty?

"Total catnip" (5-star review)

Books and Hookups

Writer Lucie's life is looking up: she has a new book deal, fabulous
friends, and a bar where everyone knows her name. The last thing she
needs is a surprise (geriatric?) pregnancy with her much-younger
neighbor.

Conspiracies and Chemistry

Secretive billionaire Tessa seeks redemption from the biggest mistake
of her life by betting it all on a groundbreaking biotechnology company,
which happens to be run by her younger nemesis. Who knew lab coats
were so sexy?

Advances and Retreats

When Bridget and her nemesis, Cole, are temporarily assigned as co-CEOs and given the chance to compete for the solo job at a corporate retreat in Costa Rica, they encounter crocodiles, sabotage, and—possibly—love.

Marriage and Trouble

After an accident, everyone mistakes woozy animal-loving cyclist Pax for Justine's fiancé. She needs a husband, and he needs cash to keep his animal rescue afloat. When real feelings start to develop, their marriage is anything but convenient.

Sugar and Spice

Invisibility is Savannah's superpower. West is the one person it doesn't work on. Inconveniently, he's also her (younger) roommate.

BOOKS IN THE SYNERGY SERIES
CAN BE READ IN ANY ORDER

Work with Me

She's got a checklist for every occasion. He's never met a bad decision he didn't make. Can straitlaced single mom Alicia find a way to work with billionaire tech genius Jackson and save her business—without falling for him first?

"Slow burn magic!" (5-star review)

Friend Me

Romance-obsessed executive assistant Marlee has a plan to woo her crush, icy and aloof San Francisco tech executive Cooper Fallon. But it all goes wrong when her fake date, instead of making her crush jealous, sparks more-than-friends feelings. Kissing the wrong guy? Not in her plan. Neither is falling for her best friend.

"Un-put-down-able" (5-star review)

Trip Me Up

Nerdy computer scientist Samantha Jones didn't mean to end up on a book tour trying to pass off her artificial intelligence-written novel as one written the old-fashioned way. And she certainly didn't mean to fall for her flannel-wearing, poetic tour partner. Opposites attract in this road-trip romance.

"This book had me hooked right from the start and up until the wee hours devouring their story!" (5-star review)

Boss Me

Frosty billionaire philanthropist Cooper Fallon would never start a fling with his off-limits assistant, Ben...or would he?

"OMG...If you like forbidden romance this is the book for you!!!" (5-star review)

Forget Me

She doesn't remember their night together. He can't forget it. When Mimi's prospective boss mistakes Mateo for her boyfriend, she's shocked when he rolls with it. But when their fake romance becomes real, will buttoned-up Mimi let down her guard for love?

"I absolutely love this twist on the grumpy sunshine trope." (5-star review)

Tempt Me

When a gaffe caught on camera threatens her company, a no-nonsense tech CEO calls on her bestie's little sister for help. But falling for her sunshiny public relations assistant could get her into even more hot water.

"THIS WAS FUN!!" (5-star review)

CREDITS

Edits and Proofreading

E&A Editing Services

Cover Design

Kari March

9 781961 373075